"DROP, DROP!"

Carlton waved his hand at the girl, hoping she would know what he meant. She raised her head to stare at the wall.

"Drop yuh garments, girl." Ella's arrogance made Carlton's mood change as quickly as his father's had. Placing his hand on the front of her loose-fitting dress, he pulled, and the garment tore. Hayes sucked on his teeth with a greedy hiss as Ella stood naked on the balcony before them.

"Right, son," commanded Hayes as Carlton stood in front of the girl, apparently studying her eyes. "We see she's a prime filly to look at. What does she feel like? Touch her, boy, touch her!"

Carlton hesitated, trying to ignore Ella's stare of contempt. It was he who felt degraded. He grabbed her shoulders angrily, running his hands over her body as roughly as he could. He bounced her breasts. He spun her around to run his fingers over her. His hands rested on her buttocks as he wondered what he should do next.

His father did the rest. Steadying her with his left hand behind her back, he plunged his right hand between her thighs, jamming his fingers into her.

"Fine filly!" repeated Hayes, his eyes glazed. "Cross her with one of my prime young studs over there, and we would have a sturdy buck all right . . ."

The Bondmaster

by

Richard Tresillian

WARNER BOOKS

A Warner Communications Company

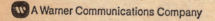

"Roxborough Estate in the Layou Valley was the most productive of Dominica's sugar plantations until it declined at the end of the eighteenth century when the Todd family started the first slave warren in the British West Indian islands.

"The Bondmaster, Mr Carlton Todd, is reputed to have made a considerable fortune by his selective breeding of enslaved Africans for sale to the plantation owners of neighbouring islands.

"A Roxborough slave became renowned throughout the West Indies as the elite of that subjugated race, and it is said that many of today's native citizens of prominence have descended from the line begun by the Bondmaster of Roxborough."

From: *A History of the British West Indian Islands by* Sir Verne W. Bisset, Bart. Published by Shankland & Box, London & Cambridge, 1913.

THE
BONDMASTER

Prologue

Chapter 1

Captain Loring eyed the shore eagerly. It was an unexpected landfall, but he knew better than to ignore his bones. When his knee started to twinge, it was time to haul down sails and put into the nearest bay for shelter.

"Row, yer damned jackanapes!" he yelled at the two men in the skiff. Sweat oozed on their swarthy faces as they strained at the oars. Loring could feel the dead heat of the afternoon closing in on him. One of the sailors broke the rhythm of rowing to wipe the sweat off his brow with the back of his hand.

"Dam' yer blood!" roared the Captain. "Cox'n!" he inclined his head to the stern of the skiff as the helmsman answered him sharply.

"Cap'n?"

"I want this man in irons if he bams us again. Ye're here to row, boy, so row!"

The skiff slid easily through the dark water of the river mouth. Captain Loring considered himself fortunate to have found such a secure anchorage. The sandbar stretching over most of the entrance to the vast river would protect his ship from the effects of the rough sea he was sure was brewing.

The ocean was deceptively calm, but the livid clouds hanging over the high hills of the island's interior told him his bones were right again. And the rapid current of the river, as it carried broken branches and coconuts in their heavy fiber shells down to the sea, showed the storm had already broken inland.

Now the schooner was anchored behind the sandbar, it would ride out the storm calmly enough and the Frenchies he had on board should be grateful to him. His ship was a sturdy one which used to ply the treacherous New England coast before her Liverpool owners bought her for the West India trade. If he had had niggers on board he would have stayed on course, but the Frenchies were paying him well to escape from Martinique and he could afford to oblige them and heave to until the foul weather passed.

The skiff broached the shallow waters of the shore as his men shipped their oars. Captain Loring cursed them automatically as the spray splashed him. One of the sailors stepped into the water and guided the boat to the bank. Standing amidst the rotting leaves at the river's edge, he held the skiff steady as the Captain leaned on his shoulder. Shoving himself ashore, the Captain sent the seaman tumbling backwards into the water. "That'll cool yer off!"

Brushing down his frock coat with his hand, then straightening his hat, Captain Loring looked at the tiny river town with interest. In addition to his own, there were five vessels anchored in the bay. That meant that there would be sport in the hamlet tonight. Already from the shadows as the clouds blended with the fast descent of the tropic night he could hear the delighted shrieks of women and the raucous laughter of seamen crowding into the casinos.

"Cox'n!" called the Captain. "Mayhap I'll sleep ashore tonight." He glanced at his ship. "Tell the mate to batten down 'fore the rain comes. And a double watch to see she don't drag."

The response of his coxswain was whipped away by the breeze which sprung up with the sudden fall of night. The Captain knew that his mate, with the promise of booty when they delivered the refugees safely to Jamaica, would watch the ship well. Turning

11

confidently to face the wooden homes of the town, he strode through the riverside vegetation to reach the track running alongside the riverbank.

"G'night, Cap'n." A mulatto wench sidled up to him as he reached the track. "I bin waitin' fuh yuh."

The woman tried to slip her arm into his. In the gloom of the evening and the overhanging vegetation which obscured her sallow skin and crinkly hair beneath her madras headpiece, she could have been white.

"Damn yer blood, wench!" Loring growled, slapping her hand away.

"I does be free," boasted the woman, nonplussed by Loring's attitude. "My lovin' is de bes' dere does be. Only two bits, sah!"

"I'll not give ye half-a-bit fer yer pox!" Loring shook away the wench and strode into the town.

Lanterns were being lit in the shacks lining the mud path running through the hamlet. Loring had a thirst on him. He ignored the twinge in his knee as he approached a shack where laughter indicated he would find grog inside. He pulled himself up into the shack, which stood on wooden stilts, as heavy drops of rain began to pound the hard mud outside.

By the light of the single lantern dangling from a roof beam, he observed three sailors standing at an upturned barrel serving as a counter. In a corner, a fourth man was busy with a brown-skinned wench, her long dress bunched up around her hips. The laughter of the men stilled as they contemplated the Captain. An old man bereft of hair and his face so wizened it was impossible to tell if he was white or mulatto croaked a welcome from the shadows as he placed a pitcher on the barrel top.

"Grog!" barked the Captain. The old man handed him a glass and indicated that he should serve himself from the pitcher.

The Captain poured a half-gill, swilled the cloudy liquid in the glass, then plunged it straight down his throat. He looked at the other men at the bar as though seeing them for the first time, offering the pitcher to them. The tension caused by his unexpected arrival vanished as the men helped themselves to the rum. Smacking his lips, Loring nodded appreciatively at the flavor of the grog.

"Dat be a fine brew, sah," the old bar man wheezed. "Dat be Roxborough rum. Ain' no rum dat better."

Loring nodded his head, mellowing as he poured himself another shot. "Aim to get meself drunk tonight," he remarked to the bar in general. "Damn storm."

"Aye," agreed a burly seaman with an evil scar torn down the side of his sunburned cheek. "It'll blow a fair force tonight, season for it."

"This here's the best anchorage, though," said his companion. "Safer here than Prince Rupert's Bay."

"Dis be Layou, Cap'n," interrupted the barman. "Bes' anchorage in Dominica when a storm be blowin'. Brigs, schooners, dey all does come yere."

The man who had been on the floor in the corner stood up to join them. He nodded toward the wench still on the floor and one of the seamen, fiddling with the front of his breeches, crouched down to her. The man poured himself a rum as the barman watched him expectantly, his monkey face stretched in a grin.

"I done say she does be good, not so?"

"Aye, aye," said the man, draining the rum with a gulp. "When you've been at sea four weeks, any wench is welcome. Even a half-bit black-arsed nigger scratching on the floor of a slavey's rum shop."

The burly seaman guffawed. "Such like as your poxy daughter ain't for the Cap'n here, John-James," he addressed the barman. "He'll he bound for May Gregg's."

"May Gregg's?" Loring, his immediate thirst satisfied, was eager to see what this shore town had to offer. It might be the last chance to relax before he unloaded his Frenchies in Jamaica. "Where's that?"

"Straight down the trail. Best casino in Layou," the seaman told him, enjoying the sulky expression of the barman. "She's a white whore, too."

Captain Loring laid a bit on the counter and turned to go. The old Negro snatched it up, put it in his teeth and tried to bend it, then slipped it quickly into the pocket of his pantaloons. The Captain hawked noisily and directed a well-aimed glob of phlegm at the head of the black wench squirming on the floor. He stepped out of the door into the mud of the road, pulling his hat firmly on his head in the rain.

Glancing back across the river mouth, he tried to pick out his ship by the lights bobbing on the water. The Captain was going to enjoy his night of freedom away from his crew and those Royalist Frenchmen. He had landed fifty at Roseau to join the thousands already there, all refugees from the new republic in Martinique. The wealthier ones were staying on board, bound for Jamaica, where they hoped to start a new life. It was a relief for the Captain to get away from the panicky bluebloods, especially that vixen, Mademoiselle de Champigny.

Having located May Gregg's, Loring shoved his way abruptly to the back of the casino through a knot of drinkers blocking his path, brushing them with rain from his coat. They cursed him irritably, but May Gregg, for it could only be she, saw him and got up from her chair perched on an empty salt-fish box where she could keep a watch on her slaves and her customers. She stepped off the box toward him, forewarned by the cut of his jib that here was a man to whom a special welcome could pay dividends.

"Welcome to May Gregg's, Cap'n! This bad weather has brought you to a good port."

She clapped her hands. "Rippin," she told the boy who danced to her side, a broad grin on his face as he watched her with apparent devotion, "take the massa's coat and put it in the parlor to dry."

"Mighty kind of ye, I'm sure, ma'am." Captain Loring appraised the stout build of May Gregg appreciatively. "But right now it's drink I crave. Grog's enough to warm a man in a storm." He waved the slave away.

"May's the name," she said, inviting him to join her as Rippin put out a stool for him by the barrel which served as a table. He placed a small jug on the barrel and the Captain reached over greedily. He poured himself a measure and drained it, feeling the rum scorch his throat.

"What kind of brew is that?" Loring gasped, his mouth watering.

"That's Roxborough special," grinned May. "Old rum, and I adds some peppers. Puts life in a man, it do."

"This man don't need no life," he growled, "though it's a fair brew, I'll grant."

For May Gregg, Captain Loring was a change from her usual clientele of cutthroats and illegal slave traders. Because of its location halfway along the Leeward coast between the established harbors of Roseau and Prince Rupert's Bay, Layou was where vessels evading the port authorities dropped anchor. No one asked questions in Layou. Ships came, unloaded their cargoes at the small jetty by the river mouth, took on water and provisions, and departed. By the time the customs officers in Roseau heard of a ship's arrival, the vessel was already in St. Bart's, or heading for the Spanish Main.

Seamen flocked to May's casino for the rum and black wenches she supplied. They drank, gambled, danced, and fought, and some died. She had lost count of the corpses Rippin had tossed out of the open back door into the sea. May herself had been born in a bawdy house in Cheapside over thirty years before. With her doting slaves Rippin and Sam and the pygmy Bambute to protect her, she had won the respect of the roughest of her customers. May Gregg was famous from Dominica to the Coromantee Coast. She picked her associates carefully, using them for their influence and gold. This Captain, who had swaggered through her bar as though he always liked to have his keg well filled, seemed just the type of man she needed. She smiled to reassure him and called over one of the girls.

"Cap'n," she murmured into his ear, "this is Cloe."

Loring raised his bleary eyes at the black face of a girl regarding him coldly as he fumbled with her mistress.

"Bah! I don't want no nigger wench!"

"That's right, Cap'n." May was tactful. "Cloe will take you to my parlor. I'm coming soon. Got to push these lazy Negroes of mine. Most everyone is asleep now, anyways."

Cloe led Loring out of the bar, stepping over the bodies of the men who had passed out. Some were still struggling with their wenches, determined to get value for their money. In the parlor, Cloe indicated the coconut fiber mattress laid out on the floor. Loring peered at her drunkenly, then slapped her away from him in a sudden fury.

"Git yer mistress!" he slurred. "Git me that May Gregg!"

Chapter 2

The wind battering the bar that night did nothing to disturb Captain Loring. With May Gregg beside him, he sailed through dreams no storm could upset. But in the morning, as the buzz of mosquitoes plagued his ears and the wind dropped its hammering, his head recoiled. He lay on the mattress conscious of the formidable woman beside him, listening to the noise of the Negroes clearing out people from the bar so that the day could start. His mouth was parched and his head under assault. He stirred, and the woman's hands crept over his body until, half an hour later, when he opened his eyes, dawn began to seep through the cracks in the shutters.

"Powerful grog, that! Man needs an eye-opener after a kegful of that brew."

May stood up and shook down her long skirt, scratching her crotch contentedly. She yawned. Loring listened to the crash of the sea against the wall below the casino. He got up from the mattress eager to see the weather and concerned now about his ship. May had gone through into the bar and he could hear her ordering the slaves to clean up the place. Loring checked his clothes. He still had his leather purse with its assorted bits and pieces and one doubloon. He retrieved his pistol intact from under the mattress where he had stowed it when the wench had brought him into the parlor the night before.

"The rain ain't eased up yet," said May. She was standing by the door open onto the road as Loring emerged from the parlor. The morning was still a dark gray, accentuated by a single lantern burning in the tavern. "Wind's dropped, though."

"Aye," said Loring, reaching for the pitcher of rum and a pewter cup the pygmy was holding out for him. " 'Spect it will be done by full light. Sea's up, though." He cocked his head to listen to the noise of the waves, then drained the rum down his throat. He shook himself as he felt the rum coursing through his body.

"Ah!" he growled, moving toward the door.

"You ain't going out already, are you?"

"Want to see me ship. Passengers all right."

"Carrying passengers?" May spoke idly. The information might come in useful.

"Always do when I can. Royalists running from that new republic they have in Martinique."

"Heard about them." May was disappointed. "Sometimes I think those Frenchies planning to take over this island again. Been nigh on ten years since I came here when we chased them out, and look, there's more Frenchies here now than English. Not counting Negroes, of course."

Pulling his hat over his greasy locks, Loring bobbed out through the door. May placed her arm on his. He stopped.

"Not leaving, are you?" There was a hint of menace in her voice.

"Lor' no!" Loring grinned. She was a tough bitch all right, he thought. No one could foist a die on her. "Me credit not good, then?" he teased.

"Don't know nothing about credit." May stood up straight, her arms akimbo. "It's cash or kind for May Gregg. No one ever left Layou owing me." She paused. "Unless they was dead."

"Don't doubt it, May." To soften her, Loring stepped back into the tavern. He had glimpsed his ship bobbing securely out in the river. The morning light was filtering through the vegetation surrounding the village. If it were not for the clouds and the rain, the sun would soon be over the crest of mountains bordering the river. He decided there was no need to go back on board until later. At his request, May sent a slave to wait for the skiff from his ship and to bring the mate to meet him at the tavern.

"Ye're a mighty charming woman, May." Loring led her by her arm to sit in a corner.

"I know what I am, Cap'n," May retorted. "There's no road 'round me but the one that's paved with gold."

May took Loring's hand and smoothed out the thick black hair on the back of his fingers, wet with rain. She needed a man like him. A fine business she had, and no child to share it with after all these years. She wiped her eyes quickly so Loring would not see.

"I'd be obliged for twenty bits, Captain."

Loring drew out his purse, shook out some bits, and passed them to her, his eyebrow raised.

May stood up and beckoned Loring to follow her back into the parlor. "To show you I want you to come back again, Captain, perhaps you can give me something to remember you by."

When a seaman came for him later, Loring cursed him and sent him back. The rain had eased off, but the wind could return, Loring reasoned. He sent word to the mate to let the passengers come ashore if they wished. He would not sail until the next morning when he could be certain the storm had passed. May smiled. If the Frenchies came to her casino that night, she would set up a game of brelan for them. And she would have her arrogant Captain for a second night before he left for Jamaica.

Loring was intrigued by the activity which the morning had brought to the ramshackle town. A wagon drawn by two horses was making slow progress down the mud track, stopping at most of the shacks while two Negroes unloaded barrels and replaced them on the wagon with empty ones. Children, a mixture of every color from the faded white of an octoroon to the midnight black of a pure African, clustered around the vehicle. The tavern owners stood outside their premises welcoming the wagon with a smile.

No money seemed to change hands but behind the wagon a Negro walked with a ledger under his arm. At every delivery point he paused to make an entry. When the wagon reached May Gregg's, three large casks were rolled in while the Negro entered the consignment in his log.

"That's the Roxborough rum that you enjoy so much!" May said with a wink, amused at the Captain's interest. The rain had stopped, and they sat on a bench outside the bar with the sun steaming the puddles in the mud.

Loring was not so much interested in the rum, but in the Negro with the ledger. Impressively built, he had the rare demeanor of a slave who was a credit to his master. Had he been younger, Loring would have been keen to buy him. A slave who could read and write and be trusted with a wagon loaded with rum would fetch a fortune in Jamaica.

The Captain turned to May, scratching his heard as a thought occurred to him. "What's this Roxborough I'm always hearing 'bout? Seems like Roxborough owns this whole whore-ridden hamlet."

"Oy! Oy!" exclaimed May indignantly. "No one owns us in Layou. That's Roxborough right there." She gestured across the track to the trees behind the cabin opposite. "All the sugar cane around as far as you can see," her hand described a half moon in the air embracing north, east and south, "and up to those hills the other side of the river."

Loring frowned. "Plenty of land there. How come one man owns so much?"

"That's Hayes Todd." May settled back on the bench. She liked to gossip and could tell a thing or two about Hayes Todd if she felt like it. "Settled here in seventy-six. Bought up all the estates around. You know, when all the English planters got scared of the French and fled for England. They got scared of hard work, if you ask me."

Loring watched the grog wagon turn at the end of the track and creak back toward the river, still followed by laughing children. The Negro with the ledger, his face serious with the importance of his work, mounted the wagon beside the driver.

May saw Loring's interest. "Every three days, they send our rum. The still is up the river, 'bout a mile. Any piece of cane you see growing 'round here is Hayes Todd's. Hundreds of hogsheads of sugar he exports every year. Direct to England. They have launches bring the casks down the river to the ships. You should see this town when it's the season!"

May's eyes gleamed. "Never knew men who could drink so much rum and ride so many wenches!" She leaned over to Loring and tapped him on his knee. "That's when a woman needs a man to look after her. It's a good life here. Ever thought of settlin' down, Cap'n?"

"With all these acres, he must have lots of slaves?"

"What? You mean at Roxborough? Sure they have slaves. Needs them with that cane. Todd buys sometimes from the traders." May was trying to follow Loring's thinking. " 'Cos in this village most of the blacks is free. That's why they're here."

Loring stood up. "Think I'd like to take a look at Roxborough."

"Whatever for?"

"Don't know. Might pick up a Negro or two. And I could always purchase some of that powerful Roxborough grog to ship to Jamaica."

"Hayes don't take kindly to strangers," warned May, looking up at him. "I suppose it's because he don't like this settlement. Says that all these free Negroes around is dangerous. He was in Alabama, you see. Things were different there."

"How will I get there?" Although Loring's knee had stopped troubling him, he did not view kindly the prospect of having to walk in the mud through the dripping bush in search of the estate house. "It far?"

"Fair way," answered May. "Can't say I've ever been there. Thought I might go to the funeral when his wife died, but I had only been here a few months then. Didn't rightly know him then, except professionally, of course." She winked.

"Aye," nodded Loring. He understood that this Hayes Todd, whoever he was, was not the kind of man to have a wharfside whore, even if she was white, inside his home. "Yer have any kind of conveyance will get me to the house?"

"There's old Mister Belle has a kittareen. He used to be owner of one of the estates until Hayes paid his mortgage and pensioned him. Works as shipping agent when sugar's ready."

A slave was dispatched to present May Gregg's compliments and ask for the loan of the kittareen for the day. Loring passed the time listening to May describing Hayes Todd's dead French wife, whom she had never seen. When the slave returned, he was leading a kind of one-horse chaise with a raised awning over the seat.

Loring looked askance at the contraption. "Bah! That thing's for spinsters going to church!"

"Then you'll have to walk if you don't want it," laughed May. "And a gentleman don't arrive on foot, do he?"

It being about two miles uphill to the plantation house, Loring decided to hell with his pride and climbed into the kittareen. It was really quite comfortable. He refused May's offer of a slave to accompany him. He preferred to go alone so that no reports of his visit would come back to her. Waving at May for the last time, he took the reins, jerked them experimentally, and then felt the contraption lurch forward as the horse started along the track.

The trail to the plantation house was well established, and though the rain had made it muddy, it was in good repair without ruts. The sight of a gang of slaves digging a ditch to drain away the surface water struck him as unusual. In these islands, no one paid much attention to maintenance work. It was customary for a road to be left until it became impassable before anyone bothered with it. This Hayes Todd, Loring decided, must be a remarkable man.

A fork in the road led him, he assumed, either to the river on the right, or up to the house on the left. Thick foliage and bamboo growing near the river obscured his view completely. He took the left fork and noted the gradual uphill climb of the path. Peering through the bush on his right, he made out the shapes of some solid stone buildings. He could hear the regular swish of the water wheel and the shouts of a work gang which indicated the location of the sugar mill.

The trail appeared to be skirting around the hill where the cane was growing and met another one running perpendicular to it. This was equally well maintained and looked like a main thoroughfare. He halted the horse and called over to the young driver who stood behind the gang. The Negro trotted up obediently.

"Which way to the house, boy?"

"Straight up de hill, massa sah. Please sah."

"Bah!" Loring found the slave's civility rather irritating. "Where does that road lead?" He pointed in the opposite direction.

"Dat road, sah? Please sah, to de river, sah."

"River?" Loring gave another snort of disgust. "Road too damn good to go to the river, boy." He raised his whip threateningly.

"Yas, massa, sah. De river, sah. It does cross de river an' does go on goin', sah."

"Ah-hah! Now ye're talking. Stupid bugger. Yer could have told me that in the first place. Goes south." Loring thought aloud. "Must be the road to the port."

"Yas, massa, please, sah."

The boy, although he had his own whip for driving

23

women, cringed before the white man in the carriage. He stayed on the road until the stranger, still snorting, touched the horse with a flick from his whip and drove on up the house road. Then he turned back on the women in the field.

"What you does be watchin'? Bend yo'self low an' root out dem weeds 'fore I does lash yuh plenty!" He cracked the whip in the air, feeling the end curl around one of the women.

"Stoopid booger!" He echoed the white stranger, relishing the words as proof of his authority.

The horse cleared a bend in the road and Loring looked up the path to the top of the hill in amazement. The tangled bush had given way to an avenue lined with royal palm trees growing at regular intervals, straight and tall. On either side cane stretched as far as the eye could see, covering the hillside and the hill lands beyond. To the west, the Caribbean shimmered before him, telltale white waves indicating that the sea still had not calmed from the night's winds. To the east, the hills rolled inland, climbing higher to the mountainous peaks covered in dense tropical forest, clouds crowning their summits. To the south, behind him, was the vast river.

Confronting him, at the top of the hill, at the end of that imposing avenue of trees, was Roxborough Hall.

Chapter 3

"Ma Phoebe! Ma Phoebe!"

The child's voice cut through the clatter of the kitchen as Phoebe stirred the soup cooking on top of the stove. Quickly, she laid down her wooden spoon on the table and bustled to the kitchen door. A boy burst through and, colliding with her huge bulk, stopped in surprise. He was panting so much he was unable to speak.

"Lord, chil'," clucked Phoebe, easing herself down to his height and placing her hands on his shoulders to calm him. "What's all dat noise for?"

Seeing the awesome face of the cook level with his, the boy hesitated, wondering how his news was going to be received. "Someone comin'," he panted. "Someone comin' up de hill."

Phoebe released the child and stood up, perplexed. "Yuh sure, boy?"

"Yas, Ma Phoebe. I done run de whole way."

"Where from you run?" Phoebe was still doubtful. The master always told her when a visitor was expected.

"By long field, Ma Phoebe. A white man in dat pretty cart de sugar man does come in. He ax Mercury de. way to de house. He comin' up de hill dis very minute."

Phoebe looked in the direction the child was pointing. She could see the horse and trap belonging to

Mister Belle, but the boy said it was another white man. She turned, clapping her hands to emphasize her decision.

"Pool," she addressed the youth squatting on the floor by the back door, "run tell Massa Hayes we does have a stranger does be comin'. He does be down by topside."

"Yas, ma'am," the youth answered quickly. He put the pot which he had been cleaning down on the ground, and a dog came over to sniff it as he hurried off.

"Dido!" Phoebe turned to face the girl sitting at the table, her eyes bright at the excitement of an unexpected visitor.

"Dido, get up off yuh backside an' bring a slice o' dat smoke' pork dat hangin' in de pantry."

Remembering the child still standing at the door, she handed him a cake of coconut cheese from a big earthenware jar. "Dat's sweetmeats I done bake for Mas Carlton. Now git back to yo' place, boy. You know you got no rights lingerin' in white folks kitchin?"

When Hayes Todd strode through the back door of the kitchen a few minutes later, there was no sign of commotion. Fowls pecked at the dirt of the floor as Dido sat at the long table chopping chives. Phoebe, the flesh shaking on her huge arm, stirred the pot on the fire, peering through the steam at its contents.

"So we have a stranger coming, then, Phoebe?" said the tall white man as he strolled across the kitchen. Joining the cook looking into the large pot, he put his arm around her waist. "Smells good," he humored her, glancing at the trail through the open window.

The kittareen was almost at the house, and he could make out the firm weathered features and the heavy black beard of the man it was carrying. "You did right to call me. Our unknown visitor looks as though he expects a cordial reception."

Hayes had little trust in people. He had no friends, not even the neighboring estate owners, and the only contacts he had outside his plantation were business ones. He held the settlers in Dominica in considerable contempt for their dilettante approach to work and their fear of the French and the runaway maroons. So when he saw the tanned stranger alight from the kittareen with an agility belied by his size, and felt the callused grip of his strong handshake, he was intrigued.

"Captain Loring, master of the *Falconer*, en route to Jamaica and anchored in the river mouth," the visitor announced in a gruff voice.

"Hayes Todd, Bondmaster of Roxborough, at your service, Captain!"

The two men eyed each other before Hayes, withdrawing his hand, led the way up the front steps. "Come up, Captain. My place is simple, but you are welcome." Hayes indicated some wooden chairs on the balcony which extended around the entire house and afforded an uninterrupted view of the cane fields right down to the river.

Loring gazed around. "Like being on the bridge!" he joked. "I do declare I can see me vessel down there at the river mouth. If yer has a spy glass, Mister Todd, I could see what that mate of mine is doing when he thinks I'm safely ensconced in some whore's arms ashore!"

Hayes looked at his visitor in surprise. When he caught the glint in Loring's eyes, he let out a hearty laugh. Phoebe, who had come out of the kitchen below the balcony, raised her eyebrows at the sound, a rare one at Roxborough. She had done right. The man would certainly be staying for dinner.

"Bo'jack!" Hayes's shout disturbed the Negro polishing cutlery in the dining room. "Bo'jack!"

The old Negro put down the knife carefully and shuffled out through the drawing room onto the balcony, straightening the sash holding up his black breeches. "Yas, Massa Hayes, sah?"

"Where the hell have you been, Bo'jack?" Hayes raised his voice angrily. "Don't you know you're supposed to be here when I come in?"

"Yas, Massa Hayes, sah. I does be here, sah. I does be settin' de table, sah. Phoebe don't say you done come home, sah."

"Sleeping, more like it! A flogging will help you keep awake. That's the trouble with niggers today." Hayes turned to address the Captain, who was still standing at the balcony railing as though on his ship, scanning the panorama below him.

"Slaves get lazy if you keep them in the house too long. Especially this Negro here. Reckon I should send him to the fields."

"Really?" The Captain turned politely, ignoring his host's annoyance. He glanced quickly at the offending slave, who, he noted, was dressed in a patched but clean uniform. His face was pleasing enough, not scowling, although he was far too old for Loring's tastes.

"Damn you, Bo'jack!" said Hayes as the slave tried to speak. "I'll lick some respect into you before I finish. Now mix two punches for us, and be sharp about it."

"Yas please, massa, sah." Bo'jack backed out of the gallery, wondering if the danger was past.

"Have a chair, Cap'n." Hayes again waved at the wooden chairs that had long flat arms designed to hold one's glass while he stretched out with feet up on the balcony rail.

"This is a fine spot for keeping an eye on the slaves in the field, especially with a glass of punch in your hand. You will take a glass, won't you?"

"Oh, aye," Loring smiled. "I've tried some of yer famous Roxborough grog already. Mighty powerful it is, too."

Hayes was pleased at the compliment. "We age our rum proper. Least two weeks 'fore I sell it. Got some fine rum aging in casks right now. Put a pound of beef in it, I do, and some prunes. Saving that rum for a special occasion."

As he spoke, Hayes tried to figure out the reason for the Captain's visit. The man still peered at the view intently, although he had settled into a seat with apparent pleasure.

"What a superb lookout, Mister Todd."

"I built the gallery right 'round the house," explained Hayes. "If we want to watch the sunset after day is done, then we go to the back. If we want the sunrise, then we sit right here. Not that we have much time for sitting. Always something to do if you have Negroes. Like cattle, you see, not like human beings. No brains, can't think for themselves."

Bo'jack came onto the gallery with two pewter mugs on a tray. He hesitated. "Please sah," he tried. "De punch, sah!"

"Right, Bo'jack. Captain Loring, I hope you'll like our punch. You put plenty rum in, Bo'jack?"

"Oh yas, Massa Hayes. Like you does say, I does make de bes' rum punch on de Le'ard coast." He stood as the men sipped the concoction.

"Hm, not bad," said Loring. "Very refreshing."

Hayes was satisfied. For once Bo'jack had not let him down. "All right, Bo'jack," he said. "Set an extra place for Captain Loring. You will stay to dinner, won't you, Cap'n?"

"I'm much obliged to yer, Mister Todd." Loring felt the punch warm his stomach and relax his body after the bouncing of the ride to the house.

"And tell Phoebe that Captain Loring is staying. She can prepare extra."

"She done do dat a'ready, Massa Hayes, sah. She raisin' hell in de kitchin. Done sen' Pool to de river for crayfish, and Dido, she a-gratin' coconut to squeeze de water in de sauce."

Hayes was embarrassed by the details, wondering how the Captain would view Bo'jack's familiarity. Did the crew on a ship behave that way with their captain? He dismissed Bo'jack quickly, turning to Loring.

"You see," he apologized, "that Negro has been my house servant since I came here. He and Phoebe. Bought them the same day when they were youngsters.

But he's getting out of hand now. Trying to impress you."

"Good slaves are a mite hard to find nowadays, I know." The Captain sipped his punch again. It was excellent. And the prospect of dinner as described by Bo'jack sounded even better.

"When yer git a good one, I suppose yer be reluctant to sell him?"

"Depends," answered Hayes cautiously. "What kind of cargo do you carry in that vessel of yours, Captain?"

"I follow yer, Mister Todd. Mine's a merchantman. I plies the islands where I'm wanted. Right now, I've got a party of Frenchies bound for Jamaica. Royalists out of Martinique. But I'm not a slave trader, Mister Todd, if that's what yer thinking. Leastwise, not any more. Started as a boy sailing from the Congo to Jamaica, I did. Many's the Negro owes me for his passage to the West Indies."

Loring chuckled, bending his head forward toward Todd. "Might be on the lookout for a couple of bright boys, though. Yer know, niggers that is housebroke. Creoles, not Africans."

"You're right," Hayes spoke thoughtfully. "Those Africans need a lot of seasoning before they're good. As soon as they get down to work in the fields, they take sick and die. Change of air, I suppose, though you would not think that that would affect them, their skins being so thick. Still, it happens with other cattle, too, cows and suchlike."

Loring was about to add something when he was distracted. A boy was running up the front steps to the gallery. Loring took him for a half-breed. His skin glowed with an almost golden hue and his limbs, Loring was quick to notice, were lean and muscular. He wore no shirt or shoes, and his pants were patched.

The boy's features attracted Loring most. He had fine lips and a slender nose, and his long blond hair was bleached by the sun. The boy walked confidently onto the balcony, training his eyes, which Loring saw were a piercing green, onto the Captain with curiosity. Loring tried to hide his excitement with a cough, hardly able to contain himself at the sight of the most gorgeous slave he had ever seen.

"My son, Captain Loring."

The boy was holding out his hand, and Captain Loring took it in a daze. Clasping the firm hand, he sized up the boy's adolescent beauty. The boy withdrew his hand, squatted casually on the balcony rail and continued to stare at the stranger.

"You come for slaves?"

"Carlton!" reprimanded Hayes. "Captain Loring has only just arrived. It's not polite to ask a visitor his business."

"Don't know much about politeness, Da. Sorry, sah." The boy turned to Loring again, who was absolutely fascinated.

"That's all right, lad." Captain Loring bent forward in his chair to pat Carlton's leg as he swung from the railing.

"I didn't know yer had a son, Mister Todd. Yer must be mighty proud of the boy." Loring squeezed the lad's leg, assuming that he must be the offspring of the Bondmaster and one of his slave wenches.

"Sure am proud," beamed Hayes. "He is the spitting image of my wife, Monique. She was blond too. Dead ten years now, since Carlton was three. Grown up a bit wild he has, with no mother to soften him. Out on the plantation whole day. See? he's as brown as a nigger, ain't he?"

Carlton was bored with his father's talk. "What you a captain of, sah?"

"Merchantman. The *Falconer*, down in the river mouth. Thought I'd come and pay me respects, seeing as I haven't put into Layou before."

"Boy wants to know everything," shrugged Hayes, proud of his son's interest. "Not much chance of proper education here, being so far from Roseau. Not that I'd want him to go to them church schools anyway. Got to learn how to grow sugar, run the plantation, handle

31

Negroes. That's more important than any schooling."

"I agree," said Loring. "All I learned, I learned at sea. Not a man to better me in me trade."

It was Carlton who announced that they should go in to dinner, casually slipping off the balcony rail and strolling through the door into the drawing room. His father and the Captain followed him into the dining room beyond. As he entered, Loring was astonished by the sight of the loaded table and then by the glimpse he caught of Carlton sparring with a light-skinned Negro youth in the corner of the room. Carlton stopped as soon as the two men entered and took his place at the center of the table. Captain Loring was placed at one end, while Hayes Todd sat at the head.

"We don't stand on ceremony here, Captain," said Hayes, drawing his chair into the table. "Don't hold with religion myself, but if you want to pray, you can. These victuals be for eating, so help yourself."

"Yer set a fine table, Mister Todd." The Captain's pleasure increased Hayes's own. "Yer have a cook who must be worth her weight in gold!" He ladled the stew onto his plate, glancing quickly at the Negro boy whom Carlton had called Prince.

Carlton burst into laughter. "You hear dat, Da? Our cook Phoebe does be so fat she de weight of two cows. You need plenty gold to balance with her on de scales."

Carlton winked again at the Negro youth who was moving round the table filling their glasses with sangaree. Loring studied the slave's youthful grace and strength. He made a perfect partner for Carlton. "Prince does be my playboy," explained Carlton when he noticed the Captain's interest.

"We are fortunate here," said Hayes, filling his plate. "This is a fertile island. We grow enough to feed our slaves here. We don't have shortages like other islands. And I'm not one of them prissy yellow-livered Englishmen who say they can't eat local produce. Why not? My wife was French, from New Orleans; she knew how to cook. Taught Phoebe all she knew.

32

The English say it's cattle fodder, only good for slaves."

"Don't take no notice of Da," said Carlton with relish. "He does be English, too."

"Boy's right," said Hayes, his mouth full of smoked pork. "That's why I came here from Alabama. Didn't want no independence, just a chance to work hard and live well."

"An' make a fortune," added Carlton, again exchanging winks with Prince hovering at his side.

After the ample meal, Carlton begged leave to be excused. "Has to see all de field hands done stow de tools proper and everything," he explained.

Carlton left the room, his arm over Prince's shoulder, while Bo'jack cleared away the plates. Hayes led Loring through the back door of the dining room onto the gallery, where there was a pair of chairs identical to those at the front.

"Me and Carlton," he said, "generally sit like this as the sun goes down. That's after he's checked the niggers. He's a good boy, likes to work, helps me a lot. Be very pleased if you could stay the night, Captain Loring. Seldom we have guests, not often I meet someone I see eye to eye with, like with you."

"Well, I don't know." Loring was flattered by the invitation. He wasn't planning to sail until tomorrow, anyway, but nights on shore weren't to be wasted on conversation with garrulous old planters.

"Know what a man wants, I do," said Hayes chuckling. "Got a nice brown-skinned wench for you, if you like."

"In that case," said Loring, joining in his host's laughter, and reaching for the pitcher of rum held in front of him by Bo'jack, "it would be mighty impertinent fer me to refuse yer hospitality, Mister Todd!"

As a man gets older, thought Loring later that evening as he unstrapped his belt and contemplated the naked girl stretched out on his bed in the candlelight, he appreciates the finer things in life. He had dined lavishly, drunk strong grog in abundance, and been treated kindly by a gentlemanly planter host. And, mused Loring, easing off his breeches before moving toward the girl on the bed, he had discovered the most perfect pair of boys in the West Indies, the white son of the Bondmaster and his Negro playboy Prince.

"Well," he thought, sitting on the bed and casually rolling the girl over onto her stomach, "I can't have the white boy, but I sure as hell am going to have that black one!"

Chapter 4

A musket shot shattered Captain Loring's dreams as he slept in the large fourposter bed. He reacted immediately, sitting up wondering if his ship was under attack, until he realized he was on shore. The wench who had been with him had disappeared. Suspicious, he swung his legs over the edge of the bed and stood up cautiously, waiting for the follow-up fire. None came. He groped in the darkness for his pistol under the pillow and then moved toward the shutter. He opened it rapidly. Outside, it was not so dark, and he sensed daybreak was not far off. A shape darker than the dawn moved along the balcony.

"Who's there?" Loring demanded urgently, preparing to fire.

"Bo'jack, sah!"

"What do yer want, boy?"

"Nothin', sah."

"What was that shot?" Loring was undecided. He had heard of slave uprisings and of planters being murdered in their beds. It happened frequently in Jamaica, and he knew that Dominica had bands of runaways living in the interior.

"Dat be daybreak, sah. Time for dem niggers to git to de fields, sah."

Loring relaxed his grip on the pistol as Bo'jack came level with the window. He was fully dressed.

"Does you want somethin', sah?"

"Bah!" Loring was annoyed at his own foolishness. He turned back into the room and decided to lie on his bed until there was sufficient light to dress himself. He had been given the guest room at the back of the house with a view over the hillside out to sea. Although it adjoined the dining room, the entrance door was from the gallery.

There was a flight of stone steps leading down to the ground floor at the other end of the balcony, as well as the front entrance steps. Loring had been told that the kitchen, stores, and quarters for the house slaves were in the lower part of the house, which was built of stone. The upper part was constructed of timber with a shingle roof.

Hayes Todd had explained to Loring the night before that there were two guest rooms with their doors opening onto the gallery. This was to enable visitors to have wenches in their rooms without disturbing the rest of the household. Hayes had his room at the front of the house, with a dressing room adjoining it. His son had a similar room opposite. Loring had seen Carlton go to that room the evening before, accompanied by Prince. The two seemed inseparable. Hayes had explained that the boy had slept in Carlton's room since his mother died.

Loring's thoughts lingered on that playboy. Prince was his name, and princely he seemed. He was probably a year or two older than Carlton and had a refinement unusual in Negroes, perhaps from being brought up in a white household. Loring pictured Prince in fine livery as a gentleman's fancy body servant in Jamaica. He would surely fetch a high price.

"Yes," thought Loring, rubbing his crotch, "I must have him."

When Loring joined Hayes for breakfast later, he was disappointed to see that there were only two places set at the table, and that Bo'jack, not Prince, waited on them.

36

"Carlton not joining us?" he asked, hoping to appear casual.

"No," said Hayes, "that boy's off in the fields somewhere. I don't have an overseer, prefer to do the work myself, but Carlton takes a lively interest. Have some coffee," he urged. "It's our own, grown on the plantation."

Loring sipped the steaming black brew. "It's excellent."

Hayes beamed. "I grow a little coffee on land I bought from one of those Frenchies. French specialize in coffee, but there's too much disease and the market is poor, too."

Loring nodded, but planter's talk was not of interest to him.

His host continued. "The English planters stick to sugar. I've done all right out of sugar myself, but then I have the right location, you see. We just send the sugar down to the river, where it goes direct to England.

"Nigh on twenty years I've grown sugar here. Have to dung the soil, though. Beginning to wonder how I can keep it up. Need sugar, I do, but would not object to growing another crop, too."

"Forgive me, Mister Todd," said Loring, seizing a break in the conversation, "I'm not a planter."

"But you've sailed around the islands, Captain. Surely you know what people are doing in other places. Jamaica and that Trinidad, for instance. Are there any new crops what make the money and don't drain the soil like sugar?"

Loring put down his coffee cup. The word money had caught his attention. "There's one crop that I see gits the money, Mister Todd, but that's livestock, not sugar nor coffee."

"Cattle!" Hayes was disappointed. "Cows need plenty of pasture, get sick too easy."

"Not cattle, Mister Todd. Leastwise, not the four-legged kind. Livestock, though. I mean Negroes, Mister Todd."

Hayes was puzzled. "Negroes? Got plenty of them. They costs money, not makes it. Costs so much to keep a Negro, Captain, burns me the way it reduces profits."

"Aye, Mister Todd. Don't doubt you." Loring poured himself a second cup of coffee. "With respect, sir, consider where yuh would be without yer slaves."

"Huh?" Hayes did not understand what his guest meant. Surely he was not one of those damned abolitionists? "Can't survive without slaves, Captain! No Negroes, no work, no sugar, Captain. And no profits, none at all!"

"Exactly!" Loring sat back triumphantly. "Yer've got plenty of Negroes here. Now, me point is that one day there might not be any Negroes to do the work."

"How do you mean?" spluttered Hayes in alarm.

Loring realized he was on dangerous ground. "It's the way things are shaping, sir. Look at what's happening. Denmark banned the slave trade last year."

"First I heard of it."

"It's true, although the law don't take effect for another ten years. But just think what will happen if traders can't ship Africans to the colonies no more." Loring leaned back to watch his words work on Hayes.

"Makes no neverminds to me," said Hayes, his confidence restored. "I've got so many of those black buggers, doubt I need to buy another African again. All my Negroes be seasoned, too, better workers."

"That's wonderful, Mister Todd." Loring leaned forward to face Hayes across the length of the table. "Well, what about the other planters here? Are they as fortunate as ye be? What 'bout them in Jamaica, Antigua, Trinidad? Them planters can't git enough Negroes even now. In ten or fifteen years, with none comin' over from Africa, they'll pay a fortune for a creole nigger."

The silence which followed as Hayes chewed on the final crust, his eyes resting on the Captain, was broken by a whoop of delight as Carlton ran into the dining room.

"Morning, Cap'n, Da!" he said breathlessly. "Run up from Long Field. Coffee done finish'?"

"No, Mas Carlton," said Bo'jack, bustling across with a second pot. "I done save yours for you, an' de bread."

Carlton remained standing as he poured himself a cup. "You sailin' today, Cap'n? Wind done blow itself out now."

"Captain Loring's been telling me Denmark banned the slave trading, son," said Hayes, before Loring could reply.

"Dat so?" Carlton shrugged his shoulders.

"Means nothing to us, does it, son?" Hayes continued thoughtfully. "But the Captain says that Negroes might get scarce. What you really suggesting, Captain Loring?"

"Ye asked me 'bout a crop to make yer profits, Mister Todd. Livestock, says I. Negroes, says I. Raise Negroes to sell, Mister Todd, and ye'll do better than yer ever done out of sugar. Why, I can get hundred pound sterling for a prime field slave right now! In ten years a seasoned Negro will cost double."

Hayes sank back in his chair, his breakfast forgotten. The last time he had bought Negroes, he got a mixed coffle of ten for two hundred pounds from an illegal trader who had put into Layou. He had begrudged spending so much money at the time. He had about two hundred slaves in all. He was not sure, but it represented a fortune, if this Captain Loring was to be believed.

"Don't seem nothin' in it," said Carlton, ignoring his father's silence. "Niggers plentiful. Don't need no special care. Can sell what we don' need fuh de plantation. Make profit all roads."

"Aye, ye've a bright lad, Mister Todd." Loring reached up and ruffled Carlton's hair. "But hogs that run wild ain't never as sweet as those fattened in the pen, are they, son?"

Carlton grinned. "Ain't no one plannin' to eat our niggers, Cap'n."

"Mayhaps the Captain's right," interrupted Hayes. "What kind of Negroes them people wants down in Trinidad and Jamaica?"

"Seasoned, of course. If they are creole born, less likely to be rebellious. Trinidad wants strong bucks for field work. But Jamaica wants slaves what are housebroke and respectful, more fancy."

"Dat's all talk," said Carlton. "We know about dat. You not de first man dat come an' want our niggers."

"Carlton!" warned Hayes, angered by his son's impatience. "The Captain isn't trying to buy our niggers. I asked his advice on what we could raise alongside sugar. No future in relying on one crop, son. Interesting suggestion, it is."

"Raise niggers?" Carlton still did not see any sense in it. "De niggers does raise demselfs, anyway."

"Let me show ye what I mean, Mister Todd. And yer'll see too, lad," suggested Loring. "Yer slave, Prince, where he be?"

"Down by de kitchin' I expect," said Carlton sulkily.

"Mister Todd, would ye permit I send for the boy? Like to give yer all a demonstration."

Intrigued, Hayes ordered Bo'jack to go down to the kitchen and send the slave up to them. As they had all finished breakfast, he invited the Captain to sit in the drawing room. Joining them reluctantly, Carlton was puzzled by what the Captain had in mind. He regarded Prince as his friend rather than his slave and was pleased when he saw Prince trotting up the stone steps at the front of the house. He walked out of the drawing room to meet him, but before he could speak, Hayes rose up from his seat.

"Hold it, boy!" he barked. Both Carlton and Prince stopped, neither knowing which one he was addressing.

"Why are you coming up the front steps, boy?" demanded Hayes, pointing his finger in accusation at Prince. Carlton, glancing at his father's face, saw his brows heavy with anger. From his own seat, Loring watched Prince's pretty features mottle with concern.

"But Massa Hayes, sah, Bo'jack done say you wants me quick, sah. Lef' my breakfas', sah." Prince looked at Carlton for support.

"Since when you have right to come up the front steps, boy? Don't you know that niggers use the back steps?" Hayes turned away to stomp back to his chair, addressing no one in particular. "What do we have back steps for?"

Prince, poised on the top step, did not know whether he should come in. He opened his mouth to speak.

"Hush!" said Carlton, waving his friend away. "Go down an' come up back steps," he urged him. Prince turned and ran down while Carlton went back into the drawing room. "He don't mean no wrong, Da. Believe' you want him quick."

"Ain't no hurry can cause niggers to forget their place, Carlton. Remember that. Them niggers inclined to please themselves too much, and when we have company, too."

Hayes had settled back in his chair now. Captain Loring, embarrassed at the show of authority which Hayes had put on, apparently just for him alone, tried to get the situation in calmer waters. "When yer buys a slave, Mister Todd, what do yer look for?"

Hayes thought. "Strength, I suppose," he replied, stroking the stubble on his gnarled cheek. "I'm buying the slave to work, right, so I want one that be strong. And bright," he added as an afterthought. Hayes looked up at the gentle tap on the door which separated the drawing room from the dining room. Prince stood there nervously. "Don't want no troublesome bugger, either."

"Please, sah," said Prince, refusing to be chastened. "I does be sorry, sah."

"Damn you, boy!" roared Hayes again. "When white folks are conversing, you just keep your damn mouth shut. Carlton!" Hayes turned on his son. "That slave of yours gettin' too fresh these days!"

"Yes, Da," answered Carlton, wary of his father

41

when he was in such a mood. He would explain to Prince afterwards that his dad was only trying to impress their visitor.

Captain Loring, who was much attracted by Prince's arrogance, beckoned him to come over to his chair.

"With yer permission, sir?"

Hayes shrugged, greatly put out by the slave's behavior.

Loring stood the boy in front of him, gripping his wrists with both hands. "How do yer test a Negro before yer buy him, Mister Todd?"

"How?" Hayes was surprised. "Well, I use my eyes. Mayhap, I'll get him to jump. Easy to judge if I like him or not."

"That's right, sir. That's the best way. If yer going to buy a slave, ye wants the best, ain't it? So, if yer going to raise niggers to sell, then yer've got to breed the best. Yer son here reckons niggers raise themselves anyway. But ye should make sure they only breed good niggers, not scrawny runts yer can't sell for ten bits.

"Now look at this young specimen here. With me eye I can see he is mighty pleasin'. Not an ugly black boy, right. Nice bright skin, nose not too flat. Open yer mouth, boy," said Loring, releasing the slave's wrists and standing up. "Right, seems like he has fine teeth."

Loring slid his finger into the boy's mouth and passed it over each of his teeth. If Prince was tempted to clamp his mouth shut in disgust at the proximity of the captain's pockmarked face and his foul breath, he showed no sign.

"If yer inspect a nigger carefully 'fore yer buy, ye know yer gettin' what ye think yer gettin'."

Loring withdrew his finger and looked at Todd and his son, both watching with fascination. "Now, the boy looks strong, right, but ye must check his muscles." Loring began to pass his hands across the boy's chest and, holding him close to himself, reached over to

42

feel his shoulders and back. "Yes, feels fine. No marks on his skin, neither. Very important, is that."

Loring sat down again. "With slaves gettin' scarce, the gentleman who buys from ye will want a Negro who is going to breed for him, right?"

Hayes nodded thoughtfully, but Carlton still did not see what all the fuss was about.

"There's some niggers don't give yer no young ones at all. Got to check before yer buy. Boy!" He looked up at Prince watching him. "Step out of yer trogs!"

Prince hesitated, glancing quickly at Carlton standing behind the Bondmaster's chair.

"Go on!" growled Hayes, annoyed at the slave's hesitancy, even though he himself was surprised at the Captain's request.

"Ah!" said Loring as Prince stepped out of his pants and stood naked before him. "See what I mean?" He tapped Prince on his buttock to make him stand sideways.

"The prick," said Loring, reaching out his callused hand to grasp Prince's penis.

Carlton gasped, his eyes on his friend's body. Prince was too scared to resist.

Loring skinned back the head, feeling the boy's penis throbbing in his rough hand. "Ye must check the prick be clean. And the bollocks." He cupped Prince's testicles in his hands, bouncing them. "See! They are heavy. Boy's a breeder!"

Loring noticed Prince's rising erection with satisfaction. "Bend over, boy!" he said, leaning forward in his chair as Prince bent down. Loring placed his finger in between the boy's buttocks. "Got to check for piles," he explained to the astonished Hayes.

"Well, I never did!"

Loring gave his finger a sudden thrust. Prince yelped and stumbled forward onto the floor.

"He's not bad," smirked Loring. "Raise niggers like him and ye'll be famous from Alabama to the Spanish Main. Quality, seasoned niggers."

Loring, his dissertation concluded, sat back in his

chair, idly passing the finger he had inserted into Prince's bottom under his nose. Sniffing, he glanced first at Hayes, who was sitting as though unable to believe his eyes, and then at Carlton. He noticed with amusement the bulge Carlton was trying to hide by covering his crotch with his hand.

"Here!" Loring grinned as he kicked the discarded pants across the floor to where Prince was still lying, clutching himself.

"Git them trogs on, boy!"

Chapter 5

Prince, rushing pell-mell to the stairs to tell Ma Phoebe how the stranger had inspected him just like he had heard they do at the vendues, crashed into someone blocking the gallery. It was the stranger himself.

"Oh, sah!" he stammered, breath knocked out of him. "Excuse me, sah. Don't mean no disrespect, sah. You a'right, sah?" In his panic, he dabbed at the Captain's coat with his hands as though to brush away evidence of the fateful collision.

Loring had been waiting to intercept Prince and grabbed his hand eagerly. He squeezed it. "Look at me, boy!"

"Yas, sah," whispered Prince. "Don't hit me, sah! Please, sah!"

"Shut up!" Loring gripped the boy's hand tighter. "Ain't goin' to beat ye. Now do as I say, and look at me."

Prince raised his head from the level of the stranger's chest to look up at his face. It was old and tanned, pitted with scars under the eyes. His black beard, flecked with gray, was sticky with globs of saliva. Prince was scared to look into the man's bloodshot eyes which were searching his face eagerly.

"Do ye know who I am, son?"

Prince relaxed as he sensed the man was not vexed

with him. There was something else about him. He was puzzled. "No, sah."

"See that ship out there?" Loring rested his hands on the boy's shoulders, spinning him around to look along the gallery out to the river mouth. "The large schooner there. She's mine. I'm the captain of that vessel."

"Yas, sah." Prince looked politely. He was used to the sight of ships, and he had often watched the vessels being loaded with hogsheads of sugar for shipment to England.

"I sail to Jamaica, boy. A land such as yer never did see. People dressed in the finest clothes, goin' to balls and such like. Big roads, coaches, enormous great houses, thousands of people. A boy like ye could be dressed in fine silks, work in one of them great houses for rich ladies and gentlemen."

The Captain's voice was low, speaking directly into Prince's ear. He felt his body tingling with excitement. "Sah?" Prince wriggled under the pressure of the man's fingers fondling his backside.

"Yes, boy?"

"Is true dat I be mighty pleasin', sah?"

Loring cuffed him on the side of his head. "Ye bugger! Yer want to come with me, boy? Yer want to dress in fine silks and ride in a big carriage?"

"Oh yas, sah!" Wait until Ma Phoebe heard about this, thought Prince. "Yas, sah!"

"Right, boy. I'm goin' to buy ye. Yer go'n be me slave. Sail with me on me ship, mess with me. We'll do a lot of things together, boy." The Captain released Prince suddenly. "Where yer goin' now?"

"Mas Carlton done sent me to de kitchin fuh breakfas'."

"Mas Carlton, eh?" Loring nodded his head. Soon he would have this stripling calling *him* the master, not some brat still wet behind the ears. "Be off with ye! I've got words to have with Mister Hayes Todd!"

Loring found Hayes still sitting in the drawing room where he had left him a few minutes before. It seemed strange, even to Loring who hardly knew him, for Hayes to stay so thoughtful for so long. He did not look up as the Captain returned, but kept drumming his fingers on the long wooden arm of his chair.

In the two decades he had been in the island, Hayes Todd had worked hard. He had come to this British possession with his French wife as a refugee from the War of Independence. He was fortunate to be able to buy the Roxborough plantation from its English owner who had grown bored with the relentless struggle of making the estate profitable.

After years spent building up his cotton plantation in Alabama, Hayes was not put off by the so-called hardships of growing sugar in Dominica. With the money he had brought with him, and greatly aided by his wife's own inheritance, he acquired slaves by the score. He prowled the free port of Roseau to get the best bargains from the Guinea factors, buying Negroes destined for other islands so that he could get the best. By mixing seasoned slaves with new imports direct from Africa, he had been able to build up a strong and well-disciplined herd.

Learning from his experience in Alabama, Hayes was kind but ruthless with his Negroes. They responded by working hard under his direction. He recognized his slaves as a key to prosperity and refused to hire an overseer who might ill-treat them. Instead, he worked alongside his Negroes, clearing the forest right up to the plantation boundaries. While his neighbors had trouble with their slaves, his own learned to respect him. He built them cabins to live in and gave each group a plot where they could grow their own provisions to supplement the supplies of salt fish and flour which he allocated them every week.

Two years after he arrived in the island, the French invaded Dominica and stayed five years. Those were hard times. The Marquis Duchilleau, as Governor, led his French officials in a campaign to reduce the value of the island in order to have it ceded to France at the end of the war. Most of the English inhabitants quit under the oppression of the French. But it made no difference to Hayes. He provided the soldiers with cattle when they demanded and abided by their laws. His wife's being French helped him to avoid their plundering. He was even able to acquire neighboring lands and add them to the Roxborough estate.

With the lands went more slaves. Hayes took them all. Sugar was hard to work. At best, he could hope for seven good years from a slave in the cane fields. After that, if he had not taken sick and died in the wet climate, the nigger was put to work maintaining the plantation roads, or looking after the cattle. More slaves were always needed, although he had never had any slave run away into the hills, and the bands of maroons never bothered Roxborough.

The plantation had prospered during the years. The soil had been rich to begin with, and there was plenty of sugar to ship to England. But after twenty years the soil was getting worn out, and Hayes sometimes felt that he was, too. Since his wife had died just after the French left, Hayes had worked unceasingly to bring up Carlton to take over from him. But with the decline of sugar, Hayes had begun to think that he would have only a herd of slaves to leave his son and no means of livelihood. Now, if this Captain Loring was to be believed, it appeared that these same niggers could be a bigger inheritance for his son than sugar or any other crop.

"I do declare," said Hayes, turning to face Loring, who had returned to his chair. "If what you say is true, and there are people who will pay a hundred pounds for one slave, then I have a fortune here at Roxborough, quite without considering fifteen years hence."

"Indeed, ye do, sir! Indeed ye do." The Captain leaned forward. "Only with prime stock, mind ye. Worked-out niggers ain't no good. That's why yer got to breed. Boys like that Prince are prime. Could get a hundred pounds easy for him."

"Really, Captain?" Hayes was intrigued but doubtful.

"It's a fact!" protested Loring. "Why, I wouldn't mind giving the hundred pounds meself." He paused, looking at Hayes to see how he would react. "If I had it, of course."

"Ah!" said Hayes, as though Loring had provided the lie to his tale.

"Yes," Loring pressed home. "Would yer take a hundred pound for that buck?"

"Captain Loring," Hayes said with a smile, "surely you don't take me for a fool. I know you are a man of the world. If you put down a hundred pounds in gold on that table for that slave, it's because you can sell him for double!"

The two men's laughter attracted Carlton, who came in from the gallery.

"But," continued Hayes, "I've got to see your gold!"

"Gold fuh what, Da?" asked Carlton.

"Son! This is business!" Hayes looked at Carlton standing framed in the doorway, the estate stretching away into the distance behind him. The boy's young face was bright with curiosity.

"Come in, Carlton," Hayes relented. "When you're Bondmaster, you'll have to buy and sell slaves same way as we do with our cattle." Carlton walked over to stand beside his father's chair.

"Captain Loring here has offered me a hundred pounds for that Prince."

"Da!" Carlton was shocked. "You not sellin' Prince, Da. You can't sell Prince!"

"And why not? Prince is a slave, ain't he? He's mine to sell, if and when I take a mind to."

"But he be my own slave, Da. I done have him since I was a babe. He does play wid me, we does do everythin' together."

"I know, son," sighed Hayes. "I know you don't want to lose your playboy, but you're growing up now. You should be learning, not playing. That slave ain't no use to you again. 'Cept as a body servant, mayhaps," he conceded. "But you ain't sick and you ain't a fancy English boy what can't fasten his own britches. You're nearly a man, Carlton."

"Yas, Da," he said softly. "Yas, Da."

"Anyway, Carlton," Hayes put out his hand to rest on his son's arm, "it's just an offer the Captain is making for Prince. Haven't decided if I'll accept it yet. You got the gold, Cap'n?"

"No, sir! Won't fool ye. Ain't got it." Loring felt that he had seen a way out of his difficulties. He wanted that nigger bad.

"But I'll make a deal with ye, Mister Todd. Yer say I can probably git more than a hundred I'm offerin' yer. Mayhap I can. What d'ye say to a partnership?"

Hayes had a feeling that a partnership with Loring would be as good as a pact with a privateer. He was impressed by his swashbuckling guest but could not see a way to trusting him. "How's that?" he ventured.

"I guarantee ye a hundred pounds for that boy. If I sell him for more, then I give ye half me profit when I come back."

"So when does Da git de one hundred pounds?"

"Carlton!" Hayes was amused rather than angered by his son's apt interruption.

"Aye," mused Loring. "Yer son be mighty sharp, sir. He be a credit to yer. Got much education, has he? Can he read and write and so on?" Loring knew that it was an impertinent question, but he decided to risk it.

"Want to learn," said Carlton immediately. "But Da can't write more dan sign his name so don't have no one dat can learn me."

"Boy!" his father was angry now. "You too damn fast. Hold yo' tongue 'fore I take off my strap and thrash you."

"I ask yer to forgive me askin'," said Loring, "only I got a lady on me ship as is lookin' for a position. Nice and respectable, not a young slip. Related to the late Governor General de Champigny of Martinique." Loring bent forward, lowering his voice. "They say she is his daughter by his mistress." Loring sat back

50

again. "White, of course. Very educated, and speaks English. She used to be tutor to a family in Martinique."

"Why are you telling me this, Captain?"

"Was just thinking as how ye might be needin' a tutor for Master Carlton here. Seems right that he should be learning just as yer says. Mighty cultured is M'selle de Champigny. She could learn him plenty."

"Captain Loring," said Hayes slowly, "I know I'm an ignorant planter. If you've got a proposition to make, then for God's sake oblige me by making it. No good trying to fool me with sweet talk."

"Aye, Mister Todd. I respects ye for that. I'm offerin' to 'change M'selle de Champigny for that slave of ye'n."

Hayes sat back in his chair. He would have to pay a tutor about fifty pounds a year. It was no bargain. He shook his head.

"Wait, Mister Todd," said Loring, leaning forward again. "I told yer she is well connected. She won't want no payment at all. Say we values her at a hundred pounds, right? Give me that slave in 'change and if I sells him for more, I brings ye half the profit. And ye still git yer tutor for yer son Carlton here." He sat back in his chair. "What ye say?"

"Seems like you are mighty keen to have that slave," said Hayes. "First time I sold a nigger to a stranger. Watched that boy grow, I have." He checked himself. "Carlton, call Prince here."

There was no conversation between the two men as they waited for Prince, each considering in private the advantages of the transaction. Captain Loring had no doubt that he could persuade the Champigny woman to teach the heir to Roxborough, while Hayes was delighted by the merits of swapping a slave for a white tutor.

Prince entered through the dining room and stood before them. Carlton watched.

"Boy," said Hayes, "you've been a good slave and a true companion for my son. Ain't sold a slave before, leastwise not to a stranger, but Captain Loring here mighty keen to have you, so I'm selling you to him. He's your new master. Wherever you go, I want you to remember all you learned at Roxborough. You hear, boy? You're Roxborough born and bred, and don't you bring no bad name on us."

"Yas, sah! No, sah!" Prince was confused. "I does be a good nigger, sah. Please' to be goin' wid my new master, sah, but I be sad to be leavin' you an' Mas Carlton an' Ma Phoebe, sah."

"For God's sake, shut your mouth!" Hayes stood up. "Come on, Carlton, we got work to do. All those damn niggers will be idling if we don't get behind them. Captain Loring!"

The two men shook hands to confirm the arrangement, and then Hayes spun suddenly round and strode out of the room onto the gallery.

Carlton paused for a last look at Prince, but the Negro had turned to watch his new master. Annoyed, Carlton ran down the steps, clearing his throat angrily and sending a stream of spittle after a chicken scratching in the dust.

One day, he thought as he trotted obediently after his father, he would be the one to say who was to be sold and who was to breed. He would show those slaves! One day he, Carlton Todd, would be the Bondmaster of Roxborough.

BOOK ONE

The Roxborough Breed

Chapter 6

"M'sieur Hayes! M'sieur Hayes! Oh, what shall I do!"
The shrill voice of the Champigny woman jerked Hayes Todd suddenly out of his afternoon nap. Fists were pounding on the closed door of his chamber. "What the devil does that French wench want in the middle of the afternoon?" Hayes wondered.

"Yes! Yes!" he called, easing himself up to swing his legs onto the floor. It could not be more than an hour since dinner, he thought. He shook his head and glanced out through the open shutters of the window. There was a long line of Negroes working peacefully in the fields at the bottom of the hill. Everything appeared to be quiet. The banging on his door continued.

"Oh, M'sieur Todd! Forgive me for my disturbance, but I am so troubled."

"Damn the woman!" Hayes cursed quietly to himself. For two years she had been living at Roxborough tutoring Carlton. Surely by now she knew better than to wake an Englishman when he was taking his afternoon nap. He stood groggily on his feet. "Perdition take her!"

"Well, what is it, woman!" he shouted, staggering to the door and throwing it open.

Mademoiselle de Champigny was startled. She stepped backwards into the drawing room until she collided with a chair, which she grabbed quickly for support. Hayes noticed that her face, normally so carefully composed, was pinched with worry. Even her hair, which she always wore swept back from her forehead and gathered in a tight knot at the back, showed signs of her concern, strands sticking to her brow, wet with perspiration in the afternoon heat. With a nervous gesture she tried to push the strands back into place.

Hayes watched her curiously. The complete change in the woman, who had constantly appeared to be incapable of emotion in all the two years she had been at Roxborough, puzzled him. He forgot the anger he felt at her boldness in disturbing his afternoon routine. Instead, he steadied himself in the doorway and waited while she dabbed at her face.

"Oh, M'sieur Todd!" she blurted out, her eyes pleading with him. "What am I to do?"

"What have you done?" snapped Hayes. Seeing a pitcher of sangaree on the dresser, he poured a deliberate measure before turning to contemplate the woman again.

"You realize, m'selle, that to disturb an Englishman in the middle of his post-prandial repose is tantamount to insolence. If you were a nigger, I'd have you strung up to that flamboyant tree and thrashed. How would you like that, eh?" He raised the cup in his hand, gulped down the wine and smacking his lips defiantly.

Mademoiselle de Champigny caught her breath. How she hated this vile man with his English arrogance and stench of rum and black women!

"M'sieur Todd!" She paused, delaying the pleasure the full effect of her words would have when she uttered them. "M'sieur Todd, please forgive my interruption, but ze French, M'sieur Todd, ze French, my people, zey are 'ere."

"The French, m'selle?" Hayes was unimpressed. "Are they not here all the time?"

"But zey 'ave invaded, m'sieur. With a big army."

55

"They would need, m'selle, a very big army indeed."

Hayes glanced quickly across the balcony to the cane fields below where he saw with satisfaction that his Negroes were still working. The long line of blacks, bent double, advanced slowly across the field where the cane had been cropped. The drivers were watching them, whips silent in their hands. If there was anything afoot which should concern him, his slaves would be the first to show it. The hush of the afternoon would be broken by the slice of the whip and the cries of the slaves. Hayes could read the signs of trouble before he even knew what the trouble was.

"It's a ver' big army, M'sieur Todd. I 'ave ze information 'ere." Mademoiselle de Champigny was baffled as she waved her piece of paper at the odious Todd. "If only it will unsettle him," she thought, "it will make my own predicament more bearable."

"A piece of paper, m'selle! For a piece of paper you want to disturb my household with your barging and caterwauling? I follow signs, m'selle—my nose—not scraps of paper!" Hayes snorted, flinging himself down into a chair and sticking his legs out straight in front of him.

"And what does your precious piece of paper say, m'selle? What does it say!"

"It's in French, m'sieur. I will translate."

The paper was a leaflet printed in Guadeloupe and it announced the invasion of Dominica by citizen Victor Hughes, the Commissioner to the West Indies from the French Revolution. The leaders of the invading expedition, Rameau and Caneaux, by this proclamation announced a penalty of death for any French inhabitants of Dominica, even naturalized and adopted subjects, who would bear arms against them.

"Hah!" chuckled Hayes Todd when the woman had finished reading. "That's a most impressive proclamation, m'selle. Where'd you get it?"

"A boy brought it from my friend in Colihaut."

Hayes considered the situation. He knew the woman had a colleague tutoring the daughters of an English family at their residence near the village of Colihaut, a few miles farther north along the coast. If a boy had brought it, as she claimed, it would account for his own slaves not having heard about this so-called invasion. It it was a French business, his own Negroes would only hear of it when runaways spread the word through Layou. The proclamation was obviously printed before the invaders had arrived, if they had actually arrived at all.

"But, m'sieur," demanded Mademoiselle de Champigny, disappointed by the lack of concern being shown by Todd, "what will you do?"

"What will I do!" Hayes laughed. "Woman, what do you expect me to do? Prime the cannons and arm the niggers?"

"Bue ze revolution, m'sieur. Zese people, zey are not like us. Zey are not reasonable. Zey come from France to free ze people."

"In that case," said Hayes watching the woman carefully. "I would say that you are the one to worry, not me. You left Martinique, did you not, to escape the revolution? And now your revolution may catch you here!" He guffawed.

"Oh!" The woman clasped both hands to her head as the reality of the situation returned to her. "Zat was why I wake you, m'sieur. What can I do? I am so afraid. You do not know zese people, m'sieur. If ze French 'ere fight zem, zey will kill us. If we do not fight zem and zey win Dominique, zen zey will kill us."

"Kill you, m'selle? What nonsense."

"Yes, m'sieur. I am known, you see. I am a relative of the great Governor of Martinique, General de Champigny. I am aristocratic."

The sounds of commotion down the hill where the slaves were working drifted up to the house. Hayes glanced quickly out of the open door and across the balcony into the distance. He frowned. Something had unsettled the niggers; perhaps the boy who had brought the paper had spread the news. Hayes remained in his seat, determined not to let this French chit see that he was concerned. The cries of pain which followed the first hubbub from the fields satisfied him. With the whips caressing their backs, the slaves would get on with their work.

"M'selle!" Hayes drew in his legs and leaned forward to face the governess. "I have lived in Dominica under the French, and under the English. The soldiers fight; I grow sugar and make fine rum. My neighbors are French, my wife was French. If the French take this island, so be it. You say these are the revolutionaries and that your Victor Hughes and Rameau and Caneaux have come to free the slaves and kill the aristocrats. Fine sentiments. Free the animals and shoot the farmer. How do you then live? Come." Hayes stood up and beckoned the woman to follow him out onto the balcony.

"Look," he said, waving his arm to encompass all the land stretching below them right down to the river mouth. "This is Roxborough plantation, damn fine land with damn fine Negroes, all well fed and good working animals. Ain't no kind of government, be it English, French, Danish, or Spanish going to destroy what's bringing in prosperity. I have a fine estate here for me and my son, and we makes money. I goes along with whoever be running this island and welcome them all. Roxborough is my island, and I make my own peace treaties."

As he spoke, Hayes noticed his son racing up the hill from the lower field. M'selle de Champigny had done a good job with the boy, he would grant her that. Now he could read and write English and French as well as he could speak it, and do enough arithmetic to check the accounts, too. The woman had been worth it, even though she seemed to despise him because he was an ignorant planter. He turned abruptly, striding back into the house for the sangaree jug, speaking over his shoulder at the woman trotting after him.

"You'll do as you please now, m'selle. If you want to stay here, we'll guarantee our full protection. There

ain't nothing going to happen to molest you. Invasion will come, invasion will go, you'll not notice any changes here." Hayes watched the last of the wine mixture trickle out of the pitcher into his cup. He raised the cup to his lips, staring over the brim into the eyes of the woman. "And if you want to go," he said softly, "you goes."

Savoring the sangaree in his mouth, Hayes wondered why his son's tutor was so troubled. The glance she gave him before she swept back onto the balcony was one of disapproval, even contempt. Hayes watched her bob quickly down the front steps to head for her quarters, a wooden cabin he had built for her when she first arrived. She had refused to live in the house with him and Carlton, although they had enough rooms. She had insisted on her own quarters, putting a partition in her cabin to use the front as the schoolroom and the rear for sleeping. She had even rejected the slave Hayes had assigned her, saying that she had no need for one.

Her evenings, as far as Hayes was aware, were spent idly in her cabin reading in the flickering light of a candle. There was no church in the vicinity, so her Sundays were spent in meditation. Occasionally, she journeyed to Colihaut to spend a few days with her colleague, but otherwise appeared to have no interests. Now, words on a leaflet had revealed emotions to him which Hayes had not believed she possessed. Perhaps the threat of these invading French revolutionaries would drive the strait-laced miss to seek personal protection from him in the nights to come. Hayes chuckled at the thought.

From the gallery, he could see his son reach the top of the long path from the lower field and jog easily toward to the house. Mademoiselle de Champigny, who was walking to her cabin, saw Carlton too and beckoned him to come to her. Hayes watched the boy hesitate as his response to his tutor's discipline made him contain his eagerness to continue toward the house. Hayes watched the two in conversation,

Mademoiselle de Champigny's hands frantically flying to her head. Carlton listened briefly, then left her standing strangely fragile and alone as he ran up the front steps to his father.

"Good afternoon, sir," greeted Carlton. "I'm pleased to see you are not still abed."

"I would be, Carlton, if it weren't for that damned French tutor of yours. Come!" Hayes held up his hand to silence his son before the boy could speak. "Give a shout to Bo'jack to bring another pitcher of sangaree. That woman's exhausted me with her talk of invasion."

"It's true, sir," said Carlton, following his father into the drawing-room. "It appears that the French have landed a few hundred men from Guadeloupe. They have come to take the island for France. They have issued a proclamation for the French here to join them, sir. There is great consternation in the village."

"Forsooth, son! Consternation in the village means more trade for the rum shops. Are the niggers restless?"

"Not here, sir. But it appears that in Colihaut an army is being gathered to join up with the French. Frenchmen and slaves, sir, to fight the English."

"So," said Hayes, rubbing his hand over the stubble of beard on his face. "I think I divine the reason for the consternation in the heart of your French tutor, Carlton. This friend of hers in Colihaut whom she has visited. You know her?"

Bo'jack bustled in with a fresh pitcher, filled a glass, and passing it to his master, who took it without his customary upbraiding for the slave's slothfulness. Carlton was grinning mischievously.

"It's not a she, sir, but more of a buck."

Hayes stopped stroking his beard. "A buck with pretensions to intellect, I'll warrant?"

"Yes, sir, a schoolmaster he is, from France. And it is he who is leading the other Frenchies."

"Where to, son? Where have the French landed?"

60

It was the first time that Hayes had felt concern about this invasion.

"Pagoua Bay, I do believe, sir." Carlton sank into the seat opposite his father. He had reckoned that his news would bring some excitement to life on the plantation. "Should we not make preparations, sir?"

"Of course, son. Thrash the Negroes when they stop working. This invasion is of small consequence. What support can a band of clerks, bookkeepers, and schoolteachers from Colihaut give an invasion? And how will they get to Pagoua Bay? That's right the other side of the island, on the east coast. They'll die before they reach the French, and the French will never cross the interior to take Roseau."

"But sir, with respect, sir, our defenses are reputed to be very poor."

"Not at Roxborough, son. Idle niggers are more of a threat than French radicals. Tell the drivers I want every nigger working until nightfall this evening. Anyone who shows reluctance, throw him into the cell and I'll deal with him myself."

Carlton glanced at his father, who mulled over the cup of sangaree still in his hand. His father was not old, but he had the defeated look of a man who had lived his life in too much of a hurry. Carlton knew his father had worked every day with his own hands for years to build up Roxborough into the finest plantation on the coast. Now he had achieved that, he seemed to be letting his energy drain out of him. Perhaps he had no more left. If there was a Negro in the cell tonight, Carlton wondered if his father could still exert the will to punish sufficiently to defeat a rebellion.

His father seemed to have nodded off, his eyes closed and his head falling forward on his chest. Carlton took a quick swig of sangaree and silently trotted out of the room and down the front steps to harry the drivers.

Chapter 7

"Da! Da!"

His son's voice dragged Hayes out of his sleep for the second time that day. He jerked himself awake in his chair as Carlton's feet pounded on the wooden gallery and the boy burst into the room.

"Da, come quick! It's M'selle de Champigny, Da." In his excitement, Carlton lapsed into the slave talk he had learned as a child. "She done die, Da. In de schoolroom!"

"You sure, son?" Hayes was already walking out of the room and down the front steps. "Perhaps she's in a swoon or something."

"She dead all right, Da. She done kill herself."

"By the devil, I'll string up that fat Phoebe by her thumbs and lash the blubber off her if she doesn't stop that wailing!" The cook blocked their way at the bottom of the steps.

"Massa, massa, oh mercy, massa!" Phoebe reached out her hands to grasp Hayes around his knees before he could move from the step.

Phoebe's shrieks had disturbed Hayes more than Carlton's news. He drew back a step, disentangling himself from the cook's arms, then brought his right foot down with a satisfying crunch into the woman's face. Phoebe stared at him in surprise, but stopped her shrieking.

"What's the matter with the wench?" he asked Carlton as he stepped over the slave, who had crumpled at the foot of the step. Her wailing had brought Bo'jack running to the front of the house. "Keep that bloated carcass quiet, Bo'jack, and don't you start, or I'll skin you alive!"

"Yas, Massa Hayes, sah!" Taking this as his authority to beat Phoebe, Bo'jack cuffed her in the face himself.

Hayes, with a muttered word of relief, followed his son toward the teacher's cabin. But behind him the crying broke out again as Phoebe, rising from the ground, drew herself up to her full height and hit Bo'jack a blow which felled him to the ground. Satisfied, she directed her attention to wailing again, clasping one of the kitchen girls to her wide bosom for support.

"My god, Carlton. Sometimes I don't know what to do with those niggers. Any excuse and they start to bellow."

"Yas, Da," said Carlton, dancing beside his father and trying to urge him to hurry. "Dat m'selle, she does look strange when she dead."

"Dead, son? We'll see about that."

They reached the door of the cabin and Hayes brushed aside a gang of naked children squabbling for the right to peer inside. The shutters were open and the room was gray with vague evening light as the sun began to set far out to sea. There were two desks in the room made by the Roxborough carpenter. One was raised off the ground for the governess, while Carlton's was at a lower level. A book was open on it. Hayes looked at his son quizzically.

"I done tell de drivers what you done say, Da, an' den I done come here for to do study before sunset. De place does be so quiet I don't know she does be in dere." Carlton indicated the room behind the partition which divided the cabin.

"Suddenly I does hear dis moan, low, low, low. Den a loud cry. Den it all does go quiet. I does be scared,

Da, but I does wait an' den I does look in de door and dere she be, dead."

Carlton stood behind his father as he pushed open the door. The shutters were closed in here, but he could make out the shape of his governess on the bed, exactly as when he had left her. He watched his father kneel uneasily beside the woman's body as though to listen for her heart.

"I told you she was dead, sir," said Carlton, reverting to English as he lost his nervousness. His foot kicked something on the floor, and he bent down to pick up a small vial. "It must have fallen out of her hand.

"Aye," said Hayes, picking up the woman's legs and heaving her fully onto the bed. "Not much of a swoon is that, son. More like a permanent death to me. Learned your lessons well, have you, son?"

Hayes was leaving the room when he saw the paper on the floor. He picked it up and strode out into the classroom. Carlton looked back at the body of his governess before following his father, who was smoothing out the paper on his son's desk and squinting at it.

"Don't suppose we'll be getting you another tutor, Carlton," Hayes said, studying the paper. "This one didn't like all she read in them books and papers. Do you know what this says?"

"I haven't seen it before, sir." He held out his hand for the paper, but his father crumpled it quickly into a ball and lobbed it out of the window.

"It's a proclamation, son, signed by two Frenchies. Funny woman, your tutor. Better get Sharp to make her a box. Can't bury her now, it's too late. Sun's down already. Get the small gang to dig a hole at first light. Put her in it before breakfast."

"Where, Da? She's the first white woman to die here since my mam, ain't she?"

Hayes paused at the door of the cabin. "True, son, true. She weren't no Negro, that's a fact. Said she was aristocratic. French like your mother, too. Best she goes up the hill with her. Not close, but in a servant's place."

A small crowd had gathered outside the cabin watching Hayes silently. Phoebe had stopped crying and held her breath as she wondered what the master would do to her. Phoebe knew that she was the one responsible for the m'selle's death, and she expected that Hayes would know it, too. If she had known, she thought to herself, that the m'selle was going to drink the poison, she would not have given it to her. That very afternoon she had asked her for it to kill the rats in her cabin, and now she was dead. Still, Phoebe thought, her potion had worked, and now all the niggers would know that she could work powerful obeah. Master Hayes could do what he liked, thought Phoebe, putting her hands to her face and starting to howl again.

The noise stopped Hayes as he stomped back to the house, his son walking doubtfully behind him.

"You can tell that Phoebe," shouted Hayes above the din, "that she'll really have something to wail about if we don't get our supper tonight. And tell her to get Congo Venus and the other women and wash down the wench and lay her out nice. That Congo Venus laid out your own mother, Carlton, and she attended the doctor when you were born. She can deal with white folks right nice."

No one slept early that night at Roxborough. The lanterns burned late in the big house, and the slave huts stayed open to the night. Although they did not have candles, the slaves thronged the front of each wooden shack, people detaching themselves from one group to another. After a long day cutting cane in the fields or working in the still by the river, not many of the slaves stayed awake much after sunset. But even though they had been forced to work an extra hour that evening, no one went to sleep early. Children stood at the edge of each group, sucking fingers in awe as they listened to the whispers of the old people.

Although the slaves had heard about the invasion

from the slaves who had returned from the village, the news of the death took precedence. The tale of white men who had taken their slaves to meet an army at the other side of the island was no concern of the Roxborough Negroes. No one was interested in a long trek in the bush at night with all the jumbies and spirits abroad. Besides, what had happened at Roxborough was more important.

In every hut there was talk about the death of the white lady. Gradually, the slaves began to understand how it had happened, shrinking a little with fear inside themselves as they realized that what Ma Phoebe could do to a white lady she could most certainly do to them. Somehow, so the story was told among themselves, Ma Phoebe had found out that the white lady was planning a proclamation. No one was certain what a proclamation was, but some of the men had heard Master Hayes himself say something about it. Whatever it was, Ma Phoebe knew about it and so she had given the lady a powerful potion to stop her wickedness. The potion was so powerful that the white lady died as soon as it touched her lips. Ma Phoebe's reputation as a majah obeah woman soared.

Carlton knew from the days when he was a child and had to eat in the kitchen out of the way of his father that Bo'jack repeated everything he heard in the drawing room to Ma Phoebe's eager ears. So Carlton waited until Bo'jack had left him and his father alone on the gallery before raising his doubts. Downstairs, Ma Phoebe was puzzled that the matter had not been discussed. She was finding that the fear of the punishment she was expecting was even worse than the punishment itself.

"Sir," began Carlton tentatively.

"What is it, boy?"

"Don't you find it passing strange, sir?"

"What riddle is this, son?"

"M'selle de Champigny, I mean, sir."

"Forget the woman, son. I told you why she killed herself."

66

"It ain' that, Da. Where do you think she got the stuff to do it with?"

"Lord, boy! That's easy. Just crush a few leaves together. Any one of them slaves from Africa can tell you that. There is so much poison growing all around us here in the jungle, even you and I could take a draught in our broth and be dead before you know it. That's why you've got to have good Negroes in the house, Carlton. Them you can trust.

"Bo'jack may be slow and lazy, and as for that Phoebe, well, she's a fat sow, but she's a damn good cook. Both of them creole, born in the island, so they was partly seasoned from birth. Your mother trained them. Get a good slave when he's young, keep him away from the field niggers, beat him twice a week, and you have a chance of getting a loyal Negro.

"Shouldn't wonder that governess of yours went to some old black crone in the slave quarters and bought a potion from her. Maybe Congo Venus herself, who knows?" Hayes suddenly broke off and chuckled. "That m'selle was so mean, shouldn't wonder she told the nigger she'd only pay for the potion if it worked!"

Carlton laughed at the joke so his father would not see that he was not satisfied by the explanation. He still felt that there was something strange about the affair.

Hayes stood up, cocked his head to the wind, and then walked the length of the balcony to the corner. He leaned over the railing and took a deep breath.

"Huh! Carlton, come over here, I want to show you something." He sniffed the air again as Carlton got up and joined him. "Take the air, Carlton. Tell me what you smell."

Carlton tilted his head upwards and breathed in deeply. The night air flooded into his lungs, making him feel light-headed.

"Try again," his father urged. "Take the scent?"

"It's kind of . . . well . . . not really like the rest of the night." Carlton gestured to the spot where they had been sitting in front of the house where the pure air of the sea constantly wafted around them. He was not sure what his father wanted him to say.

"Mark that stench well, son. Kind of sweaty, ain't it? That's Negroes. We're downwind of the slave quarters here. Any time them niggers aren't in their shacks at night, I can tell. The breeze carries the message to me right here. They be sittin' outside their shacks tonight considerin' and figurin'. They won't do much figurin' because they born stupid and they'll die stupid. And they won't do much considerin' because they scared."

Hayes walked slowly back to his chair. "I'll say one thing for your governess, Carlton. She done us a real favor by dyin' today. Saved us a puncheon of rum, anyway."

"How's that?" Carlton found it difficult to follow his father's reasoning at times.

"If the slaves got too excited about talk of invasion, I reckon I might have had to broach a puncheon of nigger rum for them. Whenever you've got a crisis like that, rum is the answer. Whipping one or two is all right; it makes them a bit more scared, but rum and water fools them as long as you don't give them an overdose. They can't find no fault with massa then. Now, your governess, she done gone and made them forget all about the invasion, done the job of a puncheon right nicely."

Carlton shook his head in disbelief. The old man was so wily, he seemed to know what the slaves were going to do before they knew themselves. He scratched the curls at the back of his head thoughtfully, then smoothed down the locks which tumbled around his shoulders.

"So you are worried about the invasion, then!" he suddenly realized aloud.

"Me, son?" Hayes turned to look at Carlton, studying him curiously. The boy was in the full bloom of youth with his hard sunburned body filling out and muscles beginning to build up across his shoulders and chest. He was dressed as always in a ragged shirt, breeches torn off below his knees, and no shoes. His hair, its fairness accentuated by the long hours spent in the sun without a hat, was unkempt. His face had lost its childish plumpness and was beginning to shape up, with the defiant cut of the Todds to his jaw.

"Son, what you know you never show to your slaves. You are thè Bondmaster. You are invincible. Those slaves are animals, Negro animals. If you don't keep on top of them, they'll snap off your balls. Never let them know what you're thinking. Never let them catch you unawares; always keep ahead of them."

Hayes watched his son frown. "It's not difficult, son. Negroes don't have brains like you and me. They don't have learning, either. Know your slaves and you'll know what they are going to do next."

Chapter 8

The small gang, those Negroes who were too young or too old to work in the field gangs, had been allowed to come up the hill to watch the burying of Mademoiselle de Champigny. As Carlton glanced idly at males and females watching his father mutter a prayer before the box was pushed into the hole, his eye fell on Harriet.

She was a small girl, about two years younger than Carlton, with a skin the gorgeous color of highly polished red cedar. The calico frock she was wearing was scarred with dirt, but it did nothing to lessen the attractiveness of her childish breasts. Carlton, meeting the girl by accident near her mother's shack one night, had already handled those breasts, squeezing them in his hands until she had cried out in pain. The squeal had carried to her mother, who had called her to come in, but Carlton, left tense and uneasy, had vowed to have her. She was his wench.

Harriet, suddenly aware that someone was watching her, raised her head and stole a glance at the white man and his son. The Bondmaster had come to the end of his speech and was waving to the men to push the box into the hole. Carlton was watching her with his pale ghostly eyes, just like a jumbie's. Quickly, Harriet ducked behind one of the older women, wondering what she had done. If Carlton reported her to her mother, she would get another beating that night.

Harriet breathed a sigh of relief when the burial business was over and the Bondmaster turned to go. She peeped around the edge of the crowd as their driver called the small gang together. She watched Carlton strolling down the hill a step behind his father. He looked so fine with his lovely hair flowing in the early breeze and with his clear white skin.

Carlton fell in step with his father as they headed toward the kitchen.

"Now that's over, son, we've got to keep the niggers occupied. I'll ride into Layou this morning and go 'n' see Belle. He'll know what this French nonsense is all about. He's such a coward that if there's any truth in what they're saying, he's probably ridden to Roseau already and holed himself up in the fort!" Hayes slapped his hip as he chuckled at the weaknesses of some of his white neighbors.

"We won't cut no more cane until next week, Carlton, so you can keep your eyes on the slaves this morning. They have to clean Long Field. Will is a good driver, and he has got Dukey and Thomas with him. Tell them to give the Negroes a heavy touch of the lash if they slack off at all. Long Field's near the ferry so they may hear any news before you, but you can watch from the house gallery to see who's using the ferry and send a boy down for messages.

"Your learning's finished now, Carlton, so it's time to take on your share of the work!"

"Yes, sir," said Carlton. He felt he was at last growing up. The days of having to wash his face and go for his lessons before breakfast had died with the tutor. Now he could ride around the plantation all day and do as he pleased. Even his father had as good as told him to get a wench. There was nothing stopping him from having Harriet now.

"Oh, Da?" said Carlton as casually as he could make it. "What are we going to do with the m'selle's cabin? I could use it to keep my books and that in, if you like."

71

His father seemed to take a long time to reply. Carlton bit his lip nervously and looked up at him. Hayes stopped a few yards from the house, where they could see Ma Phoebe bustling around in the kitchen. Carlton felt his father's hand on his shoulder.

"Son, when I was your age, or even a bit younger, I was workin' my way to America. Some English gentleman met me in Bristol and got me a passage on board ship with him. There wasn't nothing I wouldn't do for that man. Oh yes, I was popular, and there were plenty of women to amuse me, too, so that was all right. You see, son, I might seem old to you, but I was your age once.

"If you want that woman's cabin for keeping your books in, then that's all right. But 'pon my soul, I'll wager you'll be studying more than books before long!"

With a gruff chuckle, Hayes propelled Carlton forward. He fell with a crash against the thick timbers of the door.

"Oh my gawd!" shrieked Phoebe. "Mas' Carlton, you done scarify me! I does think is dat Bo'jack tumblin' down de stairs wid your da's sangaree."

"Mornin', Ma Phoebe!" Carlton rushed to the cook and embraced her.

"Oh my gawd, Mas Carlton! What you done do dis mornin'? What you so larky for at dis hour? De coco tea don't have time boil an' dem bakes only now burstin' up like de sunshine an' you a'ready to hug Ma Phoebe like you starvin'!"

"That's it, Phoebe. Daybreak funerals are hungry work," said Hayes standing in the doorway surveying the kitchen.

"Beg pardon, Massa Hayes, sah."

As Phoebe addressed him, Hayes sensed her ebullience fade away. That was usually a sign that there was something wrong. He glanced quickly around the kitchen again.

"Where's Bo'jack?" he asked sharply. "I'm gettin' tired, Carlton, of forever askin' where's Bo'jack. The best thing I can do is send him out to the fields under Will, then I'll know where he is."

"Please, sah, don't send me to de fields, sah." Bo'jack appeared at Hayes's elbow, the empty rum pitcher in his hand. "I does be cleanin' de wares, sah."

"Draining the rum, more like it. Bo'jack, you are the laziest slave I ever did see, and I'm not going to stand more of it, do you hear?"

"Yas, sah. I does hear, sah."

Carlton, who saw this performance between his father and his old slave take place every day, was studying a girl cowering in a corner of the kitchen. She was watching open-mouthed as Hayes was speaking, her eyes wide but not, Carlton was puzzled to observe, with fear. Her glance seemed to be one of disdain at his father's behavior.

"Who's that chit?" he demanded quickly.

Phoebe looked in the corner of her kitchen as though she saw the girl for the first time. Realizing that she had become the object of attention, the girl tried to crawl under the table. Phoebe bent down and laid her massive hands on the girl's ankles and dragged her out. She lay quivering on the floor, her frock ridden up round her thighs, her buttocks, naked under the loose garment, almost uncovered. She raised her head, but Carlton was watching the girl's body heaving under her dress, the long brown legs splayed wide on the floor. His mouth dried.

"What for you crawlin' under de table like a cucaracha, gel? Don't you know yuh massa does be askin' you somethin'? Oh my gawd! Wha' does dey t'ink Ma Phoebe does have in her kitchin, only de mice an' de cucaracha!" Phoebe gave the girl a hefty kick in the side with her bare foot and then smiled sweetly at Carlton. "Dat girl jest come from de quarters, sah."

"Phoebe's so dam' fat, son," chuckled Hayes observing his son's interest, "she eats chits like that for breakfast. Come on, son. I sent Bo'jack for the horses, we've got work to do."

"Yes, sir." Carlton looked down at the girl on the

73

floor again. He smiled at her encouragingly. Her eyes watched his own, sending a shiver of annoyance through him as he realized again that it was not fear in the girl's eyes but a kind of boldness. He drew back his foot and let her have a sharp kick in her stomach as Phoebe had done. He was rewarded by a surprised cry of pain from the girl and a glance of pure hatred as he spun around and ran after his father.

The small gang were weeding the path in front of the house. Four boys cutlassed the ditch while the girls worked in the path. The laughter that Carlton heard as he rode up the trail, stopped as soon as the slaves caught sight of him. He saw Dutchip, the driver, waddle down toward the girls and give one of them a token switch with her whip. Dutchip looked up at him for approval, and he realized that the girl she had lashed so tantalizingly was Harriet.

"Mornin', Mas Carlton, sah!"

Carlton reined in the horse. The girls in the gang bent lower to pull out the weeds, casting furtive glances across at each other and trying to suppress their giggles. One of the boys muttered something in patois which nearly set them off giggling again. Carlton missed the words but took the sense of the expression. Joseph, Little Cudjoe, Johnny Garraway, and Henry were his age. Before Prince was sold, he and his playboy used to chase those same boys in the bush and beat them when they caught them. Now Carlton was their Bond-master, not playmate, and could really lash them.

"Hand me that whip here, Dutchip!" He held out his hand.

"Yas, massa, sah. I does drive my gang well, massa. Dis be de best small gang, sah."

Carlton leaned down from the horse and snatched the whip from the woman. It had a short handle with a slender leather thong, about ten feet long, cut out of a single piece of cowhide. He tested it, flicking the handle gently. The thong spun out, and curled around a seed pod hanging from a flamboyant tree. There was a crack, and the pod dropped to the ground.

Satisfied, Carlton tried again, sending the whip snaking toward Little Cudjoe in the ditch. With Prince, Carlton had often practiced to see who could wield the whip with greater dexterity. He had not forgotten the technique. Little Cudjoe jumped back in alarm, rubbing his cheek where the lash had stung him.

"Hah, my fine Cudjoe! That will learn you to move. Take your punishment like a man, not like a little boy."

"Sah, sah! I don't do nothin'!" Little Cudjoe dodged back into the ditch as the whip scorched past his ear.

"What! Answer back your master, would you? This isn't a little boy's game any more, Cudjoe!" Dutchip's shriek of laughter distracted Carlton. With a backwards flick, he had the thong wrapped around the driver before she could move.

"How does the nurse like her medicine?" he mocked as he withdrew the whip slowly. "This gang of yours seems in need of a stronger dose, Dutchip. Perhaps the fields is the best place for you and those boys?"

"Please, not de fields, sah. Massa Hayes done say I too sickly for de fields." Dutchip rubbed her body but, as Carlton knew, her pride in front of the gang had suffered more than her rump. He felt that he had shown them that he was the master, not a boy any more. Casually, he let the whip snake out again low over the girls who had stopped weeding the path in their nervousness, their giggling forgotten. As though by accident, Carlton let the thong caress the shoulder of the brown-skinned Harriet.

"I want you to send a girl to clean up M'selle de Champigny's cabin, Dutchip." He flicked the whip again, allowing it to fall on Harriet's backside as she bent down. "That one will do."

"Yas, Mas Carlton, sah. I does do what you does tell me, sah."

"Good, she can go now." Digging in his heels, Carlton urged his horse forward, scattering the girls in front of him, throwing the whip casually down on the ground at Dutchip's feet. He was confident that whatever the slaves wanted to say about him now, they at last knew that he was bound to be the Bondmaster of Roxborough and was going to be as strict as his father.

He rode the horse back to the barn and dismounted, shouting for Marmaduke to stable the animal. Without waiting to see where the cartman was, he walked over to the cabin which until the day before had been his schoolroom. Someone had latched open the door and the shutters, and the breeze from the surrounding hills had blown away all evidence of his late governess. Apparently his father had given orders for the cabin to be cleaned, because the few possessions which the Frenchwoman had kept in her room had all been removed. Even a clean coverlet had been placed on the bed.

Carlton studied the small cabin. It would be ideal for his purpose. He could really do some reading in peace in here. It was not his intention to abandon his books just because he was supposed to keep a few Negroes under control. What he had managed to read so far had been fascinating, and his governess, dour as she was, had given him the key to the delights to be discovered through books. But right now, he thought as he closed the shutters of the cabin, he had other delights on his mind.

Although it was bright daylight, closing the shutters made the cabin quite dark. It was perfect. He stepped back into his former classroom and sat in his teacher's desk. He observed for the first time that the tutor's desk had been so positioned that it afforded an uninterrupted view across the cane fields to the ferry. From there, Mademoiselle de Champigny had been able to watch the commerce of the river and, perhaps, had seen her schoolmaster revolutionary traveling between the capital and his village sanctuary. Through the shutter he had left open, Carlton caught sight of Harriet, the object of his own desire, running with obvious eagerness toward the cabin. She reached the door and peeped in before withdrawing her head quickly.

"Come, Harriet," said Carlton softly, "don't be frightened."

"Oh, Mas Carlton, sah, you done startle me." Harriet stepped into the cabin and looked around her, finally raising her head to regard the young white master sitting at the high desk.

"It's quite all right here, you know. What's dead is dead and buried."

"Yas, Mas Carlton." Harriet stood waiting.

"Sit down, Harriet."

She looked about her, wondering if he meant on the floor or on the only other seat in the room, which was behind a desk smaller than his own. She moved toward it.

"That's right. You're the pupil and I'm the master today." Carlton's eyes gleamed as he discovered that from his raised seat, he had a chance to see under the loose front of her dress. "I hope I did not hurt you with the whip this morning."

She shrugged her shoulders, not certain whether she should speak or not. It seemed such a strange remark.

"There's no one else here now, Harriet. I want you to speak to me when I ask you questions. I don't have a whip to beat you now."

"No, sah." Harriet was intrigued by the quiet tone of his voice. It reminded her of the time when he had held her outside her mother's home.

"When Prince was here, I used to practice with the whip all the time. But I had to stop when I started my learning. Now the governess is gone, too, so I'll be coming 'round the plantation every day now. I'm going to be the Bondmaster one day, Harriet."

She loved to hear his voice. It was soft, like his skin, it seemed to flow on and on like his hair. His legs looked so fine and strong in his breeches. She felt she could reach out and touch them under his desk, but he was the buckra and she was an ugly black girl with a flat chest and skinny legs. She could not do anything like that, for he would certainly strike her and even whip her until she was dead. She shuddered.

"You're frightened," said Carlton coolly, suddenly aware that he had complete power over the girl. He could do anything he wanted with her. He owned her. "Stand up!"

Harriet hesitated, intrigued by the harsh edge in his voice. She rose slowly, pushing back the small bench she had been sitting on. It toppled over with a startling crash.

"What, girl! You dare to make a noise!"

"I does be sorry, sah, Mas Carlton, sah."

"I should punish you for that, Harriet." He stood up, feeling the constraint in his thighs. She lowered her head as his pale eyes seemed to burn into hers. "Go in there!" he ordered, pointing through the door leading to the back room. His hand clenched around the heavy wooden ruler which lay on his governess's desk. He lifted the ruler slowly and rapped it down with a sharp crack on the desk top.

Harriet felt herself trembling inside. She shuffled over to the door he indicated, pausing at the threshold of the darkness within. She raised her head to look back at him as he stood silhouetted against the open shutter, his finger pointing imperiously. She entered the darkness of the room.

Carlton quickly stepped across to the cabin entrance and swung the door closed, fastening it inside. He walked toward the dividing door and saw Harriet, with her back to him, standing in the center of the room, her head down. He gripped the wooden ruler tightly in his hand, tension making him croak as he began to speak.

"I am going to punish you, Harriet."

"Yas, sah." She hardly dared to breathe.

"Take off your dress!" He banged the ruler against the wooden partition to emphasize the urgency of his command.

Harriet fumbled with the tie at her shoulder and shook the garment down over her body until it fell at her feet on the floor. She stepped out of it, keeping her naked back facing him. Carlton steadied himself on the door jamb.

"Bend over the bed," he croaked.

As the smell of Harriet's body seeped through the closeness of the room, Carlton gripped the ruler tightly in his hand to control the passion he could feel rising in his own body. He watched the girl step forward and lower herself across the bed, becoming a darker shadow on the dimness of the coverlet. She tilted her head to one side and he could imagine her eyes open, anticipating his movements as he advanced toward her. He found the greatest difficulty in speaking. He raised the ruler above his head and poised his arm.

"Harriet!" he shrieked, bringing the flat side of the wooden shaft down on to her buttocks with all the strength he could muster.

"Aye! Aye!" Harriet arched her back. The blow seemed to tear through her flesh. "Mas Carlton!" she screamed as the pain became an ecstatic glow cutting through her whole body.

"Harriet!" The ruler fell again on her naked flesh, and again she arched her back at the ruthless cut of pain.

"Aye! Mas Carlton!" She tensed her body across the coverlet, preparing herself for the next blow. It never came.

Carlton paused, his arm raised, listening.

"Mas Carlton," sighed Harriet.

He let the ruler fall on the floor with a clatter, kneeling beside her. Gently, he put his hand on her bottom, running his soft finger along the welt left by the ruler. He bent forward, rubbing his face in the warm flesh of her buttocks. Harriet dared not move. He cupped his hand around the curve of her cheek, squeezing it slowly at first, increasing the pressure so that Harriet squirmed.

"Mas Carlton!" she whispered.

Fascinated, his fingers began to explore her flesh in the blackness. He clenched her body in his hands and pushed her over on the bed so that she faced him. He ripped at the fasteners on his breeches and peeled them off down to his knees. Harriet saw him looming above her in the darkened room and waited, her eyes on him adoringly. He threw himself on her with a groan.

"Harriet!"

"Massa! Massa!" she shrieked as he rammed into her viciously. "Massa! Oh, Massa!"

Chapter 9

Roxborough Hall, as Hayes called his home in moments of cynicism, was designed by him on the lines of the houses he had seen on the cotton plantations of Alabama. The limits of the local skills and lack of imported materials had defeated his attempts to emulate very closely the luxury of the great houses of Alabama, but the basic plan of the house preserved the convenience of its design. The kitchen, store and house slave quarters were built of stone while the upper rooms were constructed out of local timber sawn by a carpenter whose labor had cost a hundred pounds even in those days.

The attraction of the house was the gallery which ran around all four sides, and the back steps which gave secret access to it. The two guest rooms were both entered from the gallery and, although the main bedrooms—now occupied by Hayes on the west and Carlton on the east—had their access from the drawing room, they were both served by a dressing room which could only be entered from the gallery. There was a connecting door between each dressing room and its bedroom.

The beauty of this arrangement, as Carlton appreciated when he began to smuggle Harriet into his room at night, was that a wench could enter the dressing room without anyone in the house being aware of it.

She could be dispatched in the morning before dawn and neither Bo'jack nor his father would be any the wiser. Perhaps Carlton had overlooked the fact that it had been his father who designed the house and was quite aware of its conveniences. Prince himself had slept in Carlton's dressing room for years, and the slave's presence in the upper part of the house at night instead of in the quarters below had never disturbed Hayes or the occasional guest. Indeed, far from feeling that he should reprimand Carlton for Harriet's presence at night, Hayes was content that his son had discovered the uses to which the accommodations of Roxborough could be put.

"You are growing well, boy," Hayes said to his son one night, as they sat in their customary places on the gallery. Bo'jack had brought them their decanter of rum and departed for the kitchen. Carlton poured himself a measure, not for politeness any more, as Hayes observed, but for enjoyment. Their evening sessions on the gallery had developed, over the months since Mademoiselle de Champigny had died, into a review of the day's work on the plantation.

Carlton glanced down at his body as he stretched out in the gallery chair, his legs on the balcony rail. What his dad had said was true, he could see that. His muscles were stronger now, his waist was firmer, and riding each day around the plantation had developed his legs. His hair, too, was shorter, the boyish locks chopped off one afternoon by Sharp, the carpenter, who was also the plantation barber. Carlton had discarded the tight breeches of his boyhood for the baggy pants of a grown man. On the plantation he wore a loose shirt, not yet affecting the jacket and hat which his father preferred to wear when inspecting the work being done by the slaves.

Carlton was proud as he appraised himself. "Thank you, sir," he said, smiling at his father.

"I did not intend to compliment you on your strength, Carlton," retorted Hayes. "It was my wish to make an observation concerning your conduct."

Indeed, sir?"

The old man had funny ways at times, thought Carlton. He hoped the session would not be prolonged this evening, as he had ordered Dutchip to send up a new girl from the small gang. She was probably waiting in his dressing room at that very minute, if she had managed to slip in while he was having supper.

"I hope I have not given any offense, sir?" suggested Carlton to fill the silence as he waited for his father to speak.

Hayes had been wondering how to put things. "Sometimes," he began, pouring himself a glass from the decanter, "the Bondmaster is the last to know what is going on among his slaves. If he is, then he can count his days as being reduced to the minimum, Carlton. Do you understand me?" He sipped his rum cautiously.

"Not really, sir."

"A man who has slaves should never make the mistake of thinking that because he is a carefree, jolly fellow, his slaves love and respect him. They don't, Carlton, they don't. There are thirty thousand niggers in Dominica, my son, and only a thousand white men— and some of them are French, be damned! Last year, the French tried to invade the island and turn the slaves against us for their own ends. They did not succeed, but they might do so again."

"I know that, Da. You've always told me to use the whip when I have to, just to keep the niggers respectful."

"Aye, son. The whip's a punishment, and there are other punishments you don't even know about yet. But slaves do, and it's the fear of them that keeps them back. Show signs of weakness to a slave and he'll remember until he can use that weakness against you. The Bondmaster has to know everything that is happening, because if he doesn't, if he misses signs of trouble as soon as they show themselves and doesn't stamp them out, then very soon the slaves are going to get him."

"You're not afraid of a few vile-smelling blackies, are you, father?" Carlton tilted his glass down his throat to indicate his lack of concern.

"Afraid, son? Of an animal? Not I. But I might be afraid of my own stock." He put down his tankard with a deliberate clatter on the table and sat back in his chair. Carlton, surprised, leaned forward.

"You mean me, Da? What have I done?"

The sounds of night embraced the two men on the gallery. Crickets and other insects chirped in the bush. There was a distant cry of a baby, but otherwise not a murmur came from the scores of slaves huddled in their cabins down the trail from the house. The rushing of the river where it narrowed was a background to the forest noises. Fireflies darted among the trees bordering the yard at the front of the main steps. A creak, as if caused by a nervous footfall on the gallery, reminded Carlton of the wench coming to meet him that evening.

Hayes sighed, the heavy sigh of a man desperately tired but unable yet to give up. "As the Bondmaster, son, I must know everything. Damn it all! Did I not build this house with my own hands? Monique, your mother, never knew. When she had the room which is now yours, son, I had my little black visitors in the night, creeping in to the dressing room for me to let out the venom in me. If I didn't let go all the passion I had into those niggers, I would have destroyed Monique. The heat does something to a man, makes him a beast. How I would have shamed Monique!" Hayes gripped the arms of his chair, sitting upright, unseeing.

"Da, what is it?" Carlton poured his father a rum, tapped his hand, and made him accept the tankard. The action brought Hayes back to the present. He glanced at the tankard, then grimaced at Carlton to excuse his own foolishness.

"You see, son. A weakness. I mean, I know all

about you, Carlton," he continued, his tone resuming its authority. "I've no objection to you having a black wench in your bed. A white man needs relief. But, Carlton, you must remember that those black chits you ride at night are not human. They are property. You must do what you have to do to them, and then let them go."

Hayes held up his hand to silence his son. "Not only that, son, you must watch this weakness. You are white, and your seed is white. Sow that seed in a black furrow that's rotten and you'll get a poisonous shoot. That's the stock you've got to watch."

Carlton watched his father with horror before leaping up in agitation and gripping the balcony rail firmly as he stared out into the night. He gulped, then turned around to face his father. "Da," he said slowly, "I have a wench with a full belly already, maybe another as well." He shrugged his shoulders.

Hayes snorted. "At last, son, you tell your da. I'm the Bondmaster and I have to know everything. From the moment you started off Harriet in that schoolroom and then brought her up here into the house, I've known what you've been about. I can smell nigger, Carlton, whether it's in my house or on my son's limbs. But that's all right. The Bondmaster tills the soil first at Roxborough, or his son does. Mount every dam' filly on the plantation if you like, but keep whelps and romance out of it. You hear! Romance is for white women, not slaves."

Hidden beneath the front steps where she could hear every word spoken by the Bondmaster and his son on the balcony above her head, Ella, the kitchen girl, fingered herself. Mas Carlton was her god and it troubled her that skinny toads like the one she had seen creeping up the backstairs to his room should ever taste him. Ella wanted Mas Carlton for herself. She pictured how she would claw the hard white flesh of his back with her nails, her legs locked around his waist as he pierced her.

Ella touched herself with mounting speed and pressure as she looked up and saw Mas Carlton staring out into the night. From the lantern throwing its gleam around him, she could see the golden color of his hair and his troubled frown. As her fingers raced over her body, she longed to cry out to him, begging him to come down to her.

A soft moan escaped her lips and she sank to the earth. She clawed at the stones of the kitchen wall as her body bucked involuntarily. Her eyes were closed tightly. Suddenly, horror overtook her and she cowered in the corner as still as the night, wondering if her cry had disturbed Ma Phoebe. She listened. Above her head, footsteps sounded and someone went off the gallery into the house itself. She thought that it must be Mas Carlton himself going off to his bedroom to meet that toad. She listened again, praying that Ma Phoebe had not heard her cry. There was no sound from the house, nor from the kitchen. Slowly Ella relaxed, gratefully abandoning herself to the mysterious sounds of the night.

"Aye!" she sighed to herself, curling up in the dark corner, her eyes closed, seeing Carlton. "Aye!"

A shaft of light fell on her and she opened her eyes in panic. Mas Carlton stood over her! He was swinging a lantern inches from her face. "What have we here?" Ella tried to wriggle away, but Carlton's foot fell on her body, trapping her. "Stay!" he commanded as he peered closer.

"Why! It's our little kitchen cockroach!" Carlton laughed. "Why are you sleeping like a cur at the foot of our steps, cockroach, eh?" He rolled her body in the dirt with his foot. "What have you done, cockroach, to be cast out here with the rats and the lizards?"

Carlton chuckled as he continued to boot the girl's yielding body, yet the expression of disbelief on the girl's face, rather than that of fright, puzzled him. He recalled the first day he had seen this slave in the kitchen, and how she had seemed to be challenging him even then.

He released her body from his foot. "Stand up!"

Ella got to her feet immediately, but with an unexpected dignity.

Carlton placed his lantern on one of the stone steps and sat down beside it. "Come!" he beckoned to the girl impatiently with his finger. "Stand here in front of me." He looked at her and then placed the lantern higher up, level with her eyes.

"Now, cockroach, what's your name?"

"Ella."

"Ella, is it? Ella alone? My, you are a lively cockroach, to be sure!" He gripped her wrists tightly, forcing her hands to rest on his knees as she faced him. "Let's try it again. Now what's your name, cockroach?"

"Ella." She paused before adding, "Mas Carlton."

"Fine!" He nodded his head mockingly, amused by the provocative quiver of her lips. "And what is your business lurking in the dark recesses of Roxborough Hall?"

"Sah?"

"Why you does be hidin' under de step, girl?" Carlton ground his hands around her wrists, chafing them. The girl returned his glare, taking his lapse into slave talk as an indication that his anger was not yet severe.

"I does be goin' to my sleepin' place, sah."

"An' where does dat be?" he taunted.

"Behind de store room, sah. By where Ma Phoebe does sleep, sah."

"Yes, yes." Carlton relaxed the pressure on the girl's wrists, still perturbed by the blazing confidence in the wench's eyes.

Where he sat on the step, the girl's face was level with his own. She was tall, with an arrogant tilt to the way she held her head. Her limbs were long, and her body, not yet fully filled out, had a boyish quality to it. She reminded him of Prince. Her face was distinctly African, a sensitive nose spreading above full lips which seemed soft and vaguely inviting in the light of the lantern. It was the thought of kissing those lips which made Carlton cling to the girl's wrists more in alarm now than any desire to frighten the creature. He had never wanted to kiss a slave before.

"Ella, what's your age?"

"I does have sixteen years, sah."

"How can you be so sure?"

"My ma done tell me I does be born de same year wid you, sah. Ma Phoebe say dat you does be sixteen years, sah, an' you jest like your da."

Carlton frowned. It had not occurred to him that slaves expressed opinions about him among themselves. It was almost human. He released his hands from her wrists, but Ella, instead of drawing rapidly away from him, kept her hands resting on his thighs.

"You're damn curious!" he said, brushing her arms away from him gently.

"I does be Batutsi."

"What's that?"

"Batutsi does be my people. My mam, she done be born in Africa. She done tell me I does be pure-breed Batutsi 'cos my da does be Batutsi like her."

"Niggers is niggers."

"Yas, sah. Batutsi be de best of niggers."

Carlton was intrigued by the wench. It was the first time he had heard any slave talk about different kinds of Negroes. To him, the only kinds were those who could work and those who were sickly.

"Who's your mother, Ella?" His voice was softer now.

"Fria, sah. She done die las' year, a big tall lady she was. She be home now."

"Home?"

"In Africa, sah. She done join my da. He was be a prince in Africa."

Carlton shook his head in disbelief. He had heard that slaves had their own fantasies and that some of them still believed in Africa. At Roxborough, though, most of them were creoles who had been born in captivity, and Africa was as unreal to them as England was to him.

"Was your father a Roxborough slave, Ella?"

"Oh no, sah. He was be a free man in Roseau. He done meet my mam when she done be at de factor's. He was be a pure-breed Batutsi. Dat be why de factor does put him wid my mam. Massa Hayes bought her when she be full," she added, as though explaining something to a child.

"How do you know all this?"

"Because I does be Batutsi! My mam done tell me all dat she does remember about her homeland and her people. Batutsi does be special Negroes, she say, not like de Pawpaws or de Coromantins."

"What are they?" Carlton asked, even more perplexed.

"Dem's different people. Bo'jack does be a Pawpaw."

"What about Ma Phoebe?"

"She does be creole, but perhaps she does have Batutsi blood in her, too," Ella allowed. "Dat's why my mam done sent for her when she know she goin' die an' ax her to take me into de big house."

"She knew she was going to die?"

"Yas. Batutsi does know all dem thin's. Dat's why dey be special."

"Huh!" said Carlton. "That's all superstition. And I don't believe what you're telling me, either. Some niggers be good and some be bad, that's the truth. Roxborough niggers don't be too bad because my da seasoned them all properly. With the whip."

"Yas." Ella stood upright and proud in front of her young master. Her mother had told her that she need never be afraid of a white man. She came from the noblest race on earth, and no white man could ever take that away from her. If she was ever punished so much that she had to die, then she should be happy because she would be going home to meet her ancestors.

Carlton scratched his ear, not sure what to make of this slave. If Prince was still around, Carlton knew he could ask him if what she said was true. This wench was the first Negro he had talked to properly since the day Prince was sold. With the other slaves on the plantation, it was always "Do this" or "Do that."

"What other niggers at Roxborough are Batutsi?" he demanded.

Again those full lips opened in a proud smile. "Only me does be one, sah, Ella."

"You been mounted yet, Ella?" The question excited Carlton as he asked it.

"No sah! My mam does say only a Batutsi does be for me."

"And what about the Bondmaster?"

For the first time since he had caught her, Ella lowered her eyes from his. "And de Bon'massa, sah," she whispered.

Carlton laughed triumphantly. "Go on, girl. Get to your bed!"

He swung himself around and stood up on the step, still chuckling. The girl had sense. He looked down at her as he reached for his lantern. The deep brown eyes enhanced by a thick black line of dark lashes seized his and forced him to cut short the laughter in his throat. He paused, returning her stare, trying to fathom the meaning in her eyes. He blinked, then she was gone. He snorted in disgust at himself and climbed the steps slowly.

His father's snores could be heard rattling the jalousies. Carlton peered down into the darkness below the gallery deep in thought. Ella would be curling up in a corner in Ma Phoebe's quarters, he supposed, trying to squeeze some comfort out of the hard earth floor.

What dreams did she have, this Batutsi Princess? Carlton shrugged his shoulders and turned away. Batutsi! he thought, and Pawpaw! What names! As though the slaves had some kind of identity. Were they not property just as his father had said, to be used at his pleasure? Carlton retreated from the balcony and it was only when he had carried the lantern to his room and opened the door that he remembered the slave girl who was waiting for him there. The dividing door off to the dressing room was open, and he held up the lantern to study the black shape stretched out on the floor. "What girl is this?" he asked himself softly. "Is she good breed or bad breed? Batutsi or Pawpaw?" He scratched his head. "Damme, I can't even remember her name."

"Wench," he said aloud, digging his boot into her side. "Get up!"

The girl opened her eyes, closing them again as the lantern dazzled her. She rolled away his boot squealing. "Don't hit me, sah!"

"Damme, stop whimpering, girl! I'll tie you to the bedpost and thrash you till daybreak if you want something to whimper for! Who sent you here, girl?"

"Dutchip, sah. She done say dat you does want me for de night, sah."

The girl dragged herself to a sitting position in the corner of the tiny room. Her thick hair was knotted in squares all over her head. She was small and seemed to be wearing the same loose-fitting garment she had been wearing in the fields that morning when Carlton had spotted her. She was about twelve. As he looked at her frightened eyes, Carlton recalled the bold eyes of Ella.

"Dutchip was mistaken, girl. Here!" He held out his hand. "Here's a bit for you to spend on something pretty for your hair. Take it!" He walked over to the door that opened onto the gallery and held it for the girl to pass through. "Now go back to your quarters. Run now, for jumbie not to hold you!"

The moon, which had been hidden by the clouds swarming over the top of the hills, began to cast its pale glow over the cane fields and woods surrounding the house. Carlton, aware of being caught in its unexpected light, stayed on the gallery looking over the railing to the river beyond the fields. He bit his lower lip slowly, sucking in the air as he considered his strange action in dismissing the girl. He would like to have believed that he was taking his father's advice seriously, but the eyes of that Batutsi Ella kept staring the words out of his mind.

Sighing loudly, he turned back off the gallery into his room as Ella, watching from below in the moonlight, smiled to herself and went to hers.

Chapter 10

The morning gun woke Carlton. He listened to the dawn before opening his eyes. The heavy splatter of rain on the shingles of the roof and the sounds of water filling the barrels underneath the gallery reminded him of the clouds that had secluded the moon of the night before and shadowed his encounter with Ella. He was tired this morning. Birds, delighted by the rainfall after days of dry, hot sun, larked in the trees surrounding the house, chortling loudly. The bed was comfortable. It had been his mother's bed when this room was hers. He supposed that he had been conceived in this very bed, where he now brought those stinking black fillies who took his fancy. He was the one who had sullied his mother's sheets with nigger wenches.

To love a slave was not permitted, he knew that. A nigger, at best, was a different species of human from a white man. There could be no romantic attachment between black and white. Yet he felt this strange attraction toward that girl Ella. His thoughts had surely been full of her the whole night. In truth, she did not seem like the other slaves. She was not dead behind her eyes like the rest of them. She did not speak to him meekly because he was the son of her owner. Rather, she seemed to defy him. But what nonsense she did speak about the different slave peoples, Carlton thought as he struggled to get up.

Later, when he had dressed and taken a turn around the plantation on his horse and seen that all the gangs were working in spite of the showers of rain, he had a chance to discuss with his father what Ella had told him. His father made him change his wet trogs and gave him a draught of rum to drink before they had breakfast. The rum made him bold enough to question his father. Bo'jack, serving the freshly baked bread and omelets to them, pricked up his ears.

"Of course the niggers have different people, Carlton," said his father. "We white people have Frenchies and Spanish and English and so on, so why shouldn't the Negroes have their own, too. Africa is a very big place, you know, son."

"Are some slaves different from others, then, sir?"

"Yes, yes. There are some factors who say they can tell good nigger blood just from the face of the slave. I don't know much about it. Of course, planters prefer seasoned slaves who have been broken in, or a creole actually born on a plantation who doesn't know enough of any other kind of life to want to make trouble. It's the Africans you have to choose carefully."

"You ever buy from a Roseau factor, Da?" Carlton accepted another omelet from Bo'jack.

"Bought my first stock from a factor twenty years ago. Not much since, though, 'cept here and there, like."

"Ever bought a Batutsi, Da?" Bo'jack, who had been about to go down to the kitchen for a fresh jug of coffee, decided to pass around the omelet plate again.

"Batutsi, eh? Yes, son." Hayes smiled indulgently, exchanging a glance with Bo'jack. "We had a Batutsi wench here once, didn't we, Bo'jack?"

"T'ink I does remember dat wench, sah."

"Damme! You'll never forget her, Bo'jack! Carlton, you see that ear of Bo'jack's what lost its lobe? Not me that cut that off, son. It's a Batutsi what chewed it right off his head one night!" Hayes shook with laughter, and Carlton was amazed to see that Bo'jack put down the omelet plate on the table to join in the chuckling.

"She was a vicious tiger, sah, dat wench!"

"Ah, Bo'jack, you met your match then," spluttered Hayes, forking more omelet into his mouth. "Was in the good old days, son, a few months before you were born, I s'pose. I went to Roseau one day and saw this fine female at the factor's. The factor said she was full, but no one believed him. I took a chance, though, and paid the man's price. It was high, but the filly really was prime. I put her to Ma Phoebe to season because your mother was going to drop you and we needed a new maid about the house."

Hayes looked at Bo'jack again. "She was a fine female, as I remember, proud as hell but a winning wench in bed, eh, Bo'jack?"

"I does not recall, sah." Bo'jack picked up the omelet dish but still did not leave the room.

"You damn liar!" laughed Hayes. "Well, son, this oaf Bo'jack here takes a fancy to that Batutsi wench, but she doesn't want anything to do with him. Says he's a creole pauper, or some such nonsense."

"Pawpaw, Da."

Hayes looked at his son curiously. "Yes, maybe you're right. Something of that nature. Anyhow, Bo'jack tries to rape the wench but she's not having it and chews off his ear. You never did hear such screaming that night—and Bo'jack was the one crying!"

Hayes again collapsed into laughter while Carlton waved Bo'jack away, indicating his empty cup of coffee. The slave appeared reluctant to leave.

"Bo'jack!" said Carlton sharply. "Git my coffee 'fore I does have cause to lash you."

"Yas, sah." Bo'jack sidled out of the room slowly.

"Where did you hear about that Batutsi, son?" asked Hayes, plonking his fork down on the table.

"Oh, just some slave talk. What did you do to the wench?"

95

"That's it, son, what could I do? The Batutsi was splendid in the house, but your mother didn't take to her. And I needed Bo'jack, so we had to separate them. I sent the Batutsi to the quarters to work in the fields. But she couldn't tolerate it, went into a decline. That's what them Africans do sometimes. I left her be, although sometimes she made some baskets out of dry grass, fine things. The other niggers were scared of her, said she was an obeah woman. But to me she was one of the finest nigger wenches I ever did know." Hayes lapsed into silence, his eyes distant.

Bo'jack entered then and glanced at his master, wondering what had been said in his absence.

"Was that because she was a Batutsi, do you think, Da?" Carlton held out his coffee cup for Bo'jack to fill.

"The factor did tell me that Batutsis were the best Negroes that money can buy. They had their own nigger aristocracy, you see, and were supposed to be among the nobs in their own country. That's what made them so spirited. Not like this Pawpaw, as you call him here."

"Are there many different breeds of nigger, Da?"

"Lord! I suppose there are. Don't know much about it, really. Best thing is for a nigger to forget his background, son. Make him a pure field slave, that's the best breed!"

"Da?" said Carlton tentatively, emboldened by his father's good humor. "You remember when that Captain Loring was here, the one that took Prince away with him? You and he talked about breeding niggers to sell. I said they breeds anyway, so what's so special about that? But seems to me that if we're going to breed niggers, we should really pick out the best stock to do it."

"What are you driving at, son?" Hayes was impressed by the boy's interest in something at last. He had been disappointed that the boy did not take much notice of sugar. Cane harvesting had never meant more to his son than riding around the plantation cursing the slaves.

"Well, say we does go in for breeding niggers, special like. Then we wants good stock, right? Batutsi s'posed to be the best, so shouldn't we try to get some more of them? And there must be other breeds what make the best slaves. Let's get some of them, as well."

Hayes put down his coffee cup. "You can go now, Bo'jack," he said to the hovering slave. "Get this room cleared up when we finish." There was silence between the two men as Bo'jack shuffled out. Carlton fidgeted impatiently.

"So, son," said Hayes when Bo'jack finally closed the door, "what's this? We have close on three hundred niggers running 'round this plantation costing more than three thousand pound a year to feed and clothe, and now you want us to buy more! Sugar fetching less and less, son. Can barely cover costs these days. We got no cause to buy more niggers at all, no sir!"

"It's just what the Captain said," ventured Carlton, intrigued by the ideas which were entering his head as he spoke. "If slaves getting scarce on the plantations in other islands, we could sell some of our useless stock to the traders at good prices. Then we could use the money to buy prime Negroes ourselves and breed from them. Could season the slaves right here."

"Wait, Carlton." Hayes put his hand on Carlton's arm. "I see you got this thing on your mind right bad. All right, son, I'm not agin it, so no need to charge at it like a nigger in cane with a blunt cutlass. Now, what be the reason to sell slaves just to buy more to breed, when we have prime niggers right here? Batutsi ain't the only special breed, son." Hayes sat back in his chair, a plan forming in his own mind.

"You agree to breeding niggers then, Da?" Carlton was surprised.

"Of course, son. Been thinking about it for over three years. Needs planning, son. Like I told you, our own slaves are good. I know that because we've always treated them proper. I punish when it's necessary and not otherwise. The niggers know that. And I feeds them well; they get their salt fish once a week and a piece of meat now and then. And look at all the fish they gets down in the Layou river." He paused, scratching his chin.

"That reminds me. There be some kind of nigger what makes good fishermen. The factor told me that, and I bought a dozen from him. Happy fellows, always singing. Wageny, or some such name. They the ones what live nearest the river. Unlikely to work much good in the cane, but they sure are good fishermen. That nigger on the ferry, he's a Wageny, too."

Hayes pushed back his chair and stood up. "You finished your coffee, son?"

"Long time, Da."

"Come on, let's take a look around." Hayes rested his hands on the balcony, temporarily lost in thoughts of the Alabama plantations when he had been a bright young buck himself, chivvying along the slaves to put in extra work so he could get a bonus for a good cotton harvest from the owner. He would have liked a gang like that, to look after them, work with them, sport with them.

Carlton glimpsed a figure moving at the foot of the back staircase. He walked to the end of the gallery and saw Ella below. She had the coffee cups that he and his father had been using that morning in her hands. She was holding them lovingly. She carried them over to the trough where one of the kitchen boys was already pouring out water for her to wash the wares. Perhaps she sensed Carlton on the gallery above, for she suddenly lifted her proud head and watched him for a few seconds before lowering her eyes to the trough. The casual arrogance of her gestures was the most puzzling thing about her. She knew that Carlton was the son of her Bondmaster, able to do with her what he wanted, and yet she had an air of defiance which none of the other slaves ever showed.

"Come, boy!" called his father. "Stop watching those kitchen sluts and let's see what we can sight from the front of the house."

Carlton shrugged his shoulders and tried to dismiss the girl from his mind. His father was pointing to a group of Negroes in the distance, walking along by the river bank.

"Them's the Wagenies. Not in the fields, you see. Didn't expect them to be. They'll be going to their nets. The quarters will need fish for dinner today, and we've got plenty of niggers around to cut cane." Hayes eased himself down in his chair while Carlton remained standing at the balcony rail looking out to the river.

"Often wonder why some slaves are fishermen and others are better as domestics. It's all down to their kind, I suppose," mused Hayes. "Those Wagenies sure like to fish, though."

"Da," said Carlton, turning to face his father. "I think I see what you mean. We've got some slaves here who are good workers according to what they have to do. They the kind to raise, right?" His father nodded encouragingly.

"But Da, that's just the stallions. What about the fillies for them to mount?"

"You picks them, son. Take them young, fourteen, fifteen. Look for the fresh, lively ones with clear eyes, fine teeth, firm legs, wide hips. Inspect them yourself."

"Inspect them?" Carlton was overwhelmed at the prospect of inspecting all the plantation females.

"That's what they does at the factor's," Hayes recalled. "Have the filly strip and look her over. Bounce her bosom, see she's regular built. Finger her. Know how to finger a filly, son?"

Carlton looked at his dad in amazement, retreating to the chair beside him to cover his embarrassment and the familiar stirring he could feel in his crotch. He crossed his legs, keeping his eyes on the distant palm trees growing alongside the river. "Of course, Da."

"Don't think you do, son." The old man looked at

Carlton and shook his head with a sigh. "It's not some kind of game to make you come off. It's what you have to do to judge the quality of your stock." Hayes sat up in his chair and gazed out over the railings. "I'll show you, son. Call that wench up here."

"That one?" Carlton was startled. Hayes had picked out Ella as she was carrying a pail of water in front of the house.

"Sure, why not? I'll get Ma Phoebe up here instead, if you like, and have her strip down. Methinks you'd prefer a filly to an old nag, though!"

"Oy! Oy!" Carlton called, determined not to let his father notice anything wrong. All heads within earshot froze as they heard his call, none daring to look toward the balcony. "You, slut. Put down that pail and come up here!"

Ella stopped still. She raised her hands above her head and eased off the pail of water and placed it gently on the ground in front of her. Watching the ground, she moved toward the steps leading to the balcony.

Carlton felt sick. "Back stairs, wench! And hurry."

Hayes contemplated the girl as she came around the corner to stand in front of them. She was tall and moved easily. He stroked his chin, recalling the days when he used to have fillies like that by the score. "Well, son, go ahead!" he snapped.

"To do what, Da?"

"Inspect, damme! Finger! See if she'll breed, you dolt!"

Carlton appraised his father, trying to assess his mood. It changed so often from good humor to anger, it was always best to do what he said so as not to provoke him to greater exasperation. Ella stood before him impassively.

"Drop, drop!" Carlton waved his hand at the girl, hoping she would know what he meant. She raised her head to stare at the wall behind Carlton's chair.

"Drop yuh garments, girl."

Ella's arrogance was troubling Carlton and made

100

his mood change as quickly as his father's did. Anger whipped through him and he stood up, determined to cut this fast little bitch down to size. Placing his hand on the front of her loose-fitting dress, he pulled. The girl resisted him slightly with her body, then swayed forward to the pressure of his hand.

"Stand up!" He tugged again, and the garment tore away in his hand. He ripped it to the waist, then let it go.

"Drop!" He brushed the dress off her shoulders and it slid down her body to the floor. Hayes sucked on his teeth with a greedy hiss. Ella stood naked on the balcony before them.

"Right, son," commanded Hayes as Carlton stood in front of the girl, apparently studying her eyes. "We see she's a prime filly to look at. What does she feel like? Touch her, boy, touch her!"

Carlton hesitated, trying to ignore Ella's stare of such contempt that it was he who felt degraded. He grabbed her shoulders angrily, running his hands over her body as roughly as he could. He bounced her breasts and when she showed no concern in her haughty face, he thumped her suddenly on her chest with a blow which would have felled a weaker woman. He spun her around to run his fingers over her shoulders and down her back, conscious of the stimulation of her rounded curves. His hands rested on her buttocks as he wondered what he should do next. His father was wheezing.

"Oh, yes, she's built to bear a dozen whelps, Carlton. Fine filly, fine filly. Come here, wench!" He beckoned her hastily with two fingers of his right hand. She stepped out of her torn dress lying on the floor and moved to the Bondmaster's side. Hayes remained seated, her abdomen level with his eyes. He reached forward and placed his left arm around her buttocks. She stood erect.

"No, girl," he said. "Open your legs. That's it." Steadying her with his left hand behind her back,

101

Hayes plunged his right hand between her thighs, jamming his fingers into her.

"Right," he wheezed. "Right!" The girl staggered back against the rail as he released her. Carlton sat down quickly in his chair. Hayes nodded knowingly, unconsciously rubbing the fingers of his right hand under his nose. He signaled with his left hand for the girl to pick up her dress and get out.

"Go on," said Carlton, finding his voice. "Get back to work."

Ella's bouncy pride had left her as she bent down to grab her dress and walk naked around the balcony to the back stairs. Tears filled her eyes, but she was determined not to let the Bondmaster and his son have the satisfaction of seeing her cry.

"Fine filly!" repeated Hayes, his eyes glazed.

"That's the Batutsi, Da."

"You don't say."

"I mean, she's bound to be one of the best if she's a Batutsi."

"Best for what? Too much of an animal. Like her mother. But cross her," Hayes added thoughtfully, "with one of my prime young studs over there, and we would have a sturdy buck, all right. Tell you what, son, if you are so interested in this breeding idea, I'll give you an opportunity to try it out.

"Those bucks in the top field, they're young. I gives them a ration of rum and water every afternoon, and they work well. I'm going to give them to you. You can find any fillies on the plantation which takes your fancy. Make sure you inspect them properly first, don't want no pygmy stock. Then you can let those stallions mount your fillies and we'll see how things work out.

"Mark my words, though, Carlton," Hayes added, wondering if he had already gone too far when he thought of his son's lack of interest in sugar. "No good any black-bummed bozal jumping your fillies. You will have to do it all regular like. And you don't want your studs wasting their seed and weakening the breed.

"No, son! Must pen them at night. You can have the old barn for that. Son," he cautioned finally, "if what they say be true, then you could make as much from this crop as I ever did from sugar, even more. It takes time. You've got to be serious. I'll help you, but I don't know much about this stock-rearing. Sugar's been my life, leastways since I left Alabama. We going to stop shipping sugar, son. I want a rest. Keep a little cane for the rum, that's got a bit of profit and I can handle that. You can have the stock."

The shock of the encounter with Ella still affected Carlton. He heard his father's words without taking them in fully. For the first time he had been conscious of doing something which made him ashamed, and it was worrying him. Ella was property just like a cow you would inspect to see if it was healthy, he tried to reason. She had a brand mark on her thigh like all the Roxborough slaves, burned into her flesh by his father. She was an animal, and now a source of profit if he could put her to breed with some of the bucks his father was giving him. But wasn't she also a person?

"Da?" he said. "That wench, that Batutsi. I'd like her if I can have her?"

"Of course, son," said Hayes. "I thought that was what I am telling you. Pick the fillies you want."

"No, Da, I don't mean for breeding. I mean for me. Like you used to have when you were a young man, a bed wench."

"Glory be! You bounce the chit's suckers and you want her to move into your bed!"

"She works in the kitchen already, Da. Ma Phoebe's been training her for nigh a year now."

"Has she, son? You noticed all that, then? Can't say I did. When you've got three hundred niggers about the place, can't remember one from the other sometimes. Want her for your wench, do you?"

Hayes paused, wiping his face again, sniffing his

fingers. "Huh! Don't see why not. She's a fair piece. Wonder if she's like her mother. Better watch your balls in case she is. Don't want them lopped off like Bo'jack's ear, what!" He leaned over and clapped his son heavily on his thigh.

"Tell you one thing, son. Always make sure a nigger washes herself before she comes to your bed. Sometimes this house fair stinks with the riffraff straight from the fields which you pulls into your chamber at nights. 'Bout time you had a regular wench and stop sticking it into any black hole you see!"

Hayes chuckled, clapping his hands loudly. "Bo'-jack!" he called. "Where's that old bugger? Thought he'd be hiding 'round that corner when you had that Batutsi stripped down. Hey, that reminds me. If she's coming in to the house, better get a decent dress made for her, especially now you tore her own." He chuckled again. "Tell Ma Phoebe find one of the women that's a seamstress come and fix her up. She can wait át table. Be pleasing to have her to look at when we're eating, instead of that old joskin."

Carlton declined the rum which his father was pressing him to have. He felt nervous, more on account of Ella than because of his new responsibility. Pairing off the slaves was going to be much more interesting than riding in the hot sun watching the niggers sweat. But what about Ella? If what his father said about the girl's mother was true, then Ella herself would be a very different proposition from the field slaves he had mounted before.

"All right, sir," he smiled, shrugging off his doubts. "I'll have a punch."

"That's right, my boy. Helps you handle the slaves, you know. You forget their contrariness when you have a gill of this inside you."

Carlton nodded. He relaxed as the rum concoction seeped through him, sending a warm glow to his head. The rain of the morning had stopped and the sun filtered through the trees, a slight breeze rustling along the balcony. He would ride to the quarters that very afternoon and start making a list of all the slaves on the plantation. Even his father did not know how many there were. He would list their names, their jobs, and their quality. And that night he would have Ella.

He raised his glass to his father, smiling happily as the old man poured him another measure of rum.

Chapter 11

"Oh mah gawd!" The ladle fell from Phoebe's hand onto the stone floor of the kitchen. "Girl, you sick in yo' head? If Massa does see you in dat state dere will be one big rampage in Ma Phoebe's kitchin. Dose white buckra don't like no naked nigger in deir food."

Ella stood straight and haughty at the kitchen door as Ma Phoebe rushed toward her. She was enjoying the commotion.

"So we does be born, Ma Phoebe."

"Dat's right," said the cook, swooping down to grab a piece of cheesecloth from the table. "An' so we does die if buckra claps eyes on you naked in his place. Put dat bit o' muslin 'round you, girl. Quick, nuh! Oh my gawd!" Phoebe thrust the cloth at Ella, but she brushed it aside and pirouetted gaily on the step.

"Den come yere, den!" Phoebe grabbed the girl's wrists and pulled her roughly off the step down into the kitchen. In spite of her size, Ma Phoebe moved swiftly, dragging Ella behind her. Ella struggled to regain her balance, but Ma Phoebe was too much for her and she stumbled and fell at the big woman's feet as Ma Phoebe came to a halt at the head of the long working table. The cheesecloth fluttered down on her.

"Hear dis now, chile," said Ma Phoebe, placing her

hands squarely on her hips, her gigantic bosom heaving as she caught her breath. "In dis kitchin we does wear clothes 'cause it be white men we does be dealin' wid."

"But Ma Phoebe," said Ella pulling herself to her feet and wrapping the muslin around her chest, securing it so it covered her body, "it does be white men done tell me take off my clothes."

"Oh mah gawd! Hear de gel!" Ma Phoebe sat down abruptly.

"It does be true, Ma Phoebe," said Bo'jack, sidling in through the door, his face split into a wide grin. "Massa Hayes an' Mas Carlton dey both fingerin' de girl. Mayhaps dey does be plannin' for to sell her."

"Sell!" Ma Phoebe's hands shot up in the air in surprise. "Dere ain' be no sellin' a' Roxbra ever, not ever."

"Oh no?" said Bo'jack filling a pitcher of punch from the small cask kept locked in the pantry. "What about dat Prince, den? De one dat Mas Carlton done have sleepin' wid him all de time. Done sell him."

"Dat was be exchange for de governess." The thought of Mademoiselle de Champigny calmed Phoebe. "Dey does want de punch a'ready? Cane cuttin' in de top field, Massa Hayes, does be go up dere?"

"No," said Bo'jack. "He done tell me go come wid de rum. Dey can see de top field from up dere where dey be."

"Massa Hayes be sickenin' fuh somethin', dat's sure. He does always check de sugar when de boys does be cuttin'."

"Ah does tell you," said Bo'jack as he walked toward the kitchen door to go upstairs with the rum. "Dey be plannin' to sell deir stock. Ah hear dey does say dey does wan' to sell you, but you too dam' black an' ugly!" He darted out of the door as a bread roll whistled past his ear.

"Wait till you come back yere!" Ma Phoebe shouted after him. "When you hungry you'll see who black an' ugly! Now, girl." Ma Phoebe hitched up her long skirt and settled back on the bench, pulling Ella down beside her. "You jes' tell Ma Phoebe all de things what dey does do you on de gallery an' all dat dose buckra does say."

Ella recounted her experience, omitting to mention her own fascination at the procedure until Massa Hayes stuck his fingers in her. That was brutal, and she was still hurting. Ma Phoebe put her heavy arm around her, pulling Ella's face down onto her bosom.

"Child, dey does be plannin' to sell you in true. Is dat dey does do at de vendue." She patted Ella's shoulders. "But Ma Phoebe does be going fix dat for you. You don't have to fear of dat, chile."

Ella pulled her face away from the suffocating bosom. "Ah don't fear dat, Ma Phoebe. An' ah don't think dey does be plannin' for to sell me, now."

"How you know what dey does think? Dose buckra don't think straight like Negro folk. Dey have deir own partic'lar ways. Don't never know what dat Mas Hayes and de boy does be thinkin'."

"Mas Carlton does like me too much for to sell me."

"Oy oy oy! Chil', white men don't like niggers! We people not deir people. Ain' no likin' in it, no, sah!" Ma Phoebe hauled herself to her feet and went over to the grate. "Ella, girl, don't know where dat useless boy be. Git me some o' dat wood for de fire. It does be dyin' too low." Ma Phoebe shook her head as though seeing her future in the glow of the embers under the grating.

"Dey be wantin', Ella, but not likin'. Dey wants dis, dey wants dat, dey wants yuh body, but dey don't like you."

Ella carried over some small logs and fed them into the stove as Ma Phoebe held open the door with the tongs. She closed it quickly when the fire began to dance.

"Another thing, Ella," said Ma Phoebe, as she bent down to sort through a pile of dasheen and tania on the floor, putting some into a basket. "I tell you

108

another thing." She sat down on the bench with the basket in front of her.

"Buckra be de Bon'massa, an' we de bondage. What buckra does say, we does do. Dat's de way it be. Hush, chile!" Phoebe picked up the basket and held it for Ella to take. "I does know what you be thinkin' 'cause yo' ain't no quashie like dat Bo'jack or dem niggers in de cane. You does have de spirit."

"What's dat, Phoebe?" said Ella, taking the basket from her.

"Ah does be Ma Phoebe to you, girl."

"Yas, Ma Phoebe. But de spirit, Ma Phoebe?"

Phoebe looked vague. "De spirit? Lord, ah done talk too much a'ready. Go clean dat food for dinner, an' take care dat muslin don't fall and reveal yuh nakedness." Phoebe rose, but Ella confronted her, her young face searching Ma Phoebe's.

"What, chile? You jes like yuh dam, I does declare. Clean de food, girl! Den tonight," added Ma Phoebe, her tiny eyes dancing in the fat flesh of her face, "maybe I does remember something about de spirit. Now go quick. I does have de meat to beat 'fore Mas Hayes does beat me for keepin' him waitin' for his dinner."

Dinner at Roxborough was taken in the afternoon, when the dead heat of the sun was at its fiercest. It was the main meal of the day, and Ma Phoebe always tried to prepare something special for her Bondmaster. Madame Monique had begun to teach Phoebe herself as soon as she came to Roxborough, and it was always Phoebe's aim to prove that she could cook better than her white mistress. Yellow fever had carried off Monique three years after Mas Carlton had been born, and Ma Phoebe had reigned supreme ever since.

The Roxborough slaves accepted Ma Phoebe's position on the plantation. She had added power to her authority over them by her knowledge of plants and their uses which, along with her massive size and strength, gave her a reputation as an obeah woman.

Phoebe knew that her influence on the slaves contributed more to the peaceful management of the plantation than any whip or chains brandished by the white Bondmaster.

If Hayes Todd was aware of her power he had never given her any sign of it. He had always been a sensible man when it came to managing the plantation, and his determination and energy had won him respect where other white men in the island were hated. Ma Phoebe had long ago reasoned that if things were going well for her Bondmaster, then things would go well for his slaves. Fortunately, the years had favored the plantation, and sugar had brought in more rations, new cabins in the quarters, calico by the yard, and a routine which few of the slaves wanted to disrupt.

The question that puzzled Phoebe, as she busied herself ladling the dinner into tureens, was what attitude young Mas Carlton was going to take. Oh yes, she knew that Mas Carlton did respect his slaves, but he was young and hot. He could do anything. Ma Phoebe had seen the signs and it was worrying her. The boy was getting to be a man and could disrupt the tranquillity on the plantation which she had schemed so hard to achieve. Already, she knew, Mas Carlton had developed a taste for putting his nose in where it was not wanted, hauling wenches into the schoolroom to mount them, beating them like ponies while he did so. If there was much more of that, the Negroes would get restless. It was unsettling.

Ma Phoebe looked up as Bo'jack came into the kitchen, wiping the sweat off his forehead. Dinner was all prepared.

"Ah does be warnin' you, Ma Phoebe," he said, slumping down on the bench. "Massa Hayes and dat Carlton boy dey does be plannin' some wickedness."

"Oh my gawd!" She raised her eyes to the heavens. "Look a' de man. Dey be near ready fuh dinner an' he does sit down an' harangue. Go call dat Pool come an' help yuh carry de things up for de table."

"Dey don't want me serving dem now, Ma Phoebe. Ah done hear dem say dat Ella more sweet dan me an' dat she be de one for to serve dem."

"Hah! Dat's wha' you does git for saying dat Ma Phoebe does be black an' ugly!" Ma Phoebe shook with delight. "Now git yuh backside out of mah way an' go 'n' serve dem buckras."

As was her custom, Ma Phoebe stood at the foot of the back stairs while dinner was served. She quizzed Bo'jack and Pool, each time they came back down the stairs, pleading to know how the buckras liked her dinner. Every day it was the same. Sometimes, if she had prepared something really special of her own invention, she would creep up the steps and onto the gallery, being careful not to let the boards creak under her massive weight, and crouch under the window. To hear Mas Hayes express pleasure at the flavor of a sauce, or to listen to Mas Carlton commenting on a dish, was her reward. She knew then that she was a better cook than a white woman could ever be. It was her secret.

"Ma Phoebe," cried Bo'jack, tumbling down the steps. "Come quick! Dey does want you!"

"Oh my gawd! Something done happen. You don't go 'n' throw dat red pepper in de sauce?"

"No, Ma Phoebe, ah done nothing. Dey jes' take de food and deh Mas Hayes he done tell me for to git you quick."

"Oh my gawd!" Phoebe wrung her pudgy hands anxiously in front of her bosom, reviewing the preparations she had gone through for dinner.

"Don't vex yourself, Ma Phoebe," said Ella, coming to stand beside her at the foot of the step. "De Bon'massa does call, so de nigger must jump."

"Fah!" Phoebe snorted, pulling herself up the staircase. Bo'jack and Ella and Pool nervously watched her progress.

"You goin' up, too, Bo'jack.

"No, sah, Ella, not Bo'jack. Dey does tell me stay away."

Pool and Bo'jack sat down disconcerted on the lower step, their ears poised to catch any angry shouts from the dining room above. Ella, tired of waiting below, tried to push past them to climb higher up the steps.

"Stay 'way, girl, dey don't want no nigger girl in dere. Dey goin' sell you for sure."

Phoebe's huge figure appeared at the top of the steps. They tried to read her face, but she gave no clue as she stepped down. To Ella, she appeared almost regal.

"Ma Phoebe, what happen?" she asked before the cook reached the final step. She sensed a smile on the old woman's face.

"Dey does like my cookin'," she chuckled. "Wants for to tell me dat de kitchin never lets dem down." She tried to look coy. Bo'jack snorted with disbelief. "Not like de serving. Get up dere, Bo'jack, an' bring down dose empty dishes for Pool to wash. Ella, you go by Mally Ibo at de quarters. Tell her Ma Phoebe does say she to come an' carry some calico make a serving dress for you dis af'noon myself."

Ma Phoebe lowered herself into the big chair she had had installed in the kitchen so that she could driect her helpers whenever she felt too tired to stir the pots herself. She sighed contentedly. Mas Carlton's decision to make Ella his regular bed wench was the opportunity Phoebe had wished for. With Ella to tame him, Mas Carlton would stop his running wild and disturbing the niggers. She had listened to all they had told her in the dining room. Get clothes for Ella, tell her to bathe, dress her nicely, send her up into the house, and teach her to serve at table.

"Oy, oy, oy," she sighed softly to herself, her head slumping forward as sleep overwhelmed her, "de buckras done do right."

It was a busy afternoon. Mally Ibo sat under the gallery hastily stitching a dress for Ella. Ma Phoebe dispatched Ella to the river to bathe, giving her a cake of sweet soap which she had been saving in the

112

locker of her own room. Dutchip was ordered to send one of the women from the field gang to accompany her. Pool was sent to the quarters for Cleo, a child about ten years old, because Ma Phoebe said she needed someone in the kitchen now that Ella was going into the house. Bo'jack was sent to the stockman to try to get some fresh milk so that Ma Phoebe could make special cocoa tea with canelle spice to drink for supper. Little Cudjoe was called over from the small gang to run up the valley where the river narrowed to pick some leaves from a bush which grew there. Ma Phoebe herself spent an hour in her own quarters making some private preparations, coming out only to send off Pool for a *crapaud* from the bag of frogs stored under the cellar.

In the late afternoon, the rain began to fall again. Neither Hayes nor Carlton ventured out into the rain and, as it looked as though it had settled in for the night, the slaves were dismissed and told to go back to their quarters. Bo'jack was soon ferrying rum back and forth to his masters while the word about events at the big house was spreading among the slaves. Ella, now dressed in her new frock, which hung easily from her shoulders, was delighted to be the center of attraction. Mally Ibo was proud of her work.

"She plenty pretty now wid dat fine dress."

"No," said Congo Venus who had been ordered by Ma Phoebe to come and plait the girl's hair. "It be de locks in she hair!"

"Dat be you," said Ma Phoebe, taking a pot off the grate where she had been brewing the leaf which little Cudjoe had found for her. "Now ah does wan' mah kitchin clear." She placed the pot on the table and then dipped a ladle into the light green liquid, pouring it into a clay mug. " 'Cept you, Ella."

Ma Phoebe noticed with satisfaction that night was beginning to fall. She beckoned Ella to follow her along the passage which led to the slave rooms under the house. Ella had never been permitted to enter

Ma Phoebe's room, although she used to sleep in the passage outside her door. She was nervous now as she followed the woman waddling along in front of her, bearing the cup with the steaming liquid she had prepared. Ma Phoebe threw open the door to her chamber and stood aside for Ella to enter. She pushed her gently. The room was dark.

"Now, chile, you jest do as ah say," Ma Phoebe told her, bustling into the room and closing the door. "Remove dat dress first."

Ella obeyed without hesitation and when she was naked in front of her, Ma Phoebe gave her a thrust which made the girl fall backwards onto the pallet on the floor which Ma Phoebe used as her bed.

Crouching down, Ma Phoebe fumbled on the floor and then scooped up the giant frog Pool had brought her. It squirmed. She pressed it into Ella's hands, forcing her to hold it. "Don't let go, now!" she cautioned.

"I won't," said Ella, clenching the slimy frog, which suddenly gave a croak.

"Ah!" Phoebe was satisfied. She plunged a knife into the frog's neck and neatly sliced off its head. The blood trickled on Ella's hands as the *crapaud's* body twitched in her fingers. Ma Phoebe caught the drops of blood in the cup so that it mixed with the liquid she had boiled. She began chanting words that Ella recognized as in a language that she and the other slaves instinctively knew, but were unable to utter. Ma Phoebe threw more things into the cup.

"Drink dis, now!" she hissed at Ella. "It does give you de spirit of obeah, de spirit of your ancestors, de spirit of de power over buckra."

Ella grabbed the cup, letting the decapitated frog fall between her thighs. Ma Phoebe eased herself down to crouch in front of her, keeping her own hands around the cup and forcing Ella to drink until every drop had drained down her throat. Ella grimaced at the foul taste. Her head spun and she fell backwards onto the pallet, her legs stretched open before her.

114

Ma Phoebe smiled, her fat lips stretched tightly across her teeth. Ella could just make out her bulk in the gloom of the room as she saw the cook's head go down to meet her outstretched legs. She felt her lips nibbling at her naked thighs, plump fingers digging into the soft flesh of her buttocks. Ma Phoebe's tongue began to rasp against her skin, over her stomach and down between her legs. The spinning in her head passed, and Ella arched her back off the pallet in eagerness as Phoebe's tongue dived into her.

"Mas Carlton," she sighed, gripping the cook's head. "Mas Carlton!"

Ma Phoebe's hand clasped the wet body of the dead frog. She brought it slowly up Ella's leg, rubbing it against her soft flesh, lubricating her gently with its blood. Suddenly, she plunged the headless frog deep into Ella, thrusting it in and out with a frenzied rhythm.

"Mas Carlton, Mas Carlton," sighed Ella as she fell back on the pallet in a swoon.

Chapter 12

Kingston hurried up the road to the house as fast as he could, his ledger book tucked tightly under his arm. He had been counting hogsheads in the still room when Pool had run in and said that Mas Carlton wanted him urgently and he was to bring the plantation ledger. Ever since Master Hayes had put him in charge of the ledgers six years before when the white bookkeeper who used to do the work was killed, Kingston had carefully recorded all the plantation's business. He had been taught to read and write as a boy in Jamaica, where he was born some fifty years before. When his old master had died, while he was still a youth, Kingston had been sold to an island trader who had sold him to Master Hayes. Massa Hayes trusted him and he worked well for him, so why Mas Carlton should have cause to send for him he could not fathom.

"Boy," he said to Pool who was striding along in front of him impatiently, "wait a while. Let me ketch mah breat'." He paused and gazed up the road to the house.

"Mas Carlton done say you sure got to haul yuh black arse up to de house right quick." Pool, as a house slave, felt himself superior to Kingston, even though the old man knew writing and figuring and had his own quarters down by the mill.

"If you not comin' I go tell Mas Carlton." Pool was impatient; he wanted to get back to the kitchen so that he could hear Ella tell about her first night with Master Carlton. She had not come down to the kitchen until nigh on breakfast time, and Master Carlton had risen so late he did not have time to ride around the plantation before breakfast as he usually did.

"Dat Mercury, de driver, he done come to de house dis mornin'," Pool boasted, showing off his knowledge. "Massa Hayes done tell him where to work. Dere does be plenty happenin' dis mornin'."

"I comin', boy," muttered Kingston, starting up the path again. "I does be more steady in my ways dan you young pups. I have to preserve my strength for my figurin'. You does be workin' in de house a long time now, boy. It does be recorded in dis book." Kingston flourished the ledger at Pool as a symbol of his authority. "Perhaps you have some information on de matter of dis come-quick business?"

Not wanting to reveal that neither he nor Bo'jack, nor even Ma Phoebe herself knew what was going on in the big house today, Pool remembered something he had heard Bo'jack say the day before about Ella. It was not true, in view of Ella being taken up as Mas Carlton's bed wench, but it might impress the old nigger. "I hear dey does be plannin' to sell de stock," Pool confided.

Kingston stopped in his tracks. "Day say dat! Boy, you lie!"

"Well, I hear dat Bo'jack say dat Massa Hayes and Mas Carlton, dey done strip dat gel Ella down an' finger her jest like dey does do at de vendue."

"Ella?" Kingston started up the hill again, repeating the girl's name to himself. "Ella? Yas, she de one does have de Batutsi dam what pine away an' die. Thought I hear last night dat Massa Carlton done take her for his bed wench."

"You done hear all de happenin's, now," said Pool sulkily. He increased his pace and left the old man

117

to walk at his own speed when he glimpsed Mas Carlton hanging over the balcony railing watching them.

"Mas Carlton up dere," he said over his shoulder to Kingston. "Best you hurry yourself lest he does sell yuh at de vendue wid de others."

As Carlton watched them, he felt as though a change had come over him. He felt in himself the uncertainty that the old man must have and knew he would have to explain his new job to Kingston very carefully to get the cooperation he needed to succeed. What puzzled Carlton was that he should even think the gray-haired old nigger should have feelings of any kind.

Ella had somehow stirred in him this new feeling of consideration for a slave. She had looked after him with such tenderness the night before when, overcome by the sangaree and rum punches pressed on him by his father, he had collapsed on the floor before he could even get into bed. Ella had made him drink some obnoxious concoction which she promised would cure him. This morning, when he woke, he had no trace of the effects of the drinking of the night before, and he had taken Ella tenderly instead of in his usual brutish fashion. Strangely, the regular twitching in his crotch this morning made him feel as though he had been the one who had been deflowered, not Ella. He shook such thoughts out of his head as the old Negro neared the house.

"Good morning, Kingston," he called. "Please come up here. Use the front steps," he added as the slave started to pass around to the back of the house. Pool, who had reached the kitchen, turned back and watched in amazement. Ma Phoebe nodded her head knowingly as she overheard from her open window under the gallery.

"Come in here," Carlton led the way into the dining room, "and put the ledger on the table." He reached for the book while Kingston stood apprehensively. Carlton began to turn the pages.

"You have a very neat hand."

"T'ankyuh, sah."

The first pages of the book contained a register of the slaves on the plantation. Against each name was a date, and some names had two dates. Each name was numbered, and there were over a thousand names in all. The ledger must have been started by Carlton's mother long before he was born. Other hands had written in the book until Kingston's distinctive style showed where he had made his first entry in 1791.

"Whenever a chile does be born or whenever Massa Hayes does purchase a new slave, den I does enter de name an' de date in dis column here, sah." Kingston stubbed his finger proudly on the page when Carlton asked him to explain. "An' when one does die, I does enter de next date against de name."

"What happens when a slave is sold?"

"Sold, sah?" Kingston's eyes grew wider, the whites flashing in panic.

"Yes, when we sell a slave, do you enter the date of the sale, too?"

"Ah," Kingston hesitated. "Well, yas sah."

Carlton looked through the pages again. He realized he would have to know the year in which a particular slave had been born for the register to be of any use. He had always assumed that Prince was the same age as himself, so he looked on the page representing 1780. Running his finger down the list, he was surprised to see the number of names which already had two dates against them.

"I see from this list, Kingston, that a lot of the children born here die very young."

"Yas, sah."

"Why is that, Kingston?"

"I does not know, sah." Kingston was really concerned now. Did this young master suspect that he had killed the children just to fill the pages of the ledger?

"Ah, here it is." Carlton paused at the entry reading Prince, 1780, 1793, holding his finger against the name of his fondly remembered playboy.

He looked up at Kingston, who bent over the book as he spoke. "How do you know from an entry like this who has died and who has been sold?"

"I does remember, Mas Carlton, sah. I does have a good head for rememberin'."

"I'm sure you do, Kingston. But look at it this way. If someone else is looking at the book and you are not there, how will he know what has happened to a slave listed in this ledger?"

"Not here, sah?" Kingston scratched his head nervously. "Beg pardin, sah. Where Kingston does be?"

Carlton clucked his tongue in amused exasperation. "I'm illustrating a point, boy. Of course you'll be here, but I mean I might have the book and you might be in the still. You see what I mean?"

"Yas, sah." Kingston was worried. Why should the young master have his book? He wished he could sit down.

"I think that we will have to be more specific in these entries. If a slave is sold, then you will write *sold* beside the date. Same thing if he is bought, then write *purchased* beside the name. Also, I think we could put down who he is bought from, and who he is sold to. It preserves a kind of record. Perhaps we should also note down the price in each case, as well."

"Yas, sah!"

Carlton looked up at the troubled face of the slave. "Just like with the hogsheads," he smiled gently. "When you take the wagon down to Layou, you record each sale and the price paid, not so? We will do the same thing for the slaves."

Kingston began to understand, but already the master was giving him some more instructions.

"When a child is born here, it would be interesting to know something about it, don't you think so, Kingston?"

"Yas, sah."

120

"I think we should write down the name of the sire and the dam. That way we can read from the ledger who is producing pups and who isn't. And see," said Carlton indicating the lists, "there is no sex indicated. We must be able to tell if it's a male or female whelp."

"I does know, sah."

"Oh yes, Kingston, I'm sure you know. I know, too, when I read these names. Little Cudjoe here is a colt, while Patience here is a filly. But if we inscribe male or female against each name, it's easier to take a tally of what we have."

Kingston's face brightened. He understood about tallying. It was what he was doing most of the day, checking the barrels of rum or hogsheads of sugar.

Carlton was sucking his finger thoughtfully. "We seem to lose a lot of whelps each year, Kingston. Yet the fillies does be bearing all the time."

"Yas sah. Some of de chil'ren does be born sickly, an' deir dams don't take no care ob dem neither."

"Why is that?" Carlton was appalled, for he suddenly realized that each whelp lost was the loss of a slave who could be sold for a hundred pounds a time.

"A dam does drop her chile in de field, sah, an' when she does finish work, sah, de chile done die a'ready. If de babe does live, sah, de mam does give de chile to an old woman, sah, an' de chile might not eat, sah, an' take sick quick. De young nigger don't have much chance to live, sah."

Carlton bent forward in his chair, resting his head on his hands. Standing behind him, Kingston felt concerned for the young man, his youthful shoulders hunched up under his shirt as he tried to solve some kind of problem. Kingston hoped that this young master would be good to them all.

"Is there much sickness in the quarters, Kingston?" asked Carlton suddenly.

"No, sah. De quarters does be healthful, sah."

"Then why don't the whelps survive?"

Kingston tried to help. "Seem like deir dams don't want deir chil'dren to live, sah."

Carlton frowned. He raised his head to peer up into Kingston's eyes to see what he could read there. Was it insolence? Was this a way the slaves defied their Bondmaster, dropping a whelp and letting him die? If it was, then the mothers must be made to see the advantage in raising more stock. A new dress, or something, for every healthy child. Better still, he thought, a place must be built to raise the new stock, with some of the old Negroes as stock keepers. When a dam drops, thought Carlton, she could have free time from the fields to suckle the whelp for a few days before the child goes into the stock pen. It would be raised there, trained right from birth to be an obedient and willing slave. What a high price such a well-seasoned slave would fetch!

Carlton stood up. "Yes, Kingston," he said, guiding the slave out to the back steps. "We are going to make Roxborough famous in the West Indies. No," he added as the slave looked back for his precious ledger, "you can leave that with me for a few days. I want to compile a new register of all the slaves we have here. You can help me, of course," he added, again seeing the alarm spreading across the old man's serious features. "I will want you to tell me the occupation of each nigger, as well."

"Dere be another ledger in de still room, sah, which I does have. It does have de name of who in de fields, or in de mill or in de hot house, or here in de great house, or wherever he does be."

"You must know everything about every nigger at Roxborough?"

"Oh yas, sah."

Carlton looked across the back balcony. "You see those colts over there, in the cane. Those six bucks, what's their age?"

Kingston peered across the vegetable garden to the edge of the cane. He made out the shapes of six or more men working in the field gang. "I does be sorry, sah. I jest can' remember every slave on de plantation but if you does give me de name, I sure to know something, sah."

"Yes, yes," said Carlton. "That's all right. I'm going to pick out some prime young colts today. I'll make a list of their names and then we can begin a stock book on each one. The fillies, too," he added with a chuckle.

"You go down to the kitchen. Tell Ma Phoebe I say to give you a portion of breakfast. And I wants you at this hour tomorrow morning, do you hear?"

"Yas, Mas Carlton, sah." With a quick look through the open window across the dining room at his ledger lying open on the table, Kingston gave his young master a salute and started down the stairs.

Carlton turned back. There was one point that was still troubling him in the scheme that was forming in his mind. He knocked on his father's door, gently at first, in case the old man was still sleeping. Hearing a low groan, Carlton pushed open the door and went in. Hayes had the room still in darkness.

"Da, you'll suffocate in this heat."

"Oh, son, don't open them shutters. Light's too bright for me eyes this morning."

"You must be losing your spunk, Da," said Carlton, opening one of the shutters to let in some air. "Can't take a good brew like you used to. Here, I'll block out the light with the curtain." He pulled the curtain on the bedrail until it closed down one side and blocked off the glare from the open window.

"I'm feeling so sickly, son. Might be dying."

"Nonsense, Da. You had plenty of rum last night, that's all. So did I."

"I s'pose so, son. Everything all right on the plantation?"

"Yes, Da. I was wondering." Carlton sat down on his father's bed. "I've been talking with Kingston. I got the ideas and I'm going to pick out my colts and fillies. But what I don't know is how I set my colts to

123

my fillies. I mean, how do I regulate them, keep one filly for the same stallion till she takes."

"What!" Hayes tried to sit up. "That be troubling you?" He held his head. "Them fillies supposed to have a dam, right. Let the dam do it. You'll see." He tried to chuckle but caught his breath suddenly.

"You feeling queer, Da?"

Hayes tried to nod his head, deepening in color as the blood rushed to his temple. He let out his breath again. "Bit of constriction, son," he gasped. "Must be the Madeira in the sangaree. Not Roxborough rum, anyway." His chest heaved. "Tell me about Ella. She pleasurable?"

"Da," said Carlton, "that little thing's a tiger, in truth! I still feeling her." He touched his crotch, causing his father to attempt a loud guffaw.

The laugh swiftly turned to a choke. Hayes tugged at the sheet wildly, trying to catch his breath. Carlton watched in horror as he saw his father's eyes stare at him in panic, his normally florid complexion turning deathly pale. He dashed to the shutter and flung it open.

"Ma Phoebe! Ma Phoebe!" he shouted. *"Venez vite.* Come quickly, please come quickly! My da dying."

Chapter 13

Like fire crackling relentlessly through the bush in the dry season, word of the events at the big house spread through the plantation. Kingston's mysterious conference with young Master Carlton boded no good for the future, the slaves declared, especially as it was followed by the sudden collapse of old Master Todd himself. The days slipped by, and the slaves restlessly waited for developments, but the news which filtered through to them was slight. Ma Phoebe herself aided by Ella, was reported to be nursing Master Todd. Some of the older slaves were surprised that Master Todd did not send for the white doctor from the capital.

"When buckras does be dying," Mally Ibo told Dutchip as they sat in the shade of a mango tree, "dey does send quick for de buckra doctuh come physic dem." She glanced up to the house where Carlton could be seen on the balcony, a big book in his hands.

"Mas Carlton does be doin' plenty readin'. Kingston does say dat be de plantation register he does have wid him all de time."

Congo Venus had been sitting with the two women as they rested after their day's toil. She stood up to leave. "Dat buckra ain't be dyin'."

"How you know dat?" Mally Ibo looked at the old

midwife, eager to hear her opinion, which should be more reliable then most.

"Like you does say, Mally Ibo. No buckra doctuh dere, so massa not dyin'. Ma Phoebe done fix him good."

"She powerful obeah woman for sure," chuckled Dutchip.

"Does not be de obeah dat does do it," said Mally Ibo. "Ma Phoebe does know all de bush dat does grow here. She done make Massa Hayes de bush tea an' he done cure."

"Ma Phoebe does be learnin' Ella plenty obeah, you know," said Dutchip not to be outdone. "Pool done tell me Ella does be in de quarters wid Ma Phoebe every night before Mas Carlton does send for her."

"She mam done give her de obeah way," concurred Congo Venus.

Suddenly Congo Venus held up her hand. Even the boys stopped and listened.

"Hear dat?"

"It de conch!"

The plaintive moan of someone blowing a conch shell wafted over the fields. The birds seemed to be stilled as the mournful note reverberated through the cocoa trees and down to the riverbank. An answering call came from the mill, and then the sound was taken up and repeated by the first player.

Mally Ibo burst into a low wail, echoing the note of the conch. "De Bon'massa done die!"

"No, sah!" said Congo Venus with equal certainty. "See de house. Ain't no one does be wailin' dere."

"But why dey blowin' de conch, now?" Dutchip could see Pool standing at the top of the grand steps, puffing and blowing, straining each time to get a note out of the shell. From the mill, Kingston, who had been expecting the signal, urged his own conch trumpeter to blow harder.

"Dat be de call for all hands," said Celestin to Juba

and the other boys with them. "De massa does want every one of us at de house."

"How you know dat?"

Celestin, normally the quietest of the gang, flushed as he felt the eyes of the other boys on him. The three women were also standing around waiting for his answer as the moan of the conch wailed overhead.

"Dat be de signal Kingston done tell all of us to listen for. Dat day he done come an ax all of us our names."

"Den is a vendue!" Dutchip clapped her hands. "Pool done say dere be a vendue."

"What's a vendue?" Asaph, the youngest of the five youths, demanded.

"Oh my gawd!" said Mally Ibo, who had forgotten her hysterical crying in the excitement of all the noise. "You soon see. A vendue is when buckra does buy and sell all of us."

"I hear dat, now," said Juba. "I go'n git de top price!" With a whoop of delight, Juba beckoned his gang to follow him as he jogged back up the hill.

People were running to the great house from all directions, encouraged by the drivers whom Kingston had instructed in advance about the assembly planned for that afternoon. The old men and women were ushered up the trail by the younger ones from the quarters while the old mill gang who lived by the river accompanied Kingston. The Wageny fishermen loped easily along the path, one carrying a string of fish from his shoulder as a gift for the kitchen. The infirm in the hot house who could still move crawled over the mud floor out from the corners where they had been left to die and crouched in the open where they could see buckra on the balcony.

From this vantage point at the head of the steps, Carlton was astounded by the sight of the Negroes emerging from all parts of the plantation. Some ran, others stepped nonchalantly out of the bush or toiled in chattering groups up the path from the ferry. Although it had been his idea that all the slaves should be assembled in front of the house, the sight of three hundred Negroes of all ages swarming up the hill to confront him was unnerving. Bemused, he turned away and went through into the drawing room. Ella came over with a glass of lime juice sweetened with molasses. She handed it to him without a word.

"They're coming," he said, taking the glass and smiling at her. "I didn't know I had so many." He drank the juice gratefully, and passed the glass back to her. "I have to tell them now."

"You be good for dem," she said. "Dey be interested in you now."

He searched her eyes, wondering what mockery her words contained. Their few nights together had brought him a contentment as well as a complexity of feelings he still could not understand. Her tender concern made her seem human. He had talked to her sometimes as they lay in his bed after he had mounted her, and he was ready to believe that she was sharing his own emotions. It was impossible, of course; she was black and a slave.

He peered through the shutter over the balcony and saw the huge crowd. "Tell Pool to stop now," he instructed Ella. "And tell Ma Phoebe to be ready."

The assembled slaves jostled around the foot of the grand steps, bartering rumors about why they had been summoned. None of the older ones, even those who had been on the plantation for twenty years, could remember such a gathering. They watched Pool standing at one end of the balcony and then broke into more speculation as Bo'jack, dressed in his Sunday clothes, suddenly appeared out of one of the doors and stood at the other end. Many of the younger slaves had never seen Bo'jack before because he kept himself aloof from the field hands. Impressed by the sigh of expectation which had greeted his entrance, Bo'jack drew himself up to his full height and folded his arms across his chest. Ella could see him from the window of Master Hayes's room and smiled to herself at the sight of a Pawpaw trying to look dignified.

Carlton stepped through the drawing room door onto the balcony. Over the heads of the mob of slaves, he gazed out at the bamboo walk by the river, coconut trees growing between the bamboo supporting the feathering of the fine leaves. As the herd hushed itself to silence, Carlton deigned to look down, picking out individuals whose faces he recognized. Few of the men, except the older ones, wore shirts, while the women were dressed in the drab gray of dirty calico. A Madras head-tie worn by one of the older women was a spot of color, but overall the effect was one of drabness amidst the overpowering lushness of the scenery around them. As he surveyed them, Carlton wondered what kind of lives his slaves really led.

He shook his head to straighten his thoughts, looking for a beginning. "Well," he muttered, his voice vanishing in the late afternoon breeze. He cleared his throat and then projected his voice louder, to reach the far edge of the herd.

"I summoned you all here today for an important announcement."

"You see," whispered Mally Ibo to Dutchip, "de Bon'massa done die."

"No he ain't!" said Dutchip. "Does be a vendue."

Carlton looked behind him into the house. His father's door had opened, and Ma Phoebe waddled out.

"I want you all listen very close." Carlton lapsed into dialect in the hope that they would all understand better. "Dere be plenty old talk does be flyin' around, an' dat don't be good for de work."

"Aye!" A piercing shriek cut him short as Mally Ibo caught sight of the figure edging toward the doorway behind him. Others took up the cry, some weeping, some laughing as Hayes Todd brushed aside Ma Phoebe's supporting arm and stepped through the doorway onto the gallery. He clutched at the railing to steady himself, pale and tired but was quite clearly alive. He began to speak in a quavering, uncertain

129

voice as the Negroes edged forward nervously to catch his words.

". . . new master now. I'm old and tired. I have given every one of you to my son, Master Carlton here. He is the Bondmaster of Roxborough now. You must obey him in everything. If you don't, you will be punished. . . ."

As his voice trailed off, Carlton helped his father back inside, handing him to Ma Phoebe. It was all over so quickly, Mally Ibo wondered if she had dreamed it. She glanced around and saw the rest of the slaves watching the gallery dumbfounded. Carlton had stepped back onto the gallery, and he began to speak again.

"Kingston, come up here," he called. From the table beside him, he picked up the plantation ledger and handed it to the old bookkeeper as he reached the top step. He himself opened another book on the table and sat down in front of it.

"Now, Kingston here will call out the name of every one of you. When you hear your name, I want you to come up the step right here so I can look at you. I am the Bondmaster now, and I want to know every head I have on this plantation. We'll take the males first, then the females. When you have come up the steps and I have seen you, then you go back to the quarters."

Confusion broke out in the crowd, no one quite understood. They listened again while Mas Carlton explained in patois, and it still seemed a strange thing. Massa Hayes had told them never to use the grand step, and now Mas Carlton was checking their names on it. Reassured by the sight of Kingston with his big register, the slaves began to file forward slowly when Kingston shouted their names: "Will, Taumany, Smart, Short, Love, Dukey . . ."

It was easy for Carlton to assess the quality of his stock at a glance, and he was dismayed to see how many were old and feeble. He wrote down the names of those who appeared to be younger and more robust than the rest and added the names of hands whom Kingston described as tradesmen, the carpenters, drivers, boilers, distillers, and coopers. The women came next, the young girls giggling and clutching at their frocks as they stood before him. This was interesting, and he carefully noted their names, inking in a tiny star by the names of those who appealed to him most.

It was nightfall when the exercise was over. Bo'jack was passing around the house lighting the oil lamps while Ella was setting up the table. Carlton made arrangements with Kingston to work on the lists the next day and carried all the books under his arm into the house. He looked into his father's room and saw that the old man had drifted off to sleep, a contented smile on his face. Carlton instructed Bo'jack to sleep that night on the floor outside his father's door in case he should want anything. He took the cup of sweetened tea which Ella gave him and then, unable to drink it, made the girl close up the shutters and follow him into the bedroom.

"You bathe today, gel?"

"Smell me, Mas Carlton. I does have de sweet perfume what Ma Phoebe does make from vine."

Carlton chuckled, placing the books on top of his dresser. "Ella, how did that assembly go?" he asked anxiously, surprised at himself for seeking her opinion.

"De people like it," she replied, smiling. "But you done say nothing about why you keepin' de special book."

"Ah, yes," he said, unbuckling his belt. "Get out of that shift, girl, and I'll show you what them niggers in that book have got to do for me."

Ella lifted her shift gracefully over her head. A few nights before, she would have let it fall to the floor, but now she placed it on the end of the bed and stood naked in the center of the room. Carlton, still in his shirt, lunged at her. She stepped aside. He lunged again, and again she sidestepped with a laugh. He paused, a wave of fury swamping his features like a spoiled child denied his comforter. She put out her hand to beckon him as she leaned against the bed, and he rushed at her brutally, forcing her back across the mattress. He buried his head greedily in the smooth blackness of her supple breasts.

Inspired by their closeness, he panted into her ear, "We go'n stop growin' sugar at Roxborough, Ella."

She squirmed as his breath sent a shiver through her body. Carlton thrust himself gently inside her, feeling her legs lock around his waist.

"We go'n set dose colts mounting dem fillies, an' give me a whole herd of de best niggers yo' ever done see," he exclaimed.

"Like dis!"

Chapter 14

Changing the purpose of the plantation was a gradual process. In the month which followed the pathetic abdication of his treasured title to his son, Hayes Todd slowly recovered his strength. He never knew how much was due to Ma Phoebe's mystical prowess as well as her teas, as both she and Ella were determined not to lose their old Bondmaster so easily. Ella, too, was pledged to limit the amount of sangaree and punch made available to him, to aid his recovery. He spent whole days in the great house alone while his son explored every part of the plantation recording his new possessions in the ledger he had once used for his school work. When he was not riding around the plantation or discussing his slaves' parentage with Kingston, Carlton worked in his old school cabin, converted into an office. With Hayes bedridden, it became Ella's habit to carry Carlton's dinner over to the office, where she served it for him each day.

Carlton began to look forward to this interruption in his daily routine and ordered Ella to bring enough dinner for herself as well. While he ate his dinner at his desk, Ella squatted on the floor to eat hers instead of eating outside the kitchen door with the other house slaves. It was unheard of for a slave to eat with her master, but Carlton was a victim of a need for companionship which extended beyond his lust for Ella. He discovered that he was able to discuss his ideas with her, and the information which she gave him was invaluable in helping him work out his schemes. He came to have a reluctant respect for her nimble mind with its quick grasp of his own thoughts.

"I put Juba down in the barn with his gang," he told her one day as she squatted on the floor in front of him. He had thrown off his boots when he had come in from the plantation and now rested his feet on her lap. She caressed his ankles while he spoke.

"They'll clean it up so they can live in there."

"Dat's too pretty a place for dem field niggers to live. Dey accustomed to sleep on de floor of de ajoupa where deir mam does be living. Or wid dose dey does be loving." Ella tweaked a hair from Carlton's ankle and laughed as he winced. She held onto his foot to stop him withdrawing it, but instead he eased himself further down in his seat.

"I want them all together, you see. None of this please themselves mounting every filly in the quarters. I will assign their fillies to them, and then they can sleep by them, but when they are not on stud call, then they must sleep in the barn."

Ella continued to stroke his legs. "I know de Bon'-massa does know best," she said, trying to gauge his mood. "So why don't dey jest mount de females dey does be loving now?"

"I want quality stock, Ella, that's why. If every filly on the plantation was like you, then it would be all right. But some of them got the pox, others got the rheum, and then some of them are very poor stock."

"You have to sell dem poor stock, now?"

"Who knows, Ella," he said withdrawing his feet and beginning to pull his boots back on. "I would if I could replace them with more Batutsi females like you."

"Dere ain' no more like me, Mas Carlton." Ella looked up into his bright yellow eyes, a broad grin spreading across her face. "Dere ain't no Batutsi, no

Pawpaw, no Coromantin, no creole an' no Congo like your Ella, Mas Carlton. I be yours forever, Mas Carlton."

Ella's simple conviction of her destiny surprised Carlton, but he attributed it to her Batutsi nature. His boots on, he stood up, giving her a playful kick in her side as he left the cabin. He headed for the barn where the five youths his father had recommended as pioneers for his stock farm were waiting for him. They listened carefully as he explained his scheme to them.

"From now on, you sleep here. When you finish work in the fields, you come straight here. Kingston will send over a cook from the quarters, and you'll be getting extra rations because I want you to eat plenty and build up your strength. I will be locking this barn door at night," Carlton continued, holding up the large iron key in his hand. "And I'll be the one to release you in the morning."

Juba was stunned. "Please, sah, Mas Carlton," he dared to interrupt. "We don't do nothing, sah."

"That's right," said Carlton. "And I aim to see that you don't get the chance to do nothing, either."

"All of our females, sah. Dey does be pining for us at nights."

Carlton shook his head emphatically. "You don't have females now, unless I say."

A sulky silence greeted this remark. Carlton grinned at their reaction, for these five boys were usually so full of high spirits that a man would be hard put to find a more carefree and hardworking gang. Their good humor was one reason why Carlton liked these colts. They were all his own age and, quite apart from their splendid bodies built up through work in the fields since they were ten, they were handsome in a niggery sort of way.

"Now, boys, I don't think you understand me yet. I did not say no females, did I? After a few months you will all be so tired mounting every filly I find for you that you'll be begging me for a rest."

Celestin, who always seemed to get left out when the boys were on their boisterous assault of every girl in the quarters, was the first one to see the point. "You go'n give us de girls, sah?" he asked in amazement.

"That's right, boys. I'm pairing each one of you with one of the choicest fillies on the plantation. Fillies what are being saved for me. Bondmaster wenches. Now when I give you your filly, your work will be to mount her and mount her good until she full. I want whelps out of each one of you, do you hear?"

"A chile, massa?" Juba regarded the young Bondmaster in astonishment. "Dat be our work?"

"Yes, to give me offspring. I want fine stock here at Roxborough. My slaves are going to be the best in the world. I need strong, healthful whelps for that. I'm warning you now," he said, waving the key at the five youths clustered around him. "This be serious. When I lock this door at night, it's here you must stay. I can see everything from the great house," he lied, "and I know everything. If any of you so much as touch a filly without my permission, I will," he paused, grasping in his mind for a threat sufficiently terrifying to deter them, "I will cut his grain myself."

Juba gulped. The thought of being neutered like a bull cow did not appeal to him at all. Little Rose, his girl friend on the field gang, would not like it, either! There had never been anything like that happen at Roxborough. He had known this man since they were children together. No white buckra was going to cut his grain.

"Yas, Mas Carlton," Juba said obediently. "We does understan' you good."

"I hope so. You all been living a sweet life on this plantation. Do everything my way, and the sweet life will continue."

A chorus of "yassahs" followed him as he turned to climb back up the hill to the house. His next problem was the fillies. He was going to keep the studs

136

locked up for about a week, so that after a while they would be ready to mount anything he gave them.

After his father had gone to bed, Carlton sat on the balcony thinking about what he should do about the old slaves who were no longer a source of profit. His arms folded over his chest, he stared out into the night. Apart from his father's unexpected feelings of sentiment, Carlton could see no reason for keeping on the old Negroes. The good stock, yes, but not the ailing niggers who could never work again. If only there was some way of hastening the death of the sickly ones, he thought, then he could thin out the herd without upsetting the old man.

A slight movement caught his eye. It was not the regular stirring of a branch in the breeze, but something unusual happening on the path. He saw it again. A shadow crossing swiftly from one dark patch to another. He checked the key in his pocket. He had locked the barn door securely, but he had a suspicion about what might be going on. He got up from his chair and went quietly around the gallery. Since his father's stroke, Bo'jack had been instructed to sleep outside the old man's door. Carlton found him and shook him awake.

"Come with me," he hissed. He grabbed up a long knife from the dresser. He would have liked a pistol, but it was locked in his father's room and there was no time to wake the old man. He slipped quietly down the back steps, Bo'jack following him nervously, clutching a broom in his hand.

Carlton walked easily in the moonlit night through the bushes to the barn, without carrying a lantern. The window high up in the back wall was open.

"Stand there," he whispered to Bo'jack. "See no one jumps out."

"But sah! Dose boys does be plenty strong."

"Hah! Fine houseman you are, to be scared of a couple of field niggers. Perhaps you should go and join them in the cane tomorrow."

"Oh no, sah."

"All right. Well, don't let no one out and no one in."

It was impossible to open the lock on the door quietly, and all those inside, he realized, would be awakened by the noise he was making. He wished now he had waited to take a lantern, as he couldn't see anything inside when he managed to get the lock opened.

"All you niggers," he said into the blackness of the barn as he opened the door. "Come out here now."

"We does be sorry, sah. We ain't done nothing, sah." Four figures crept out, afraid of the unknown terrors of the night as much as of Carlton.

"Let's see who is here."

"I does be here," said a voice at his elbow. It was Celestin.

"Celestin? Who is missing?"

"Ain't no one does be missin', sah."

The moonlight, which had enabled him to spot someone leaving the barn in the first place, was not bright enough for Carlton to identify the youths around him.

"All you black buggers look alike in the dark!" Carlton shouted angrily as the boys moved around him. "Someone is not here. There were four of you came out of the barn. For God's sake, stop moving about. You, what's your name?" He pointed the carving knife at the chest of one of the figures.

"I does be Asaph, sah!"

"That's two. What about you?" He scratched the chest of another with the blade.

"Ah does be Celestin, sah. Ah done tell yo' dat, sah."

"Celestin? You dam' fool! Who's this?"

"Dat does be me, sah."

"What's your name, boy?" He jabbed the knife impatiently.

"Dukey, sah."

"You?"

"Asaph, sah!"

138

Completely confused, Carlton spun around trying to identify the missing slave. He had an idea. "Where's Juba?" he demanded.

"I does be here, sah." The voice came from behind the youth standing nearest to him.

"Where you was, boy?"

"I was be sleepin', sah." Juba sounded pained by the question.

Carlton cursed and counted the heads in front of him again. There were five this time.

Chapter 15

"Damn! Damn! Damn! They tricked me, Ella, they tricked me!"

Carlton prowled around his bed where Ella was crouching cross-legged in the center.

"That dolt Bo'jack was no help. He's been in the house too long. He's soft and scared. I really must get my own boy. He's my da's man." Fuming, Carlton continued to pace the room.

"Would you believe, Ella? Bo'jack claimed that he didn't see Juba slip back, but that must have been how it happened. Juba probably heard me fumbling with that dam' lock in the dark and had time to run back before I noticed who was missing. Oh!" He struck his forehead with the palm of his hand. "I was a fool to fall for that trick!"

"Hush, Mas Carlton. Dere ain' no need for yuh to be vexed, now."

"You don't understand, Ella! How do I show them all that I am serious? I reckon Juba is about the best colt I have on the whole plantation. He's young and so full of sap it's fair bursting out of him. He ought to sire about a score of whelps that I'll raise and sell for more profit than threescore hogsheads of sugar.

"Ella, I'm not locking him in the barn for my own pleasure. I'm doing it for the plantation, to secure

140

the future!" With a bellow of despair, he threw himself on the bed.

Ella wriggled across the counterpane to reach over and stroke his neck soothingly under his collar. With her free hand, she untwisted the fasteners of his shirt, nudging his cheek with her nose. "Forget Juba," she whispered into his ear. "You does be more smart dan he."

The proximity of Ella's nakedness overwhelmed Carlton and he turned to clutch her around the waist. Giggling, she tried to wriggle away and he allowed her to drag him across the bed. Their lovemaking that night overcame the restrictions imposed by their relationship as master and slave.

In the moment of climax, Carlton cried out that he needed Ella and she, in her way, knew that she needed him. In the private blackness of his mother's bed, the curtains drawn around them, his life seemed to assume a new clarity.

"Dat Juba," said Ella as they lay on their backs, arms still entwined round each other. "I does know his woman."

Ella wanted to reward Carlton, to show him she was totally his, prepared to do anything for him, even betray a brother slave if it was what Carlton wanted.

"Huh?"

"I does know his woman. She be dat Little Rose. Her mam's cabin is where he does go when he does slip out de barn."

Carlton peered at Ella in the gloom from the candle still flickering in a corner of the room, as he opened the curtain round the bed. "Little Rose? Ain't she that yellow female with the bile showing in her eyes?"

"All Ibos does be like dat."

"Well, it ain't good for prime niggers. He can't have her. I want to mount him with that red-skinned chit from Congo Venus. She's fourteen already. He being so black could give a nice copper-skinned whelp, strong from the father, and the grandmother, too."

"Don't know how you go'n keep dat Juba at de

chile from Congo Venus. De mother might want her own, too."

"Huh." He cuddled the girl closer to him. "Ella, you do a man a power of good. I just like you like that, I really do."

"Yas sah, massa, sah!" They both laughed.

In the night, when she knew from his snores that Carlton was sleeping, Ella carefully extricated herself from his arms and slipped out of bed. She picked up her shift and went through the connecting door into the dressing room. If he awoke and saw she was not still in his bed, Carlton would not be surprised. From the second night, he had instructed her to sleep on the pallet on the floor of the little room after they had finished their lovemaking. Even after tonight's tenderness, it would seem right for her to have left him, unless he had ordered otherwise.

Ella, however, did not stay in the dressing room. She slipped on her shift, opened the door out onto the gallery, and crept stealthily down the front steps and into the shadows underneath the overhang of the veranda. She tapped three times on the wooden shutter of Ma Phoebe's cellar room.

When Ma Phoebe eased herself up off the floor and fumbled her way to the door to let Ella into the quarters beneath the house, she recounted, as she did every night, her conversation with Carlton. Ma Phoebe was overjoyed.

"At last you does have him! Chile, you go'n be de big lady in dis house one day. I know it! I mus' learn yuh all de things I does know so you can see for de Bon'massa but good."

But Ma Phoebe was worried about Carlton's search in the night for Juba. "What for dat young massa want stroll in de night wid so many wickid niggers aroun'? Dat Bob'jack scared his own shadow. Ain't no use in de dark. Mas Carlton does need a strong young buck like dat Juba to take care of him good." Phoebe let out a shriek of delight which threatened to wake the whole household.

"Wait! I does have de answer, Ella! Oh my gawd! Massa must take dat Juba as his boy! Yas, den he can watch de buck all de time. De buck can't even slip down yere in de quarters 'cause ain't no way he go'n escape in de night if I in charge of him!"

It was an hour before dawn when Ella crept back up the steps and into her pallet in the dressing room. Phoebe had instructed her on what to do and Ella would be able to get an hour's sleep before she snuggled up beside Carlton and suggested the plan. Just as Phoebe had predicted, Carlton accepted the idea from Ella and began planning how to have Juba as his personal slave.

"Don't know about my da, though," he told Ella as he pulled on his breeches. "He doesn't like field niggers in the house. Says they're not properly seasoned."

"But Juba don't have no cause for to come in de house," Ella reasoned according to Ma Phoebe's plan. "Why, he can sleep down in de quarters where Ma Phoebe can watch him de whole night. In de day, he will ride around wid you and wait on yuh in de schoolroom."

Carlton completed dressing just as Bo'jack fired the gun. It was five o'clock. "You a little black vixen," he said with a smile. "You're cunning, but it makes sense to hear you. I'll send Bo'jack to unlock them boys right now and bring that Juba to me. That will give him something to think about!" He chuckled at the thought of the fright that his summons would give the slave who had made him look so foolish the night before.

Carlton was taking his breakfast with his father when they heard some unusual commotion in the kitchen below. He dispatched Bo'jack to see what the noise was about and to tell Ma Phoebe to keep her kitchen in better order. Bo'jack came back with the news that a boy had arrived from the village.

"He done say dere be a vessel in de river mouth wid slaves, sah. De captain does present his compliments and does say he be willin' to sell to de Bon'-massa, sah."

Carlton jumped up and walked out to the gallery. There was a large schooner anchored in the bay, and he could see the crowds gathering around the tiny jetty.

"It's true, Da," he called behind him. "Looks like one of them illegal traders made it straight here from Africa! She's taking on water already. Bo'jack, is that boy Juba waiting downstairs?"

"Yas, sah! He does be tremblin' what you does be plannin' to do to him. Ma Phoebe have put de fear of gawd in him."

"That's enough!" Carlton walked back to join his father in the dining room as Bo'jack shuffled behind. "Get him some decent trogs. Give him yours, or let Pool pass on his Sunday pants to him. Anything will do. Tell Ma Phoebe to smarten him up, like, you understand that?"

Bo'jack digested these strange orders slowly. "Yas, sah," he answered uncertainly.

"Fine, we must hurry. Send to Marmaduke and tell him to get my horse ready. The messenger boy still there?" Bo'jack nodded his head as he began to sense the excitement of the occasion.

"Right. Tell Ma Phoebe give him refreshment, and then send him to say that the Bondmaster of Rox-borough will be coming to inspect his cargo."

"You aiming to buy some more stock, son?"

"I think so, Da, don't you? We're missing young stock, bad."

"I know, I know. Sometimes you can get good specimens from an illegal cargo. If the vessel loaded quickly to put to sea before the regular shippers caught them, the niggers might be less congested on board. They'll be fitter after the voyage, and the price will be easier 'cause the captain'll want to sail away in a hurry before the revenue in Roseau hear about him. Yes, son," Hayes nodded his head in agreement. "I wish I was coming with you."

"I'll do all right, Da."

"You remember how to inspect them properly? We have enough runts here, don't want more. And buy females, son. Always short of females. Might find me something, too," he added, a wistful note entering his voice.

"What about currency, Da? If he is an illegal trader, I can't ask him for credit."

"Currency? We have the finest currency in the land right here. Get Kingston to load up his cart with a few puncheons of grog."

"I know, Da. But I will need some money. If he is in a hurry, he won't want to bother with no puncheons."

Grudgingly, his father agreed and shuffled off to his chamber. A few minutes later he called Carlton to join him, giving him the key to a small chest under his bed. Carlton pulled it out and unfastened the padlock. The old man gestured him away and then knelt over the casket. He raised the lid slowly and peered under it, preventing Carlton from seeing the contents. He put his hand in and withdrew some gold coins. He looked at them suspiciously and then withdrew more, pitching them onto the counterpane of the bed. Two more handfuls, and then he stopped, peering up at his son.

"Some people puts their money in the ground, son. Perhaps I should, too, now that I'm ailing. But who can I trust here? That's enough for a coffle, I'll be bound."

Carlton helped the old man return the box to its hiding place and then gathered up the coins in a leather purse which he hung around his waist under his pants.

"Hurry back, son. Layou ain't no good for you. Too many free Negroes around. That May Gregg might invite you to take a drink with her and a pinch of her charms. What's the point? You have your grog here without water in it and your wenches, too, what don't have the venereal." Hayes shook his head slowly, wondering if he had told the boy too much.

Carlton's laugh set his mind at rest. "This is business, Da. May Gregg has nothing in her tavern I don't have at home. And sweeter, too," he added as Ella passed on the gallery. It gave him an idea.

"Ella," he called through the window. "I want you to come to the vendue. Ask Juba bring my horse here and wait downstairs."

"What do you want her for, son? Ain't no call to take along your bed wench!"

"She knows her kind, Da. She can talk to them. They won't speak English or French, will they? I want to know where they come from. I need the best breeds if I'm going to buy at all, so I'll need someone to help me. She can do it."

"Yes," said Hayes thoughtfully, "you may be right, son. These small islands get only the refuse turned down by Jamaica and Trinidad. You'll have to creolize them all; seasoning sometimes takes the best part of three years. Yes, perhaps you should take Ella. Tell her to make sure you buy singles. If you buy a pack what hunts together, they be harder to break in."

Hayes was still offering advice as Carlton ran down the steps and mounted his horse.

"Hey, son!" he called, brandishing a pistol above his head. "You best take this, too."

Carlton indicated that his father should give it to Juba to bring for him.

"No, sir! Don't ever trust a slave with a firearm, son." The old man shuffled down the steps and handed the gun to Carlton himself.

Touched by his concern and his obvious desire to accompany him on the trip, Carlton leaned forward and kissed his father on the forehead. Bo'jack held the old man steady as Carlton galloped off, Juba and Ella running behind.

Mr. Belle was worried. "It isn't customary, sir, to . . . er . . . well, take a young female on board these vessels." He looked askance at Ella, who rode with dignity in the prow. "Especially one . . . er, so shall we say . . . er . . . scantily dressed. The Negroes, sir, and the seamen, have passions, sir, which perhaps your young breast has not experienced, if you will forgive me for being so bold, sir."

"Of course, Mister Belle," said Carlton, much amused. "I am most grateful to you for pointing it out. At Roxborough, you see, we are not so formal, and I had overlooked this in my haste to come here before the vessel sails." As he finished speaking, Carlton pulled off his shirt, exposing his hard, suntanned body. He tossed the shirt over the head of the oarsman to Ella who caught it, a look of enquiry on her face.

"Cover up yuh titties, Ella. They does disturb Mister Belle!"

Carlton's shirt had the desired effect, for it transformed Ella, with her short hair, into a boyish figure when she laced it up high to the neck. Carlton relaxed in the skiff, taking in the sounds and stench of the schooner.

"Has she really come from Africa, Mister Belle?" he asked. Sweat was pouring off the agent's forehead, and it was his turn to feel ridiculous beside Carlton, who was barefoot and now wore only his breeches.

"The captain told me that she has already put into a number of ports on her way here, sir. Each time she sold a few slaves and then sailed to the next island before the revenue men could get to her."

The stench as they reached the side of the vessel was sickening, even to Carlton, who had been reared with nigger smells. "I declare, Mister Belle, that these niggers will need to bathe in the Layou River a few times before I can take any of them home to Roxborough."

The two white men were helped up the rope ladder while Ella climbed up easily by herself. She was enjoying her role as a boy, and stood patiently behind Carlton. She was aware, though, of the attention she attracted among the sailors who stood around on

147

deck. Carlton, too, came in for his share of appraisal. The Captain, who had already made Mr. Belle's acquaintance when he had first landed on shore, came over and shook his hand.

"Mighty nice of yer to come aboard, Mister Belle. But what's become of the celebrated Bondmaster? Has he decided that he doesn't want to trade with a pirate?"

Although his beard was bushy red, and not a patchy black one, the captain's manner reminded Carlton of Captain Loring. In spite of his arrogant swagger as he regarded Carlton, he seemed friendly enough.

"Likely young lad," the Captain continued. "Wants to sign on, does he? Could use him right well, what!" He guffawed, punching the mate who stood behind him, with his elbow. He took a closer look at Ella standing behind Carlton. "What's this! A wench?" He put out his hand to grab the folds of the shirt.

"Stay, Captain! If you please!" Carlton's voice concealed the sudden nervousness he felt.

"This is my slave, Captain, and my interpreter. I'll be obliged if you would not molest her. You will find plenty of niggers of that ilk in the casinos of Layou. I am," he added quickly, holding out his hand, "Carlton Todd, Bondmaster of Roxborough, and I am desirous of purchasing about twenty niggers of prime quality."

"Holy mother of Mary!" The Captain looked at Mr. Belle for confirmation.

You're the big man who owns the whole of this coast?" The Captain spread his arms above his head to include the shore and the mountains behind. "I am delighted to meet yer, young sir." He pummeled Carlton's hand with apparent warmth.

"It will be a pleasure to do business with one so . . ." The Captain appeared temporarily at a loss of words, glancing at his mate in astonishment. "So eager, shall we say, to honor Captain Delawney with his trade. I take hard currency only, you understand."

148

"I have the best currency in the island, Captain Delawney, Roxborough rum."

"No good." The civilities were over, and Carlton sensed the mettle of the man he would be bargaining with.

"I beg your pardon, sir! Our rum is of the finest quality, aged for five years in puncheons made by the best coopers in the West Indies."

"I take it back, me young sir. Forgive me. Yer rum is probably, indeed most certainly is, the very best. Some may take rum, but my currency is gold. I must bid you good day, sir, and would sail now to catch the tide." He spun around on his heel, an expression of contempt for Belle, who had so wasted his time.

"I have gold, Captain, if you have niggers."

"Gold! You must forgive me again, sir. The smell of my niggers must have hidden the sweet scent of your currency from me. Where?"

"And where are your niggers?"

The captain was amused. "I like yer looks, young sir, and I like yer spirit. Very well, you can see the merchandise. Olaf, send them up."

Chapter 16

When he saw the creatures who emerged from the hold, it was Carlton's turn to be surprised. Because they were black, he knew that they were the same species of animal as his own slaves. But these were wretched beasts afflicted with sores, some barely able to stand, others bent double with swollen stomachs and backs lacerated with lash marks. They blinked in the sunlight, struggling to stand while a gang of seamen surrounded them to prevent any of them jumping overboard. Some gazed around in sheer terror while others, with the glazed eyes of apathy, moved only when prodded by the sailors. As they staggered onto the deck, flies swarmed about them, darting at their eyes and onto the festering ulcers around their ankles. The stench of excretion, purulent flesh, and nigger sweat made Carlton retch. He spun away from the ghastly sight, clutching the ship's rail. A blast of breeze from the green hills of his home brought him back to reality.

He regarded the specimens gathered on the deck with loathing. Not a slave at Roxborough, not even those abandoned to die in the hot house, was as wretched as these black skeletons.

"Captain," Carlton said as he walked back to the ship's master, "I was told you had slaves to sell. I'm not here to purchase carrion."

"Do not insult me, sir! These niggers are fresh from the Gold Coast. They are Coromantins, renowned for their superior strength and capacity for work. Perhaps they are a little weary from the voyage, my young sir. Do not judge them by that. There is nothing amiss that a few days on shore won't cure."

"I suppose that you never knew Dr. Farley, Master Carlton?" Mr. Belle ventured in the silence which had greeted the Captain's sales pitch. He was anxious to make amends to both parties.

"Dr. Farley was the surgeon in Roseau a few years back. He made a considerable profit by buying cargoes of Negroes such as these. A few days of physic and some bowls of soup, and the Negroes were sleek enough to sell for three times what he had paid for them."

"Well," said the Captain, "if this lot don't please you, let's have a look at another lot. You can buy them singly or as a group, as you please." He signaled to the mate called Olaf to bring up more while the wretched group in front of him were hastened below. The set which replaced them were in the same emaciated state. Carlton's dreams of buying prime stock for his herd vanished.

"Master Carlton," said Mr. Belle, drawing him aside from the Captain's ear. "I have heard that you can buy these niggers for around forty pound sterling a head."

"I wouldn't give a piece of eight for this rubbish!"

"But, Master Carlton, do not consider them as they look now. A few days at Roxborough, and the chances are they will fill out and be good workers. Look at the potential, Master Carlton. You do have the facilities."

Carlton relented. He could buy a few to see how they settled in. It would be new blood. "But these look so wasted, Mister Belle, as though they've already had a dozen years in the cane."

"See the next lot, Master Carlton. Perhaps there is something better."

"Of course, young sir," agreed the Captain, indicating to Olaf that he should send up the next group. "This is my last lot of males. Mine is a small vessel, you understand, and even with stacking, I cannot ship a larger herd. The stock space is so limited."

When the third group shuffled up, Carlton despaired. There was no difference. Ella, however, stepped forward and whispered into his ear. He looked at the Negro she indicated.

"That one." Carlton pointed out a tall boy whose body showed the rigors of the journey but whose eyes darted around him with slight interest. "From where does he hail?"

"Why, Africa, of course." The Captain shrugged his shoulders.

"I desire to inspect that one, Captain. And that one, too." Carlton had seen another in the group who was dancing nervously on his feet, rather like a pedigreed horse. It seemed remarkable that he should possess any energy at all after emerging from the stinking bowels of the ship. Olaf pushed the two Negroes forward. They stumbled, but both recovered their balance and did not grovel on the ground before him as the Captain seemed to think they should.

As Ella spoke in a tongue he could not understand, Carlton recognized a few patois words and realized that Ella herself did not know much of her own language. The tall boy she addressed picked up his head immediately when he heard her. His nervous grunts seemed to satisfy Ella. She nodded her head at Carlton. He pointed to the second Negro bouncing around and refusing to stand still despite Olaf's shouts.

"Stay!" commanded Carlton when he saw that Olaf was about to strike the Negro across his rump to stop his little dance. "I want to inspect this one. Ella, see what language he speaks."

Ella asked him a few questions in her own language, but the response was not what she expected. "I don't understand him, Mas Carlton. I done hear his tongue in de quarters. Dat Juba mam, she does speak it."

"That buck looks like a Yoruba," said Mr. Belle, wanting to be helpful. "Your father has some Yorubas already. I remember that he liked them for their intelligence."

"Well," said the Captain, bored by the talk. "Do you want them or not?"

Although there was not much to see except bones almost breaking through their skin, Carlton asked that both of them be made to turn in front of him. The tall one had long slender legs like Ella and, as he studied his features, Carlton thought that he could detect the Batutsi nose and lips. The other was more negroid, with flat nose and thick lips and, although he was shorter in stature, his broad shoulders suggested a fine physique. Long accustomed to black nakedness, Carlton was not daunted by the size of their private parts. Remembering what he had seen Captain Loring do, and to impress his knowledge on Mr. Belle, he put out his hand to grasp the balls of the shorter one. The fellow stopped dancing, and a gleam of surprise appeared in his eyes.

"I'll take those two, Captain. What about the females?"

"I've got some," admitted the Captain. "A small lot. Not very good stock, though. They have not deigned to eat very much!" He chuckled. "Surely you'd prefer some more of these bucks. They'll grow into fine work animals under your care, sir!"

Ella, who had been exchanging grunts with the Batutsi, touched Carlton's arm. The gesture surprised Mr. Belle. Hayes Todd would have lashed any slave with a horsewhip who dared to touch him, especially in front of others. Belle endeavored to engage the Captain in conversation so that he would not notice the familiar way Carlton treated his female follower.

Carlton listened intently to Ella. "Dis bush nigger say dat dere be some Watutsi females on board, Mas Carlton. Dey be like Batutsi. He say dey be plenty sick. I expect dey does be pinin' for deir country."

"I'll see the females, Captain. I have all the bucks I need. Thank you for your kindness."

The women Olaf ushered up were even more decrepit than the men. Carlton shuddered as he looked at their starved bodies grown stale in the confines of the hold. Where breasts would have stood out proudly, there were folds of skin drawn tight across protruding rib cages. Their hair was unkempt and caked with dirt and excreta, and their faces were twisted in fear. Carlton was appalled. He looked at Ella for reassurance as though longing to see a transformation from these haggard crones near death to the radiant beauty of his black bed-maid.

"Ask them their age," he hissed, hoping that way to find out who was young and who was old.

Hearing Ella speak, some of the creatures assumed a more human aspect and gradually answered her with grunts similar to her own. Ella told three of them to stand aside from the others.

"Dese be de best, Mas Carlton," she said softly. "Dey be de most young, and dey say don't have sickness on de voyage like de others."

"They know each other in Africa?"

More grunts, animation spreading into the faces of the selected three. "No, Mas Carlton," said Ella, "dey be from de same country but dere be many tribes. Dat one have her sister here."

He looked at the female Ella pointed out to him and then at the five remaining women, wondering which was the nigger's sister.

"No sister," he said, wearied by the sight of such wastefulness. It would take him weeks to get these creatures into good health. His father, he remembered, had said that creolization would take three years, and he was beginning to understand why.

"They are in such a poor state of health, Captain, I deem it a favor I am doing to offer you even a doubloon for one of these sad animals."

"Young sir, I trust that your remark is intended as a reflection of your limited experience rather than

154

a criticism of my Negroes. You must understand, young sir," continued the Captain, taking Carlton by the arm to lead him out of earshot of Olaf, "that a Negro you buy off the decks of a vessel does not have the gloss of one fattened up for sale at the factor's. You will find my stock excellent and prime. Those females there are lively mounts, those males, too."

"What will you take for the two colts and the three fillies, Captain?"

"What will you offer, Bondmaster of Roxborough?"

Carlton reached into his crotch and pulled out the bag of gold. He was reluctant to display so much wealth on board, but he had no alternative. He opened the purse and took up a handful of coins which he placed on a locker top. He was pleased to notice the captain's eyes glisten. It was then Carlton realized that he should have agreed on a price before producing his money, as the Captain would surely not be content until he had extracted as much gold from him as possible. Swiftly, Carlton picked out the doubloons from the pile of pistoles, crowns, pieces of eight, and perus which his father had given him.

"Your niggers are weak, Captain, and unseasoned. It will cost me a tidy sum to make them fit for work. I will pay you two doubloons a head for your males, and one for your females."

"Double it!" said the Captain without hesitation. "Then double it again!"

"This is gold, sir. Worth more than seven pounds sterling a piece."

"You have wasted my time enough, sir. You have gold in that bag to buy all my cargo, and here you are haggling over five blacks."

"I'll double it." Carlton laid out the doubloons on the locker top. "No more."

The Captain looked at the pieces and then held a steady gaze on Carlton, who kept his own pale eyes steadfast on the Captain's bushy red face. The Captain took in the sight of the half-naked white lad who was bargaining with him and lowered his gaze, shaking his head with amazement.

"Boy," he said, "I've done business with the fiercest chiefs of the Congo tribe. I've negotiated deals for hundreds of pounds with the toughest factors in Jamaica. But I ain't never met the likes of you. A lad! Well, lad, put something on it," he added, pocketing the coins. "A token of esteem for the good Captain who brought you such prize niggers?"

"With pleasure, Captain," said Carlton smiling innocently. "Another two doubloons." He proffered the gold to the Captain. "And I will do you the honor of a favor by removing another of those prize niggers from your responsibility. A female, sister to the one I have purchased.

Biting the gold coins he had been given took away the venom of the Captain's cursing as Carlton supervised the loading of his purchases into the skiff. It was impossible for them all to go at once, so he dispatched Mr. Belle and the four females together with Ella. Mr. Belle advised him to rope the females together, and he linked the ankle of one to the ankle of another, holding the end of the rope himself. Carlton publicly gave Mr. Belle his purse of money to hold for him, as he did not intend to make himself a target for the villainous crew of the ship. As soon as another skiff came alongside, sent over by Mr. Belle, Carlton pulled the two males into it by the cord binding them and set out for the shore.

Juba was waiting for them. "I does be here de whole time, sah," he said, helping to steady the skiff while Carlton prodded the Negroes with his pistol to make them jump onto the shore. "Dat be sickly lookin' niggers, sah."

Carlton grinned, cuffing Juba proudly, pleased with his bargaining. "Aye, not like you, Juba. But your sire probably looked like this when he arrived from Africa. These niggers will blossom out. Now how am I going to get us all to Roxborough, Mister Belle?"

"I have taken the liberty of sending for a slave

156

chain, sir. You will be able to chain the Negroes quite securely so they don't run. You have your horse-whip should they be truculent."

"You are most kind, Mister Belle. I'm grateful for your help. What do you think of this morning's venture?"

"I would advise next time a more circumspect approach, Master Carlton. It seems that your very youth appealed to the Captain and he overlooked his preference for a higher price. I think you drove a good bargain, sir."

"Aye, as long as one don't die on me. You can't even eat a dead nigger, Mister Belle."

Hayes Todd was not surprised at the condition of his purchases when Carlton and his coffle, whipped along the road by an exuberant Juba, returned to Roxborough. "Put them in the quarters with the other niggers, son," he suggested. "They'll soon toughen up."

"Not in the quarters, Da," said Carlton as they watched the Negroes sitting in the shade of the trees in the yard, panting from exhaustion after their long walk. The chains still bound them.

"Don't forget why I bought them. I don't want them to start rampaging around mounting each other without my permission."

"Huh!" The old man was contemptuous. "How will you stop them?"

"Chains, sir. They'll stay in chains until they are broken in. I'll put the colts in the barn with my stallions, and the fillies can go in the hot house until they are stronger. I'll have a field cook to tend both."

After dinner, Carlton summoned Juba, who had been waiting for him like a faithful puppy below the stairs, and ordered him to bring all the new Negroes to the back of the kitchen. When Juba saw the silver iron the Bondmaster had in his hand as he descended the back step to look at the Negroes, Juba quivered.

"Mas Carlton, sah, what dat be for, now?"

157

It was unusual for a slave to have the temerity to ask such a question, and Carlton was affronted by Juba's boldness at first. He was about to chide the slave when it occurred to him that interest was perhaps a quality to be encouraged if Juba was going to be one of the sires of a new generation of Roxborough slaves.

"This is the band of bondage, Juba," he explained letting the Negro touch the iron. "That letter you have on your shoulder was burnt there by my father when you were a whelp. You won't remember. That's the letter R, which means Roxborough. It says to all the world that you are a Roxborough slave. Any time you want to run, the branded R brings you back."

"Dat not for me, sah. I never go'n run. I does be your boy, sah."

"Fine, Juba. These niggers bathe?"

"Every one of dem, sah. De buck does be from Yoruba, sah, where me mam done come from."

Carlton looked at the six Negroes, still naked, but with a softer countenance now that the grime of the middle passage had been wiped off in the river. The Yoruba boy had stopped shuffling, his energy reflected in his eyes darting around the compound. The Batutsi had even regained some dignity in his demeanor, although the females still clutched each other for comfort. Carlton handed the branding iron to Juba and told him to give it to Ma Phoebe to heat in the fire.

Next, he called Bo'jack and Pool and, as Juba returned, he told Ella to come out of the kitchen and tell the niggers to lie on their stomachs. The women began to moan with fright. The Yoruba, who was at the end of the chain, found it hard to lie still. Pool and Juba sat on his backside to hold him down, Bo'jack clearly expressing his distaste at having anything to do with a stinking African.

Ma Phoebe waddled out of the kitchen, brandishing the silver iron with a grim smile as it glowed red from the coals. "You want Ma Phoebe do de job, Mas Carlton? Bo'jack, hold dat lively one down by his neck."

So saying, she placed her foot on the Yoruba's neck, pinioning him to the ground, and plunged the glowing brand onto his left shoulder. The shriek of terror gave way to the sickening smell of burning flesh. The Yoruba bucked and threw off Pool and Juba as Ma Phoebe removed her foot from him.

"Dat be fine!" she chuckled, handing the brand to Ella, and moving over to the Batutsi, who was next in line.

"Hol' dem niggers down!" she commanded Pool and Juba. "You does be temptin' me to burn you, too."

"Give the brand here!" shouted Carlton unexpectedly, snatching the glowing iron which Ella was bringing back from the fire. "This is my job."

With a fixed smile, Carlton advanced on the first of the females struggling under the weight of Juba, Pool, and Bo'jack. He thrust the solid silver letter down on the black flesh of the nigger, gripping his teeth tightly with satisfaction at the smell of the charred flesh and the sudden shriek of pain.

"Now you are a Roxborough slave for sure!" He gave her a kick as the boys released her and jumped across onto the next one.

He was enjoying it.

Chapter 17

As far as Carlton could judge, his new purchases began to settle down to life on the plantation without any difficulty. The two males he put into the barn with Asaph and Celestin, while the females went, in the end, to live with some of the older women. Carlton unchained the boys on their second night and, as they began to lose their fear of the new-place and to receive a daily meal, they showed no sign of wanting to escape. Carlton warned the old women with whom he had placed the girls that they must be kept in from nightfall to daybreak and were only to be mounted by the stallions appointed by Carlton himself. He backed up his warning with threats of a flogging if he found that he had been disobeyed.

Despite all his menacing statements, Carlton doubted if the slaves understood his seriousness. Whenever he addressed any of them, he was always greeted with a bright smile brimming over a mouth full of impeccably white teeth. There seemed to be no dampening his slaves' good humor at having him as their Bondmaster. He suspected that, having watched him grow up on the plantation, the slaves were too familiar with him to respect him. Even the new niggers seemed to show a greater fear of Ma Phoebe then they did of him. As long as there was no flouting of his authority, however, he was content that the spirit of well-being continued.

Juba, he was delighted to see, fitted naturally in his role as his personal servant. Every morning, Juba greeted him with a cheery smile and a saddled horse ready for a tour of the plantation. Carlton allowed Juba to ride an old donkey around with him and was much amused by the style Juba showed when addressing his fellow niggers, as though being on the Bondmaster's household staff made him a Bondmaster himself. Even Juba's former companions felt the wrath of his tongue when Carlton sent him to bring Asaph and Celestin to the house some ten days after they had been first confined to the barn.

"You run fas' now, niggah," Juba said to Asaph, prodding him in the backside with his boot as he sat on his donkey. "De Bon'massa go'n lash you if yuh don't move yourself fast."

"How dat, Juba? You de Bon'massa now? Ah come when ah does be ready."

"Den I does tell Mas Carlton dat you be one fresh niggah an' he sure go'n lash you plenty."

"Mas Carlton ain't lash no one but dem gels in de field gang. He don't have de will for de punishmen' like his da'." Celestin strolled easily along the path, ignoring Juba's entreaties to walk faster.

"True!" Asaph echoed. "You ever see him cuff a niggah, Juba?"

"Dat be 'cause de niggahs don't give him cause to be vex when he does have me wid him," explained Juba to his own satisfaction. "Only you two bozals dat be troublesome so."

"Why he done send you for all of us to de quarters?"

"He go'n mount yo wid de two dem Africans he done buy."

Carlton explained the arrangements to Asaph and Celestin, amused by their eagerness for the assignment. Asaph was brought to the ajoupa belonging to Candice, one of the old plantation grandmothers with swarms of children running in and out of her old shack. She had already been put in charge of one of the Watutsi purchases, and now Carlton ordered her to let Asaph and the female sleep on the pile of rags she called her bed.

"I want to have a fine male whelp out of these two, Candice, so you see that they do it good."

"Oh yassa!" Candice cackled, showing the single tooth left in her upper gum. She prodded Asaph in the ribs. "De boy young an' de girl fresh from de Afric'. De action go'n shake my old shack to de groun', sah!"

"So long as you see that he mounts her all right, I don't worry about your shack, Candice. Don't take much time to build a new one." Carlton looked at the small ajoupa with its roundwood frame cut from the forest and covering of plaited coconut leaves. "You've got to watch this buck here doesn't take off in the night and go and chase another filly."

"Me, sah? I does be grateful to yuh, sah, for giving me dis fine niggah wench, sah. I don't take off for no other filly, no sah."

Celestin was to be paired with another of the Watutsi fillies in the shack controlled by Mary Jean, who had been recently retired from being a cook for the field gang because of her rheumatics. Three young children, the only survivors of her daughter's eight, were playing with the Watutsi girl when Carlton and Juba rode up, Celestin following behind. Seeing the white man coming, the Watutsi, who was still as naked as when she had arrived at Roxborough, ran inside the shack. Celestin caught a glimpse of her lean body. He longed for her.

"Is dis de buck you say yuh does be bringin' for my niggah? Mas Carlton, sah?" Mary Jean looked with disgust at Celestin. "My niggah hot from Afric', Mas Carlton. She does need a plenty powerful stallion to break her in, not dis chile I does know since he done suck his mother's titty. Dat buck no good for my niggah, Mas Carlton." She looked from Celestin to Juba astride the donkey. "Now, dat Juba, he does have de reputation."

"Hah, Mary Jean! You just see that they gets together. I want a bright-skinned whelp, and Celestin has the color to cancel out that Watutsi's damn blackness. Juba here will get his when I'm ready."

"I does be sure dat I does hab dose whelps you does want in me, Mas Carlton," ventured Juba as they rode back to the house later that evening. "I does feel de whelps in me, sah. Yo' don't want me to give yo' no stock, sah?"

"Yes, Juba," grinned Carlton at the lad. "Yes, I want stock from you, but not just any kind. If I have extra mouths to feed, then I want them to be healthy ones."

"My whelps go'n be healthful, sah."

"Yes, well, you must forget that Little Rose of yours for that to happen. She too yellow in her eyes."

"Little Rose, sah? Who she?"

Carlton chuckled, reining in his horse as he approached the stable. "Juba, you're smart. That's good. Yes, I think you have earned what I have in mind for you. You are an obliging nigger. If you retain your pleasing manner, I seen no reason why you should not serve me by day and serve the fillies I pick for you by night!"

Carlton dismounted and flicked Juba's calf lightly with his whip. "Tomorrow, I think I will put you to the little virgin Congo Venus has been saving for you."

"Tomorrow, sah? I does be ready tonight, sah." Juba rubbed his crotch enthusiastically. "I does give you a strong buck whelp tonight, sah. Really, sah!"

Once again Carlton chuckled at Juba's eagerness to please. He paused with his foot on the lower step before going up to the gallery. "Not tonight, Juba! I'll make the arrangements tomorrow. Go 'round to the kitchen and get your supper from Ma Phoebe, and then bed down early."

Below in the kitchen, Ma Phoebe confronted Juba.

The two were alone. Ma Phoebe had just bolted the kitchen door and held up the lantern in her hand. Juba was slumped on a settle, his legs stuck out before him.

"Come, boy." Ma Phoebe paused in front of him. "I does be closin' up dis kitchen. Bo'jack and Pool does be sleepin' long. Time for you to go to de quarters wid dem."

"Don' feel lak sleepin', Ma Phoebe."

"Oy oy! Maybe you has another thing on your mind?" Ma Phoebe's eyes glinted as she glanced down at his body stretched right out in front of her. The shirt he had been given to wear by Mas Carlton was open to his waist, the ends knotted in front of his stomach. His breeches were bunched up tightly around his bulging crotch. Ma Phoebe sucker her fat lips, her eyebrows curling up.

"You a well set-up buck, to be sure. Why don' yo' strip down out dem britches for Ma Phoebe. I does give yo' de special thing."

Juba straightened himself as the lantern glowered over him, preventing him from seeing beyond its glare. Suddenly, he felt Ma Phoebe's flabby hand grip his upper leg, fingers kneeding his thigh muscle like dough.

"What you mean, Ma Phoebe?" Juba's customary confidence faltered.

"I done be watching yuh, Juba. I does think yuh have a thirst dat Ma Phoebe does know how to quench dis very minute."

The lantern descended to the ground where it threw a circle of light over the slabs of the kitchen floor. As she placed it on the ground, she rested her head on Juba's thigh, the thick greasy hair lying like a huge spider on his leg. Slowly, her head began to creep up his thigh, until her chubby hand reached up and grabbed him.

Juba leaped to his feet, knocking Ma Phoebe backwards in his haste to escape.

"Dat ain't for you, yuh ol' witch. You keep off dat thing, yuh hear!" He brushed at his pants as though

164

trying to scrape off the recollection of Ma Phoebe's clammy hands.

Making no attempt to get up, Ma Phoebe regarded him from the spot where she had fallen. "Dat be all right, my pretty boy." Her voice was venomous. "Dat be all right."

Juba turned and ran off down the passageway to the chamber he shared with Bo'jack and Pool. He went in and bolted the door behind him, reminding himself that he was not afraid of an old obeah woman. He curled up on the floor trying to sleep, but sleep would not come as he thought of Ma Phoebe's hands and the virgin Mas Carlton had promised him.

As he lay on the floor, he heard Ma Phoebe shuffle along to her room and bolt her door behind her. It seemed hours while he waited for her to have time to fall asleep. Convinced she must be sleeping, he got silently to his feet and unbolted the door as carefully as he could. He peered out into the passage. There was no light and no sound. He crept stealthily past Ma Phoebe's room, hoping that she had not put some kind of spell on the main door so that it would squeak and waken her as he opened it. But the door opened quietly and he stepped out into the night.

It was a black night, but Juba knew that he had only to follow the path to the quarters for fifty paces and then turn off. Dutchip's ajoupa was there. He had done it so many times before. There was time for two hours with Little Rose, and then he could be back in the kitchen before anyone stirred.

Ma Phoebe had been listening for Juba to get up. Quickly she lit her own lantern and pulled herself up from her pallet. She followed the route which Juba had taken to the outside door, but instead of pursuing him, she slowly hauled her great bulk up the grand steps, edged round the outside gallery and banged on Mas Carlton's door.

"Mas Carlton, sah! Mas Carlton!"

With the white plantation owner's instinct for survival, Carlton had jumped out of bed and was across to the door by the time Phoebe called a second time. He recognized her voice and groped for his pistol on the dresser beside the bed while he spoke.

"What is it, Ma Phoebe?"

"Mas Carlton, sah. Dat Juba, he done fool me. He done go out de cellar, sah."

"Juba!" Carlton threw open the door, grateful for the light of Ma Phoebe's lantern while he checked his pistol.

That night, before he had fallen asleep, Ella had told him that she was pregnant. He was content and had been dreaming of a flourishing plantation with ships coming from as far away as America to buy Roxborough pedigreed slaves. And now Ma Phoebe was telling him that Juba, the one nigger he had hopes for, had disobeyed him!

"Where did he go?"

"By dat wench of his, dat Little Rose. It does be for you to ketch him an' punish him so he don't do dat again, sah!"

"I know what I have to do without you telling me, Ma Phoebe!" He pulled his belt tight, stuck in his pistol, and strode off down the gallery.

"But, sah, Mas Carlton, sah? You does want me to call Bo'jack and Pool help yuh fin' him, sah?"

Carlton stopped. He turned and strode back to the black mountain of a woman who was almost as wide as the gallery itself. Puzzled by his expression, Ma Phoebe began to shake the rolls of fat on her arms in consternation. Ella came out of the dressing room and stood behind her.

"Mark my words good, Ma Phoebe! I'm the Bond-master of Roxborough. Juba, you, and every one else here are all my slaves, given to me by my father in the presence of every nigger on the plantation. Mine, you understand? You are all my property and this is my plantation.

"I'm going out there now to get Juba. If I find him with a filly, then in the morning, with all my slaves

166

here, that Juba is going to get his balls cut. And you, Ma Phoebe, can haul your fat black arse off my gallery and go make some coffee!"

Chapter 18

Little Rose clung to Juba, her legs wrapped around his waist and her hands clawing at his back. His arms clutched at her tiny body, almost lifting her off the ground. She uttered a long moan and Dutchip, listening in the corner of the ajoupa, sighed as she stroked herself to join in Little Rose's climax. The couple were lying on the rags which Little Rose and Dutchip shared as their bed. Juba's outstretched legs were touching Dutchip as she crouched in the darkness where she had been put to wait her turn. Little Rose's cries grew more demanding and Juba, in response, plunged faster and faster.

There was a crash. The board which Dutchip had placed in the entrance to serve as a door, fell heavily into the shanty. A lantern was thrust through the gap. Juba pulled out of Little Rose, her cry of ecstasy abruptly changed into a shriek of terror. He raised himself up on his knees to stare in wild anger at the shape of a man behind the lantern. Dutchip tried to shrink her large body into the darkness of her corner where the lantern glow would not find her. She recognized the figure as that of their Bondmaster and saw the outline of his pistol aimed at Juba's heart.

"Get up!"

Juba's heart sunk as he heard the words and realized who confronted him. The lantern played over his naked torso, picking out the pulsation of his body as his semen spouted to the ground. Little Rose, whimpering with fright, crawled over to Dutchip and clasped her desperately.

"Get up!" Carlton gestured to the hapless Juba with his pistol.

"Massa, sah, massa!" Juba fell forward and put out his hand to grasp Carlton's leg. "Massa, it not my fault, sah!"

Carlton's foot rammed into Juba's face. The slave gasped in surprise.

"Get up!" This time, Carlton directed his foot at the soft flesh of Juba's crotch. "Stand up! Come on, quickly now."

Juba recoiled from the blow, waiting for the next one and watching the Bondmaster warily. He slowly pulled himself to his feet. "Yas sah, massa, not my fault, sah!"

When he was standing, Carlton held the lantern against his face, close to his eyes, causing Juba to blink at the glare. For a moment, Carlton searched the slave's eyes with his own. Dutchip watched in amazement as she saw the Bondmaster shake his head and sigh, a tear easing out of his eye and trickling down his cheek. The Bondmaster lowered the lantern and cleared his throat, sending a stream of spittle at Little Rose which fell against her breast and seeped slowly down to her stomach. He jabbed his pistol into Juba's waist.

"Walk!"

"Massa, sah! Juba yo' boy, sah. I does do anything for yuh, sah!"

"If you don't walk, boy, you're going to be dead."

The chill of Carlton's voice cut through Juba's pleading. Casting a last look at Little Rose cowering in the corner with Dutchip, he stumbled out, Carlton following with the lantern in one hand and his pistol in the other. As they left the ajoupa, Dutchip and Little Rose joined together in howling like helpless dogs in pain.

"Move!" Carlton prodded Juba in his rear with the gun as the slave paused at the sound of the crying.

"Yas, massa!" Juba started up obediently and followed the path, swifter now, his manner changed. "I does know I done do wrong, sah," he pleaded as he walked. "I swear I ain't never go'n do no wrong 'gain, sah."

"That's right," said Carlton, tapping him again with the pistol. "You ain't."

"I go'n be your boy, Mas Carlton, sah. Juba do what you does say, sah."

Carlton met his pleadings with silence until they reached the stable door. He was surprised to see Ella emerge from the darkness and stretch out her hand for the lantern. He gave it to her to hold while he unlocked the door of the stable. He nodded his head for Juba to go in. Carlton and Juba both realized at the same time that there was a shutter in the stable which could be opened from the inside. Carlton paused at the door, clucking to calm the horses, and looked around the stable. At one end was a small cupboard where saddles and bridles were kept. Its door was secured with a large wooden bolt.

"Down there," said Carlton.

Juba walked to the cupboard and was surprised when Carlton opened the door and told him to get in.

"But I does not be able breathe in dere, sah!"

Carlton shrugged, waving his pistol impatiently. Juba turned to Ella. "Tell de massa I die in dere, Ella. It does be too small for Juba."

"Juba, get in!" Carlton's voice was menacing.

"I does go in dere, sah," said Juba, trying another tack. "I does know you bound punish your Juba. I done do wrong, but never again, sah. It don't be my fault, sah."

When Juba was shut inside and the door bolted on him, Carlton leaned heavily against the stable wall, cradling his head in his hands. The sound of whimpering from inside the cupboard sickened him. He turned

170

away, following Ella as she led the way up to the house.

"You should not have come out, Ella."

"No, sah."

"Why did he do that, Ella. Why?"

"He too dam' stoopid."

"I've got to punish him now, Ella."

"Yas, sah."

"He did wrong, you see. The slaves have to know that when one of them does something against their Bondmaster's wishes, then he will be punished."

Ella walked with him silently up the grand stairs to his room. The kitchen was lit up and Bo'jack and Pool had been roused from their beds by Ma Phoebe. Coffee had been made, but Carlton did not feel like drinking it. He told Ella to drag off his boots and then dismissed her. She was to make sure that he not be disturbed. On top of the bed, he lay fully clothed, his pistol still clasped in his hand. He regretted the plans he had ever made for Juba, cursing the inexperience which had let him be so easily fooled by the slave.

In the kitchen, Ma Phoebe quizzed Ella on their young Bondmaster's mood. Bo'jack and Pool listened in disbelief.

"He does say dat he bound to punish Juba," said Ella. "He don't say how."

"He won't cut him," said Bo'jack. "Mas Carlton don't do dat."

"How you be so smart?" demanded Ma Phoebe. "Dat Mas Carlton, he be de Bon'massa. He does do what he does want. Dat he done tell me hisself."

"But he won't cut," ventured Pool. "De massa don't have no will for dat. I does b'lieve he does ax Mercury give Juba one big thrashin' to make him bleed."

"Best he does do dat," agreed Bo'jack. "De ol' massa done give me a lashin' hisself one time. He don't be strong as his driver, but he done be more skillful wid de whip. He lash me here an' he lash me there. I never know which way de sting does come.

171

It pain me so dam' much, I done sleep on my belly for a week. Den it finish an' de Bon'massa don't trouble me no more." Bo'jack lapsed into silence.

Ma Phoebe stacked up the coffee mugs, then ushered them all off to bed. "De mornin' does tell us what he does be go'n do. For myself, I does say de boy get what he does deserve. Let's get our sleep, now, 'fore time for de mornin' gun."

Carlton made his usual morning round alone, noting the undercurrent of excitement about the events of the night before. He instructed Mercury and Will to lock Juba into the chains kept for new niggers and to leave him lying in the stable. Dutchip was removed from her position as driver of the small gang and told by Kingston to remain in her quarters. Little Rose was also confined to the quarters.

The old females gathered around Dutchip and Little Rose to comfort them and to speculate on Juba's punishment. It was generally agreed that Mas Carlton was not as ruthless as his father and would never cut Juba as he had threatened. If he was an ordinary field hand, the women reasoned, then he might get a severe flogging. But Juba was the Bondmaster's pet and Mas Carlton had never shown a capacity for punishment, so everything would be all right and Little Rose would soon have her man back in her arms. Little Rose and Dutchip felt reassured by the comments of those around them, but they still broke into occasional wails when they felt in need of more comfort. After the first wave of scandal had passed through the plantation, the slaves settled in for a normal day.

Carlton acquainted his father with the activities of the night before when they met for breakfast.

"I heard you go out last night," said Hayes as he sipped his coffee when Bo'jack had left them alone. "And I heard you come back in again, I think," he added more slowly than before. "Then maybe I heard someone weeping, too?"

Carlton grinned ruefully at his father. "If only he

hadn't done that, Da. I had so much hopes for that nigger."

"Hopes gone now, I suppose, son?"

"Yes, Da."

"He's only a nigger, son. You've got three hundred of them. There's millions more in Africa. Do what you think best, son. Remember, though, that what you do to Juba this morning will determine what kind of man, and what kind of Bondmaster, you are. In the slaves' eyes."

Carlton pushed back his chair and stood up. He went over to the dresser and pulled out the large jar of rum which was kept in the lower cupboard. He uncorked the jar and poured some of the rum straight into his coffee cup. He placed the cup on the table, corked the jar and put it back, closing the cupboard door emphatically. He looked at his father, who was watching him sternly.

"You think you can do it, Carlton? Just another nigger, you know."

Carlton picked up the cup and tilted his head back as he opened his mouth and let the raw rum trickle down his throat. He grimaced and then smacked his lips, replacing the cup and picking up a knife from the table. He tried the edge of it with his finger, found it satisfactory, and stuck it in his belt. His boots clomped across the floorboards as he made his way to the front gallery, shouting down below for Bo'jack and Pool.

Hayes Todd sat back in his chair, sucking thoughtfully on his gums.

The blowing of the conch echoed around the plantation. Without enthusiasm, the slaves laid down their hoes and cutlasses and, urged on by the drivers, drifted toward the great house. While they assembled, Mercury and Will were sent to bring Juba to the foot of the grand steps. They dragged him, heavy chains holding both his ankles, across the yard and threw him down to lie on the earth. Ma Phoebe bustled out to gloat over him, ignoring his pleas for help. Carlton stood at the top step, as impassive and ominous as the hills looming over the plantation, watching the slaves assemble.

"Tie his hands!"

The two drivers looked at each other reluctantly as Bo'jack proffered the rope he had brought from the cellar store. Ma Phoebe, annoyed by the drivers' slowness, grabbed the cord from Bo'jack and fastened it around Juba's wrists, binding them securely behind his back.

"Ma Phoebe!" pleaded Juba, tears entering his eyes as terror gripped him. "Wha' Bon'massa go'n do me? Help me, please, Ma Phoebe. Help yo' poor Juba. I give it to you anytime you want, Ma Phoebe!"

Ma Phoebe's forearm smashed into Juba's face, knocking him back to the ground. Bo'jack and Pool exchanged curious looks. Ella, standing by herself at the foot of the steps, cast her eyes up to where Carlton was standing. A breeze ruffled the golden curls at the back of his neck in the morning sunlight; his eyes stared straight ahead.

"I want all you slaves to know," shouted Carlton to the herd, "that when the Bondmaster says something, he means it. This boy Juba here was mounting Little Rose last night, and I had forbidden him to do that. He disobeyed me, and so now he has to be punished."

There was not a slave on the plantation who did not know Juba. He had always been popular, either running happily as a child through the quarters with his pack of friends, or putting his youthful strength to work in the fields. The slaves had all been pleased when Mas Carlton picked Juba for his pet. The women's hearts had fluttered as they spied Juba riding around the plantation on his donkey, wearing a smart shirt and breeches instead of his field rags. Now he lay naked on the ground quivering with fear as the Bondmaster walked down the steps to meet him.

"Turn him on his back!"

"No sah! No sah!" Juba shrieked as he saw Carlton draw out the kitchen knife from his strap.

The crowd gasped. "He really go'n cut him!" said Asaph in horror.

"Hold him!"

The two drivers sat on Juba's feet as he tried to pitch himself free. Ma Phoebe, her tongue protruding through her teeth as her fat lips parted in a strange grin, pinioned his shoulders with her knees. Bo'jack and Pool watched the scene, their eyes wide. Ella, who had slipped up the back stairs, stood on the gallery behind Hayes.

Slowly, Carlton put his hands on Juba's prick, laying it across the boy's left thigh. He grasped the testicles in his left hand and, deaf to the shrieks of Juba and the helpless wailing of the assembled slaves, he brought his right hand down and swiftly nicked through the skin holding the scrotum. The screams of pain slicing through the air made each of the slaves shudder with fear. Some turned away and crept slowly back to the fields. Others craned forward to see Juba writhing as Mercury and Will jumped off him. Celestin watched the evil smile frozen on Ma Phoebe's face as she bent forward to splash Juba's blood on her fingers.

Holding Juba's testicles up in his hand, the blood dripping down his wrist, Carlton mounted the grand step for all to see. Then he flung the bloody scrotum onto the ground, where the dogs pounced on it. With his hand, which still held the knife, he made a gesture of dismissal and, brushing past his father and Ella, went into the house.

Ma Phoebe eased herself up off the limp body of Juba. She wrung her bloody hands in front of her enormous stomach and shuffled off to the kitchen. The drivers, uncertain what to do, backed away as three old women came silently forward and, crouching over Juba's body, began keening dirges of the Africa none of them would ever see again.

Long afterwards, Carlton realized that something in him had died that day. The easy atmosphere which had prevailed at Roxborough disappeared. The slaves still greeted him respectfully, but the happy smiles they had given him from childhood vanished. Carlton passed among his slaves as a stranger, issuing orders and waiting for them to be carried out. He built up a structure of command, relying on Kingston and such intelligent slaves as Mercury and Will, whom he used as the drivers. It functioned efficiently; and during the months following Juba's castration, the plantation slipped into the desired routine. His breeding regime began to show results with three of his fillies plugged. So, too, although he did not know it, was Little Rose.

Ella gave birth to Carlton's own child soon after the turn of the year. It was a difficult birth and caused Congo Venus, who acted as midwife, a lot of anxiety. As Ella lay on the kitchen floor and Ma Phoebe muttered, Congo Venus had to use all her skill to ease the child into life. It was a red-skinned baby, the largest Venus had ever seen. Carlton, who was working in the mill when the news of the birth was brought to him, immediately declared an issue of a half-pint of rum and water for everyone on the plantation. It was his first son.

Hayes was delighted. "You ever think of getting married?" he asked Carlton as they sat together on the gallery a few nights after the birth.

"Married! What a strange idea, Da. What do I want to marry a nigger for?"

"You numbskull!" choked his father in exasperation. "I don't mean to that Ella. I mean to a woman. When a man's your age in a place like this, he needs a wife, son. A man gets like the niggers after a time, if he doesn't have a wife."

Carlton was amused by the latest of the old man's ideas. "Where am I going to find a wife, Da? No women in the village, apart from the whores, of course."

"You'll find one, son. Man needs a wife. Man needs children."

"But I just had a son, Da."

"Call that a son? That's half-nigger, only part human! Don't forget that. Breed from your niggers if you like. He's red-skinned, which is fine because bright slaves fetch good prices. Some of those people in Jamaica like slaves with a little human blood in them, too.

"But you need a white wife, son, to give you a family. It's the only way you'll stop drifting about until you ain't no more than a white nigger yourself.

"Besides," he added, splashing more rum into their tankards, "you need an heir, someone of your own blood to carry on the Bondmaster line."

Chapter 19

Carlton and his father spent many evenings trying to decide which slaves to sell to the factors at Roseau. They knew they must winnow out the useless slaves if they were to keep expenses down. But what was a "useless" slave? Of course they would keep the old slaves until they died, and the lazier ones in their twenties who were already past their prime should be offered for sale while they were still capable of fetching a price. The children from about five to twelve, though, should they be sold?

"Now you are planning to breed, son, I don't see why you want to sell the pups at all. They'll fetch better prices when they are fully grown." Hayes had taken to smoking a pipe in the hope that it would enable him to cut down on his rum-drinking, and he had the pipe in his clenched hand as he gesticulated.

"Aye, Da, I know that. But they are not pure niggers, are they? I mean my breed. When I am established, I want to have a reputation for first-class pedigreed stock. I don't want to sell anything but prime niggers bursting with strength. Now I've seen what those traders sell after they've crossed the middle passage, planters are going to be delighted to pay high prices for my quality stock. Huh," he laughed, slapping his knee, "maybe I'll even put the slave ships out of business!"

Hayes sucked on his pipe and, finding it had gone out again, withdrew it to look curiously at his son. "Tell me, if you are only going to sell first-class niggers, what are you going to do with the others? I agree that so far things are fine. Your stallions have sired a dozen whelps, and not a runt among them. But they might produce a sickly offspring at any time. If you don't want to sell the runts because of spoiling your reputation, and you don't want them around here, what's going to happen to them?"

It was Carlton's turn to look thoughtful. "If they be runts," he finally said, "then I suppose they will just take sick and die. Pity to get runts, though. Have to sell the dam, but I'll say she can't breed. Yes, Da." He sat back in his chair, swinging his feet up on to the balcony rail. "I aim to be fair. A consumer will know what he's getting when he buys from me, so he won't be disappointed. People will demand the Roxborough breed for preference!"

The tobacco Hayes was smoking came from the plantation. The old man claimed it had a niggery flavor which he found necessary to hide by soaking it in rum and then re-drying it. It was a pleasant aroma, and Carlton liked the smell as it wafted around him. He took in the scent with a grin, his mind ranging over the studying he had been doing earlier that evening.

"I've been checking the records," he said with determination. "Some of those pups are mongrels who won't sell for more when they are fifteen than when they are five. And I am the one who has the expense of maintaining them. In ten years, Da, I'm going to have the choicest and sleekest niggers you ever did see. Those mongrel pups will be bad for business. I'm going to take about ten of them to Roseau, to get rid of them now, and I'll take another ten full-grown."

He stood up, signifying that the discussion was at an end as far as he was concerned. His father made no comment. Carlton had turned away to go to his room, so he missed the old man's smile of pleasure. Hayes was satisfied that Carlton's self-assurance and determination were at last beginning to show he was his father's son.

Preparing the coffle for sale took more than a month. Each slave had to have a new set of clothes because Carlton wanted them to look at neat as possible. Mally Ibo, the seamstress, enlisted the plantation women to help her fashion the calico pants and shifts. Each male slave was to wear a shirt and shorts; females were to have a loose shift each. The children were to be similarly dressed. Hayes was scornful about the preparations, advising Carlton to look about his own appearance instead of that of his slaves.

Carlton knew that the old man was right. He had no town clothes. He tried on one of his father's coats and it was decided that the hem would be let down to give it the length and, if he did not attempt to button it up, the tightness across the shoulders would not constrict him too much. Mally Ibo was induced to fashion new breeches for him, although she was full of misgivings, as she had never before sewn anything for white folks to wear. His work boots were polished up by Pool. Carlton, having had no experience of the exclusive social world of the English whites who resided in Roseau, was sure he would look presentable.

Proudly, Carlton led his procession down the main path, sitting astride his horse, followed by Bo'jack a few paces behind on a donkey. Then came the coffle, breaking into a jog as Mercury and Will, mounted on donkeys, whipped them up expertly. The slaves who had come to watch the departure drifted away. Only Dutchip stayed to look as Little Rose, her baby in her arms, was pulled into a jog down the path by the rest of the coffle. Ella cooed at her child to bid his father farewell while Hayes, clearing his throat, ascended the stairs. He paused at the top to gaze down to the ferry where the coffle was being split into groups to be ferried across.

Although it was only four leagues along the coast to Roseau, the journey seemed like an expedition because, at best, the road was a bridle path able to accommodate horses and slaves only in single file. More often, it deteriorated to a narrow track pitted with large holes perilous for the horses. The mountainous terrain, with the hills sweeping right down to the sea, made it difficult to keep to the most direct route along the coast, and at times the trail twisted inland, then reappeared high above a bay.

The group passed through the hamlets that bordered the rivers at Mahaut and Massacre, stopping at both for the slaves to refresh themselves. Although they had set out soon after dawn, it was late in the afternoon before the coffle reached Woodbridge's Bay on the outskirts of Roseau. As they neared the town, the road improved, and Carlton had to draw his coffle to the side to avoid having his slaves run down by a passing carriage. He was amused to see the dress of the white people who rode in it. The ladies wore wide-brimmed hats with white handkerchiefs pinned around their noses, presumably to prevent the sun from blistering their fair skins, while the men had kerchiefs pinned under the forepart of their hats, and rode in long trousers.

All the company had umbrellas to shield themselves from the dying sun. Carlton, in contrast, had his old hat perched on his blond curls. He wore his shirt open and stowed his coat in his saddle bag, to wear when he reached the town. He saluted the group in the carriage as it passed, but they chose to ignore him, leaving only the words "Nigger overseer!" hanging in the air.

Roseau was a small, ramshackle town made up of clusters of tiny houses grouped around the bay and along the cobbled roads leading out of the central market square. Since Carlton had visited the town as a boy, there had been an invasion scare, and the town had been ringed with defense works, including Forts Young and de Moullin on the coast, and Melville's and Bruce Hill batteries overlooking the house roofs. The forts and a few of the houses were stone; the

181

others were of wood with thatched roofs of Roseau grass.

Fording the river, Carlton led his coffle into the town, anxious to secure them in a factor's compound so that he could go in search of a good supper. His arrival attracted the attention of the townsfolk and he heard many flattering comments about his perky though dusty Negroes. There seemed to be an extraordinary number of French people in town, possibly, he thought, the remnants of the French revolution a few years before. He was comforted by the presence of the militia, both white and colored men, strolling around town in their smart scarlet coats faced with black velvet.

Following the directions he was given in French by a tavern keeper, Carlton led his coffle down a mud road rutted with wheel tracks dried hard by the sun, to reach a compound with a high roundwood post fence surrounding it. Though it was situated on the bay front, there was little breeze, and the dead heat of the afternoon hung heavily over the compound. The place had the stink of excreta which Carlton recognized as typical of any place where niggers were penned. That was the niggery stench Hayes had spoken of when sniffing his own tobacco. The owner of the compound must have been notified of Carlton's approach, for he stood at the gate rubbing his hands in welcome.

"Good day, young man!" The factor was short and rotund with a face reddened more by rum than exposure to the sun. Tufts of gray hair stuck out from the sides of his bald head, and he wore the greasy brown garments of a tradesman on whom bad times have descended.

"And whose coffle is this, young man?" he demanded.

"Mister Marks?" asked Carlton, dismounting from his horse and choosing to ignore the man's impertinence.

"The same, young man. And who are you with such

a tongue? Haven't seen you in these parts before."

Mr. Marks took in Carlton's dusty calico pants and open-necked linen shirt. His burnished face marked him out as a country man, probably, Marks thought, the overseer on one of the east coast plantations. He cast his eyes over the slaves, his glance telling him that here at last was the quality stock for which he had been hoping for weeks.

"Mister Marks, the slave factor?" Carlton was persistent.

"That's right, young man." Mr. Marks looked away from the slaves reluctantly. "And who might you be representing?"

"I represent myself, Mister Marks, and I'd be obliged to you if you'd take a look at this parcel of niggers with a view to us doing some business."

"On whose authority?" Mr. Marks wriggled his hands nervously in front of his belly, betraying his enthusiasm for the deal.

"On my authority!"

Again Mr. Marks was forced to look away from the slaves and suspend the calculations running through his head, to pay attention to the young whippersnapper who had brought them to him. "Now, young man, I must know for whom you work and see your power of attorney before we can discuss anything."

"Of course, but you don't expect a man such as the Bondmaster of Roxborough to do business with you on the public highway, do you?"

"Roxborough? Roxborough? Hayes Todd. He's the Bondmaster, ain't he? Haven't seen him in years." Mr. Marks scratched his belly thoughtfully under his coat, unmindful of the perspiration pouring off his brow in the setting sun.

"He's no longer Bondmaster now, Mr. Marks, but I am Carlton Todd, his son, and I would be obliged if we could step inside to discuss terms and to water my niggers. We have had a long march today."

Carlton stepped around Mr. Marks into the courtyard of the compound, motioning to his drivers that they should follow him.

"Not here! Not here!" cried Mr. Marks overcoming his astonishment. "Negroes go in the back way."

He clapped his hands, and a boy dressed only in ragged shorts popped his head around the door way immediately. Carlton smiled as he realized that the boy had been hiding behind the fence listening to their conversation. The boy looked about fourteen and had a small round face which broke into a wide and friendly smile as he saw Carlton. "Good afternoon, sir!" The boy respectfully bowed his head as though genuinely pleased to see the visitor. Carlton was intrigued.

"Claudius!" shouted Mr. Marks, no longer able to conceal his excitement at such a fine set of slaves. "Take these niggers 'round the back. Pen them good, water them, and give them straw."

"Those three," Carlton indicated the drivers and Bo'jack, "are my property and will be returning to Roxborough. They have special treatment, Mister Marks."

"Chain them good, do you mean, so they won't slip away in the night?"

Carlton looked at Bo'jack, who was regarding Mr. Marks with extreme distaste. "Not necessary, Mister Marks. They'll be traveling back to Roxborough alone anyway. I will give them a ticket in the morning. In the meantime, separate quarters for them, I think."

"Now I am going to see to my lodgings, and I'll come to you in the morrow to arrange what is to be done," said Carlton, walking to the door. "That's a lively lad you have there, Mister Marks." The boy, Claudius, was holding the door open for him.

"Aye, born in Africa, raised at Government House until President Matson left last year. Worth every bit of a hundred pounds, he is, at current rates."

"I'll buy him," said Carlton, without hesitation. "Come with me, boy!"

"But, but—!" Mr. Marks gaped in astonishment as

184

Carlton put his hand on the boy's shoulder and edged him out of the door.

"I'll bring you your gold tomorrow, Mister Marks. You have thirty of my stock here as your security."

"Yes, yes, but the bill of sale, the——"

"Tomorrow!" said Carlton firmly. "Now, boy, show me the best lodging house in Roseau."

"Yes sir, Mr. Carlton. Shall I call a carriage, sir?"

"Of course, if that's the way gentlemen usually travel."

"It is, sir."

"Good!"

With a chuckle, Carlton waved the obsequious factor out of his thoughts and followed after the boy who had run ahead to whistle up a carriage from the jetty. Carlton was beginning to relish the prospects of a few days in Roseau away from the confines of the plantation and his father. It did not matter to him if the auction took a week to arrange. Bo'jack would carry word back to Roxborough about the delay in his return, and the new slave Claudius could show him all that the capital had to offer.

Chapter 20

Carlton was delighted with his purchase of Claudius. The boy appeared to know everything and everyone of note in Roseau. He was a well-mannered buck, apparently thrilled at having Carlton as his new master. That he had a high opinion of himself, Carlton admired, so long as the slave did all that was expected of him. He had quickly found tolerable lodgings, run by a French lady and her mulatto maids, in a narrow lane off the main highway. Two of them accompanied Carlton up to his room and giggled as he watched them place towels on his dresser, fill his water jug and, by bouncing on the bed, show how comfortable the mattress was.

"These girls will make you very welcome, sir," said Claudius, wondering if his new master understood the nature of the establishment.

Carlton dismissed the maids with a wave of his hand and grinned. "How come you don't speak like a nigger?"

" 'Cause Massa Matson done educate me like an Englishman, sah. He done sent me to de school an I done learn everything!"

"All right!" Again Carlton laughed as he sat down in the chair to contemplate the buck standing in front of him. "I feel that you and I are going to get on very well. I'm not a hard master, providing you do what I say. I punish disobedience severely, as you'll learn when you come to Roxborough."

"I'm looking forward to that, sir!"

"Damme! You even respond like a human being. Boy, I think I'm going to enjoy this sojourn in Roseau."

"Anything you want, sir, just ask me. I'll endeavor to get it for you as quick as I can, sir."

"Right now, I want a sangaree and supper, boy. To-morrow, I want a tailor and a cobbler."

"What about tonight, sir?"

Carlton raised his eyes quickly to search the boy's face. There was neither insolence nor suggestion reflected there, only an apparent willingness to please. "Boy!" said Carlton frowning slightly. "I'm the Bond-master of Roxborough. I have three hundred Negroes on my plantation. I need neither nigger nor mulatto to attend me in my bed tonight."

"I beg your pardon, sir. There are some choice ladies of your complexion in the town. They do entertain gentlemen, sir, for a modest fee."

"Really?" said Carlton. "You make it sound like the governor's lady herself. But no, I'll be about my business first."

Claudius stood patiently before his new master. The moment he had seen him outside Mr. Marks's compound, Claudius had known that here was a white man he could serve well. The gentlemen in Roseau were either elderly misers troubled by gout or young blades whose abuse of their slaves was matched only by their ignorance. This young master seemed to have a serious and determined air despite his obvious inexperience of city life. This inexperience worried Claudius.

"Sir?"

"Yes, boy?"

"Your business is to sell your coffle of slaves, sir?"

"Yes."

"Through Mister Marks, sir? At an auction?"

"That's not really your concern, is it, boy?" Carlton was trying to gauge the reason for the boy's interest. "I have not yet decided."

"Excuse me for saying so, sir. Is Mister Marks a personal friend of yours, sir?"

"Never set eyes on him before this afternoon. Why?"

"I know it isn't my place to say anything, sir, but you have been very good to me, sir, I mean, buying me like that and getting me away from Mister Marks." The boy hopped nervously from one foot to the other.

"Speak, Claudius. What is it you have to say?"

"Thank you, sir. Well, I have been with Mister Marks for four months waiting for someone to pay him the price he was asking for me. I have seen his tricks, sir. He is not very honest, sir."

"That's business, boy. I'll watch out for his tricks."

"Yes, sir. It's this auction which he has spoken of, sir. He likes to auction slaves because he gets a high commission, both ways. He takes it from you and also from the purchasers. Sometimes, he keeps niggers out of the auction to sell privately for more money, sir. He can make half as much as the nigger sells for, just for himself, sir."

Carlton bit at his little finger. His father had told him to expect some kind of double dealing, and now he appeared to have walked straight into it. Could he believe the slave? He did not know what to do.

"When I was with President Matson, sir, a gentleman from Rosalie plantation wanted to buy a whole coffle of slaves. I saw him again yesterday, sir, in Roseau. He said that he was looking for slaves to work in his fields, and some women and children, too. He hasn't long owned the plantation. Perhaps he would like to buy your niggers, sir?"

Claudius, thought Carlton, was a regular bag of tricks himself. "Well, why can't this gentleman bid at the auction?" he wondered aloud.

"You would make more money yourself if you sold to him privately, sir."

"And what about Mister Marks? He has all my slaves staying in his compound, don't forget about that."

"But he charges rent for the accommodations anyway, sir. The purchaser must pay that. Would you like me to arrange it, sir?"

"Damme!" Carlton stood up and gave the boy a slap around his ears. "I believe I would! That would fix the factor, earn me some more money, and give me an opportunity to relax here for a few days instead of worrying about business."

"Well, sir, I could look for the gentleman this evening."

Again Carlton was obliged to study the youngster's features, but this time he caught hold of the boy's scrawny neck and forced the slave to look up at his own eyes. He searched the young face intently, wondering what deviousness was concealed in the innocence of the boy's startled reaction.

"I hope you ain't planning to trick me yourself, boy. If it's the slip you're planning to give me, it's death, boy. Don't think that because you were the President's nigger, I respect the President's laws. At Roxborough we have our own laws and we abide by them. Death for a runaway, boy!"

"Sir, you're hurting!" squealed Claudius with obvious surprise. "Thank you sir," he gasped as Carlton eased his grip. "I'm not a runaway, sir. I'm proud to be a gentleman's servant. I can take you to a tavern for supper, and you may meet the gentleman there yourself."

The mention of supper reminded Carlton of his hunger. He let the boy go with a push which spun him around and flying against the door. He pulled the long coat which his father had given him out of his saddle bag and eyed it with as much distaste as did the slave.

"Are you going to wear that, sir?" Claudius watched from the door where he had been flung.

"Have to, don't I, boy?"

"It is customary for a gentleman to wear a coat, sir, and white breeches and polished boots when he dines. Perhaps you will be getting all those things tomorrow, sir?" There was a note of concern in the slave's voice.

"Why, yes, nigger, I will."

"Then may I suggest that this evening you send me to carry supper here for you, sir, and a pitcher of sangaree?"

Carlton looked at the slave with surprise, and then at the coat his father had given him and which Mally Ibo had worked on to adjust to his size for a whole day. He held it to his nose. The coat smelt of the dampness of the plantation. He threw it at the slave in disgust.

"Boy," he said with a sigh, "you're dam' right. Get me supper and grog, and quick!"

"Yes, sir!"

Claudius turned out to be as good as he promised. The next morning, he escorted Carlton to a tailor where he was able to assemble a commendable outfit from the tailor's stock, and then on to a cobbler where a fine pair of boots was acquired. With the addition of a shirt and a scarf, Carlton met with the approval of his slave, who now seemed prepared to let him be seen in the Roseau taverns.

Carlton submitted willingly to the slave's suggestions, for he had learned from his encounter with Mr. Marks that in Roseau a planter from the coast was regarded with something less than respect. Seeing his master dressed to his satisfaction, Claudius led him to the tavern where he could meet the Rosalie planter who might buy his niggers.

The tavern was at least twice the size of May Gregg's in Layou and, Carlton quickley noticed, the clientèle were of a higher class than the itinerant seamen of the Layou taverns. The place was thronged with young men, many of them in the uniform of the militia, some gathered around tables playing cards, others in an anteroom where a billiard table had been set up. The raucous laughter and braying conversation, the clatter of tankards pounding tables, and the general stench of the atmosphere amazed Carlton.

"Those white bucks have been here since last night,"

explained Claudius as he urged his master to enter the tavern.

When he glanced around, Carlton sensed that the slave was using him as an excuse to gain entry to the tavern. All the drinkers were either French or English. Only the serving wenches were black.

"Where you going to wait, boy?" he asked Claudius, not wanting to offend against local custom.

Claudius's eyes showed a flicker of disappointment. "Outside, sir, I'll be there if you need me. Ah, I see him, sir. He's that gentleman in the blue coat. I'll call him!"

Before Carlton could stop him, the slave pushed into the group of men around the upturned barrels which served as a counter. Carlton watched him tug at the coattails of one of them. He was a tall fellow, a few years older than Carlton, wearing a powdered wig. He seemed not in the least perturbed to see Claudius and bent down to listen to the boy's whisper. Carlton noticed with distaste how near Claudius was standing to the white man, and he was even more astonished when the man put his arm around the slave and began to squeeze his posterior. Carlton strode over to the counter.

"I'm Carlton Todd of Roxborough," he said thrusting out his hand for the man to shake. "This is my slave here, sir!"

"So I'm hearing, so I'm hearing," said the man, raising his head. "Highly honored to meet you, Mister Todd. Dudley Botts of Worcestershire and Rosalie plantation at your service." He returned Carlton's handshake limply.

"Wait outside!" said Carlton sternly to Claudius.

"Yes, sir." Claudius smiled obediently at his master, although he obviously felt he should be allowed to remain in the tavern. He began to make his way out through the crowd.

"My, aren't you the tartar!"

"I beg your pardon, Mister Botts."

"The boy's no harm in here. I always enjoy his

191

company myself." Botts waved in the air with his hand to show his contempt for the tavern rules. "Would have bought him myself, you know, but for the life of me, don't know what he'd do at Rosalie. A drink, sir?"

Carlton accepted the shot poured into a mug for him by Botts. "You been at Rosalie long, Mister Botts?" Carlton suspected that here was one of the dilettante planters his father was always criticizing.

"Heavens, no! Only been out of England a few months. That's why I'm looking for seasoned slaves. Don't have the experience or time to creolize Africans myself. I plan to spend a week out at Rosalie every few months, you know. The place is so far from town, such a journey to get there, you know. I have a good overseer, fortunately, who loves the work, although he does beat those niggers!" Botts appeared to be enjoying himself immensely, and the shouts of the young men around him frequently distracted him as he spoke.

"I've got a coffle of thirty niggers—males, females, and whelps. All seasoned. The males have worked cane; they know their place. The women, too, all from my main gangs. Most of the children are broken already, small gangs. You want to buy them?"

It had not been Carlton's intention to make such a direct sales approach but he found the boozy heartiness of Botts and his companions very irritating. The gloom and the smoke in the tavern also made him nervous to get outside again.

"Of course, that's what I'm looking for. I suppose you don't have any fancies?"

"Fancies?"

"Oh," said Botts, "it's an American term. You know, the fancy niggers, pretty boys, mulatto wenches—anything, you know, nice."

"Mine are working Negroes, Mister Botts, not playthings."

"Pity," said Botts looking bored. "Fancies sometimes fetch high prices, you know. What's your price for the coffle?"

"Won't you see them first?"

"Glanced at them already. Went down to Marks's dirt hole last night. This is a small town, Todd. I heard about your coffle, so I took a look at them. Some are a bit old, over twenty-five, but I want a bunch of hard-working slaves without any problems. They'll have enough problems when my overseer starts on them! Marks told me that he is going to auction them for you. I'll buy them now if you tell me your price."

"Paying cash, are you, Mr. Botts?"

Botts nodded as he poured himself another rum.

"Then I'll take two thousand."

"Pounds or guineas?"

"Guineas, of course!" interrupted one of Botts companions. "A gentleman always deals in guineas. I'm Jones Farley," the young man said, nodding at Carlton. "Heard you were in town. Wanted to come and see you last night, but your boy said you were tired after the journey. Selling your niggers dam' cheap, aren't you?"

"It's what they're worth." Carlton supposed that Jones must be the son of Dr. Farley, the slave-dealing physician. He liked the fellow, whose unaffected air contrasted sharply with Botts's mannerisms.

"You advise me to take them, Farley?" Botts asked.

"I do, I do. Todd here's selling too cheap!"

Farley left as suddenly as he had arrived, his arm around the shoulders of a serving wench, as the laughter of the crowd around him swallowed him up.

"All right," said Botts, draining his mug. "Let's go and see Mr. Marks and organize a Bill of Sale."

Chapter 21

Botts was as good as his word. He accompanied Carlton to the slave factor, where Carlton was compelled to explain that he had contracted privately to sell to Mr. Botts. Although Marks was dissatisfied at the thought of profits he was going to lose, he was consoled by Botts asking him to keep the Negroes for another two weeks. Marks obviously sensed better pickings out of Botts then out of the Bondmaster. He charged a substantial transfer fee, anyway, for preparing a Bill of Sale, and also deducted the hundred pounds he was due for Claudius. Carlton was relieved when the transactions were finished and he was free to shake hands with the limp-wristed Mr. Botts and step out into the road. Claudius was waiting for him.

"If you please, sir," said Claudius, "I have a shirt in Mister Marks's compound. May I get it, sir?"

"You could have thought of that before. Don't be long!"

As he walked behind his new master, Claudius was aware of having done well out of the deal. From Mr. Botts he had collected a commission for arranging the sale, and another from Mr. Marks. He viewed the future with the Bondmaster with enthusiasm. He was sure that if life at Roxborough did not appeal to him, he could contrive a means of changing his situation.

The fact that he was a slave did not mean that life for Claudius was without opportunity and excitement. On the contrary.

"Where does society go in the evenings, boy?"

"All places, sir. The tavern where we met Mister Botts is the popular one, sir. That's where they play billiards all the time, sir. You can gamble there for high stakes, too, if you like."

"Boy, you are going to have to do something about that tongue of yours," grinned Carlton, recalling that it was the slave's precocity which had attracted him in the first place. "Tell me where the white ladies go."

The slave frowned. "This town is a bit small for that, sir." He was thoughtful. "When I was at Government House, the President did hold soirées sometimes for the visiting naval officers. He used to ask the plantation owners, sir, and they would bring along their daughters. Is that the kind of white lady you mean, sir? Or the married kind?"

"Yes," said Carlton, his heart sinking, "the daughters. Where do they gather at night? Is there a club or a hotel here where they congregate?"

"Oh, no, sir. I've only ever seen them at Government House. But they are whores as well, sir, and each one wants to mary a British officer and leave the island."

Carlton ignored the prattling and, as evening descended, concentrated on the scenes of the town. It was a sleepy little place. A pie-seller moved along the lane with a tray of freshly baked cakes and pies, while groups of free Negroes sat around on house steps, some calling to Claudius as he passed. Soldiers strolled down the main street while French refugees idled at corners in secretive groups. In spite of himself, Carlton found he was heading for the tavern where he had met Botts.

Bidding Claudius wait for him on the bench outside the entrance door, Carlton moved into the packed bar. Heated voices rose from the game of billiards going on in the side room. Drinkers clustered in groups around the upturned barrels which served as tables, and in a far corner a game of cards was under way beneath a lantern. Carlton peered into the gloom to see if he recognized anyone while he groped his way to the counter. When his eyes had become accustomed to the heavy fumes of tobacco and alcohol, he reached the bar with relief and called for a half-gill of rum. Adding a few drops of water, he began to swill it down when, in the crush around the bar, he felt himself being hugged by someone. He turned around in time to see the long-haired mulatto youth who quickly released him and began to worm his way through the crowd.

"Watch who you're bouncing, boy!" warned Carlton, but the youth paid no attention, disappearing quickly through the throng.

His cry carried to Jones Farley standing a few paces behind him. "Helloo, Todd!" he called, beckoning Carlton to join the group around him. Carlton pushed his way over, somehow grateful that Botts was not with them.

"This is the celebrated Carlton Todd of Roxborough plantation," laughed Jones, introducing him to his cronies, none of whose names Carlton was able to catch in the noise of the tavern. "Botts is tickled pink with those niggers you sold him this morning. I should collect my commission now!"

"Be happy to oblige. Gentlemen, a drink on me!"

"Botts has been looking for a ready-made field gang for some time, you know, Todd. He has a packet of money. His family bought him a plantation and told him to set to and run it."

"My slaves will serve him well," said Carlton, proud of being accepted into the group. "They're not prime, of course. Too old for that."

"Don't know much about field niggers myself," said Jones. "None of us do, being in commerce, you understand."

"I do," said a florid-faced young gentleman with

196

his hair worn close-cropped to his temples. "The only good nigger's a dead one!"

Carlton joined in the laughter of the group. "But it was you who told me I was selling too cheap," said Carlton to Farley. "Surely you know something about Negroes."

"Did I?" said Jones. "Don't you see the subject's a bore? That's the trouble with all you planters. Can't talk about anything but the price of sugar or the cost of slaves."

Again Carlton joined in the general laughter. "I trust you are not putting me in that class yourself, Jones?"

"Haven't heard much from you yet, old boy."

"Well, I would be pleased to give you a dissertation on the historical importance of . . ." Carlton paused, as though looking around for inspiration. He held up his glass with a smile. "Of rum, perhaps!"

"Beats me what you do on a plantation the whole day," said the cropped-haired fellow after the laughter had died down. "Don't you get tired of all that stinking black flesh around you day and night?"

"Ah!" said Jones before Carlton could reply. "It's the nights which aren't so boring, eh, Todd? Think of all those wenches a man can have *gratis* when he is the Bondmaster of a slave empire."

"Maybe's it's all right for the men," said another of the group, "but what about the women? What do they do with themselves?"

"Hate to think!" said Jones. "Wait for a husband to find them, I hope."

"Must be hell for them, don't you think?" the same man continued. "A man's wife is happy because she has her husband—when he's at home, of course," he grinned. "But what about the girls stuck out on the plantations? Look at the Dalrymple pair out at Portsmouth, or even those spinsters over in Marigot in the north."

"And there's the Vandy girl down in Grand Bay,"

chipped in the short-haired man. "She's most eligible for a husband."

Carlton strained his ears to hear the man speak above the hubbub. He was a curious mixture, with a skin much darker than Carlton's, whose color was due to the sun and not to Negro ancestors. "The French, of course, let their women have their Negro boys," continued the man. "But can you imagine Major Vandy permitting that?"

"But dammit all, man!" said Jones, apparently affronted. "An Englishman will marry a virgin, sir, or not at all!"

"I was referring to the French, Farley." The man spread his lips wide over a set of impeccable white teeth. "There is no accounting for a Frenchman's taste, or a Frenchwoman's, for that matter. But Sybil Vandy, I would vouchsafe, is more preserved than the Virgin herself."

"Be a lucky man who gets her," observed another man in the group. "If she were here in town, I'd court her myself. Can't stand the country, though, that's the problem."

The conversation veered onto other topics, but Carlton contemplated what he had heard about this eligible young woman at Grand Bay. No one had mentioned her looks but she was considered honorable by the public in general which, he decided, might make a journey to Grand Bay worth while, especially as it appeared that he would not be able to find a wife in Roseau. He reached inside his coat for his wallet in preparation for paying his bill and taking his leave. It was gone.

"I've been robbed!"

"What?" said Jones with only polite interest. "Not of all Botts's money, I suppose?"

"No," said Carlton, "but a large enough purse, any-way. I had it inside my coat when I came in, because I paid for my first drink. Now it's disappeared."

"Often happens, old chap," said the dark one. "A

drinker's hazard. Credit's the only way to do business in a tavern. Matters not."

"But what about my purse?" Carlton was shocked, though the loss was trifling and he still had the money for the slave sale strapped around his waist. "I think I know the fellow who did it. A mulatto bastard bumped me as I was standing at the bar. I'm sure it was he. Thought it funny at the time."

Explaining his predicament to the tavern keeper, Carlton promised to settle his bill the next day. The keeper was indignant at the suggestion that a robbery had taken place in his premises, knew no one answering the description Carlton gave him, and demanded he settle his bill immediately. It was Farley who signed the chit before Carlton could rush outside to see if he could track down the thief.

"I'm been waiting for you, sir," said Claudius, standing up as Carlton came out of the door.

"I should dam' well hope you have. Tell me, boy!" He grabbed Claudius on the shoulder, glancing along the line of niggers sitting on the bench to see if he recognized any of them. "Did you see a mulatto buck come out of here, about your height, with long black hair? Thin as a snake, he was."

"I might have done, sir."

"What the devil do you mean?" Carlton shook his slave fiercely.

"There's all kinds of boy does look like that. You have real mulattoes with white fathers and black mothers, then you have those who are nearly white because they have two mulattoes for parents. They are the kind who try to pretend they are not black, sir. When their children have children you can't see any trace of blackness in them, not like me."

"Boy!" Carlton cut short the chatter with a swipe across the slave's face with the back of his hand. Claudius staggered and fell across the boys seated on the bench. They exploded into the laughter they had been trying to conceal behind their hands.

"Tell de massa," one of them said. "Befo' he does kill yuh."

"What game is this, boy?" Carlton pulled up Claudius by his collar, lifting him up on his toes to look straight into his eye. "Tell me what you know about all this!"

"Sir," said Claudius with a wide grin, "I believe I did see such a buck as you describe. He appeared to be in possession of some money which looked familiar, sir. Seeing that I did see this money previously in the possession of my master, sir, I did relieve him of it, sir. Please release me, sir, for I have it here."

Claudius put his hand in his shirt and pulled out Carlton's purse, holding it up. There was cheering and clapping from the Negroes seated on the bench.

"Give that here!" Carlton snatched away the purse, plunging it into his pocket. He grabbed Claudius suddenly by the ear and dragged him down the steps into the road.

"Sir!" begged Claudius. "Don't hurt me. I got back your purse for you, sir. In a fight. Outside here. All those niggers there saw me do it, sir!"

"Maybe you did." Carlton tightened his grip on the slave's ear. "But you tried to play a joke on me. For that, I'm taking you to the stocks. A night locked up in the stocks in the marketplace will serve to show you that I am your master, not your comrade."

"The thief, sir. I caught the thief."

"Aye, so you say. And I'm grateful to you for it. But no one tricks the Bondmaster, not even you, my Roseau rat."

Chapter 22

In the morning, Carlton was disappointed to see that there were no small boys gathered round the stock using his slave as target practice. The only ones who showed interest in Claudius were some niggers squatting on the ground in front of the stocks, presumably commiserating with him. As soon as they spied Carlton, they leaped to their feet and took off into the market crowd.

Carlton found the jailer with his keys, tipped him, and watched him unlock the huge padlock. As he was released, Claudius sprang up and tried to stand, then massaged his ankles quickly. Looking up at Carlton with a rueful grin, he seemed none the worse for the experience.

"I trust you passed a peaceful night?" Carlton had expected his slave to be looking more contrite.

"Oh yes, sir." Claudius wondered what his master would say if he knew that he and his cronies, fortified with a little rum smuggled out to them by one of the pot boys from a nearby tavern, had been playing cards for most of the night. "Was the money all there, sir, when you counted it?"

"Huh!" It was Carlton's turn to give a rueful grin. "I trust you have learned your lesson. I'm not one of your town bucks in brocade and moccasins, me young nigger. I'm a planter and I work for my living. You were not bought to amuse me. Jokes are for those feckless habitues of the taverns, if you like, but not for Roxborough, do you hear?"

"Of course, sir. What are we doing today?"

Carlton outlined his plan to journey to Grand Bay and instructed Claudius to retrieve his horse from Mr. Marks, who had stabled it in his compound, and to make all the necessary preparations. He himself returned to the lodging house where he took breakfast, settled his account, packed his saddle bag, and waited on the balcony for Claudius. He was astonished when the boy rode upon a small pony leading Carlton's horse behind him. Claudius waved to people in the street. It seemed that the whole of Roseau knew the slave.

"Where did you get that pony, boy?" Carlton demanded when he came down the steps of the lodging house.

"This pony? It's mine, sir."

"Is it indeed? Since when did a slave own his own mount?"

"But it is my own, sir. President Matson gave it to me. Grand Bay is a long journey, sir, and I thought that you would like your slave to ride behind you, sir, as befits a gentleman's servant, not a field slave."

Carlton was dumbfounded. A slave with his own horse? He had never heard the like of it before. "That mount goes in with mine when we get to Roxborough!" He thrust his saddle bag at Claudius, who jumped down to receive it, then helped his master mount. They set off through the town, the Bondmaster in front, the slave behind, waving at the girls watching him through the jalousies where they were supposed to be cleaning their mistresses' bedchambers.

Claudius apparently knew a great deal about the area, so Carlton asked him about the Vandy plantation. Immediately the slave jerked his pony to an abrupt halt, his sunny face closed with fear.

"Not dere we does be goin', sah!"

202

"Good heavens, boy, what's the matter with you? Come on, we can't delay."

Claudius gulped, digging his heels into the side of the animal to catch up with his master. "But sir," he whined, "I'm sorry to show my disrespect, sir, but are we really going to the Vandy plantation?"

"What is it to you, boy? What's so troubling about the Vandy plantation?"

"That Major Vandy does beat his slaves something terrible."

"Good for him!" smiled Carlton, convinced that Claudius was only frightened at the prospect of a little traditional plantation discipline. "Some people are too soft on their niggers. Seems like you have had too easy a time in the past, my boy. Plantation life will beat some good sense into you."

Claudius persisted. "Major Vandy, sir, is he a friend of yours?"

"Never set eyes on the fellow."

The answer seemed to reassure Claudius. "I hear he treats his niggers awful, sir. White folks say so. I'm scared of him."

"He must be a powerful man indeed for you to be worried. I thought that you weren't afraid of any man, judging by your conduct around town."

"It's true, sir. Only Major Vandy. They say he is a little crazy at times. Beats his slaves for no reason, hangs them, too, sir. Oh, say we are not going there." Claudius rode his pony in line with Carlton, trying to will him to change his mind.

"This Vandy man appears most intriguing, Claudius. I think we should visit him and stay awhile. I might buy some slaves from him, if he has any to sell. He has a daughter, I believe. What do you know about her?"

"Nothing, sir. I only hear tell about Major Vandy, and how he does mistreat his Negroes. I heard about him when I was with the President."

"Eavesdropping as well, Claudius? What a troublesome nigger I have bought myself. I think I'll ask this Major to give you a piece of his punishment to curb your high spirits, boy."

Claudius drew back in shock. "Oh no, sir! I'll always do whatever you say, sir."

The Vandy plantation was an anachronism. Major Vandy had appropriated it ten years before, when the French owners fled the effects of the revolution. Sybil, his daughter, now eighteen, had spent the entire period on the plantation under the tutelage of a strict governess and a French riding master. Her trips out of the plantation were limited to rides in the neighborhood accompanied by her maid. Every afternoon, Sybil liked to ride the trail through the forest, galloping her fine horse as fast as she could go, brushing away the stifling atmosphere of the Vandy home from her mind. Her maid, on a slower, smaller pony, tried in vain to keep up with her mistress, but Sybil was pleased to outpace her and ride completely alone, the fronds of the trees brushing her face as she swept along the path.

The Major himself had told the maid that she must never let her mistress out of her sight, and she was terrified lest something should happen to Sybil and reveal her own inability to carry out the Major's bidding. The unpredictable Major was the most feared man in the area. All the slaves did as they were told, no matter what they thought about the Major. As Mistress Vandy supervised the cooking herself, there was no opportunity for the maid or any of the others to put poison in the Major's dinner and finish him off for good as they yearned to do.

Her mind filled with such thoughts, Sybil's maid trotted along the trail, following the direction her mistress had taken. Sybil had been out of sight for a long time, and the maid expected to meet her returning along the path. She had been riding for an hour, and was anxiously scanning the turns in the trail ahead. Suddenly, there was a shout from the undergrowth, and the bushes parted.

"Claire!"

Her mistress stepped out into the pathway.

"So this is how you dawdle along behind me!" Sybil stood with her legs placed firmly astride the path, dashing her riding crop against her thigh. Her face was flushed with anger. "Hasn't Daddy told you to keep up with me all the time? Who knows, I might be raped by a Hottentot if one were to waylay me!"

"Small chance of that, mistress," thought Claire to herself, wondering what ploy her mistress was going to try now. "Ah does be sorry, ma'am. Yo' horse does be so fast, ain't no chance me ketchin' yuh even if I does try."

"Get down from that horse, Claire." Sybil brandished her riding whip menacingly. "I declare I will have to thrash you myself."

"Rather you than the Major," thought Claire, easing herself down from her mount. "Oh, please don't punish me, ma'am," she whined convincingly. "I does be sorry, ma'am. It ain't go'n happen no more."

"I'm not so sure about that, Claire. I think this afternoon is a fine time for a thrashing. It's been a week since you had one." Sybil surveyed the path. It seemed secluded enough for her purpose. "Here," she handed the reins of her own horse to her maid. "Take the horses through the bush into the clearing. Tie them well."

"Yas, ma'am." Claire continued to snivel as she led the horses through the undergrowth, hoping that she would not encounter a snake. That would really make her cry. She came to a small space in the trees where the forest floor was itself a carpet of leaves. She tied the reins around one of the trees and then looked back. Her mistress was heading through the bush behind her, her face flushed and her dark ringlets dancing into her eyes. With an impatient gesture, she brushed her hair from her face and stood in front of her maid.

"Now, Claire, I'm going to beat you like you have never been beaten before!"

"Oh no, ma'am, please no, ma'am."

"Take off your drawers, girl!" Sybil's voice was deep, a blood vessel pounding against the side of her temple. "Come," she ordered as the maid hesitated. "Take off your drawers and lift your petticoat!"

Claire wriggled out of her undergarment as quickly as she could, gathering up her petticoat to hold it in front of her, above her waist. The boots she wore came halfway up her calf muscles, the black of the leather only slightly darker than the dark brown of her skin.

Sybil gulped. "Bend over that log!" she commanded.

"Please don't hurt me, ma'am!"

Raising the crop above her head, Sybil sliced the whip down. It switched with a delicious sound into her maid's naked bottom. Claire's yelp of pain spurred her on to raise her arm for another blow.

"No, ma'am, no, ma'am. Oh, it does hurt me, ma'am!" After the fourth blow, Claire twisted around her skirt still gathered high above her waist, and faced Sybil. "Oh ma'am, no more, please!"

"Did I hurt you, then?" Sybil's deep voice took on a note of tenderness. "Did my whip cut you?" She put out her fingers to touch the girl's flesh, passing her hands underneath to cradle Claire's bottom. She knelt down and pressed her face close to the maid's.

"It does be all right now, ma'am," said Claire, sobbing as she rested her face on Sybil's shoulder. "I does be sorry dat I make you vex, ma'am."

"Yes, Claire, I know." Sybil removed her hands from fondling the girl's buttocks and patted her on the shoulder. She sat on the ground and pulled the maid down with her. "It gets so hot in the afternoons, Claire, let's rest awhile. Put your head on my stomach for a pillow."

"Yas, ma'am," answered Claire obediently, laying her head where her mistress indicated and stretching out on the hard ground beside her. Her skirt was still tucked up around her waist.

As Sybil watched her, she felt her throat tightening

206

again. "I suppose it does be cooler like that, Claire, without undergarments?"

"Yes, ma'am."

"Then remove mine for me, Claire. I would be as cool as you."

"Oh no, ma'am, I couldn't do that!"

"Why ever not? Do you want me to tell the Major that you were deliberately dawdling behind me today? I will, you know."

"No, ma'am."

"Then I demand that you remove my undergarments for me." So saying, Sybil gave her maid a push in the shoulders which brought her face down level with her thighs. She reached down and yanked up her long skirt herself, lying back on the leaves as the maid's trembling fingers fumbled to get hold of her drawers. She tugged, and Sybil arched her back to help the process. As she felt herself uncovered, and the gentle breeze caressing her, she sighed.

"Ah, Claire, that is much cooler!"

"Yas, ma'am." Claire sat at Sybil's feet, marveling at the whiteness of her mistress's exposed flesh. Sunlight filtered through the treetops to dapple the soft black curls glistening before her.

"You may kiss me, Claire."

"Ma'am?"

"Down there, Claire, oh, down there! I am on fire, Claire. On fire! Come!"

Sybil raised her body and leaned forward to clutch her maid behind her neck, forcing the girl's head down between her thighs.

"Kiss me, Claire, kiss me, damn you!"

Sybil closed her eyes and sank back to the ground.

Chapter 23

"Ho!" said Carlton reining in his horse. "What have we got here?"

They had been riding hard for more than three hours since they had stopped for refreshments. The treacherous trail had led them over vast chasms plunging to fertile valleys and rivers below. They had negotiated the rain forests of the interior before branching out toward the coast and linking up with the broader avenue winding through the flat lands toward the sea. Side paths leading off the avenue indicated that they were nearing a populated area. Two riders emerging from the bush a hundred yards ahead of them were the first people they had met on the trail.

"A white lady and her maid?"

"Aye. And what lady is this?" He spurred on his horse to catch the riders. The woman looked around with a startled expression as she heard him approaching. "Hellooo!" he called, anxious to reassure her.

The woman appeared to speak to her slave and then urged her horse into a canter and pulled away from the black girl. Carlton's horse, tired after the journey from Roseau, was no match for this sudden burst of speed, but Carlton followed by Claudius drew alongside the maid.

"Hello, nice girl!" said Claudius. "Don't be frightened. My master craves company. Why did your mistress ride off?" He indicated the figure disappearing round a bend ahead of them. The girl stared straight in front of her, refusing to look at Claudius.

"Fie upon you, girl!" said Carlton. "Did your mistress not teach you any manners?"

"Yas, sah!" Claire looked at Carlton for the first time. "But she does forbid me to speak to unfamiliar niggers, sah."

"Hah!" Carlton laughed. "That puts you in your place, boy."

He looked more closely at the black girl on her pony. She was a tall filly with straight back and lively eyes, but a bit too lean for breeding, he thought. Not enough sap in her, but the right age group, anyway. He put her about seventeen. "And what did your mistress tell you about unfamiliar white men, girl?"

"Nothing, sah, except be respectful, sah."

"Fine, girl."

They were nearing the bend in the trail and Carlton wondered if they would see the white woman still fleeing from them or whether she had been courteous enough to wait. "Perhaps your mistress needs to heed her own lessons."

"Sah?"

"We wished no harm to the good lady, yet she chose to flee from us."

"Miss Sybil does be a virtuous lady, sah. She don't have no truck wid strange buckras, sah."

Carlton's eyebrows rose. "Indeed?" he turned back to Claudius. "We seem to be near our destination. Yes, indeed," he added as they rounded the bend to see a horse and rider waiting for them a few yards ahead.

"My apologies, ma'am," he called. "It was not my wish to frighten your horse."

Sybil glared at the stranger. First he had surprised her when she least expected it and then, instead of trying to catch her as she had thought he would, he had stayed conversing with Claire. "My horse wasn't frightened!"

"Oh?" Carlton was curious.

"And neither was I," she added hastily. "What business do you want with my maid, may I ask?"

"Your maid, ma'am? No business whatsoever. May I congratulate you on her true respect and dignity which do her mistress credit."

Sybil ushered her horse forward so that the man would follow suit. His nigger, whom she had quickly appraised as a brash boy who would be of no interest to Claire, fell in behind the man at an appropriate distance, which indicated his good training. The man himself was puzzling. He had a pleasing complexion, his blond hair contrasting with his tanned face. His eyes were his most interesting feature, reflecting a determined assurance and not attempting to conceal his frank assessment of her. By his accent, he was local, but she sensed that he was not a town buck who idled his hours in billiard taverns. This buck seemed to have more spunk than that.

"You have the advantage over me, sir," said Sybil demurely, inclining her head toward him to acknowledge his presence. "You appear to know of me, but you are a stranger to me."

"A thousand apologies. I have precious little time for the formalities of society, ma'am. I am the Bond-master of Roxborough, ma'am, Carlton Todd at your service."

"Roxborough," murmured Sybil, impressed by the authority with which the man recited his title. She looked at him again. He was scarcely more than a year older than she. Quickly she looked back to the trail to avoid his piercing eyes. He did have a most appealing smile, she thought.

"Is that a big plantation, Mister Todd?"

"Fair, and three hundred slaves to go with it."

"Three hundred!" Again she glanced at him quickly, but his eyes were still on her so she turned back to the trail. This was no way, she thought, for Sybil Vandy to behave. The young man was attractive, she supposed, and probably wealthy, too. So what? Many attractive and wealthy men had come her way before.

Even as she thought, she knew she was fooling herself. Most of the men who had found their way to Vandy Hall were either one or the other, but never both.

"You mentioned that you hoped to make my acquaintance in more fitting circumstances," Sybil said, finding her footing and hoping to put the man in his place before he realized how impressed she was with him. "Was it to see me that you journeyed from Roseau? If it was, then I must share your feelings as I would hope to receive you in a more dignified manner."

"Miss Vandy, It would be most ungallant of me to say that making your acquaintance was not the reason for my journey. Had I known that Sybil Vandy was a lady such as you, it should have been the *sole* purpose of my visit. Neither am I a slave trader intent upon the purchase of slaves. Shall we say that having a few days free and being both unimpressed with Roseau and uninformed about the south, I thought a visit to the plantation and family of the renowned Major Vandy would be most opportune."

As he followed Sybil up the steps of Vandy Hall, Carlton realized that they were not so grand as they had first appeared. The wall with its fancy balustrade was cracked, and the ornaments had broken away in many parts. The steps, too, were hazardous, with gaping holes where many stones were dislodged. There was an air of deterioration about the place which suggested that the Major's fortune was certainly not directed to his house and estate. Even though it was nearly nightfall, Carlton was puzzled by the absence of slaves.

Sybil herself opened the door to the interior after she had invited Carlton to attend her on the balcony. He glanced around him as he waited. The silence hanging over the house was unnerving. He missed the bustling kitchen sounds of Roxborough, the sight and cries of pickaninnies playing in the front yard and the cluck of chickens scavenging in the back. He was nostalgic for the songs of boys coming home from the river after a day's fishing, and the chop of a cutlass as a nigger cut wood for his fire to heat his supper.

A door banged somewhere in the house, and an English voice uttered an oath. A woman's voice answered him shrilly; there was a muffled conversation in excited tones before another door, nearer this time, banged, and then a clomp of boots announced the approach of, Carlton assumed, the Major.

Inside the house, someone jerked the balcony door and cursed as it refused to budge. After another couple of heaves, it opened inward to reveal an angry white man who kicked in spite at the open door before striding onto the balcony. The man was thin with a spiky crop of gray hair above a face whiter than any Carlton had seen before. His gray coat hung loosely from his shoulders, its hem brushing the baggy breeches which were stuffed into his unpolished boots. His unkempt appearance surprised Carlton, as did his bleary eyes peering out from behind protruding cheekbones.

"Bondmaster of Roxborough, eh?" The man did not offer his hand as he confronted Carlton, his eyes traveling from his feet to his head and then down again. His voice was tense, as high as his daughter's was deep. "You think you've finished sucking your mother's breast, boy!"

Carlton took a step backwards as the Major's foul breath wafted over him. "I beg your pardon, sir! My mother, if you please, has been dead for fifteen years, sir!"

"Not surprised, boy, not surprised." The Major walked over to the balcony railing and gripped it tightly as if to prevent his toppling over.

"Did you know her, sir?" asked Carlton, trying to establish some link of communication with this strange man.

"Of course not! What are you doing here, boy?" The Major closed his eyes, swaying dangerously. "Answer!"

"Are you all right, sir?"

"All right? Who is all right? Did you answer me yet, boy?" The Major turned to face Carlton, his free hand opening and closing as though he would have liked a whip in it with which to strike him.

Carlton decided to ignore the pathetic attempts of this old man to exhibit the authority he may once have had. "Major Vandy," he began, "I have a plantation with over three hundred acres of cane. I always need new slaves, and it occurred to me that you might have some."

"Nigger-buyer, eh? What are you doing on my balcony, boy?" The Major grasped at the railing for support again.

"Your daughter invited me up here, Major."

"Interested in my daughter, boy? Who's your father? What regiment is he in?"

"My father has always been a planter, Major, never a soldier."

"Creole, is he? A mulatto?"

"Sir! You insult me! My father is English, born in Leicester, and my mother was French, born in New Orleans."

"Aha!"

"Aha!"

"Sir?"

"French, eh? New Orleans, eh? My daughter likes you, boy."

"I'm delighted to hear it, Major."

"But I don't, neither does Mistress Vandy." The major spun around on his heel, stumbled, lurched to the door jamb for support, recovered, and went through the door into the house. There was a crash as he careened into a table and then silence as he came to rest against a chair into which he slid. Putting his head inside the still open door, Carlton was uncertain what to do. The Major was watching him.

"Never let niggers get the better of you, boy. If you haven't got the strength to beat them yourself, have two bucks who can. I have two bucks so strong they could pull this house down between them. The executioners, I call them. 'Send for the executioners'

213

is all I shout, and my niggers do what they're told. You got money, boy?"

"I have enough to buy any stock you have to sell."

"Not selling my executioners. Without them, this plantation will collapse. Think I don't know that? You must have discipline, boy. My daughter's been well disciplined. Many men have asked for her hand. Not letting you have her. Nigger-buyer!"

The Major closed his eyes tightly only to open them again immediately. "Cash, you say? Speak to the wife. She'll know, she'll know." The Major's silence seemed to indicate that Carlton was dismissed, so he edged out of the doorway to stand again on the balcony, wondering what he should do.

It was considered impolite for a gentleman to tour another man's plantation without an invitation from the owner, but Carlton was intrigued by the Vandy estate and wanted to see how things were run. The glow of a lantern shone through a crack in the floor of the balcony, and he smelled something sizzling in a pan, so Carlton decided to investigate. He went down the front steps cautiously, and then around their base toward the light. The shutter of the cellar was partly open and he peered in. What he saw made him look again in astonishment. A white woman, about the size of Ma Phoebe, in an English bonnet, and with a blue-and-white checked apron tied around her ample body, was humming to herself as she stirred a pan on top of the stove. There was no one else in the kitchen.

Wondering who she might be, Carlton backed away and decided to go in search of Claudius. Unfamiliar with the layout of the plantation, he tried to locate the Negro quarters by listening for voices. He heard nothing. Defeated by the complete darkness of the place, he groped his way back to the steps. Both the woman and the lantern in the kitchen had gone. He was relieved to see, however, that a light had been placed on the balcony. He went up the steps eagerly, hoping that he would encounter Sybil and get an explanation for her father's odd behavior.

It was not Sybil waiting for him, but the woman he had seen earlier in the kitchen, minus only her apron.

"Oh, Mister Todd!" she said, throwing out her pudgy arms and blocking his way so that he was obliged to submit to a suffocating embrace. "I'm so glad that you could come!" she said as she released him.

"Sybil has spoken about nothing but your visit for days. Cook has prepared something very special for you. Won't you come through to the dining room? I don't know what it is; I never go into the kitchen myself. We have such good slaves, you know, so well trained. Would you care to hold the lantern? I don't know where that boy is right now. Come."

Handing him the lantern with one hand, she grasped his free hand with her fat fingers and pulled him quickly into the house.

Chapter 24

A man dressed in the black coat and white collar of a cleric rose out of the darkness of the dining room as Carlton entered with the lantern held high so he could avoid bumping into the many pieces of furniture which filled the room. His hostess apparently knew how to negotiate a path through the chairs without mishap, for she continued to drag him by his hand around the room. She placed him with obvious satisfaction at the top end of the table.

"Hah!" she said as though in triumph, taking the lantern and thrusting him into the proper chair. "We will hang the lamp here, so!"

A nail had been driven into the wall in the center of the room and she stuck the lantern on it, turning around to see whom the light revealed. The room was so large that Carlton found he was on the periphery of the glow, while the cleric, who still stood at the center of the table, was reflected in full.

"Yes, yes," said Mrs. Vandy. "Patterson, you are here, then? Where's my husband? Where's my daughter?"

"I know not, ma'am. It's been my pleasure to attend them here since Miss Vandy returned from her afternoon ride, but I have not had the good fortune to encounter either."

"Vandy!" The woman's stentorian voice echoed

through the dining room and bounced out into the rest of the house. A shrill squeak answered immediately, followed by the crash of a piece of furniture and a muttered oath.

Carlton glanced at the clergyman, who gazed at Mrs. Vandy as though in a trance. The tall figure of the Major suddenly appeared at the doorway, hovered at the edge of the light and then sank into the chair at the head of the table.

Behind him, Carlton heard another door open, and he turned to see Sybil glide into the room. She had changed her outfit of the afternoon into a vaguely Grecian-style dress which accentuated the proportions of her body. Carlton rose in his chair.

"Sit down!" It was the major's squeaky voice. "It's my daughter, dammit!"

Carlton glanced again at the clergyman, expecting to see a sign of acknowledgment at the curious behavior of their host, but the man had re-entered his trance-like state. He continued to stare at Mrs. Vandy who, having seated herself carefully, was dolloping the contents of a silver chafing dish onto the plates lined up in front of her.

Sybil, who had passed out of the glow of the lamp, reappeared beside her father and sat down on a chair at his righthand side. She passed a plate to her father and then one across to the cleric. Mrs. Vandy passed one down to Carlton and immediately took up a spoon to dig into the mess on her own plate.

"Cook calls this eggs, Mister Todd. We don't have as many chickens as we used to."

"Niggers steal them all," said the Major, coming to life again. "Thrashed three of them yesterday, I did. Caught them at it."

"Caught them stealing?" Carlton was incredulous.

"Caught them thinking about it!"

"Reverend," said Sybil so suddenly that the cleric dropped his spoon on his plate with a clatter. "Mister Todd is the Bondmaster of Roxborough. Reverend

Patterson," she said archly in Carlton's direction, "wants to marry me."

Carlton was uncertain which of her statements caused the Reverend Patterson more surprise. Looking first at Carlton with astonishment and then at Sybil with disbelief, he returned his gaze to Mrs. Vandy.

"He don't have any money," said the Major, to put an end to the topic.

"The Bondmaster of Roxborough, sir? Oh yes, he does, if you'll forgive my saying so," Reverend Patterson, out of his trance, addressed the Major. "I am reliably informed, sir, that the Todds of Roxborough have one of the best sugar plantations in this country, Major, with a fortune equaled by no one. I have plans to approach the Bondmaster himself for funds to assist our church in the course of my journey around the island."

"Why wait until you get to Roxborough," asked Sybil demurely, "when you have Roxborough right here?"

"Funds you want, Reverend?" Carlton smiled graciously at Sybil. "I'd be happy to oblige."

"Funds? Oblige? This whippersnapper nigger-buyer has a fortune? Eh, Patterson? Tell me, damn you!"

"Oh, without a doubt, sir. I would say that he is one of the wealthiest men in the country right now."

"Is that so, Mister Todd?" asked Sybil. "Then you'll be able to give Reverend Patterson something really substantial for his church. If I am going to marry the Reverend, I would not want him to be a poor parson, and if I were not going to marry him, I would extend to him the same generous thoughts."

"You are most kind, Miss Vandy," said the clergyman, trying to hide his embarrassment by concentrating on the evil mess still remaining on his plate.

"Marry! Marry! Marry!" The Major thumped his spoon on the table. "Ask your mother, ask your mother. Mister Todd?" The major assumed an expression of affability. "A word in your ear, Mister Todd. Let's leave these ladies and do some men's work. Come, will you?"

The Major's chair fell backwards with a crash as he stood up and stumbled toward the door. Catching himself on the door jamb, which Carlton decided was an art the Major had practiced to perfection, he waited for Carlton to join him.

"Come, my boy," said Vandy, pushing his arm under Carlton's to grip his elbow and steer him through the darkened reception room. "I've got some fine French brandy in my chambers which might prove acceptable to you. You do drink, don't you? Old enough for it, I suppose."

"Why, yes," said Carlton, smiling at the prospect of a drink after his long journey and confusing evening.

Vandy groped his way through a door leading from the reception area and then along a corridor, feeling his way with his free hand while clinging to Carlton with the other.

"Should I get a lamp, sir?" asked Carlton politely.

"Never know when you'll be blind, boy."

Carlton's foot came up against an obstruction which suddenly groaned. He stopped, but the major pulled him on.

"Wondered where he was," chuckled Vandy. "The door's here, then. Ah, yes."

Vandy opened the door into a room where three candles cast long shadows over the walls, which were hung with swords. Carefully, Carlton stepped over the body lying in the threshold. Vandy let go his grip of Carlton's elbow, steadied himself on the door jamb again, and aimed a kick at the backside of the body. The shape groaned and pulled itself out of the doorway to lie in the dark of the corridor. Carlton realized that the creature was a dwarf.

"Purged him," said Vandy simply. "Maybe too much. Maybe he's going to die. Don't know."

"He's your servant?"

"My doormat!" Vandy went over to an old wooden closet set into a recess in the thick stone wall of the room and opened it with a key he took from his pocket. He produced from its depths a bottle of brandy together with two glasses.

"Sometimes I feel brandy will be the death of me, Todd. Who ever would have thought that poison could taste so sweet? Won't you join me?" He poured a generous measure into a glass and a small shot into another, handing the smaller one to Carlton.

"Of course, parsons are notorious liars. Had a chaplain once, always preaching about the evils of drink. Never found the evils yet. The man died stone cold sober split in two by a Carib cutlass. That was evil, Todd, evil. Not the drink. The man lied, you see. Do you think that Patterson lies?"

"About his wanting to marry your daughter?"

"Zounds, sir! About your fortune."

"Roxborough is a large plantation, Major."

"So is mine, dammit! Mortaged up to here." Vandy held his brandy glass above his head, spilling some on his forehead as he did so.

"There is no mortgage on our property, Major, neither on buildings nor on slaves."

"None on the slaves? You feed them, too?"

"Of course."

"None on the slaves and you feed them, too." Vandy was thoughtful. "Of course, when I was a soldier in Antigua, I had a successful plantation myself. Dam' mistake to come here, though. Got this estate cheap, free you might say, from a traitorous Frenchie. But can't get the niggers to work.

"Some fellows make their money easily, give mortgages on niggers, you know, at ten percent. No risk. Want to marry my daughter, Todd?" He gave Carlton no chance to reply.

"Of course you do! Ten percent interest, quite a dowry, isn't it? Ask her mother, ask her mother." He poured himself another brandy, ignoring Carlton's empty glass.

"Show you the niggers tomorrow. You don't need to see them, of course. Just advance me what you like until I sell them. Reverend Patterson could marry you. Ask her mother."

Vandy's head lolled forward and then slowly his body toppled over onto the table. His hand still gripped the brandy glass upright as he came to rest in front of Carlton. Reaching for the bottle, Carlton poured himself a substantial draught and drained his glass. The major had begun to snore. Carlton put his glass down on the table, removed a candle from its holder on the wall, and slipped out of the room. In the corridor, he bent down to examine the Negro dwarf who lay buckled up in agony, his tiny knees drawn up to meet his enlarged head. His eyes were wide open, glazed with fear.

"What ails you, boy?" He held the candle over the slave's head, crouching down to hear him properly.

"Water, sah, water!"

"No water, boy," said Carlton standing up. "A shot of the major's brandy might aid you," he chuckled to himself as he returned to the room and poured a gill of the major's precious liquor into his glass. "Here, boy."

Carlton knelt beside the dwarf and tipped the contents down his throat. In the light of the candle, he saw the slave's eyes relax and then a smile spread across the creature's face as a shudder seized his grotesque body. With a gurgle, he died. Carlton frowned, stood up, and went back along the corridor to find where he was to sleep that night.

Morning gave Vandy Hall a saner aspect than it had had during the eccentricities of the night before. Although no gun announced the dawn as at Roxborough, Carlton woke early and found his way to the front balcony. To his pleasure, he saw Claudius sitting at the foot of the grand staircase, mournfully resting his head in his hands. Carlton crept silently down the steps and clapped both hands on the slave's shoulders.

The boy gave a squeal of terror, pitching his head round in sheer fright. "Oh, sir," he smiled his relief.

"I thought you were the Major, sir. What a terrible place this is, sir."

"Really," said Carlton. "Let's take a look around." He began to walk around the front entrance pathway, as Claudius gamboled like a dog around him, delighted to see his master again.

"There ain' nothing to see, sir. Not more than ten niggers in the place and the fields all gone back to bush, sir. Only two horses, those we saw yesterday. Slept in the stable, I did; didn't have supper, either."

"We're about the same, then, Claudius. They have a cook here?"

"I don't believe so. The old man who's the groom said the only female they have left here is that maid who sleeps in the house with Miss Sybil, sir. It's Miss Sybil who does protect her from the Major. They say the Major and his wife are crazy, if you'll excuse my observation. The niggers are all scared something awful of the Major, sir. Please, Mas Carlton, how long are we going to stay here?"

"As long as I want, Claudius, remember that. I find it most pleasant here. Look at that aspect." Carlton pointed to the view down the hillside running below them where coconut palms marked the progress of a river through the valley out to sea. "It's an appealing place to have a fine house and a plantation."

"The niggers say the soil is cursed, and the great house, too."

From a shack so small and low that he took it for a chicken house came the sound of a low whimpering. Claudius pulled back in fright.

"What's that?"

"I don't know, sir."

"Claudius, what became of the brave nigger who fought the Roseau pickpockets for his master's purse, eh?" Carlton cuffed the boy's ear. "Go see who's in there."

"Me, sah?"

Carlton looked around the deserted compound. "There's no one else, is there?"

"I don't want meddle wid de Major's torture, sah!"

"What's that, boy? You know what's in that chicken house? It ain't chickens, I'll swear. More like a nigger to me."

"Yes, sir, it is a nigger, sir. He be all right dere, sah."

"Rubbish. What's he doing there? The place isn't big enough for a pig, far less a slave."

"The Major put him there, sir. The old groom told me that the Major does call that his torture chamber."

"Dammit, boy, let's see." Carlton took his pistol from his belt, primed it, and fired at the padlock holding the door of the low shack. There was a yelp from inside, and Carlton knelt down to prize off the lock where it had broken with the force of his shot. He pulled open the door and, on his hands and knees, peered into the dark inside.

"Good heavens!"

"What is it, sir?" Claudius was jumping nervously.

"See for yourself!" Carlton moved away from the doorway, revolted by the stench from inside the miniature prison.

When Claudius knelt down, he perceived a Negro inside stretched out on the ground, shackles around his wrists binding him to the roof of the prison. The roof was no more than three feet from the ground and the position of the shackles further restricted movement anyone incarcerated within might have. Urged by Carlton, Claudius reached inside and loosened the bolts holding the shackles. The Negro's arms dropped beside him. Putting his own hands under his shoulders, Claudius slowly pulled the prisoner out of the tomb-like structure, laying him at Carlton's feet.

Carlton stared in amazement. The boy was naked and smeared with excreta. Perhaps no more than fifteen or sixteen, he had the most superb physique Carlton had seen. His features showed an intelligence undiminished by his confinement. Carlton took the calabash of water that Claudius brought from the nearby trough and held it to the nigger's lips. The boy drank slowly, as though determined to savor every

223

drop. When he finished, he forced himself into a sitting position with the help of Claudius.

"Thank you, sah!"

"You all right, boy?" Carlton felt quickly over the boy's body to check for any signs of injury. He passed his hands across his chest and down his stomach to his penis lying inert on his thigh. As he gripped it in his hand, Carlton was amused to feel an immediate stiffening. He pouched his testicles, bouncing them in his palm; they were firm and full. Running both his hands down the boy's legs, he found no defects in the muscles. Quickly he rolled the slave over and inspected his back. Except for recent scratches on his shoulder which should disappear without a trace when they healed, the boy seemed the most perfect specimen he had ever come across.

"You an African?" demanded Carlton, who had noted the liveliness in the boy's eyes now that they had accustomed themselves to the light again.

"Yas, sah. I does be a Yoruba, sah."

Carlton nodded with satisfaction.

"What's your name, boy?"

"Mingo, sah!"

Chapter 25

From Claudius, Carlton learned that Vandy's treatment of his slaves seemed to be an insane persecution. Only the day before his arrival, Carlton was told Vandy had nailed a girl to a tree by her ear because he thought she had been listening outside his room. During the night, the girl tore herself free from the tree, leaving her ear hanging by itself, and fled into the mountains to join the Maroons.

Carlton well understood the need for discipline. He suspected that in freeing Mingo, he had trespassed upon his host's generosity. Had Mingo been a less superb specimen, Carlton would have had no qualms in returning the slave to his coffin-sized prison. But if Mingo was to be believed, he had done nothing to deserve his punishment, and the old groom confirmed that the Major had imprisoned him four days before and seemed to have forgotten about him.

Carlton was determined to have Mingo. He was a fine nigger who looked as though he would sire a score of whelps. It troubled Carlton as to how he should go about acquiring him from the crazy Major. He was also puzzled about Sybil. She seemed acceptable enough and had the broad hips of a child-bearer.

Though Roxborough could not boast a house the size of Vandy Hall, he thought Sybil would find it acceptable and fit in admirably. He had no doubt that his father would approve. As for sleeping arrangements, she could have one of the guest rooms, Carlton decided, for he had no intention of giving up Ella to attend his wife every night. As long as she could bear a son for Roxborough, her function as mistress would be fulfilled. He might just as well take her as any other.

Walking up the steps to the house when he returned from the village, Carlton assessed the estate in greater detail. Shutter doors hung from the casements, slates had dropped off the roof, and there were rotten floorboards on the gallery decking. Weeds clogged the drive up to the hall, and broken bottles hurled out of the dining room windows littered the house gardens. Unless the Major was a miser with a hoard of gold as secret as his bottles of brandy, Carlton thought wryly, there seemed very little prospect of a proper dowry.

"Caw!" The shout was more like the cry of an angry crow.

Carlton turned from contemplating the desolation of the Vandy residence to find the Major himself standing at the top of the steps, wagging his finger at him.

"You bounder, Todd!" The Major's voice screeched again. "You think I don't know!"

"Know what, sir?" Carlton paused on the top step almost toe to toe with the loathsome Major. Catching the man's foul breath as he spoke, Carlton skirted round him to stand upwind on the gallery.

"You've been down to the bay, haven't you? Conspirin' with those Frenchies? The Reverend told me your man was French. Got to have French grandchildren, have I? Would have killed my father!"

"Sir," began Carlton, hoping to impress himself on the Major while he was having a fairly lucid spell. "There is a small matter I would be grateful for a chance to discuss with you."

"Of course there is, boy, of course there is." The Major gripped the arms of his chair, the blue veins prominent and ugly on the back of his pale thin hands.

"I was taking the air in a casual manner this morning, enjoying the delightful aspect. I chanced upon an interesting situation. A young Negro had somehow got himself incarcerated in a most awkward fashion. Seemed he might die if he remained in that predicament, so knowing that you would hardly care to lose such a valuable piece of merchandise, Major, I was pleased to release the nigger from his plight." Carlton watched the Major swaying back and forth in his chair, wondering how much had penetrated his addled brain.

"Boy, seeing as you're a French fancyman and I was more inclined to take me a Reverend for my only daughter, I was considerin' in my mind the matter of recompense. Financial persuasion rates highly in my thoughts, and in my good lady's thoughts, too." Abruptly the Major stopped swaying and held himself ramrod straight as he fixed his gaze on Carlton. "How much, Frenchie, how much?"

"For the nigger, major?"

"For the daughter, m'sieur."

Carlton frowned his surprise. "Major, I had always believed that the prospect of a dowry was not beyond possibility in this day and age."

The Major ignored the remark, rocking forward again in silence. "What are you so interested in niggers for, Todd?" he said suddenly. "Them niggers are all mortgaged animals. If they die before the moneylenders foreclose, what do I lose? Saves me having to feed them, too. They don't work, anyway."

Carlton was confused by the kind of thinking that would cause a fine Negro like the one called Mingo to be allowed to die because of his owner's financial situation.

"Last night," he said, preparing his own attack on the Major, "you mentioned the possibility of a second mortgage on your niggers for which you would pay interest at ten percent. It seems to me, Major, that unless you have more niggers buried alive in coffin-sheds, whom I have yet to find, then you have less than a dozen slaves on the whole plantation, and of that number one is tolerably fit for work. The chances of securing a second mortgage would seem to be slight.

From traditional sources, of course, Major. From personal acquaintances, things might be different. From a son-in-law, for example?"

Major Vandy pulled himself out of his chair in the jerky fashion which had already alarmed Carlton. With another contemptuous, crow-like squawk, he careened through the door into the reception room, accompanied by the noise of a falling table.

"Ask your mother!" echoed out to Carlton standing on the gallery, as the Major made his way into the depths of the house.

It was several days before Carlton saw the Major again. Although he was unable to understand how life proceeded at Vandy Hall, meals did turn up in the dining room and Mrs. Vandy played hostess. Sybil assumed her role as bride-to-be without any suggestion from Carlton, so he supposed that there had been a family conference and that there would soon be a marriage. He tried to engage the cleric in conversation at meal times but the man seemed to be so much in awe of him that it was difficult to extract any kind of sense at all. The clergyman always took off for his own chamber after eating, and Carlton saw him only at dinner. Aware of Mrs. Vandy's double life as cook and hostess, he was nervous about embarrassing her and deliberately kept away. Sybil, on her part, seemed to be keeping away from him. It was a relief for Carlton when, after dinner on the fourth day of his stay, Sybil hinted that she might like to go riding again.

"It would be my pleasure to escort you, Miss Sybil," volunteered Carlton.

"Fie, Mister Carlton!" interpolated the Vandy mother. "Sybil has her maid to escort her."

"That's right." Sybil's reply was obedient and swift.

"I could do with a little exercise myself, ma'am. With your permission, I would accompany Miss Sybil. She could show me some of the pleasing views of this part of the island."

So it was arranged. Sybil impressed Carlton with the radiance of her appearance as they set off, Claudius and Claire attending them a few paces behind. Mrs. Vandy watched from the gallery step to see that propriety was being observed.

As the bush trail swallowed them up, Carlton felt the oppressive influence of Vandy Hall fading. Sybil's smile grew warmer, and she chatted with a gaiety he had not expected. Appraising her as a woman and fully aware of the reluctance of white women to engage in love-play, he was prepared to concede that she would make a tolerable companion for life at Roxborough. Her maid, on the other hand, was a most desirable piece of flesh and, were she not continually in her mistress's presence, Carlton would have tried to relieve his pent-up feelings on her. The strain of four nights at Vandy Hall without even the smell of a wench was beginning to disturb him.

Suddenly Sybil spurred on her horse and cantered away in front of him without a word. She gave him a cheerful wave that was almost a challenge. He looked back at Claire for an explanation. "Your mistress likes to jest?"

"She does do dis sometime," allowed Claire, having been made a party to the strategy the Vandy family had concocted for the afternoon. "My horse slow, Massa. I fear for de mistress wid nobody to escort her. Go wid her, sah."

Carlton ignored the knowing gleam in the eyes of his own slave and urged his horse to pursue Sybil, who had already disappeared around a bend in the trail. When he galloped up to the curve, there was no sign of Sybil on the long straight stretch ahead. Worried that some mishap had befallen her, he sped his horse down the trail. He had gone some distance when he saw her horse standing beside the path. A voice hailed him, and he saw Sybil lying on the ground a few yards into the bush. She was rubbing her ankle.

"Oh, Carlton! My horse threw me. I think I must have sprained my ankle."

Carlton jumped down and rushed to kneel beside her "With your permission?" She nodded her head slightly and he took her ankle in his hand and caressed it with a tenderness which surprised her. She laid her head back on the grass, breathing deeply. "Does that ease the pain?" he asked anxiously.

"Oh yes, oh yes," she said. "I feel it in my head now. Perhaps I jarred it?"

Transferring his concern from her ankle to her head, Carlton placed his hand gently on her brow. She closed her eyes as though in a swoon, waited a few seconds, and then opened them again.

"Carlton," she murmured, "you are so kind. But, Lord, I do declare, if anyone spied us like this they would soon jump to a pretty conclusion."

Recoiling, Carlton snatched his hand away from her forehead. Sybil reached out and took his hand again, placing it on her chest.

"Don't concern yourself so, Carlton, no one comes this way." Sybil forced Carlton's hand to move over her breast. "I am being destroyed by the pain I have here; wouldn't you show it the tenderness you lavished on my ankle, Carlton?"

"Madam! You are in a state of shock." He tried to withdraw his hand.

"Perhaps I am," she sighed, locking her hands together behind his neck and pulling herself up to meet him. "Perhaps I am."

She pressed her lips forward to meet his, but he drew away rapidly, ducking out of her frantic grip and rising to his feet. Her expression switched from one of anticipation to the pout of a spoiled child. Carlton retreated from the thicket back onto the road.

"Claire! Claire! Your mistress needs you!" he called down the path.

Sybil did not know what to do. The plan, which had been arranged with her father, had been foiled. Already she could hear Claire and Claudius approaching. There was no way she could trap Carlton now. It had been planned that her father would ride up and discover them together, so that Major Vandy could extract a high bridal price from Carlton. Instead, she had belittled herself in the eyes of the man she was supposed to marry.

"It's my ankle," she lied to Claire, hoping to convince Carlton that the story of her fall was genuine. "It is paining me a little."

With appropriate commiserations, Sybil was returned to her horse and the party, gloomier than they had been when they left Vandy Hall, retraced their steps. Carlton considered the situation as he rode in silence. Sybil Vandy, it seemed, was not the reluctant bride she had pretended to be. However, he had no time to dwell on his shock as, rounding the bend in the trail, he was astounded to see Major Vandy, astride an old and very mangy donkey, jogging with determined effort toward them.

"Daddy!" Sybil's shout brought the donkey to an abrupt halt, almost hurtling the Major, whose eyes were on the ground, over its neck.

"What!" The Major caught himself around the donkey's ears and looked at the ground. He struggled to regain his posture and then, as though remembering a speech, addressed the party. "Oh, my little flower! What is this? Violated you, did he, the bla'guard. He will pay dearly for this. Yes, very dearly. How much would you say, Todd? How much!"

"Oh, Daddy!" Sybil was in despair. "I hate you. I want to marry Carlton! Let's go home and get married now."

"The price, Mister Todd? You cannot do to my daughter what you did without marrying her, no sir, even if you are a French baboon."

"Stop it, Daddy! Claudius, would you lead the Major back to the Hall, please?" Carlton nodded his agreement.

"But the rape, where's the rape?"

"There is no rape, Major Vandy. If I may say so, you have put rather too high a price on your kin and too low a value on your chattels, Major." Carlton produced his own horse into a jog, slapping the Major's donkey over its rump to start it off.

"I will give you gold for that nigger of yours to liquidate the mortgage on him, plus a certain amount as your consideration. That's the only price we have to discuss, Major."

The wedding was arranged within half an hour of their return to the house. It was only when Carlton reviewed the circumstances surrounding his entanglement with Sybil several weeks later that he saw that everything was part of a plan between the Major and his wife. How else, he realized, could Mrs. Vandy have contrived to cram herself into a gown more suited for a ball than the neglected grandeur of Vandy Hall? How else could the Reverend Patterson have mysteriously appeared in the dining room with a Bible under his arm with the wedding service already marked and, it appeared, learned by heart? Indeed, it seemed that everyone had been prepared for the wedding that day except for Claudius, who confessed himself ignorant of any plot.

The Major even broached a bottle of brandy as Reverend Patterson came to the end of his performance, and Carlton seized the glass he was offered with unbecoming eagerness. He followed the first brandy with a quick second one, celebrating the removal of the strain which had been troubling him since he arrived at Vandy Hall. He now had a wife and, if the Major stuck to his bargain, he had a prime young Yoruba he hoped would sire prizewinning progeny. Carlton was in a mellow mood as he accompanied the Major to his chamber to search for a second bottle.

"It's a good thing having a French son-in-law," cackled the Major as they groped their way along the passage. "He can appreciate fine wine!"

Perhaps it was the lack of dinner that day, or his not being accustomed to the deceptive mildness of French Cognac, or his own delight at being able to leave Vandy Hall at last. Whatever it was, Carlton was thoroughly bamboozled.

At daybreak, realization began to set in. He opened

his eyes, not in his new wife's chambers as he had expected, but in the stable. His head felt as though it had been kicked by one of the horses who shared the stable straw. He was completely naked, his head resting on someone's chest. He peered through the gloom at the person lying with him. It was Claudius.

Chapter 26

Carlton jogged along the trail, his blond curls glistening in the occasional shafts of sunlight that penetrated
through the overpowering bush. Behind him rode his
wife, her eyes ablaze with dark rebellion as she contemplated the back of his neck. This ill-tempered procession was led by Claudius astride his own horse and
holding a cutlass to lop off the branches of trees which
might impede their progress. A fourth horse, laden
with a chest which contained Sybil's meager possessions, and led by the grinning boy Carlton had bought
from Sybil's father, brought up the rear.

The presence of this slave of her father's was one
of the many things on Sybil's mind that morning. She
was oblivious to the almost idyllic setting. No rain
was in sight. They were shaded from the heat of the
sun by the overhanging vegetation and, in addition,
there was a light breeze to keep them cool. The noises
of the forest around them were romantic enough with
a stream gurgling alongside the trail and the chirping
of tropical birds. If romance had been in Sybil's mind
the night before as she waited for her new husband, it
had been shattered by his subsequent behavior.

Where he spent the night she did not know. He
claimed that he had been drinking and had fallen
asleep in the stable. Her father had been in one of his
usual liverish moods that morning, unable to see, walk,

or speak clearly. It had been an exasperating departure from Vandy Hall. Her mother had done nothing but wail, and in addition Claire had disappeared. Sybil had been set on taking Claire with her, and she was determined to do so after her husband's deliberate absence on the wedding night. But in the morning Claire was nowhere to be found. She pleaded with Carlton to search for her, but he had laughed and ordered their immediate departure for Roseau, bringing that stinking nigger along with them. Even the thought of a few days in the capital, while she had her trousseau made up, did nothing to mollify her.

With the unexpected fury of a hurricane, Sybil's life had been upturned since she had taken that ride with Carlton the afternoon before. True, now she was married, but it was not on the terms she had expected. It was all her husband's fault. She scowled in her moodiness at the figure in front of her, wondering how Carlton could dare treat her so lightly.

Carlton himself, in spite of the relaxed posture as he guided his horse along the narrow trail, was far from happy. The turmoil of events had puzzled him. He regarded himself as lucky to get away from Vandy Hall with a bride and a fine nigger, but was perturbed by the change in Sybil from a robust maiden to a forward hussy in less than twenty-four hours.

When the trail widened, Sybil resolved to accost her husband again on the matter of the missing Claire. She nudged her horse alongside his. Carlton was relieved to see the sulkiness had lifted from her features.

"Are you pleased to be going to Roseau, Sybil?" he inquired politely.

She shrugged her shoulders. "I don't mind."

"You'll be able to buy a trousseau to bedazzle everyone."

"And if I get such a trousseau," she retorted, "how am I supposed to dress?"

"It was not I who sent off your maid, Sybil." Carlton believed he had at last discovered the reason for her vexation.

"That's what you say! But you wouldn't search for her, would you?"

"Sybil, if one of my slaves chooses to escape and I hunt him down and capture him, do you think that I would return him to his former occupation? A runaway suffers a slow death, Sybil, to show the others so they don't take it into their woolly heads to flee as well. Do you think that I would tolerate Claire in your service after she has clearly indicated her own mistaken preference for the life of a Maroon runaway?"

Sybil renewed her sulky pout. "You can say what you like," she moaned. "I don't believe that you ever wanted me to have Claire in the first place."

"I was never consulted."

"Do I have to consult you when I want to bring my own property?"

"Why, no, my dear! There are plenty of slaves at Roxborough, Sybil. Some well-seasoned wenches whom you'll find a thousand times better than your spoiled pet Claire. I'll give you one for yourself."

"I don't want one of your cast-off whores!"

"Sybil!" Carlton gripped the reins of his horse in surprise, bringing the animal to a sudden halt. His wife continued to follow Claudius along the trail. In fury, Carlton raised his riding whip to strike her, but Mingo, not watching the progress of his master, careened into the back of Carlton's horse.

"Oh, massa! I does be followin' dat Claudius, sah, an' don't see you does be stop, sah. Is dere anything yuh does be missin', sah?" Mingo added as he saw the confused look of anger on his master's face.

Carlton shook his head, jabbing his heels into the horse. "No, Mingo," he said softly, distracted by the slave's concern. "You ever been to the city, Mingo?"

"Me, sah? Oh no, sah."

"I'm going to get you a smart livery when we get to Roseau, Mingo, for you to be a real Roxborough nigger."

"I does be proud to serve you, sah."

Carlton nodded his head, his humor restored. A

wife, he decided as he caught up with Sybil, is a kind of animal not blessed with the intelligence of a slave. But, for the sake of his father, he was prepared to put up with this woman so that Roxborough could have the white heir the old man craved.

"Do you know where your father bought that slave?" he asked casually after they had ridden together in silence for a few minutes. Sybil looked at him blankly. "That nigger with us, Mingo."

"No idea!"

"How curious."

"What do you mean?"

"I regard it as curious that a man like your father should have a Negro of such perfect proportions and strength on his compound and never speak about him."

"My father did not like niggers. They were slaves to work and to be beaten if they did not work. They were all so lazy, they began to run away from the time Daddy took over the plantation."

"But that one Mingo didn't run, did he?"

"I suppose not." Sybil relented a little, seeing that she had already got the better of Carlton once that morning. "Mingo?" She pretended to think. "Oh, yes, Daddy brought him from Antigua when he came here. He was only a little boy then, and Mummy wanted him to work in the kitchen."

"That may account for his apparent good health, then." Carlton grinned, looking back at the boy trotting along to keep up with them. "If he was in the kitchen he wouldn't go short of rations at all. Looks strong enough to be a fighter," he mused.

"A what?" Sybil was alarmed.

"A fighter. You know, I've seen them in Roseau already. They have regular tourneys where prize niggers fight. A gentleman can make a fortune out of a good nigger."

"It sounds disgusting. I would never permit Mingo to become a fighter. To be torn apart by other niggers while gentlemen gamble."

"Oh!" said Carlton, too excited by the prospect to

have time for his wife's petulance. "First you don't know anything about him, and now you don't want him to earn his keep in a gentlemanly sport. The boy's made for fighting, just look at him." Again Carlton turned in his saddle to admire Mingo. The boy touched his forehead in a gesture of respect when he observed his new master watching him.

"I'll have none of it!" Sybil snorted, lapsing back into sulkiness for the balance of the journey.

Carlton, fired by the new idea he had for Mingo's future, rode on to discuss the project with Claudius, who confirmed that there were, indeed, some fighting Negroes in Roseau.

"A gentleman can win himself a tidy packet, sir," claimed Claudius. "I've seen it many times."

"Do you think my new nigger has any prospects?"

It was the turn of Claudius to glance back and assess Mingo. "I don't know, sir. He's built square enough. Mister Cleve Moult is the man who would know, sir. He owns the Dominican champion, a nigger called Karamantee Jack."

"Roxborough, isn't it?" boomed Cleve as he saw Carlton hesitate in the doorway of his tavern in Roseau. " 'Bout time you came to Cleve's tavern, don't you think!"

Some of the customers snorted with laughter as they watched Carlton stride through the crowd to greet the patron. Cleve shook his hand warmly. "Don't worry about these town lackeys, young man. I know about you. Knew your father. I'm proud to have you honoring my establishment!" Cleve continued to pump Carlton's hand in an elaborate handshake, without rising from his chair. He turned to the circle of young men surrounding him, indicating a chair for Carlton.

"You boyos from England may think you know it all, but there's none of you could manage a plantation like Roxborough. Finest sugar in Dominica comes from there. And rum, too! This lad here is the Bondmaster." The patronage of Cleve Moult was enough to make anyone respect the person so glowingly introduced, and the circle around Cleve nodded their heads courteously at Carlton.

"Not lace and fine clothes makes a man, boyos," said Cleve, slapping the backside of a black girl flouncing past with a tray of foaming tankards held high over her head. "Though it helps!" He looked over his tankard at Carlton, who accepted the remark with a shrug.

"I'm a planter, Moult, not a city man. Like a word with you, I would."

"Go ahead, sir!"

Carlton looked around at the circle of men who seemed to constitute Moult's council. He judged them all to be bachelors fresh from England, young dandies sent overseas to make their fortunes. The kind of specimen his father despised, and Carlton realized he was beginning to share his father's views. Well, if they wanted to know his business, he would tell them.

"We're easing up on sugar now, Moult. Interested in niggers, I am. Fighting niggers."

Moult eased himself forward as Carlton was speaking, his flabby cheeks quivering with interest.

"Got a new nigger now, young like. As you are renowned as the expert on fighters, it occurred to me that you might care to take a look at him. Maybe you could advise me whether he has prospects. Needs training and fattening, of course, but he might have something."

"Sure!" Moult was delighted. "Let's see him."

"Here?" Carlton glanced around. The tavern was packed with people. There were even some white women in an alcove who were being squired by arrogant gentlemen in powdered wigs and well-cut clothes. "Here?" he repeated.

"Why not? Just a nigger, ain't he?"

Carlton looked toward the entrance and beckoned to Claudius to bring Mingo. The crowd parted as the two slaves walked through. Seeing him in his ragged pantaloons and dust-smeared skin, Carlton felt ashamed of his nigger beside the elegant whites. But Mingo's self-assured swagger made up for his lack of raiment. He stood in front of Moult, who was shaking with excitement.

"Blow me down if he ain't a Yoruba!" said Cleve. "Must be a chief's son too, with a bearing like that."

"You rate him highly?" demanded Carlton anxiously.

"Generations of breeding must have gone into siring this boy, Todd! Chiefs in Africa are like our own Royal Family. Pedigree blood the lot of them, even though they are niggers. Of course I rate him highly. No way to judge his intelligence, but his physique is pure Yoruba."

"Think he'd make a fighter?"

"Fighter be damned! How much do you want for him?"

"Not for sale!" Carlton was pleased. "I'm never going to sell this nigger. Might fight him, though."

Moult nodded his head, and his jowls shook against the collar of his coat. "Aye, that could be a good plan. Need some more challengers for my Karamantee, I do. Jack will mash your nigger to pulp, though, which will be a shame, but there's some will back him, I've no doubt. Brelan, sir?"

Carlton had not often played cards, and never with gentlemen such as those who surrounded Moult. However, he did not want to offend, lest it affect future business between them, so he accepted the invitation to join this version of poker. He dismissed Mingo and Claudius to wait for him outside and ordered a jug of rum before taking his seat at the gaming table. Affecting an air of familiarity with the game which misled no one, he soon forgot his resolve to return to his wife at the lodging house.

Claudius peeped in through the doorway from time to time and shrugged his shoulders as he saw his master losing every hand. He curled up on the floor of the gallery beside Mingo to sleep out the night. It was almost dawn when Carlton woke him with an angry kick in his side.

Chapter 27

When Carlton staggered back to the rooms they occupied in the lodging house soon after dawn, Sybil berated him for staying out the whole night. Because he had expected this reaction, he was unmoved by her vexation. He was more concerned that this might be a foretaste of her desire to assert her will over his. In quiet anger, he threw some money on her bed and told her to go out and buy whatever fancy clothes she wanted. Ordering Claudius to accompany her, he strode unsteadily into the adjoining bedroom, drew the bolt on the door, and, with relief, threw himself on the bed.

His head was muzzy when he woke, and the room was unbearably hot. There was no sound from the bedroom next door, so Carlton assumed that his wife was still out. He eased himself off the bed, shook his head, and seeing that he still had his boots on, clomped across the floor and unbolted the door. His wife's room was empty. He walked through and opened the door into the passageway. An inert body tumbled through.

"Sah!" the body yelped.

"Mingo! What are you doing asleep outside the mistress's door?"

"Claudius done tell me wait here for when you does call me, Mas Carlton."

Carlton grinned. The nigger was already burnishing his field talk to speak like a house slave. Moult had

241

told him that Yorubas were reputed to have the best physique and intelligence of all the Negroes shipped from Africa. Perhaps it was true.

"If you want to serve me, Mingo, you have to serve me good. Hurry to the washhouse and carry me a bath. You can bathe me, boy, before I go out and see the nigger you're bound to fight one day."

Carlton was greatly refreshed after his bath. He instructed Mingo to strip down and get into the tub and wash himself in his dirty water before he threw it out. Sorting through the clothes he had worn when he arrived in Roseau nearly two weeks before, Carlton found his old pants and undershirt. He threw them at Mingo to put on when the boy emerged dripping from the tub to stand naked on the floor of the bedroom. The sight made Carlton nod appreciatively. The muscles bulged on the youth's arms, and his thighs were thick and firm.

"You sure are a gradely nigger, Mingo. When we get back to Roxborough, it's cow meat for you every day to build up your strength so you can give me a whole litter of whelps. I'm going to fight you and breed you, boy."

Carlton nodded his head again with satisfaction as he sat on the bed and buttoned up his shirt. "Get those keks on and throw out the water, and then let's see if we can find us some dinner."

Certain that Claudius was attending to his wife, Carlton strolled around the town trailed by Mingo. He was proud of the envious glances his slave attracted. Even though his clothes were ill-fitting, there was no mistaking the quality of the nigger. It was this reaction which decided Carlton to make a brief visit to the casino. He would have a quick drink with Cleve Moult before returning to the lodging house to spend the evening with Sybil. Night was falling when he located the casino. He instructed Mingo to wait outside and not move for anyone, before entering the bar.

Moult greeted him warmly from his usual seat. The casino was not as full as the night before, and Carlton was relieved to see that Moult did not have his couriers around him. He sat on the bench beside Moult and accepted a punch from the serving wench.

"I hear you've been strutting around town with that nigger of yours. Still aiming to fight him, are you?"

Carlton was delighted. "A few months' training and the pure air of Roxborough and he'll wrest that champion's crown from any nigger of yours, Moult!"

"What!" roared the big man, shaking with amusement and pounding a hefty slap on Carlton's thigh. "That's fighting talk, all right! I like that, yes, I like that. Especially," Moult added, squinting at Carlton from the depths of his pig-like face, "especially when it comes from a wealthy young gentleman like yourself with money to back up his tongue."

"I'll stake money on my nigger when he's ready, Moult," Carlton bridled.

"He won't fight Karamantee Jack unless you do, that's certain."

Time began to slip by as more people drifted into the casino, and Moult's circle of cronies grew around him. It was a convivial crowd, and each newcomer sponsored a tray of drinks as he arrived. Carlton was enjoying the company, and when a game of brelan was suggested, he was eager to join in and try to recoup his losses of the night before. The cards had just been dealt for the first time when he realized that he was being addressed by someone standing at his side. He turned irritably.

"Mas Carlton, sah?"

"Don't you know not to interrupt a gentleman when he's busy, boy!"

It was Claudius, who stood first on one leg and then on the other, his face creased with anxiety at having to disturb his master. "I'm sorry, sir. The mistress, sir."

"Lower your voice, boy," urged Carlton, glancing around to see if any of the group were listening. Each was checking his hand of cards. "What is it?"

"She says, sir." Claudius hesitated, bending forward

so he could whisper into his master's ear. "She says that she does not expect to be kept up the whole night awaiting your return, sir."

Carlton nodded his head to show that he understood, frowning at the audacity of the woman he had married. In his distraction, he played his hand without thinking and was surprised when Moult's cry broke into his thoughts.

"That's a fine start to the evening, Todd! A win first round bodes well for the night. That nigger brought you luck." Moult peered at the slave he saw standing beside Carlton. "Oh, it's Claudius, is it? Know him well. Not a trick that nigger doesn't know. Bought him, have you? You have a rare eye for the blackies, and no mistake."

The giggling which greeted the remark Carlton attributed to the lack of respect of city-dwellers for country planters. He resolved to show them that he was not the bumpkin they might think. He doubled his stake and took his cards for the next round. He won. He went straight into the third, which he lost. He lost the fourth and the fifth but came back and won the sixth. He had quite forgotten Claudius as he concentrated on the game and quaffed the glasses of punch set up on the bench beside him.

Claudius crouched down on the ground to watch his master, not daring to speak for fear he might be flung out. He liked the atmosphere of the casino, and his eager eyes took in everything that was happening. Occasionally the serving wenches winked at him, and one managed to place a cup with rum in it near him. Unobserved by anyone, or so he thought, he gulped the contents and looked back at the game. His master was on a bad losing streak. He threw his cards down in disgust.

"I'm not wagering another bit!" Carlton exclaimed, his voice gruff with rum. "Cleve Moult, sir, I'll be bidding you adieu."

"Of course, of course," said Moult. "We understand, don't we, gentlemen? No man likes to lose."

"I can bear to lose, sir!" As Moult had expected, Carlton was goaded by his words into staying on. "Deal the cards, sir!"

"Did I not hear you correctly? Did I not hear you say that you would not wager another bit?" Moult raised his eyebrow mockingly.

"Aye," said Carlton, falling into the trap. "You did."

"Then perhaps you'll wager that nigger there." Moult indicated with a nod of his bloated head the spot where Claudius was trying to blend into the shadows.

Carlton was surprised to see Claudius. The slave shook his head as though to urge Carlton not to accept the bet.

"Of course, Moult, why not? I'll wager my nigger if you'll wager . . ." He cast his eye around the bar and picked out one of the wenches attending a group of officers at a corner table, "that wench yonder."

"My pleasure."

Wagering slaves instead of gold gave the game a new zest. Others came in to join. Claudius lost track of who owned him from round to round, praying that his master would be the one who would win in the end. The game blazed on with jugs of rum circulating at a great pace. Moult was delighted at the spurt in business, visitors and residents keen to play a hand to see if they could win a serving wench or slave boy.

When the dawn broke, Carlton had passed out and lay asleep on the floor of the casino. Moult snored in his chair, and other customers lay drunkenly on benches and in corners. The firing of the morning gun roused Carlton. He groped his way over sleeping bodies, angrily kicking Claudius, whom he had lost to Cleve Moult. Mingo greeted him outside. Carlton peered at him through bloodshot eyes. He was thankful that at least he had not wagered Mingo.

"Get your mistress!" he growled. "And the horses. We're going to Roxborough!"

If Sybil had hopes that the luxuries of Roxborough Hall would compensate her for the heartlessness of her husband, they were dashed as soon as she glimpsed the wooden house which, Carlton grumpily informed her as they rode up the drive after crossing the river, was to be her home. To her, the place looked no better than an overseer's cottage. She wanted to cry, but she had the feeling that to do so would have given her husband pleasure. She bit her lip, regretting once again the foolish maneuvers which resulted in this marriage.

The sight of so many smiling slaves waving joyously to her as they rode through the plantation did not ease her. No doubt her husband had a huge number of niggers, as he had said. The vast acreage of the plantation seemed to be well cared for. Her husband's wealth, she began to realize, had not been lavished on comforts. A woman's touch, yes, her touch, could make Roxborough Hall a home.

The old man who greeted them as they arrived hugged Carlton affectionately, extending a fragile hand to shake her own.

"Son, what ails you? You look tired. Ah!" The old man broke into a wheezy laughter. "This beautiful wife of yours draining the energy out of you, eh!"

Sybil shuddered inwardly. She tried to ignore the crowd of black faces watching her as she moved up the steps followed by Carlton and his father clasping each other enthusiastically.

"You'll soon get accustomed to our simple house," said Hayes Todd when they had settled down on the balcony. An old slave brought out a jug of sangaree. Although she refused at first, Hayes pressed Sybil to accept a glass and, as she felt so utterly dejected, she agreed.

"Always meant to build a great house," Hayes Todd continued, "but after my wife died, never got around to it. Shouldn't be surprised if Carlton doesn't start now he has such a pretty wife to care for."

"Too much money, Da," growled Carlton. "Got me a new nigger, Da. This one's a Yoruba, a real fighter. I'm planning to train him and breed him, too."

Sybil closed her eyes to the chatter of the two men,

letting the sangaree work on her. She hardly noticed when Bo'jack replenished her glass. Below the house, a steady stream of Negroes passed along the trails which surrounded the place. All of them looked up in her direction. If she was being appraised, she decided, then she'd better look the part of the Bondmaster's mistress. She sat up and addressed the two men.

"Excuse me, gentlemen." She smiled coldly. "I would be obliged if my husband would show me our chambers. The ride has been long, and I would fain refresh myself."

Hayes looked at her in surprise, but quickly recovered himself. "Of course, my dear, how selfish of me. I was monopolizing my son, your husband, quite without thought to your convenience and comfort. You will, of course, share Carlton's chambers. That used to be my own wife's quarters."

"I had thought, sir, that Sybil would prefer her own chamber. The guest room would be ideal for her. It is near the back stairs so her own maid can attend her without disturbing the rest of the household."

"Very well, son, you know best."

"You will have your pick of girls to serve you tomorrow, Sybil," called Carlton after supper, as his wife went out onto the balcony to make her way around to the room she had been given. She answered him with a backwards glance of such distress that Hayes was obliged to tax Carlton about his bride's apparent unhappiness.

"I suppose I am the one to blame, sir." He related the events of the past few nights.

Hayes chuckled. "Son, you have had quite an education. I'm pleased that you are back here where you belong. I would advise you to redeem that nigger, though. He sounds quite capable. Otherwise, I declare you have done remarkably well. A headstrong woman for your wife will keep you out of mischief. She'll bear you plenty of children, son, an heir for Roxborough. Go to her now, son. Now!"

Sybil, having observed that her role as the injured party did not move her husband, resolved to accommodate him as willingly as he demanded. So when he came to her later that evening, the tensions which had grown between them dropped suddenly away. In raptures, and fired by her husband's brutal manliness, Sybil clung to Carlton with an urgency she had subdued for years. No man had ever entered her, and at last she was about to soar to womanhood.

Carlton was unprepared for such passion in a white woman, having been warned constantly about their coolness of nature. He was quickly aroused. However, considering his wife's virginity and his father's advice about caution with white women, he endeavored to restrain himself. It was useless. His wife was insatiable.

Afterwards, as he lay beside her and her fingers idly explored his chest, he thought it curious that his wife should display such ardor. He recalled her wanton behavior in the woods near her home the afternoon of their marriage. Then it struck him!

He leaped out of bed and turned up the lantern which glowed by the door. Holding it over the bed, he pulled back the sheet which covered Sybil, ignoring her protests. There was not a sign of blood. His wife was not a virgin after all.

Carlton threw open the door and stepped out onto the gallery without a word. The moon was poised above the house, its brightness causing the shredded leaves of the coconut palms to throw weird shadows on him as he stomped along the gallery to his own room. He flung open the door and stepped inside, trembling as he realized now he had been tricked. He locked the door behind him and plunged onto his own bed, horrified at his discovery. He had married a whore. Whatever airs and graces Sybil might have, she was no better than a nigger.

He rolled onto his back as the arms of Ella, who had been lying in his bed waiting, began to explore his nakedness.

BOOK TWO

Mingo

Chapter 28

Mingo stepped out of the river, shaking drops of water from his skin like a *chien*. He rubbed his hands slowly down his face from his forehead, grinding his palms into his eyes and then down his beautifully formed cheeks and under his jaw until his fingers touched above his *quaj*. He shook his head then wiped his hands slowly down his naked body to squeeze the water off his skin.

He loved the shape and size of his body and let his hands linger on his *tuli* until he felt the blood stirring within him. He shrugged his shoulders, breaking into a jog trot on the spot, raising his knees high as his master had told him to do. In the shade of the mango tree overhanging the river where the sun blinked through the leaves only when the wind stirred the trees, Mingo reveled in the development of his splendid physique.

It was his new master who had taught him to appreciate his body. Unlike the other slaves on the plantation, Mingo had no special duties apart from the exercises he was given to do each day by his master. At first, it had been difficult for him to understand, and it was only when he saw the delight in his master's face when he touched his body and saw how it was developing that he realized this was the way he could please Mas Carlton.

Every week, his master measured the different parts of his body to see if he had expanded. His thighs had thickened up, his shoulders were broader, and his arms stronger. For Mingo, it was as though a new man—a clean, strong man—had moved into his body and was replacing the boy who had dwelt there before.

Mingo continued to dance around on the riverbank, glowing warmer as he watched the water rush over the stones on the river bed, forming crystal sprays in the air. He paused in his dance and bent down to grab his calico pantaloons before running naked along the riverbank in the direction of the slave quarters. If he hurried, he thought, pulling on his pants quickly, he would have time to see Eurilla in her *kie* before returning to the big house where his master would be sleeping after dinner.

He had been by the river for an hour, so he would only have a few minutes with Eurilla, but it would be good to see his *ti-fi* again. At night, it was impossible to visit her, as the master kept him locked in the barn with the other slaves he called his stallions. One day, his master had told him, he would have his own filly and could choose the best on the plantation.

Mingo had first seen Eurilia when she had trailed after the small gang one morning as he was doing his exercises under the master's supervision in the front yard. Although he thought of her as his *ti-fi,* he knew she could only be that if his master said so.

"Oh!" said Eurilia, looking up as his shadow fell across her as she sat outside the *kie* she shared with one of the old women. "Mingo! You surprised me."

She devoured the boy with her eyes as he stood towering over her. Under his pantaloons, his *tuli* bulged, and she longed to reach up and touch it. She glanced quickly around. Ma Bess was inside the *kie* and none of the children playing around the base of the big flamboyant tree shading their home were watching. She put her hand on his knee, plying his flesh with her fingers.

251

"Mingo!" she sighed. "Every night I does be waitin' for yuh to sleep wid me. I be virgin, Mingo, jest for you."

Mingo gulped, breaking into a jig beside the girl. Her hair was newly plaited with tiny tufts adding to her prettiness. Her breasts, under the loose calico shift she was wearing, were small and barely formed. Her legs, soft and slender, stretched out on the ground in front of her. She was about two years younger than Mingo, and she watched him with a mixture of scorn and desire.

"Dose other girls does have deir man, Mingo. Me alone does wait so long."

"Eurilia," said Mingo squatting on his haunches beside her. "You does know more about de way things does be dan me. De massa say he does be keepin' me for de best filly on de plantation an' I bound to respect de massa."

"You be one big fool! So he does tell all de young men wid de pretty faces an' den he does lock dem up in de barn, but dey still does love deir women in de bush when dey get de chance."

"You too set yourself, girl! Is me dat de massa does say does go'n be de champin Dominique an' he did command me no girls when I does be trainin' 'cause dey does drain all my vital strength from my body. You can see I does be gittin' more strong every day." He flexed his arm muscles proudly.

"You does think too much of de massa. I espect yuh does be scared he go'n cut yuh grain like he done dat brudder of mine last year."

"You don' see how de massa can get vex, den?"

"All buckras does get vex' if yuh do or if yuh don't. Dat's wha' Ma Bess does say."

"Dat be true, Eurilia. I done have a massa confine me in a box fuh plenty days widout food or nothing. It was Mas Carlton done release me."

Eurilia looked at Mingo in awe. "Da's why yuh does

like de massa so?" She stroked his calf as he squatted beside her.

"Ah do anything for de massa. You don't know how all you niggers does have de best life right here at Roxbruh. Dere ain't no work here but a liddle cane an' yuh does git victuals every week to feed yourself good. Dat plantation for de Massa Majah dey don't give no food an' we niggers got to grow our provisions in our gardens or we don't eat nothing! Dat Mas Carlton be de best buckra a nigger ever done see."

Eurilia sniffed. "Yuh don't want me, dat's all."

Mingo frowned at the girl, unable to understand this strange reaction. "Of course I does want yuh. De massa . . ."

Don' tell me nothin' about de massa. You just like his fancy *neg*! Dat Pool afraid come by de *kie* whenever he does want an' he does live in de house wid de buckras. You does sleep in de barn wid de bucks. You don't be good enough for de house wid de *bekés*, no sah!"

Eurilia twisted herself around to express her pique, hoping that Mingo would respond by grabbing her shoulder and pulling her around to feed on his lips. Instead there was silence. She turned back sharply. Mingo had stood up and stepped back two paces to look at her. She noticed the smouldering rage in his eyes.

"You sure be a temptress, Eurilia. My massa does be right when he does tell me so. De quarters wimmin does be bad wimmin for a *nom* like me. Mingo go'n be champin Dominique come next year an' den I does have any of de wimmin I does wan'. Dats what my massa done tell me an' he ain't tell dat to nobody, not dat Pool. Dis Mingo go'n be Roxbruh prize nigger, de massa say. You can just keep yourself for when I does be ready, Eurilia!"

Mingo turned his back on the little girl, who had sunk onto the ground in an effort to hold him around his ankles. He began to walk with determination up the path to the house. Even when Eurilia's loud sobs filled the air and he heard the wailing of the quarter's women as they rushed to see what was wrong, he did not turn back.

When he was sure he was out of sight of the commotion in quarters, Mingo broke into a steady run up the hill. Even if his master was still sleeping, Mingo knew that after his bath he was supposed to go to Ma Phoebe for a rubdown with snake oil. Ma Phoebe was waiting for him, sitting on a bench outside the kitchen, the basin of snake oil on the ground beside her.

"Boy!" she said as he trotted up and squatted down with his back to her, "I done suspect dat you was at de quarters behind dat Eurilia chit yuh bin go'n long time."

"Ah was exercising me body, by de river, Ma Phoebe." Mingo wondered how the old cook seemed to know so much. He had never mentioned Eurilia's name to her, and yet here she was speaking about the girl as though it was a matter of daily conversation between them. He was thankful he had left Eurilia so quickly. If Mas Carlton were to find out, then there would be trouble.

"You see how long I does be waitin' for yuh, boy? See de grease done turn to liquid oil already in de heat." Phoebe dipped her large hand into the calabash containing the oil and slapped some quickly onto Mingo's neck. She smeared it over his shoulders, rubbing in the drips as it started to trickle down his back.

"You sure yuh don't pass by de quarters now?"

Mingo twisted his head to look straight into the old crone's eyes set deep into her pudgy face. They were bloodshot and yellow but peered intently into his own. He nodded his head, turning back so that she could proceed with the massage.

"I done pass by de *kie* an' say *bonjew* to de *ti-fi*," he admitted sulkily. "Da's all though," he added hastily in case she misinterpreted his remark as defiance of his master's instructions.

"Mas Carlton sure be vex' when he hears dat." Ma Phoebe pummeled his back with the side of her palm. "He done tell yuh plenty times stay way from de quarters. Lie down, boy!"

Ma Phoebe put her foot under his bottom as he squatted in front of her and tipped him up on his face. Before he had a chance to recover, she placed her massive foot on his backside, pinning him to the ground. She poured grease from the calabash down his legs and started to rub the oil into the back of his thighs.

"You sure growin' mighty pretty, boy," murmured Ma Phoebe appreciatively. "Don't surprise me none dat you hot for dat chit."

Spitting out the dirt which he had nearly swallowed when he fell to the ground, Mingo wriggled his body so that he could move his head around to see Ma Phoebe. She had her back to him now, concentrating on kneading the muscles in his leg.

"You go'n tell Mas Carlton, Ma Phoebe?" Mingo addressed his plea to the cook's fat backside, which was all he could see of her.

"Who tell yuh dat, boy? Here," she eased herself off his body, "roll over your carcass so I can do yo' belly."

When Mingo had first been ordered to have his snake oil massage from Ma Phoebe, he had been surprised. Now that he had undergone the treatment for nearly four months, he thought he understood his master's reasoning, for Ma Phoebe had the strength and dexterity of any man. As she was also a powerful conjure woman herself, Mingo assumed that she would impart a superhuman strength to him with her daily massages. Even though she was a woman, Mingo was never embarrassed by the lavish attention Ma Phoebe was accustomed to paying him. Today, lying on his back gazing at the roof of the house, he was conscious of Ma Phoebe's hands being heavier on his stomach than usual. Her fingers began to slide under the tie holding his pantaloons and slipped into the short curly hairs of his *puel.*

"A boy like you wid all de red meat I does feed yuh, does need to drain heself, though, boy." Ma Phoebe was gurgling, her flabby arms moving like the cogs of the waterwheel at the mill.

"When you does feel de heat on yuh, boy, is yo' Ma Phoebe dat can cool de blood, not one of dem chits from de quarters. Yuh know dat, boy?"

Ma Phoebe turned her massive face to look directly at him, spraying his chest with perspiration pouring from her forehead. She punched him with her clenched fist on his stomach, but he saw the blow coming and tensed his muscles to take it.

"Lay it in to him, Ma Phoebe! He'll never meet a man can give him blows like you."

Looking up, they both saw Mas Carlton watching from the back gallery. He began to walk down the steps toward them.

"Yuh want I should tell him, den?" hissed Ma Phoebe.

"No, Ma Phoebe!"

"Da's all right den. Yuh leave it to yo' Ma Phoebe."

"How's he shaping up today, Ma Phoebe?" demanded Carlton, as the cook got up off her haunches and stood behind him. He took out a handkerchief to dab his nose as the smell wafted up to him from Mingo stretched out on the earth.

"Get up, boy!" ordered Ma Phoebe. Mingo struggled to his feet and took the calabash reluctantly as Ma Phoebe proffered it to him. "Drink dis! When he does drink de oil he does build de bones stronger, sah," she explained to Carlton, who wrinkled his nose at the disgusting smell of the snake grease.

Doubtfully, Mingo held the calabash to his lips, trying not to breathe in the stench. He drained the grease down his throat, flexing his muscles for his master to see the progress he was making. Ma Phoebe took the calabash from him so he could stand with his hands on his hips to enable Mas Carlton to feel his muscles.

"I'll vouch you smell more rank than a rotten rat, Mingo, but you are coming along splendidly."

Mingo felt the gentle touch of his master's hands on his hard muscles, the whiteness of his masters fingers contrasting vividly with the blue-blackness of his skin.

"Why you can't leave that nigger alone and come and give your wife some attention I don't know!" The voice startled Ma Phoebe and Mingo, who both looked up at the gallery. Mas Carlton, on the other hand, continued to feel Mingo's biceps.

"Pawing that nigger is indecent, that's what it is!"

"This nigger, my dearest one," said Carlton softly, between clenched teeth, "is going to make us enough money to be able to build the great house you crave."

"That nigger is just your fancy slave to go and fight in the Roseau taverns. I'm sick and tired of the time you spend with these depraved Hottentots. A husband should spend time with his wife, not playing with his niggers all day!"

Mingo watched Mistress Sybil raise the glass she was holding in her hand, tip it up to her lips and, finding it empty, hurl it down at Mas Carlton. His master sidestepped as the glass crashed to the ground.

"I want a drink!"

Mingo felt his master's fingers release him as though he was reluctant to go. He walked back to the stairs to go up to the balcony.

"Keep on with your training, Mingo," he told him. "May you never have to fight a man as vile as she." He grinned ruefully, indicating his wife with a tilt of his head.

"Yah sah, no sah!" Mingo replied, puzzled.

Ma Phoebe grabbed his arm and pulled him inside the kitchen. "Keep yo' nose out of deir business!" She banged the door shut and secured it with the iron bolt.

"Now, my buck! Let's see what you does have for yo' Ma Phoebe!"

She lunged at his waist and pulled at the tie holding

257

his pantaloons. The loose garment fell easily down to his ankles, where it stayed as Ma Phoebe lowered her head.

Chapter 29

Mingo sensed that, for some reason, he was a cause of the friction between his master and his mistress. If his master wanted to build up his muscles and finger him, it was not for him to resist, and it concerned him that Miss Sybil should despise him for it. Even though his master always smiled at him and treated him well, Mingo suspected that trouble was brewing for him.

Usually, Mingo took no notice of the gossip in the kitchen when Bo'jack and Pool relayed the scraps of conversation they had heard upstairs to Ma Phoebe. He was anxious only to eat his meat and provisions quickly and then get out to the barn before Ma Phoebe detained him for one of her sessions. He was surprised when he heard the stupid Bo'jack mention his name after he had brought down the dirty supper plates.

"Nothin' left tonight for no hungry nigger!" Bo'jack was saying as he slammed down the tray on the table.

Ma Phoebe waddled over to peer at the empty plates. She banged her hands together, beaming around the kitchen. Mingo ducked his head down and scooped up the mess on his plate, hoping she wouldn't notice him. Instead, Ma Phoebe addressed Ella, who was bouncing her child on her knee as she sat in the corner, feeding him from her own plate, a quiet smile of complacent happiness on her face.

"You does see how de new white missy does like my cookin'. Every little morsel does be dere does be done. She go'n come more plump an' happy wid Ma Phoebe's victuals!" Ma Phoebe nodded her head proudly, her many chins shaking in agreement.

"Don't think nothin' else go'n make her come plump," chuckled Bo'jack, winking at Ella. "Is Ella da' gittin' de real meat!"

"Oh my gawd!" Ma Phoebe threw up her chubby hands in the air and collapsed on a stool in her mirth. She clapped her hands together, chuckling, her head rolling and tears beginning to stream down her cheek.

"Yuh does be right! Yuh does be right!"

"She feelin' de need for him somethin' fearful," added Bo'jack. "She does be harassin' Mas Carlton about dat Mingo again tonight."

"She does say," added Pool, wanting to show that he was part of the conversation too and so that Ma Phoebe would stop laughing. Mingo kept his face down in his bowl, listening with growing apprehension. "She does say Mas Carlton does do nothin' but talk of de niggers de whole day. He behavin' like he don't marry wid her an' she say she does regret de day Mas Carlton take Mingo along wid dem from Vandy Hall 'cause Mas Carlton he does care more about Mingo dan her."

"Oooooh!" breathed Ma Phoebe. "Does yuh hear, Ella? Dat missey vex'. Mas Carlton neglectin' his rightful duties to his woman, I does declare."

"Dat not concern me." Ella placed her plate beside her on the bench and wiped her child's mouth with the loose fold of her dress.

"I does think yuh done something to dat Mas Carlton, Ella," said Ma Phoebe as though discussing a patient with a fellow practitioner. "Likely it does be more wise to let Mas Carlton bed his wife sometimes. If de massa does git too much harassment from his wife, there ain't no way of knowin' how it does break out on us niggers."

260

"Not me," said Ella, still playing with her child. "He de massa, I de wench. You don' hear wha' Pool done say? De missey vex' wid da' buck' not wid me!"

"Dat's true say," chipped in Bo'jack, looking up from devouring his own supper. "Mas Carlton done say he does plan to mount Mingo wid one of dem fillies. I does not recall which one," he added to stall Ma Phoebe's immediate question. "And when she hear dis, Miss Sybil she bang down her dish an' she start to cry something terrible. Mas Carlton he don't take no never minds but Massa Hayes he comes over her side de table an' he pat her on de back and she hush de noise. He ax she why she cry dis way, and den Mas Carlton done tell his father leave de woman to weep!" Bo'jack paused to watch the impact of his words on Ma Phoebe, Ella, and Mingo, but only Ma Phoebe was watching him, her mouth open in astonishment.

It was Pool who continued the story. "I hear she say dis Mingo more lucky dan she does be and why don't Mas Carlton give her for Mingo to mount 'cause Mas Carlton ain't giving her nothing!"

Ma Phoebe was dumbfounded. She looked at Pool and Bo'jack to see whether they were lying. Both nodded their heads with alacrity to ward off her gaze. Next, she looked at Ella, but Ella still smiled complacently and cooed at her baby. Mingo, who had looked up in horror when he heard Pool's words, shifted nervously under Ma Phoebe's scrutiny.

"Dere be no good things brewing in dis place since dat woman done come here," wailed Ma Phoebe. "Mingo sure does be a pretty nigger, but dere ain't no right for a white woman what does be marry wid de massa to know de boy so."

"Wha's wrong wid dat?" asked Ella suddenly.

"Oh my gawd!" Ma Phoebe shook with indignation.

"De white men does bed wid us black wenches, though. Why don't a white woman bed wid a Negro buck if she like it so?"

"Ella, yo' brain done go soft like de snake grease

I does rub Mingo wid? It ain't right for a white woman to have a black baby in her belly, dat's why! Dat's disgrace. If dat ever happen, den it be de end of us all. Only one man can give Missy Sybil a baby, an' dat be Mas Carlton himself!"

Ma Phoebe glared defiantly at Ella and then included Mingo in her wrath, yelling at him to get up and go to the barn with the other bucks. "You keep out de mistress way, yuh hear!"

Mingo scuttled gratefully out of the kitchen and into the dark surrounding the house. On the gallery at the front, overlooking the path he had to take to the barn, there were several lanterns which threw their weak gleam down onto the open front yard. Mingo kept close to the wall of the house to see if he could skirt the pools of light without being noticed by the buckras sitting upstairs. As he passed under the steps he caught the mention of his own name. He paused, terrified. It was the old master who was talking.

"Sybil really upset tonight over that Mingo nigger of yours, son. What are you two so fired up about? You not doing your duty by Sybil, son? It's a baby she wants, Carlton, a baby."

Mingo waited to see if he would hear his own name again, straining his ears to catch what Master Carlton replied as the punch jug clattered down onto the tray.

"I do my duty when I have to, and that's the truth," Carlton was saying. "Once a week is enough, surely, father. You told me yourself that white women don't like the thing so much. But this one, she already had plenty of men before she married me, and now she can't stop."

"You know that for certain sure, son?"

"She wasn't a virgin, father."

Mingo could not see the old man shake his head thoughtfully, but there was a pause before Master Hayes spoke again.

"You may have made a mistake there, son. It's none of my business, I know, but I like your Sybil. She keeps me company here on the gallery some afternoons when you are busy training that nigger of yours. She talks to me, you know.

"I think you must be mistaken about her, son. She assures me that she has never known a man up to the time she met you, never. She says her father was very strict. Even when she went riding around the estate, the Major always made her have a chaperone with her. She tells me she liked riding. That could have done it, son."

"Done what?"

"Broken her maidenhead, son. It's not unusual. If a wench is always riding around a plantation instead of doing her samplers at home, it could happen. It's not a very ladylike occupation, I know, but I've come across it in my youth, especially in America. Some of the women there are more like men—hard workers, too."

"Do you mean that, Father?"

"Of course. I told you, I like Sybil. The girl has a lot of spirit. She has had a strict upbringing, though, just to save her for the man who would be her husband. The Vandys are an old family in Antigua. I know their reputation."

Again there was silence, this time such a long one that Mingo was about to continue his journey to the barn when Carlton's voice made him stop again.

"If that is true, Father, why is she demanding so much of me? Seems that she must have had experience before. She's more passionate than a nigger, father!"

Hayes gave a throaty chuckle. "Bless my soul, Carlton! You've met your match in a crinoline, have you? Let me tell you, son, she's your wife. If you do not satisfy her, someone else will."

"I ask you to withdraw that remark, sir!" Mingo heard the bang of a glass being slapped down on a table in anger.

"Hush, son. I'm only saying what will happen if you want to lose her. Take care of her, Carlton. Don't mind her funny ways, she'll change when she gets the attention she needs. Perhaps," there was a short pause, "perhaps if you mounted her as though she was a nigger wench, you'd satisfy her what?"

Chapter 30

Hayes passed the letter back to Carlton. It had just been delivered by a swarthy young Negro who had been instructed to wait downstairs in the kitchen to see if there would be any reply. Hayes eyed his son cautiously while Sybil waited for the letter to be passed across to her. Carlton looked at it again and then leaned over to where his wife was sitting on the balcony with them and gave it to her.

"Men's business, my dear, of small consequence to you," he told her lightly. "What do you think, Father?"

Carlton had not long come in from touring the plantation. Sybil had ridden round with him, as she sometimes did now, and they were all anxiously awaiting dinner. From the dining room could be heard the sounds of Bo'jack as he shuffled around setting the table. The dour tones of Pool, muttering at his task of carrying up the dishes which Ma Phoebe and Ella had prepared, confirmed that dinner would soon be ready. Hayes smiled benevolently at his son and daughter-in-law, leaning forward with the punch jug to urge Carlton to fill his glass again. Both he and Sybil refused.

"Come on, Sybil, a drink will do you good after all that riding this morning," urged Hayes.

Sybil returned the letter to Carlton while she smiled demurely at her father-in-law. "No, thank you, Mister

Todd. I'm not tired after the ride, but if I have your punch, then I'll surely fall asleep after dinner and not wake until supper time! And we've so much to do this afternoon, haven't we, Carlton? There's six new babies in the pen, and we want to transfer two who've been weaned."

Hayes listened as though he did not understand. It was hard enough to adapt himself to Carlton's ideas on rearing Negroes as livestock even though he was well aware that they were all as one with cattle anyway. Yet whenever he heard Sybil engaging in a discussion with his son about the breeding potential of various Negroes on the plantation, he was flummoxed.

"Well?" Sybil distracted Hayes from his thoughts, repeating his son's query. "What do you think?"

"Humph!" was his first reaction, and it caused Carlton's heart to sink. Carlton valued the old man's advice, but when it went against his own assessment, he was ready to argue against it.

"How long have you been training that Mingo?" Hayes asked thoughtfully.

"Over a year now, Father."

"You think that's long enough?"

"Of course. Mingo is as strong as a horse. He's been drinking raw eggs and eating some kind of porridge that Ma Phoebe has been feeding him for months."

"I don't doubt his strength, son. I've seen that for myself."

"I shudder whenever I see him," added Sybil. "He's like an ox!"

"I don't doubt his strength." Hayes peered into his punch glass. "I'h just wondering if he's wily enough. I've seen these fights between niggers in my young days in Alabama. It isn't necessarily the strongest buck who wins the match, you know. And suppose Mingo loses? You'll have to kill him, because he'll be almost dead anyway. It will be a pity to see such a valuable buck cut up and killed."

Carlton was staring at the letter. It was addressed on the outside to Mr. Carlton Todd, The Bondmaster of

Roxborough, in such a fancy handwriting it was almost illegible. The letter came from Cleve Moult and contained a challenge for Carlton to bring the young buck known as Mingo to fight the Dominica champion, Karamantee Jack, at Mr. Moult's tavern at a date to be arranged.

Carlton looked back at his father. "You see what Moult has written about that slave Claudius? He says he'll wager Claudius against five hundred pounds."

Hayes nearly choked on his punch. "That could mean you not only lose a prime nigger, but a fortune as well."

"It could also mean," smiled Sybil rising from her chair, "that if Mingo wins we gain an excellent slave worth five hundred pounds for nothing."

Carlton stared after her open-mouthed as she swept off the balcony to supervise the serving of dinner. "I never thought she would favor the idea at all," he observed. "I suppose I'll never understand her."

"She's right, of course," said Hayes, stroking his chin. "I'm just worried that he might not be ready."

"Oh, Father! If he's not ready now, I don't know when he ever will be. That nigger is like a pedigreed racehorse. If he doesn't have a real fight soon, I think he'll take on the whole crew of a privateer. He's already cracked so many skulls I daren't let any of my bucks fight him now lest he kill one."

"Dinner's ready!" Sybil called them. "Fresh river crayfish the Wageny brought up this morning. Don't let the dinner get cold for the sake of that Mingo!"

"Come on, son. Help me up." Hayes took Carlton's arm and eased himself up out of the chair so that he could hobble across to the table. Halfway through the drawing room, he paused. "Tell me something, son." He beckoned Carlton to stand close to him so he could whisper in his ear. "You breed from him yet? Got any whelps out of him?"

Carlton chuckled, amused by the old man's deference to Sybil's presence. "Of course, Father. Crossed him with the best fillies we've got. Three have taken already, but none dropped yet. I'd let him mount Ma Phoebe if I thought it would produce another cook like her," he added, contemplating the dishes set up on the table.

"No more talk of Mingo, if you please!" Sybil clapped her hands for silence. "It's dinner now, business can wait until afterwards."

They all sat down at the table and began to help themselves to the plates being circulated by Pool and Bo'jack.

"I was thinking," Sybil was the first to break the silence, "that my wardrobe is getting rather depleted, Carlton. Why, only last week I had to discard a dress that I have had for far too long. I know we don't have occasion to call on people, nor do we have many visitors," she added wistfully, "but one does like to look presentable for one's husband."

"You're delightful to me, my dear, whatever you wear. Why can't Mally Ibo sew something for you?"

"A slave seamstress!"

"Sorry, my dear. Perhaps there's someone in Layou. May Gregg would know."

"I don't think the wife of the Bondmaster of Roxborough should patronize the whores' dressmaker, do you, dear?"

Hayes gurgled on his soup. The chattering of his son and Sybil, since they had overcome their original suspicion of each other, was something he looked forward to at meal times. Although he was of the opinion that Sybil took too great a part in the running of the plantation and not enough in the supervision of the house, he never tired of her wheedling of favors out of Carlton. He saw the direction she was heading now, and decided he would give the whole project his blessing.

"If you decide," he interrupted, "to fight that Mingo, then Sybil could accompany you to Roseau. I'll be quite all right with Bo'jack and Ma Phoebe to look after me, and there is nothing on the plantation that needs your constant attention right now."

"Well, I'll be damned!" said Carlton. "A capital idea!"

The training of Mingo was accelerated. For a few weeks, he had been put to a creole slave girl of mixed ancestry whom Carlton found pleasing enough to think she could produce a salable offspring. Although Mingo protested mildly that perhaps the filly had not yet taken, he was ordered back to the barn to spend his nights. Hannibal was instructed to wake him at five every morning so he could take a run, and Carlton himself rode behind him each day. A quick bath in the river and a special breakfast of raw eggs and manioc followed. After that, he was put through his weight-lifting exercises. If Carlton was attending to other business on the plantation, Sybil supervised the work-out from the balcony.

Some of the other slaves were brought up to help Mingo as sparring partners, but their enthusiasm for the job was dampened by Mingo's superior strength, which soon had them bemoaning their bruised chests and battered faces. Carlton permitted Mingo an after-noon rest after he had eaten a double portion of din-ner, but his regime was far from finished. In the after-noon, there were exercises to strengthen his stomach and arm muscles before another run, this time at speed with Sybil chasing him across the savannah on horse-back, twitching her whip across his shoulders to make him run faster. Another bath in the river followed be-fore Ma Phoebe gave him his snake oil massage.

Involving herself so closely with Mingo's training had brought Sybil closer to Carlton through their shared interest. She and her husband now scarcely ever disagreed. The peace which descended on their marriage brought tranquillity to the plantation. As though in response, the slaves themselves started to breed and Carlton's program of raising slaves to sell showed signs of succeeding. Carlton was content and even prepared to put up with what he regarded as his wife's eccentricity in taking so much interest in the running of the plantation, especially if it contributed to their marital happiness. He saw his wife's interest in the training of Mingo as an extension of her desire to be involved, and saw nothing strange now in leaving Sybil in charge of Mingo.

For her part, Sybil became acutely conscious of Mingo's body. She knew every muscle of it. Even though she regarded the great size of his thighs and biceps as grotesque, his body held a fascination for her. She made him exercise naked in the afternoons by the river, watching him closely as she sat astride her horse in the shade. He was a monster compared with her husband. Aware of his mistress's interest in him, Mingo was careful to preserve the correct relationship at all times. It would be death for him to do otherwise.

The weeks of training reached their peak, and the day came for the journey to Roseau. Mingo had never looked better. His skin radiated positive health and confidence. Even the skeptical Hayes noticed it, remarking to Carlton as they prepared to leave that it would need an exceptional fighter to beat Mingo.

"But he must be wily," he cautioned Carlton as he embraced his son. "If the boy don't have that killer instinct, he's lost, you know. He's lost."

The journey to Roseau was uneventful. They were all riding, even Mingo, so that he should not tire himself unnecessarily by having to walk the whole way. A suite had been reserved at the hotel, with two bedrooms and an adjoining room where Mingo was to sleep. The presence of a male slave, sleeping in his own room inside the hotel, caused consternation. It was the custom for male slaves to sleep in the cellar, although female slaves were permitted within the hotel itself. Carlton would have nothing of it and intended to be able to keep his eye on his fighter at all times.

They had not been in the hotel more than ten minutes when there was an urgent knock on the door. Carlton gestured to Mingo to open it while he assisted his wife in unpacking their luggage. They had brought very little because Sybil wanted to buy more fashionionable clothes in the capital.

A shout of delight came from the doorway. "Is it true? Is that Mingo? In such a fine raiment? Let me feel your arm. Hard, *garçon*, hard! But you look so dainty. You're not even ugly!"

Carlton looked into the hallway to see what the commotion was about. "Claudius! I might have known it would be you making all that noise! Come in, boy."

"Yes, sir. Oh, what a pleasure it is to see you, sir. And m'lady. May I say that you are looking in the pink of health, madam? And you, sir!"

"Oy! Oy! Claudius. Cleve Moult has given you a fancy tongue as well as a new suit of clothes, I do declare."

"It is a pleasure serving him, sir, I will admit. But I am waiting to come back to you, sir." Claudius paused, looking at Mingo standing quietly by the door. "You think Mingo will win me back, sir?" He sounded doubtful.

"Why!" exclaimed Sybil bustling over. "You are the one who should know. You're familiar with this Karamantee nigger, aren't you?"

"Yes, ma'am."

"Well, what do you think?"

Claudius shuffled uneasily, looking again at Mingo in the pantaloons which Mally Ibo had fashioned for him. His hair had been slicked down with grease. He was barefooted and his dark golden skin glowed. His eyes shone with innocence.

"He looks like a babe, ma'am, compared with the Karamantee. I don't say that Mingo won't win the fight, ma'am. But when you see him, and see the Karamantee, you just have to feel a little doubtful, ma'am."

"Enough of this talk!" Sybil struck out and cuffed Claudius quickly across his ear. The blow surprised everyone in the room. It caused Claudius to stagger and fall against Mingo, who steadied him.

"Sybil!" Carlton spoke in alarm. "There's no need to hit the slave so hard."

"I hit him hard, did I? I'm sorry, Carlton. I suppose

I don't know my own strength." She winked at her husband.

"Did the blow hurt you, Claudius?" asked Carlton.

"That's all right, sir."

"I should damn well think it's all right!" Carlton snorted. "I'll give you another blow for insolence next time. Did you see that, Mingo?"

"Yas, sah."

"What did you see, Mingo?"

"I done see de mistress fell dis uppity nigger, sah."

"Were you surprised?"

"Beg pardon, sah?"

"You did not expect that, did you, Mingo?"

"Oh no, sah. De mistress does look too gentle for dat, sah."

"Right," said Sybil, smiling. "Now, Claudius, just because Mingo doesn't look ugly like your Karamantee doesn't mean that he can't beat him. Skill is important in these things, I'm sure. You've watched the Karamantee training, haven't you?"

"Yes, ma'am." Claudius was meeker now, regarding the white lady with a new respect.

"Then we want all the information you can give us on the brute. Is he fit? How does he train? What does he eat? Can he see properly? Is he right- or left-handed?"

Carlton watched Sybil in amazement. Her eyes were bright with excitement. "Sybil?"

"Carlton, my darling." She put her hand out to clasp his. "We're going to win this fight, whether it's by strength, wiles, or subterfuge. We are not going to let some numbskull pulverize our precious Mingo!'

Chapter 31

In spite of her concern over Mingo, Sybil declined to accompany Carlton to Cleve Moult's tavern on the night of the fight. A lady, she informed Carlton, would not be seen in such an establishment, and Carlton, who had been taken aback by his wife's intense interest in Mingo's fight, had been relieved. Sybil would have loved to see the fight but feared that Mingo might lose. At least she hoped that his defeat would cure Carlton of his desire to fight niggers and that he would settle down to a peaceful life breeding them instead.

She was so sure that Mingo would lose that she had already resolved that he would be buried in style in Roseau. It would give the people in Roseau something to think about when they saw how well a Roxborough slave was treated. Mingo had been so loyal, it would be unwarranted to have his corpse dragged away by scavengers without another thought. She broached the subject with Claudius on the afternoon of the fight when the slave came to give Mingo some last-minute hints.

"If he should lose, Claudius, you must make sure that a factor is sent for to give him a proper funeral."

"I pray, Mistress, don't consider such a thing. Mingo must not lose."

"You really want Master Carlton to win you back?" Sybil was amused by the trust of the wily nigger.

"Of course, ma'am. But it's not just that."

"What else is it?"

Claudius hesitated. He had no intention of prejudicing his own future when he might be a Roxborough buck instead of a tavern fool. He changed his mind about what he was going to tell her. "A lot of people hope to make money out of Mas Carlton, ma'am," he said instead. "A man who fights a nigger against Cleve Moult is expected to back his fighter with gold. If Mingo does lose, it will be a prodigious amount for Mas Carlton to pay, ma'am."

Sybil smiled, patting Claudius on his shoulder. "Go Claudius, and remember what I have told you. I will pay all the funeral expenses."

Claudius saw a ray of hope, and his dejection at the thought of Mingo failing cleared. "Yes, ma'am," he answered cheerfully, scampering off to locate Mingo in the hotel courtyard.

Claudius had invested his life's savings in Mingo to win. It was punishable for a slave to have money of his own, which was why he had hesitated to inform Sybil about his bet. If Mingo lost the fight, Claudius lost his savings. But now his mistress had offered to pay all expenses if there was to be a burial, so he would be able to recoup his own loss.

Mingo was in superb condition. His body glistened with the snake oil rub which Claudius was persuaded to give him before he returned to the tavern. Mingo listened carefully to the last-minute advice which Claudius gave him.

"You jes' rem'ber, niggah, keep on de move. Don't let dat Karamantee hold yuh. He such a big giant yuh go'n git yourself crushed if he does git yuh in he arms."

"Dat's nuthin'." Mingo was amused that this town slave should be telling him how to fight. "Ah'm primed proper for de fight. Mas Carlton does want me to win, so ah go'n win."

Claudius shook his head. "Dis ain't no joke, *neg*! Dat bozal go'n kill yuh if yuh take no mind of what I done tell yuh. You must kill him firs'."

Mingo scratched his massive chest thoughtfully. "I does have to kill him?"

"Ayeeee!" Claudius slapped his forehead in despair. "Dat's de only way yuh go'n win dis fight. Nigger, dis is life or death, I does be telling yuh now!"

"Ah ain't never killed no man before."

Claudius frowned. "Never?" He thought again, his spirits sinking. "Yuh does know how to kill, though?"

Mingo, who had been flexing his muscles proudly while Claudius addressed him, paused and scuffed the earth with his foot. He looked at Claudius doubtfully without answering.

"Nigger!" exclaimed Claudius in exasperation. "I does have all my freedom money on yuh to win. If yuh lose I does be a slave forever! Yuh got to hold dat nigger in de throat or de grain. Dat's de only way yuh sets me free!" Claudius shook his head. "I goin'. I'll see yuh tonight. An' don't forget, stay way from de Karamantee before he squeezes de life out of yuh."

As soon as he saw Karamantee Jack, Carlton realized he had made a mistake. Cleve Moult had welcomed him with open arms when he stepped into the tavern, even rising from his seat to embrace him. He had pressed a drink on him before ushering him through the tavern to the arena which had been set up at the back. It was already crowded with gentlemen talking about the upcoming bout. Cleve Moult was a born publicist and the buildup he had given Mingo would have surprised Carlton. But Moult knew that only something very special would draw the crowd to watch his Karamantee Jack again. His nigger had slaughtered six challengers already. It was difficult to find someone who would fight him, especially someone as wealthy as the Bondmaster, who would meet all the wagers.

Carlton's heart sank. Karamantee Jack was locked in a bamboo cage like an angry tiger. He paced about the confines of the small prison, occasionally charging the bamboo and shaking it in his eagerness to get out. He really was an animal, snarling at any white man who came near. Two Negroes stood by the cage with cudgels which they prodded at the fighter, serving to make him more angry. The brute was naked, and his glistening blue-black body was scarred with welts where others had clawed at him in earlier fights. His nostrils flared with an evil anger that made Carlton fear for his own life, quite apart from his slave's, if the beast was loosed. He realized that Mingo could never beat this monstrous beast.

I have Claudius here as my stake, Carlton," said Moult, clapping his arm around Carlton's shoulder with a huge shout of merriment, "but where is your money? Five hundred pounds, is it not?" A shout of delight went up from the assembled young men who had been gleefully watching the country bumpkin planter.

"I'll wager another hundred on the Karamantee," yelled one. "Fifty for me," said another. Several mocking shouts joined in as Carlton faced them. He felt wretched, but the thought of what he wanted Roxborough to be sustained him. He could stand being beaten in a fair fight, but was not going to slink away to the jeers of these Roseau popinjays. He was the Bondmaster of Roxborough with a plantation which was rearing the best slaves money could buy.

He faced the crowd. "I'll meet any wager you gentlemen," he emphasized the word *gentlemen* deliberately "care to make, providing it is in cash, of course."

"Where's yer nigger?" called one, turning to Mingo who stood at the edge of the circle quietly contemplating the scene. "Hey, boy, go and bring your master's fighter."

What had roused Mingo, Carlton did not know. As the man spoke, Mingo swaggered into the center of the arena to stand by Carlton. "Ah am de one," he shouted. "Ah am de one dat go'n make you gentlemens lose yo' purse if yuh back de Karamantee!"

Whoa! Such a shout went up from the arena that people in the streets from the bayfront to the fort could hear it. Many made their way as fast as they could to the tavern, only to find the doors were already barred, for the place could hold no more. Claudius, who had been collecting the admissions, deposited his takings with the white man who managed the bar for Moult and squeezed through the throng so that he could be at the front to watch Mingo.

Claudius had given Mingo a rum to drink in an effort to give him some more spark. It had worked, but the boy still looked puny beside the Karamantee who rushed the bars of his cage in a theatrical attempt to get out. It was obvious he could burst right through the bamboo if he wanted to. Moult had trained him well.

"This fancy lady's nigger goin' to broke me?" laughed one of the men as the commotion died down. "I'll wager another hundred."

One of Moult's henchmen had been appointed to note down the wagers, and he passed around collecting the names of all the gentlemen who wanted to bet, checking with Carlton to see if he wanted to accept the wager. Each time, Carlton nodded silently, hoping his misgivings would not show in his face. He turned to Mingo beside him.

"You spoke boldly, boy. I would thrash you for that at Roxborough."

"Yah, sah," replied Mingo meekly, lowering his head. "Dat's what I does know. Claudius done tell me say dose things."

Carlton grinned. Claudius wasn't going to let him down even if Mingo did seem destined for failure. "He seems a nasty brute," said Carlton, wondering what words of encouragement to give his slave. It suddenly occurred to him. "When we get back to Roxborough, I think you should have that Eurilia wench. Her mam saving her virgin for me, but I think you are bound to burst that maid. If you win, of course."

Mingo pursed his lips together. He needed no bribe to whet his desire to win this fight. He had seen his master's honor being challenged by these stupid *bekés* in their fine clothes who couldn't ride a horse without

277

assistance. He knew that kind. His master was different. He tore off his shirt, still pondering the insults he had heard being hurled at his master. He would be ashamed to serve those people! No wonder Claudius wanted to leave the town and come back with him, he stepped out of his pantaloons. There was a murmur of interest from the crowd as he flexed his muscles.

Suddenly, before he realized it, the door of the bamboo cage was thrown open and the black bozal was charging him. bellowing like a crazed bull. Quickly, Mingo stepped aside, and the Karamantee, unable to stop himself, tripped over Mingo's outstretched foot and hurtled into the crowd. Claudius smiled approvingly, while Carlton wondered where Mingo had learned that trick. The crowd roared their delight.

Slowly, Mingo pirouetted around to face the champion, seizing confidence from the crowd's obvious pleasure in his body movements. This time, the bozal was not going to be fooled. He came at Mingo with both hands outstretched, leaping at his throat.

"Stay way! Stay way!" shrieked Claudius, edging closer to Mingo.

But Mingo brought up his knee and let the bozal crash into it, winding himself. Now the Karamantee's anger was genuine, and he lunged at Mingo and caught him rapidly in a body lock. He began to squeeze him. The crowd sighed, feeling that the end was very near, as no one had been known to survive a crushing in the champion's massive arms.

Claudius was in despair. The fight was practically over before it had begun. Mingo's face was turning a deep purple as he struggled in vain to release himself from the bozal's grip. The snake oil on his body helped him to wriggle, but his antics only amused the crowd and delighted the bozal. As though in contempt, the champion suddenly released Mingo, threw him on the ground, and then picked him up and held him above his head. He walked proudly around the ring as though asking the crowd where he should throw him.

Completely without hope, Carlton began to wonder how much this escapade had cost him. His boy was too young, too refined, too silly. Carlton looked up. The bozal was standing over him, holding Mingo above his head. He was cackling. Everyone in the crowd was laughing as Mingo lay completely still in the champion's arms, not even struggling to break loose. Moult, standing beside Carlton, turned to face him with a triumphant smile on his fat cheeks.

"You concede, young Roxborough?"

Carlton lowered his eyes, catching sight of Claudius as he did so. The slave was shaking his head emphatically. Carlton looked up at Mingo in the bozal's arms. The slave winked at him.

"Concede? Damme, Moult, the fight's only just begun!"

And so it had. Finding that his theatrics produced no effect on the stripling in his grip, the bozal threw Mingo to the ground arrogantly. It was what Mingo had been waiting for. He twisted his body and landed neatly on his toes, leaping away as the bozal rushed at him and aiming a kick which landed with a satisfying crunch on the champion's nose. The bozal staggered. Mingo slipped behind him and threw himself at the champion's back, sending him crashing to the ground. He leaped on his shoulders, grabbed his head in both hands, and began to pound it on the hard earth.

Claudius crawled around the ring of the excited crowd. Mingo glanced up as Claudius hissed at him. "Git his eye! De eye!"

As the bozal began to shift and throw Mingo off his back, Mingo slipped his two forefingers into the brute's right eye. He gouged it out. It hung loose in front of the champion's face. blood streaming down his nose. Mingo jumped away and the Karamantee staggered to his feet. Carlton wondered how much punishment the bozal could take before he gave up.

With the rage of a wounded animal, the Karamantee grasped blindly at Mingo. Each time, Mingo slipped away, forcing the bozal to chase around the ring after him. The crowd jeered, convinced that Mingo was frightened and wanted to escape. But Mingo sensed that the bozal was tiring and wanted him to use up his strength before he closed in. He crouched and waited.

"Stay'way!" warned Claudius when he saw what Mingo had in mind. "Don't let de *makak* hold yuh!"

It was no use. Either Mingo did not hear, or he had forgotten. The Karamantee caught Mingo as he jumped at him and held him easily. He engulfed him in his long arms, wrapping them around him and slowly squeezing. The crowd sighed. This was the end. The fights always ended this way. The Karamantee had lost his eye; the challenger would be killed. It had been a good fight, and they had won their bets. Cleve Moult arranged good entertainments.

Now Mingo wriggled. What oil there was left on him was caked with dust, and it formed a protective shield to his body enabling him to squirm against the bozal, making his body-hug less effective. Mingo could sense, too, that the Karamantee's strength was not so powerful as before. Even so, his bones were hurting and he felt that he was being crushed alive. Blood was streaming onto his head from the bozal's nose. He could not see his face, only his neck, which was stifling his own nose, making it difficult to breathe.

It was then, as he felt himself passing into unconciousness, that Mingo remembered the last words of advice which Claudius had given him. Slowly, he opened his mouth and parted his teeth. The pressure of the Kamarantee's bear-hug was such that the flesh of the brute's neck popped easily into his mouth. In an effort to distract him, Mingo raised his knee and jammed it into the bozal's balls, gathering more and more of his neck into his jaws at the same time. He held his breath and closed his teeth.

The sudden spurt of blood surprised him. It coursed out of his mouth and down his body. He felt the Karamantee's grip relax, and then his arms dropped away from him and the champion slid slowly to the

ground. The fight was over. Mingo spat out a mouth-
ful of flesh and blood onto the dead man's body and
collapsed on top of him.

Chapter 32

Sybil had been talkative and eager to contribute something, anything, even though it might have been silly nonsense, to Carlton's dedication to the work at Roxborough, but she was now silent. It had not been a sudden sinking into unhappiness, and it was some time before Carlton realized that there was any change in his wife. She still sat with him and his father on the balcony at night and busied herself with a sampler. To her quietness was added a certain radiance which Hayes noticed long before Carlton.

Ma Proebe knew, of course, before everybody else. "I know the signs," she announced to her kitchen, now increased in staff by Claudius since Carlton had brought him back from Roseau.

"He done get her full!" Ma Phoebe leered at Ella, whose job it was to prepare the morning meal. Ella's son, Caspar, was playing with Claudius, both of whom were completely unconcerned by the news.

"She don't say nothing about that." Bo'jack was offended that this important piece of news had been withheld from him. Ma Phoebe might think that he was not listening carefully enough at the table.

"She will," said Ma Phoebe. "It's her first, so she'll need his comforting."

"Be a son for de Bon'massa," contributed Pool as he prepared to take up a tray with the breakfast dishes.

For the first time, Ella reacted, turning from the stove with her eyes blazing. "It don't be a son," she hissed, a strange menace in her voice. "Caspar does be his son."

Embarrassed, Pool shuffled out quickly. Bo'jack stood up and started to button his shirt in preparation for waiting on the table. Ma Phoebe sat with her huge bulk fixed in her chair, nodding her head wisely. Claudius, holding Ella's boy in his arms as he swung him up off the ground, was not the kind to be intimidated by the prognostications of the kitchen staff.

"Oh-ho, my young gentleman!" he addressed the child. "My master's son, but who's his heir, eh?"

"You hold yo' tongue," snapped Ma Phoebe. "You done come here less dan three months an' yuh think yuh does know de everything."

"But I do, I do!" he laughed, jumping to his feet and placing young Caspar on the ground. "Just like you!"

Claudius skipped out of the kitchen and walked boldly up the back steps into the house. He knew that Mas Carlton was in his counting-house checking the books. He walked around the gallery, gave a token knock on his master's door, and walked in. Claudius's role at Roxborough was that of personal slave to the Bondmaster, and he relished the post. He felt superior to any of the slaves on the estate and was certainly not cowed, as the others were, by Ma Phoebe. Quite apart from the training he had received from the island's society people, Claudius was bolstered in his self-confidence by the fact that his master had returned for him, and that Mingo had won him back. He also, of course, had won himself enough to buy his freedom any time he chose.

Since the evening when she had stayed alone in the hotel room hearing shouts from the crowd at Cleve Moult's tavern, wondering which way the fight was going, Sybil had thought of Mingo almost constantly. She had been torn in her emotions that night. If he lost, all complications would be solved and she would have her husband exclusively again. If he won, Mingo would still be there for her to watch. She could not endure the thought of his body being mauled by an African jungle animal, and then tossed carelessly aside.

The chorus of shouts from the tavern, as it drifted over the rooftops of the squat houses of the town, told her nothing. She had regretted not asking Carlton to send a messenger to her with the news of the result. Reluctantly she had gone to bed aware that if Mingo had won, then Carlton would spend the whole night drinking in the tavern, and if he had lost, he still would not return until morning.

Mingo was in her dreams when she felt strong hands holding her, kisses smothering her face. She opened her eyes drowsily, to see her husband beside her on the bed. The wooden shutters kept out the morning light, although the cries of the street vendors penetrated to disturb them. She responded to her husband's fierce lovemaking, sharing his triumph and passion with an inspired emotion of her own. But, to her surprise, it was of Mingo she was thinking, of Mingo who had killed a man by biting through his neck.

That morning her child was conceived. It was as though when the seed was implanted in her, some spirit had whispered the name of Mingo and it stayed with her. She had grown to love her husband since the day of their contrived marriage and appreciated the understanding which now existed between them. She certainly did not love Mingo. In fact, she found him altogether repulsive. The very idea of bedding with a slave was unthinkable and, with one so colossal as Mingo, it was impossible. She shuddered as she considered him. Carlton had told her that Mingo had sired three offspring. She wondered how his females coped with Mingo. What did they know about love? They were just animals.

Since his victory over the Karamantee, Carlton had let Mingo roam the plantation quite freely. The one stipulation was that Mingo should only mount those fillies approved by Carlton. Carlton had pruned his stock and sold many of the poor-quality young females to intinerant traders, retaining only the better ones. This way he hoped that all who were of childbearing age would produce quality whelps from his hand-picked studs.

A hand-picked stud, thought Sybil, as she closed the door again and sat once more on her bed. Mingo.

Chapter 33

"Yo hear about dem Ibos?" Claudius asked, referring to two slaves who had been found dead that morning. Mingo nodded his head, uninterested.

"Dey killed demselves because dey believe dat's de way deir spirit does go back to Africa." Claudius dropped his field talk and slipped easily back into his master's English. "I told Mas Carlton that, but he just laughed. But he wasn't vexed. He said the Ibos were so cheap he could afford to lose a couple. Do you believe that you will go back to Africa when you die?"

To Mingo, Africa was a place he had never really left. First there were the hardships of life with the Vandys, and now he had the boredom of his existence with the Bondmaster. His mind was still the same. "I does not know," he shrugged. "Is de mistress better?"

"Why don't you go see her?"

"I can't do dat!"

"Why not? Is you she does like. You've more right to visit her than any of us. You're the prize buck in the plantation. It's you who can do what you like at Roxborough. The mistress likes you and the master likes you. Ain' nobody going to punish Mingo at Roxborough, no way!"

Mingo looked at Claudius curiously. "How you know dat? Yuh hear Mas Carlton speak about me?"

"All the time, Mingo." Claudius laughed. "He was going to lose more than five thousand pounds because of you. Instead, that's what he won. You think he don't respect you? It's you, nigger, who's the master where the Bondmaster does be concerned."

Claudius scrutinized Mingo doubtfully. "Why you skulking here like that, anyway? Look at you. Tell the master that you want a new set of clothes. Tell him you want to look respectable when you visits your mistress. Tell him what you want. He sure got to give it to you."

Claudius stood up. "I'm going down to the quarters. I've got to tell that boy of Kingston's that the Bondmaster says that none of those Ibos got to kill themselves again or he does kill them himself."

There was no avoiding the air of excitement as sugar time approached. Other than reminding Mingo to do his exercises daily, Carlton had little time for his prize nigger. He worked with Taumany and Harius, the boilers, in preparation for the harvesting. Every morning, Carlton left the house before breakfast to go to the mill where he spent his time in the boiling and curing houses and in the distillery overseeing the preparations.

He joined Sybil for breakfast, but had no time to linger before riding around the plantation with Harius, who had to be shown how the cane had been raised, its species, the kind of soil it had been grown in and whether it had been arrowed, bored, or rat-eaten. This kind of knowledge enabled Harius to determine how much lime to use in tempering the juices, how long it would have to boil, and what kind of quality he could produce.

Although he sensed the excitement, Mingo was unsettled by lack of interest in him showed by both his master and his mistress. As soon as he had heard from Bo'jack that Miss Sybil had recovered, he expected that she would send for him again. But there was no word.

So he found reasons to pass the house and linger near the back steps, but if his mistress saw him at all, she did not call him.

Mingo did not know that Sybil watched him constantly, peering through the shutters of her chamber or out of the dining room window. Each time she saw him, Sybil marveled again at his size and his doglike loyalty to her and Carlton.

A few days before sugar time, as Mingo was returning from taking a river bath, he heard a commotion coming from the quarters. He walked toward the cluster of slaves in the distance as a small boy detached himself from the group and began running up the hill toward him. The boy was so intent on his errand that he did not see Mingo blocking the path and ran straight into him. Mingo caught him around the waist and lifted him off the ground.

"Hoa! My li'l *garcon*. Where does yuh be goin' so fast?"

The boy gazed down at Mingo in terror as Mingo held him above his head. He struggled to regain his breath. "To de house," he managed to reply.

"What business does a pickaninny have at de house?" Mingo demanded, still holding the boy above his head.

"Candice done tell me run to de house and tell buckra dat de nex' Ibo done kill heself again."

"Dat so?" said Mingo thoughtfully, setting the boy back on the ground. He remembered what Claudius had told him a few days before. "Dat's not de way to behave, at all. De massa done be vex' when yuh tell he dat."

The boy hung his head sulkily. "It does be true. Candice done tell me so."

Mingo looked down the path to the quarters. Judging by the number of slaves gathered around in a bunch, he thought that it probably was true. "All right," he told the boy, twisting him around with his hand. "You run back to de quarters an' tell Candice dat yuh done give me de message an' dat I does be carryin' de news to de house. Yuh know my name, boy?"

The boy looked at Mingo in disbelief. "Yuh does be Mingo!"

"How yuh be so sure? I could be Claudius or Bo'-jack or any of dem niggers from de house."

"I know you ain't dem," retorted the boy in disgust. Yuh too ragged for a house slave. An' I see yuh already where my sister does sleep. It's you dat done give her a whelp what make Mas Carlton give her some cloth to make plenty new dresses."

"Dat so?" Mingo shook his head thoughtfully, then pushed the boy on his way. He turned and trotted easily toward the house, feeling the morning air quickly dry his wet skin. He wore his usual tight cotton pantaloons and, pausing at the back corner of the house, ran his fingers through his thick matted hair to squeeze out the water to make himself more presentable.

"Morning, Ma Phoebe," he said, poking his nose around the kitchen door. Everyone was sitting down to breakfast while Ella was busy serving them. Only Bo'jack was missing, so Mingo assumed he was upstairs.

"What yuh want?" retorted Ma Phoebe as she put a huge piece of smoked pork in her mouth.

"I have a news for Mas Carlton. I taking it up to de Massa myself."

With her mouth full of pork, Ma Phoebe was unable to protest as effectively as she would have liked. She was going to tell Mingo that he must let Claudius carry the news upstairs or at least tell her what it was all about first. But Mingo did not wait for her. He dashed up the back stairs two at a time. Claudius slipped out of his seat to follow him.

Reaching the balcony, Mingo paused, then tiptoed as quietly as he could to stand at the open door to the dining room. He peeped in. His mistress was sitting directly opposite the door and raised her head to gaze at him, a strange expression in her eyes. Hayes, who was accustomed to ignoring the ways of niggers when they attempted to disturb him while he was eating, pretended not to notice anything unusual. Carlton, expecting their intruder to be Claudius, was surprised when he turned and saw the near-naked Mingo standing in the doorway watching them.

"You came running up those stairs like an ox, Mingo. What's your business, boy?"

"Please, sah," Mingo scratched his stomach nervously, wanting to please his master and mistress but certain that the information he had for them was not the kind to make them happy. "De quarters, sah."

"Yes?" Carlton was amused that the nigger who had fought so bravely in Roseau should be so nervous in his master's dining room. "What about the quarters?"

"Not de quarters, sah. De Ibo in de quarters. Candice done tell a pickaninny to tell yuh dat the next Ibo done kill himself."

Hayes now condescended to abandon his breakfast, banging his knife down on the table and making Mingo flinch. "Dammit! I told you that would happen. Ibos the worst kind of nigger. Just now that whole parcel of Africans will kill themselves and you won't have none left. Good thing, too! Waste of good gold, though."

"No, Father," said Carlton, pushing his plate forward and getting up from the table. "I know what to do. Mingo, go down to the kitchen and tell Ma Phoebe that I want her to give you the sharpest cutlass she has, you hear?"

Be quick, now."

"Yassa!" Mingo turned and ran down the steps. For the first time in weeks, he was feeling happy. He burst into the kitchen and shouted his master's orders at Ma Phoebe, still stuffing her mouth with smoked pork.

"De massa does say dat you must git up off your fat ass an' give me de fastest, sharpest cutlass you have."

Commotion broke out in the kitchen at his words, the noise penetrating to the dining room upstairs, adding to the tension which Mingo's news had created.

"What are you going to do, Carlton?"

"That's not for you to know about, dear." Carlton kissed his wife on the forehead. "I'm going to stop those Ibos killing themselves, that's all. You see, they are only doing it because they think that when they die, they go back to Africa. As they've only been here three days, it's going to take them time to settle in. Ibos are wild. I hear it said that they are cannibals in Africa. I'll show them that they can't go back to Africa, even when they're dead!" He strode across the drawing room, his boots pounding the wooden floor. Claudius was waiting for him at the door.

"I've got your horse ready for you, sir. Shall I come, too, sir?"

Carlton glanced at Claudius, marvelling yet again at the boy's efficiency. "Of course. Come." Claudius fell into place behind his master as he ran down the steps.

"What do you make of this affair, Claudius? You ever see it before?"

"It's them Ibos' habit, sir. They are determined to die at any time, sir. I remember when I was at the factor's in Roseau and Mister Marks had a coffle of them he bought cheap and they all started to die, sir. We were pleased in a way, as that meant the factor was losing money. Every time he thought an Ibo was going to die, Mister Marks had him whipped, sir, but that didn't stop him. Sometimes, the Ibo just hung from the ceiling and died while he was being whipped. They only seemed to be happy when they were dying."

Carlton glanced at Claudius, marveling yet again for Mingo. "Where's that boy with the cutlass?" he muttered, then turned back to Claudius. "Well, what did your factor do then?"

"That man smart, sir. When he found out that they thought they would go back to Africa if they died, he took them to the Roseau river. He had maybe twenty of them. He told them all that when they walk in the river and cross over and cross back, then they would find they had all returned to Africa.

"He had a lot of people there with whips and we all drove them Ibos into the river and the white men on their horses rode into the river with them. Well, they did like Mister Marks told them and they cross over and they cross back, and then one of the creoles who could speak Ibo said 'Welcome to Africa' and they all went back to the stockade, sir. It fooled them niggers for a while, and then Mister Marks got to sell them before any of them died again."

"Fine," said Carlton, as Mingo came around the corner with the cutlass, pursued by Ma Phoebe heckling him. She stopped her cackling as soon as she saw Mas Carlton.

"Oh my gawd!" she said. "I done tell de boy hurry but dese niggers dey don't want to do anything but thieve all de smoked pork."

"Huh," she added to herself as Carlton, ignoring her, gestured to Mingo to jump up behind Claudius, and then galloped off. "Dat Bon'massa," she said to Bo'jack, who was watching from the safety of a corner of the house. "How he think he go'n stop dem Ibos from dying? Hey, hey! I don't think I could do dat myself!"

The dead Ibo was naked. Someone had arranged his body in reverential manner according to Ibo custom with hands placed neatly, palms facing upwards, level with his head. How he died did not concern Carlton, for there were countless ways a slave could kill himself if he wished. It was the desire to do so which Carlton knew he had to stamp out immediately, before death ran through the quarters like a plague, decimating his stock.

Claudius and Mingo had ridden up and Carlton took the cutlass out of Mingo's hand. "It sharp, boy?" he asked, rubbing his thumb across the edge of the blade.

"Yassa!" grinned Mingo. "Ma Phoebe does be real vexed when I done tek it. She done say dat it be she best cutlash for cuttin, de meat for yo' dinnah, sah."

"Fine. That's what I want." Carlton looked around him. Heads were appearing from the hiding places the slaves had chosen, all eyes watching him anxiously. Across the trail, a few yards from where the Ibo's body lay, was a group of about a dozen Negroes. They were squatting morosely on their haunches. None of them had flinched when Carlton had ridden up. This was the mourning party. All of them were Ibos, although some Carlton recognized as being Roxborough slaves for years. This was proof enough of the demoralizing effect of the Africans' suicides. Carlton addressed the group, ignoring the low moan which came from their direction.

"I tell you, boys, and I tell you good. When a nigger dies he does not go to Africa. He does not go anywhere. He stays right here."

The change in the pitch of the moan to murmurs of disagreement told Carlton that at least he had been understood, if not believed.

"Here!" said Carlton, lashing at a sapling with the cutlass and cutting it cleanly at the base. "You see this young tree? I cut it off from its roots."

As he spoke, Carlton pared the sapling rapidly until it was just a stake which he rammed into the ground. "Now it's a stick in the ground."

The Ibos watched him with interest, supported by the other slaves who began to emerge from their hiding places. Carlton swung around to include them in his speech.

"At Roxborough, it is a good life. Slaves don't have to worry for nothing. But when you are dead, you have to worry about everything. There is no way that the Bondmaster can look after you if you're dead, and there is no point in being dead before your time. This nigger here," Carlton kicked the corpse in the side to a loud moan of anguish from the mourners, "was a stupid nigger. He thought he could go back to Africa;

instead he killed himself. He's like that stake in the ground now, without a head."

This puzzled the slaves. They could see that the Ibo had a head. He couldn't go back to Africa without a head.

"Without a head!" Carlton's voice rose to a shriek and he brought down the cutlass onto the neck of the dead Ibo with all the strength he could muster. The blade was fine and almost severed the head in one blow. Carlton hacked at the body a couple of times and then flicked the head free. He picked it up, ignoring the mess of blood and torn flesh, jamming it onto the top of the stake. The Ibos were stunned into silence. Claudius felt like retching.

"Neither that dead Ibo nor any one of you niggers is ever going back to Africa," Carlton shrieked. "That Ibo is a stake in the ground now. That's what happens when you kill yourself. There's no Africa. There's only Roxborough. I'm the Bondmaster of Roxborough and I own every one of you on this plantation, you understand? If anyone does something without my permission, I will punish him. That Ibo killed himself without my permission. Now he is a stake in the ground!"

Carlton flung down the cutlass suddenly and turned away to jump on the horse which Claudius was holding for him. The crowd watched him in horror-struck silence. He stared carefully from face to face of everyone present. The defiance in their eyes died.

"Not me!" burst out one of the Ibos who had been on the plantation for years. "I ain't in dat at all!" He stood up rapidly and left the group of mourners, walking over the body and kicking it as he had seen Mas Carlton do. Then he turned to the stake and addressed the gruesome head on it. "Yuh don't see what a stoopid nigger yuh does be? Yuh don't even have no body, jes' a stick in de ground."

A rumble of agreement spread through the crowd. Many began to drift away, unconcerned by the foolishness of a few Africans who had not been seasoned properly yet.

"Tomorrow," announced Carlton from his horse, "we start cutting cane."

Chapter 34

At the mill, four Negroes were responsible for stuffing in the canes. After the juice was squeezed out, the pithy remainder of the cane, called trash, was conveyed to a place below the boiling house to keep the fire going constantly. In the boiling house, there were nine cauldrons, three of them merely simmering the juice carried to them by the slaves. Scum and useless particles were floated to the top during this simmering, after which the pure liquor ran to the first boiling cauldron and so was conveyed to another until it granulated. At that stage it was carried by a large gutter into a trough, called a cooler, from where the Negroes took it in pails to put it in the hogsheads.

The famous Roxborough rum was made by a similar process. The hogsheads had large holes bored in them at the bottom and stood on stands to allow the coarsest part, called molasses, to run through. The molasses was used in the distilling of rum. It was a tedious exercise and only the fact that it improved Carlton's chances of financing his breeding ventures encouraged him to keep going.

His slaves had no such encouragement. On the twenty-four-hour work system necessary to keep the boilers going, there were many casualties. Although the slaves were relieved every twelve hours, it was not unusual for some to fall asleep on the job. Taumany, the head boiler, watched constantly to judge the sugar quality, while other boilers assisted him. Carlton prowled around exhorting the niggers to keep at their jobs. On the third morning of cropping, as he was standing by the hogsheads watching them being filled, he heard a loud shriek. He looked inquiringly at Taumany, but the old Negro just shrugged his shoulders. The screaming rose to a frightening crescendo.

"De mill done git de next one," said Taumany.

Carlton dashed out of the boiling house and ran across to the mill. He was in time to see the driver snatch down the hatchet which was kept hanging on the wall for this kind of emergency. He attempted to hack at a slave's arm where the slave was trapped in the grinding stones. The stones had already consumed the slave's limb up to his shoulder and threatened to engulf his whole body. Asaph, the driver, was doing his best to sever the arm but the writhing of the slave and the excitement of the other Negroes who came running to see the commotion made him falter.

Carlton grabbed two of the slaves and pushed them in the direction of the gutter conveying the juice to the boiling house. "Quick," he urged, "Unhook the gutter so that the juice throws onto the ground. I don't want no nigger blood in my sugar."

The juice was turning crimson as the mill extracted the life from the slave's body. Asaph made a frantic effort to cut off the arm, but the slave twisted in agony and the hatchet slipped and hacked into his head instead, spilling his brains onto the ground.

"Cut off the nigger's arm, boy!" shouted Carlton. "You're holding up the sugar."

"Dis nigger worse dan ol' codfish, sah!" grinned Asaph, as he managed to cut the limb now that the slave had stopped wriggling. The body slid to the ground while the arm passed through the grinders and emerged as bloody pulp plopping to the ground on the other side.

"Get that carcass out of here quick," ordered Carlton. "You," he addressed two of the slaves beside him, "go carry water and sluice the grinder. Wash out all the blood and let's start feeding in the cane again."

It was the same every year, Carlton thought wearily to himself as he rode up to the house later that day. There were always the niggers who dozed off and got themselves trapped in the mill or boiled alive in the sugar. He hated to leave the mill at this time. Taumany and Kingston were getting old and could not watch everything. It was only natural that work would slow down as soon as his back was turned. As he wondered what to do about it, Carlton's eye fell on Mingo sitting in the shade of a big mango tree, watching the activity at the mill.

"Mingo!"

"Yassah!" Mingo's reply was quick, but he sounded worried.

"Look at you, Mingo!" Carlton paused and gazed down at the Negro. "There you are in top condition, muscles bulging all over you, and nothing to do with your strength. I'm thinking that those niggers at the mill need a little touch-up now and then. Seems they don't have respect for the drivers, else they wouldn't fall asleep and stain my sugar.

"Yes, that's it, Mingo. I want you to patrol the mill, and the boiling house, too, and just lay into any of them niggers what's idling or falling asleep or slowing down in any way. I can't be there all the time, and I don't want them to slow up. I must get this damn sugar out quickly this year. Drive the niggers for me, Mingo, and they sure will work better."

"Yas, sah!" beamed Mingo, his eyes growing wide as the sense of the responsibility hit him. "I be please' to do dat, sah."

"Of course, that's exactly what I need. And if you get any trouble, just run straight up to the house and call me. Take this whip for now." Carlton handed him his own supplejack. "I'll send Claudius with the bullwhip from the house later."

Mingo's pleasure at being given something to do was lost on Carlton, who was completely occupied with his own thoughts. By involving Mingo in disciplining the herd, the nigger could also serve him as an extra pair of eyes on the plantation to let him know whenever trouble was brewing. The episode of the Ibos still troubled him. There had been a defiance in the quarters which he had not expected. If something like that happened again unchecked, it could be dangerous.

The sugar season passed in a confusion of sleepless nights and days of irritations, just as it always did. Carlton lost a total of three slaves, and five were injured. The loss of the slaves would add to the cost of producing the sugar. One of them was a prime buck who toppled into a cauldron of boiling sugar when he was stirring it. Carlton had ordered Taumany to have the slave's body fished out and the sugar boiled again so that there was no loss. When he checked his ledger, Carlton found that the slave had sired four whelps so that the loss of the stallion would be compensated in years to come.

Each day, Carlton relayed news of the progress of the work to Hayes, as the old man rarely left the house. Having completely relinquished all responsibility for Roxborough to Carlton, Hayes, it seemed, was content to decline into old age without a struggle. There was nothing physically wrong with him, as far as Carlton knew, but his father showed a determined reluctance to exert himself in any way.

"After twenty years like the past few days, son, you'll want to do the same," he told Carlton when his son joined him on the balcony as the boiler fire was being damped down and the weeks of work came to an end.

"I'll not have twenty years of it, Father," said Carlton wiping his forehead. "My God, I seem to smell of sugar. If I snatch an hour's sleep I wake up screaming sugar. My clother are full of dust, and my nose is stuffed with the smell of niggers and molasses. It won't worry me if I never see another hogshead in my life!"

"As long as there's Roxborough, there must be sugar, son," nodded the old man. "It needs sugar to keep it going."

"For a few years, Da, that's all. Until my niggers are grown. When my crop is ripe, then we'll be able to reap real dividends."

Claudius entered the balcony without being asked and proffered a tray to Carlton. "A glass of my punch, sir?"

"Claudius, my boy! I don't know where I would be without you. It's just what I want. How's the mistress?" he asked almost as an afterthought.

"She has spent the day thinking of you, sir. I believe she is preparing to join you on the balcony."

"Good heavens! I must scrape off some of this sugar from my skin."

"Tch!" said Hayes. "What are you worried about a little scum for? Tell the mistress that Mas Carlton says sugar has finished for this year. She'll be pleased to hear that, son. She's been missing you these past few weeks, and the baby not long to go."

"Aye," agreed Carlton. "You know, Father, I've got fifty whelps in the pen now. Imagine, fifty! If they fetches a hundred pounds sterling a head, that's five thousand pounds, Da. They'll fetch double that in ten years. Ain't that better than sugar?"

"You've got to feed and season them, son. That takes money."

"I know, Father, but not so much as sugar takes to raise. Look at the risks with every crop. Hurricanes can finish it off, or disease, and then the market can fail, or there is the chance of losing the whole cargo in a storm at sea.

"Livestock looks after itself. The niggers even season themselves. That Claudius, he is a first-class house

300

nigger. Couldn't find better than him, I'll wager. I'll put the whelps to him when they're ready. And Ma Phoebe and Ella can train the fillies to clean and cook. A trained domestic might even fetch three hundred pounds in the future!"

"You know best, son," said Hayes shaking his head doubtfully. "You know best."

Producing the sugar and then shipping off the cargo in the hogsheads from the tiny jetty at Layou meant that Carlton was fully occupied during the final months of his wife's pregnancy. Sybil had shown no sign of any weakness and seemed to glow with health. She spent her time preparing clothes for the baby with Mally Ibo, the old seamstress and her assistants. Sybil even enjoyed the domesticity into which she was settling, and it made up for the times when she used to accompany Carlton around the plantation. She looked forward to doing so again, but now her thoughts were centered around the birth of her son.

Plans had been made for the confinement. Her parents had returned to live in Antigua, driven away from Vandy Hall by debt, so she would have to do without the presence of her mother at the birth. However, it had been arranged with Doctor Farley that he would hasten to Roxborough to stay for at least a week as soon as her time approached. It was Sybil herself who confounded all the carefully made plans. About a month before she had calculated the baby was due, she awoke in the middle of the night with pains that could only mean one thing. Her cries brought her maid, who slept on the floor outside her door, running into the room.

"Take the lantern, girl," gasped Sybil. "Call Mas Carlton quickly."

Although her mistress's face was ghostly pale and her eyes pleaded for help, the maid was slow to realize what was amiss. She ran to Mas Carlton's door and banged it loudly and then, in her anxiety, rushed downstairs to tell Ma Phoebe, to whom, she had been taught all events must be confided. The whole household woke quickly. So unexpected was the labor that it was probable that the good doctor would arrive too late. Nevertheless, Claudius was dispatched to rouse Mingo and to bid him ride immediately for Doctor Farley. Ma Phoebe decided to assume control of the confused situation.

"Pool," she ordered, "stroke up de fire an' boil water. Quick, Ella, you an' me all of us go'n help de mistress an' her son. We does know all de tricks, Miss Sybil, so don't yuh worry about nothing. I done born plenty ob me own whelps an' look dis Ella here she has her own already. Don't fret. I go'n call dat Congo Venue from de pen."

"That's the nigger's midwife," said Carlton.

"Jest so, Mas Carlton," beamed Ma Phoebe proudly. "She has born all your whelps in de pen an' not lost one."

Sybil, who had begun to moan softly, was appalled by this talk of a nigger midwife and the thought of Ma Phoebe and Ella birthing her child. She was a white woman, mistress of Roxborough, and she wanted the nice white doctor Carlton had promised, to deliver her son. But she was in such agony, and out of breath, what could she say? She just wished everybody would stop staring at her as though she was going to die, and let her bring her son into the world herself.

"Ayeeeeeee!" she screamed.

"Now, all you jest go out of here!" Ma Phoebe bustled toward the door. "Beg pardon, Mas Carlton, but dis is de woman's work. Where dat Bo'jack?" she asked at the same moment as Bo'jack entered the room supporting Hayes.

"Massa Hayes, sah," said Ma Phoebe, "dis ain't no place for you, sah. De mistress does be confinin'. Please Massa Hayes, why don't you an' Mas Carlton go on de balcony an' Ma Phoebe go'n sent dat Claudius to yuh wid coffee or de punch as soon as he comes back from wakin' dat Mingo."

"But where's the doctor, where's the doctor?" croaked Hayes in concern. "My grandson must have a doctor here. You did, you know, son," said Hayes turning on Carlton as they both found themselves propelled through the door. "It's not right. Niggers have no right to birth a white boy, leastways, not the heir to Roxborough."

"I'm going back to my bed!" Carlton was irritable. He had been on the point of mounting Orphelia, a thirteen-year-old from the quarters, when Sybil's labor had interrupted him. "Ain't no point in fussing here."

"Bed? Now" Hayes was taken aback by his son's tone.

"Right. Mingo is riding to Roseau for the doctor, but he won't be here for twelve hours at least. More like a day. If Sybil's going to have the baby now, the niggers will just have to birth it. There ain't nothing you and I can do." Carlton paused at his bedroom door. He towered above his father now. It seemed that as he grew, his father shrank. The old man looked scrawny and frail in his nightshirt.

"Don't worry, Da. If you don't want to sleep, Claudius will keep you company."

The old man nodded his head silently, watching Carlton open his bedroom door and enter his room, quickly shutting the door behind him. He shuffled across to a seat and sank into it, watching the closed door of Sybil's room. Bo'jack was dispatched to call Congo Venus, and Pool brought up a small cauldron of boiling water which he handed around the door to Ma Phoebe.

"Ayeeeee!"

Hayes heard the scream and winced. He listened again. To his surprise, it seemed to have an echo. There were tiny yelps and animal grunts coming from Carlton's own bedroom. It was a few seconds before Hayes understood what those sounds meant. He shook his head sadly. His son's concern for his wife seemed no greater than if she had been one of his slaves herself.

The bed in Carlton's room creaked loudly, as Sybil screamed again in hers.

Chapter 35

As dawn broke, pitching its eerie light over the ridge of hills in the east which dominated Roxborough Hall, groups of Negroes congregated in front of the house. The women in their shapeless calico frocks and madras head scarves made a lowing sound together as they watched the light flickering in Mistress Sybil's room. They knew that Congo Venus, Ma Phoebe, and Ella were all with the mistress, and they were hanging on for any movement or sound which might indicate the progress of the birth.

The men idled in more practical groups, curious at this new diversion. With the sun throwing more light into the sky, the number of slaves increased until there was a discernible hum of concern and chatter rising up to the rooms of the hall.

Carlton frowned as he heard the sound. He rolled over onto his back as he lay in bed to listen again. It was an unmistakable Negro noise and he wondered immediately if his son had been born.

"Hey, get up, wench!" he said, pushing the slender coffee-colored girl out of bed so she landed with a startled thump on the floor. "Go back to the quarters, wench. I'll send Claudius for you when I want you, you understand?"

The girl's wide eyes watched him as she sat up on

the floor, her eyes level with the bed. The moaning from the yard continued its persistent pitch.

"Take your dress and get out, you hear!"

"Yes, massa," the girl stammered, groping on the floor for her garment and struggling into it. She opened the door onto the balcony casting a last look at the white buckra in his bed, the first one she had ever slept in, with his lovely golden hair and soft white skin. She saw the bloodstains of her virginity on the white sheet and felt proud that now she was a real Roxborough nigger.

"Get out!' Carlton's boot clumped against the door as she closed it quickly.

There was no one in the drawing room, so he assumed that his father had gone back to bed. He crossed over to his wife's room, but Claudius rose up out of the shadows where he had been waiting and barred his way.

"Good morning, sir. Excuse me, sir, but Ma Phoebe said that no one is to enter the mistress chamber, sir."

"What!" snorted Carlton with a flash of anger, making to push Claudius out of his way. The boy resisted and Carlton kept his hand on his shoulder. For a moment his eyes blazed as he thought of striking the nigger but then shrugged off his irritability and turned away from the door.

"These times are for the women, sir. There's nothing to be done."

"She's not had it yet?"

"Oh no, sir. She been screaming a little. All women do, sir."

"Hah! Young Claudius, since when have you been an expert on confinement?" Carlton sank down into one of the chairs, sticking his long legs out in front of him. Again he was conscious of the constant murmuring below the balcony.

"What's that damn noise all about?" He scratched himself.

"It's the niggers, sir," said Claudius, standing obediently beside his master. "They are waiting for the birth."

"Oh, are they? And where's Kingston and Asaph and the other drivers. Isn't there work to do today like every other day?"

"I suppose they thought they should pay their respects, sir."

"Respects? Claudius, you have a pretty turn of phrase for laziness. If I go out there, the first three niggers I see, I am going to string up from the flamboyant tree by their ankles and flog, baby or no baby. Tell them to disperse, and tell Kingston that it's my son and I am going to work so anyone not on his job today can expect no quarter from me. That includes him!"

"Yes, sir!" Claudius smiled encouragingly and trotted off through the dining room and down the back steps.

The pitch of the murmuring below the balcony changed to a whining and then urgent shuffling as voices started to shepherd the slaves to the fields and roads where they were supposed to be working.

Now Carlton stood up, going purposefully over to Sybil's room. He placed his hand on the latch and opened the door slowly until it came up against the bulk of Ma Phoebe barring his entrance.

"I does be sorry, sah! Dis not for gen'lemens, sah."

"She all right, Ma Phoebe?"

"Yassa, she be fine. Not long now."

Carlton grinned. "If yuh give me a niggah whelp, Ma Phoebe, ah does know you done put your own dere." He patted the cook's enormous stomach as she tried to suppress her laughter.

"Oh my gawd! Yuh'll git a goldin boy like yuhself, sah." Ma Phoebe closed the door resolutely and turned back to face the bed. Ella was bathing Sybil's forehead with bay rum while Congo Venus was regarding the mistress professionally.

"It does be comin'," she said to Ma Phoebe in a whisper.

Sybil was in a trance. She closed her eyes to shut out the three black faces looming over her like carrion crows. A divine force seemed to have taken possession of her body, and she submitted willingly to it. While strong hands were holding her down, she arched and churned and, in the moment of release, gave a scream of such pain and deep satisfaction, that its crescendo carried it far beyond the house and over the tops of the palm trees where it fell on the safe ears of the niggers going to their work. Ma Phoebe braced herself with Ella while Congo Venus assisted. The rattling of the door, which Ma Phoebe had bolted, served to rouse Sybil from her trance.

"What's going on in there. Let me in, damn you!"

"It does be all right, Mas Carlton," said Ma Phoebe, restraining Sybil. "Yuh wife does be having de babe dis moment, sah!" Ma Phoebe glanced at Congo Venus, who nodded. The baby had been born.

"Lord!" whispered Congo Venus. "How we does cut de cord?"

"De cord?" Ma Phoebe was puzzled. "De usual way."

"But she a white lady. I cain' do dat."

Sybil heard the voices of the niggers around her and sensed their alarm. She wanted to ask what was wrong with her son.

"Here," said Ma Phoebe pushing Congo Venus out of the way with her great body. "If you can't do de thing, Ma Phoebe can." She bent down over Sybil and bit into the cord with her teeth, neatly severing it. She raised her head and spat eloquently on the floor as Sybil, her eyes open wide in terror, watched.

She had forgotten her child now; only the sight of Ma Phoebe raising her head from her own body and spitting out her own blood was in her mind. She twisted her head to where Ella smiled reassuringly at her, but all she could see was a ghostly shadow grinning wickedly. Blood seemed to drip from Ma Phoebe's fangs while Congo Venus, a shriveled black harridan like a devil's prune, poked at her as she lay helpless on the bed. Sybil saw the three ugly niggers consuming her and knew, as she lapsed into merciful unconsciousness, that now she was no better than a nigger slave herself.

Congo Venus held up the pink child in awe. Ella gasped. "Eh he red!"

"Dat's de way white babes does be," Ma Phoebe said authoritatively. "Dey don't have no skin at all." The child began to cry. "Yuh does see dat!" she was delighted. "He jest like de massa."

"Ain't no he," said Congo Venus, "for sure. De massa does have a she for his son!"

"Oh!" sighed Ma Phoebe. "He does be vex' for sure, though."

"Why dat?" said Ella. "A daughter bound to bring him plenty sons, if he does want more."

"More? Your's don't count," said Ma Phoebe. "Yuh does know dat."

"Don't he?" said Ella, smiling. "We'll see. We'll see."

Congo Venus cackled. "Dat was be a good confinin', first rate. Don't need no doctor here at all. Don't never have a doctor."

"You ain't never birthed a beké before, neither," said Ma Phoebe, taking the child from her. "I got to take dis pickaninny to she fader. See if he not vexed. Ella, you clean up here an' soothe de mistress. She pass out now. I does be back." Ma Phoebe wrapped the child in a sheet and stood while Congo Venus opened the door for her. Carlton was waiting on the other side.

"So there's my boy," he said, watching the wizened face of the child.

"De buck does be a filly, massa, sah."

"Filly!" exploded Carlton. "What do you mean? White people don't have fillies!"

"I does be sorry, sah." Ma Phoebe cowered at his rage, thrusting the baby at him to protect herself. The child started to cry. "He does be a girl, sah," she tried again.

"I don't believe you," said Carlton, ripping away the sheet from the child as Ma Phoebe held her. He scowled. "A daughter!" he said in disgust.

"Mistress Sybil does be all right, sah," said Ella coming out of the room and smiling sweetly at Carlton. "Let me hold de baby, Ma Phoebe. You go'n clean up." She indicated the trickle of blood still on Ma Phoebe's face.

Ella's presence soothed Carlton. "A daughter, Ella, you see that. Ma Phoebe said a filly, and I suppose she was right. I wanted a son, Ella, you know that. I never expected a . . ." He hesitated. "A filly."

"You has a son, Mas Carlton. Don't forget Caspar. He does be growin 'big just like his da.' He does be very smart, too."

"Yes," Carlton nodded, "Caspar. Hah! Well, this is Sybil's child all right. Hear her bawl. Take her to her mother, will you? I'm going to check on them niggers in the ratoons."

It was left to Hayes to show his concern for Sybil's well being. While she seemed fine physically, and the baby could not have been better, Sybil herself appeared to be in a prolonged state of shock. She hardly stirred the whole morning, although she did respond when Ella roused her to feed the child, but immediately went back to sleep again.

"She does be all right now, Massa Hayes," Ella assured the old man. "See how she does be peaceful now. She be sleepin' good now, dreamin' pretty things."

Hayes was not so certain. Something had happened to change Sybil. He could see it in her face as he sat beside the bed holding her hand and feeling it squeeze his own. He remembered how Monique had been so cheerful when Carlton was born. And so proud. Sybil's mood was not like that.

Sybil, aware that Hayes was with her, felt more secure. The horror of the black women who had hovered over her and devoured her child had passed.

She knew now that if she was no better than a nigger herself, then she was going to behave just like one. She uttered a massive sigh of despair, then lapsed into an untroubled sleep. The smile which crept over her face reassured Hayes, and he stole away from her bedside leaving Ella and her maid to watch over her.

There were no joyful bells ringing over Roxborough that day. The slaves found that they were obligated to work just the same, with Master Carlton riding among them, brandishing his long leather whip, fashioned from a single cowhide, and flicking it lazily over their naked backs. There was no extra rum ration as they had expected. When Asaph dared to congratulate him on the birth of his daughter, Carlton had only snarled.

Claudius, as discreet as ever, had kept quiet. He served Hayes and Carlton their dinner as usual, while Bo'jack shuffled around the table and Pool carried the dishes.

"Seen Sybil?" asked Hayes, breaking the silence, as they came to the end of their meal. "She's looking much more rested now. Still sleeping, though."

"Aye," said Carlton, "I seen her. What do you think of the granddaughter, Da?"

"Granddaughter, grandson, makes no difference to me, boy. You're young yet. Got plenty of spunk to make a dozen children."

Carlton nodded without speaking. He pushed back his chair and went across to peer into the bedroom. Ella was sitting by the bed. He smiled at her. The sound of the door had disturbed Sybil, who twisted in her sleep. She was dreaming of a black man pursuing her up the hill to Roxborough, invading the house and entering her chamber. He was taking her hand into his strong black fingers. She wondered who was this man, this slave, being so forward. She opened her eyes quickly.

Carlton was smiling down kindly, holding her hand

311

in his, but behind him, in the shadows of the room, she was sure she could see the face of the man in her dreams. It was the face of Mingo.

Chapter 36

Sybil loathed Laura. At first, her reaction to the birth of her daughter had been one of indifference, but as she recovered from the physical effects, this changed to a dislike for the baby. She went through the role of motherhood with extreme reluctance, which Hayes was not slow to notice. Laura, as she had been dubbed by Carlton without consultation and with the same lack of passion as when he named a slave child, seemed not to mind. She appeared robust, with the Todds' independence, Hayes was certain. It was Hayes, not Sybil or Carlton, who showed concern for Laura's welfare.

Carlton, of course, was caught up in his breeding program, spending his entire days in his office or touring the plantation. Sybil continued to mope around the house as though completely lost, sometimes bouncing Laura with her when compelled to feed her. It was urgent, decided Hayes, that something be done for the child. He taxed Carlton about it.

"Ain't any of your niggers just had a whelp, Carlton?"

"I know," said Carlton shaking his head as his father offered him the rum pitcher. Claudius, lingering on the gallery after serving them their usual evening drinks, paused to take in the conversation. Sybil was already in bed, her child in a cot beside her.

"I can read your mind, Father. You think the baby needs a wet nurse. Caspar didn't have a wet nurse."

Hayes was confused. "Who's Caspar?"

"Ella's son."

"Oh," said Hayes frowning. "You mean the boy Ella had for you. Well, he's a nigger whelp, ain't he? Niggers know how to suckle their children proper. White women don't always make good mothers, you know. You can't blame Sybil for that. Besides, the child ought to have a nurse."

"I'm not denying it, Father." Carlton accepted the drink which Claudius poured out for him, forgetting his earlier refusal. "Trouble is, I don't have one suitable right now. Seems its not the niggers' season. Oh, I've got them with bellies out to here, and I've got whelps in the pen that's weaned already. But a dam that could come into the house is a different matter."

"It might be worth going to Roseau, son, to see the factors. Maybe they'll have something."

"It's difficult now, you know, Father."

"Excuse me, sir."

"What is it, Claudius!" Carlton had grown used to that quality in Claudius which, in other slaves, would be looked on as impertinence. When Claudius had something to say, it was often of importance. Hayes, on the other hand, could not understand his son's softness toward the slaves, making one into a useless ox of a fighter and now this one his tame black lackey.

"Please, sir," said Claudius, including Hayes in his remark. "I hear that in Layou there is a slave who had a child last week but the child wasn't strong, sir, and it died. She could be for sale, sir."

"How do you know that?" asked Carlton.

"The word just passes around, sir. Layou is not far, and the niggers always know what's going on in the village, sir."

"Bless my soul!" said Hayes. "Those niggers know more about the place than we do."

"Not surprising, is it, Father? They have nothing to do anyway. I wouldn't be surprised if some of them

314

go there at night. Of course," added Carlton quickly to calm the growing agitation of his father, "if we caught a Roxborough nigger in Layou without a ticket, then he's just like a runaway. That's a whipping matter, for sure."

"Aye," said Hayes. "That's what you say. You've got that ox Mingo strolling around not doing much. Let him work out on a nigger's hide sometimes."

"The girl, sir." Claudius wanted them to forget about how he might have heard the information. He had himself been in Layou the night before, gambling a few bits in one of the casinos. "She's a Fulani, sir, I believe."

"Fulani, Sultani, what's the difference?" scoffed Hayes. "That boy seems to have learned too much from you, Carlton. Looks at a nigger's tribe! Never done that in my life. Niggers is niggers."

"Not really, Father," said Carlton, eager to discourse on his favorite subject. "If you know the slave's background before you buy him, you can get a clue what he is going to be like. It's true, Da. I've been following this up a lot. It's like breeding horses. I suppose. Some have a better pedigree than others. Trouble is, nowadays when the slaves are born here, there ain't much trace of where their dams come from, so you don't know where you are, unless you have a trained eye and can tell by their features. I don't know much about Fulani, though."

"President Matson had a Fulani girl, sir," interrupted Claudius.

"Huh!" sniffed Hayes, impressed in spite of himself. "What did those English gentlemen know about slaves?"

"Well, he owned Claudius," said Carlton grinning, "so he certainly wasn't a bad judge." He punched Claudius in his stomach.

"Yes, sir?"

"Where's this Fulani wench? You don't know what she looks like, I suppose?"

Claudius knew very well what she looked like, as he was the one who had fathered her child, which had not died as he had said but was about to be given away for expediency. "She does work for Madame Gregg, sir, in the lady's house, not the casino. I hear tell how she has a clear complexion and nice hair," he ventured.

"Huh!" said Hayes again. "Sounds like more old talk."

"Might be interesting, though, don't you think, Father? I don't mind another filly, and if she's house-broke, Sybil might take to her."

Many of the events which were to happen at Roxborough during the coming years could be traced back to Tita's arrival at the Hall, as a result of the conversation between the two white men and their slave that evening. Claudius and May Gregg had worked out the scheme between them when Tita's baby had been born just before Laura.

May Gregg had been given the girl, Tita, by the captain of an illegal slave ship who had broken her in during the voyage from Africa. It had not taken May Gregg long to season the girl, and she developed a strong attachment for her. Because of her experiences on the voyage through the middle passage, Tita had developed a fierce dislike for white men, and so was quite useless to May Gregg for entertaining her clients in the casino. Instead, May Gregg took her into her own house and bed, and they passed nights of hectic lovemaking together which delighted the old whore as much as the Fulani.

It was when the dapper nigger from the house on the hill caught her attention and Tita began to entertain Claudius in May Gregg's house that May Gregg saw possibilities in selling the girl to the Bondmaster. She urged Claudius to use his influence to push the sale through, emphasizing Tita's rare features, the reddish brown, almost Mediterranean complexion, her straight hair and straight nose and slender build. The Bondmaster could not fail to be captivated by her.

And so it was. Never one to put sentiment before

316

money, May Gregg drove a bargain which was satisfactory both to her and to Carlton. She had gold and the pleasure of knowing she would still be able to lie down with her Fulani girl whenever the wench had a chance to visit the village. Carlton was delighted at the girl's appearance and bearing, and her full breasts would be perfect for his mewling daughter. That Claudius and Tita were also overjoyed at the way things had turned out was of no consequence to anyone but the slaves themselves.

When Sybil set her eyes on Tita, she could hardly believe her good fortune.

"You like what I've brought you?" asked Carlton diffidently, ushering the wench into his wife's chambers. "A christening present."

"She's mine?" Sybil spoke sharply to cover her amazement.

"All yours," said Carlton. "I bought her just for you. She's yours to do what you like with."

"You breeding from her?" Still the sharp, anguished tone.

Carlton shrugged his shoulders. "I would be surprised if a wench like she is remains without a buck for long."

"That's different," said Sybil sniffing. "I'm asking if you are going to tell her who to breed with?"

Carlton shrugged. "No, I don't think so. All my bucks around here are prime. But she's yours, I really mean that."

For the first time since the birth of Laura, Sybil looked directly at her husband. The sincerity in his expression impressed her. She put out her hand from where she sat in the bed and gripped him around the waist. He stepped closer to her, bending his head lower. She kissed his cheek as Tita watched.

"Thank you," she murmured.

Laura, who had been sleeping in her cot, suddenly awoke and decided to cry. Sybil and Carlton both saw Tita's frown of concern at the sound and, without waiting to be told, she stepped over to the cot, picked up

317

the baby, and began to nurse it. The crying stopped, Laura sensing a warmth she had not known before.

"You can feed her," said Sybil. Carlton smiled. For once his wife was happy.

Over the months Sybil's disposition changed from her sour exasperation at Laura's birth to sweetness. Carlton attributed it to the effects of motherhood itself. Hayes, too, was delighted when Sybil bounced Laura on her knee and showed off like any proud English mother. With her slave Tita always at her heels, Sybil began to take an interest in the management of the house, sending for cloth and brightening the rooms with new cushions and curtains that the seamstress made up at her direction. She also began to converse again, although she shunned the rum and would take to her bed early.

"That child," pronounced Hayes one evening after Sybil had taken off for her chambers, followed by Tita, "has changed your wife completely. Now she seems to be a wife worthy of Roxborough."

Carlton looked up from the book he had been reading. Claudius, who had been holding the lantern low so he could see the print, stood back and hung the lantern on its hook. Carlton closed the book with a sigh.

"It's true," he said, "and she seems to have taken to Tita all right, which is pleasing to me."

Had he known, Carlton would have been surprised just how much his wife had taken to the wet nurse he had bought her. Even as he spoke to his father, his wife, in the privacy of her bedchamber, was urging Tita to hurry in removing her clothes. The lantern in the chamber had burned down very low and, as Tita was unfastening her garments, she urged the maid to brush her skin with her lips.

"Oh!" she moaned, "suck me, suck me like a child." Sybil held Tita's head between her breasts and then, as she lay back naked on her bed, pushed the slave's head down to her thighs. She linked her ankles behind

318

Tita's neck, locking the slave girl into her loins. Tita responded willingly, marveling that a white woman should be so demanding.

Their lovemaking that night, as it did every night, drained away the frustrations of the life she was being forced to lead at Roxborough. Sybil clutched Tita closer to her, vowing never to let the Fulani leave her, making her swear that she would never know a man again. Tita, trusting her mistress, obeyed.

Chapter 37

The tranquillity which followed the arrival of Tita
at Roxborough grew from days to months and into
years. Because of the state of the roads, the Todds
could spend months without seeing anyone from Roseau
or hearing news of the activities in the capital. They
had better information of events outside Dominica
through vessels anchoring in the Layou basin. This
link with the rest of the world enabled Roxborough
to be completely self-sufficient. The vessel which collected their sugar brought their supplies, and the plantation was so fertile that they were never short of
local produce. Far from feeling frustrated at this lack
of communication with others, Carlton relished it.

At Roxborough, he ruled like a feudal lord over
his own domain. When he did venture to Roseau or
any of the neighboring villages, he found conditions
so inadequate that he was relieved to return home. His
attachment to Claudius grew each year, and he became
increasingly dependent on him as the link between the
big house and the slave quarters.

Together with Ma Phoebe and Ella, the boy provided
Carlton with an intelligence service which enabled him
to anticipate reactions before they happened. Of course,
this was at a cost, and although the Bondmaster was
unaware of it, he was now as much a slave to Claudius
as Claudius was to him. In subtle ways, Claudius was

able to manipulate his master more than anyone else on the plantation, even Ma Phoebe. None of the slaves resented this, regarding Claudius as their own safety valve which would prevent something setting off the Bondmaster on a rampage.

Claudius, of course, was not averse to charging for his favors. The slaves were happy to have Ma Phoebe intercede with fate on their behalf, and Claudius to perform a similar function with the Bondmaster. Claudius's private stock of gold and trinkets began to increase, and he had his own open invitation to any house and daughter in the slave quarters. Ella, too, was fond of Claudius for the way he looked after her son. He had become Caspar's adopted father, spending hours playing with the boy, influencing him with his own personality.

"Don't know why Mas Carlton don't put da' boy in de pen wid de oders," observed Bo'jack one day as Caspar darted between his legs where he was playing with Claudius on the kitchen steps.

"Dis is one nigger ain't go'n be sold, da's why," Ella retorted.

"How you know dat?" replied Bo'jack, aiming a cuff at the child's head as he darted back. "Mas Carlton don't seem interested in him."

"I know," said Ella." I tell yuh I know plenty things."

"You an' Ma Phoebe!" Bo'jack gave up trying to catch Caspar and sank down on a bench. "You does think yuh know every liddle thing. S'pose yuh want tell me dat one day dis nigger child go'n own dis plantation an' de white man be workin' for him! Heh, heh, heh!"

"Could happen," broke in Claudius. "Anything is possible. Look, Bo'jack, how many free Negroes are there in Dominica right now?"

Bo'jack shook his head. The idea of a free Negro did not seem right to him.

"There's lots already. There's the maroons in the hills."

"Dem maroons?" Ma Phoebe eased her bulk forward in the chair where she had been napping while Ella prepared the dinner. "Dem maroons? How dey free? Dem's runaways. Dem's briganditti or some such. Dem not free. Don't bring da' kind of talk to Roxborough, Mas Claudius. We does be happy niggers at Roxborough. Don't want no runaways."

Claudius chuckled. "All right, Ma Phoebe, don't gobble so, you'll break the chair. It's not runaways I am referring to. I mean those slaves who have bought their freedom, or got it through birth. Look at Caspar here." He caught the boy as he ran past and held him close to him. He was a fine-looking lad with an almost yellow complexion and his father's soft hair, although it was black like his mother's. He had hazel instead of niggery-brown eyes and a perceptive stare.

"No one can tell me that this boy is going to be a slave like all us. He's half-free already."

"Hold your tongue!" It was Ella who spoke.

"You does see," chortled Bo'jack. "De boy's mam does have no mind of your nonsense. I does still say dat de massa must send him to de pen wid de others. He does have a hundred or more of dem dere now."

"Eighty-three, to be exact."

"Oy, oy, Claudius! You does know dat better dan de massa."

Claudius shook his head. "Master Carlton knows. That's money for him. Every day he counts them. You never notice how he sells the old field hands and doesn't buy more? There ain't many able-bodied men left on the plantation now. It's those young niggers who are the new crop for Roxborough. But this boy Caspar isn't one of them."

It was true. Bo'jack nodded his head sadly. So many of the friends he had known for years had gone, either sold or died. He rarely went to the quarters now; everyone was younger than he and no one offered him a drop of rum they had managed to get from the stillman.

"You does be all right," accused Bo'jack. "You does take off to de village at nights wid Mingo. Likes of me an' Ma Phoebe here has to stay here at nights. Ain't got no one to welcome us no more."

"Dat's right," said Ma Phoebe. "Yuh better take care dat de massa don't ketch yuh sometime."

"Where I goes when I goes to my bed is my business!" Claudius laughed. "Give me the goblet of cool water, Ella. Come, Caspar, let us go'n see your father in his office."

As they walked around to the front of the house and across the yard to the cabin which Carlton still used as an office in the day, Claudius instructed Caspar. "Always look after Mas Carlton properly. Try to think what he's going to want before he does. Now, did you hear him send for a drink?"

"No."

"Not no, boy. No, sir."

"But ain't you a slave?" Caspar looked up at the man beside him in his bright orange pants and white shirt. "What for I does call yuh sir?"

"Everyone's a slave, Caspar. But you must still have respect. Now, Mas Carlton did not send for a drink, right? But it is nearly midday, you see by the sun, so he is certain to have a great thirst in this heat. He has some old rum in his office, I know, because I put it there myself. If he fancies a little drink now, then he'll welcome this cool water. He'll think better of us for remembering it before he does."

The child nodded gravely. He adored Claudius, and whatever the man told him to do must be right.

"Knock on the side of the house and tell him good day."

Caspar wrapped on the wall of the cabin by the open door. "Good day, sir!" he piped up loudly. Claudius grinned.

Raising his head from his ledger, Carlton gazed out into the sunlight at the little boy, preparing to reprimand him for disturbing him, but when he saw it was his own son, he mellowed. "What you want, boy?"

Caspar looked up at Claudius, who was hidden by the door jamb. He looked back at his father. "Excuse me, sir. I have brought de cool water in case you does want a drink, sir."

"I'll be blowed!" exclaimed Carlton. "That Claudius put you up to this, I suppose." He jumped down from his stool, and bade the boy enter. Claudius came in behind him.

"That's it, Claudius," he said, accepting the pitcher of water and splashing some into a glass with rum. "Got to train the boy early. I wonder what his age is now? Six? Seven?

"He'll make a fine servant for someone. See his bright color?" Carlton patted his son's cheek. "Boy, you'll fetch a fine price when you are another two or three years in age. Especially at auction. You must learn everything Claudius can teach you."

"Does I have to call him sah, sah?"

"If he's your teacher, yes. If he's your servant, no."

"Please, sir," said Claudius, "may I have a word with you?"

"Of course," said Carlton, settling back onto the stool and waving his son away. The boy laughed at Claudius and then ran off across the yard.

"It's something I heard, sir."

"Well, let me know what it is, Claudius."

"I'm not sure if it's anything important to you, sir. President Matson always told me to keep my ears open, and this kind of information he would have paid well for, sir."

Carlton frowned, his dark eyebrows almost joining in a line across his forehead. His temper, which was not so quick now that he was getting mature, nevertheless bubbled to the surface on occasions such as these. Now he almost exploded. "What! You trying to sell me information, are you? I'll see you whipped alive first!"

"Oh no, sir," said Claudius, surprised at himself for starting off on the wrong foot. "I just meant to explain, sir, that this kind of information would have appealed to the President, sir, but it might not be of any interest to you, sir."

"That's for me to decide. Get on with it!"

"It's the French, sir."

"What French? We don't have French here."

"Not at Roxborough, sir, but there's plenty in Layou. And in the other villages, sir. I have heard things."

"Get on, get on!"

"I hear that a big invasion is planned, sir. Any day now. The French navy are going to sail into Dominica and capture the island, sir. That must not happen, sir. I know the French. They are not good, sir."

If Carlton had cared to enquire into the dislike of his slave for the French, he would have found it based solely on commercial motives. Claudius felt that the French were more attuned to the wiles of life in the tropics and so were less easily fooled than the English. But Carlton, surprised by the tenor of Claudius's information, immediately wanted to know how he had come by it. That was what Claudius had feared.

"Well, sir, sometimes when I go to Layou to do a message, sir, or to see Mr. Belle, or check on the wagon, when it carries the rum, sir."

"That's Mingo's job, isn't it?" interrupted Carlton, seeing something amiss in his carefully planned schedule for the running of the estate.

"It is, sir, but I accompany him sometimes, when there is nothing for me to do here, sir."

"Did I authorize that?"

"No, sir."

"I see."

"Sir, when I'm out," continued Claudius rapidly, "I always listen to what people are saying, like President Matson told me to do. There are so many French people in the village, sir. It is said that they are preparing for the invasion. Some of them say that one day they must own this plantation, sir."

"What! Carlton thumped the desk. That could be why the French were interested in Layou. There was a perfect anchorage in the river mouth for a few ships of the line, and there were no defenses. They could have been sent to spy out the land for a surprise attack. But there was always talk of the French coming to attack Dominica. How certain could he be that this rumor was any more true than any of the others?

Carlton leaned forward on the desk, resting his chin in his hands and peering with his pale eyes from his vantage point on the raised dais into the deep brown eyes of his slave. Under his searching gaze, Claudius shifted nervously.

"So, my fine Claudius, a likely story. First you confess that you have been going to Layou without my knowledge, and you back this up with some cock-and-bull story about an invasion."

"It's true, sir."

"You say I am lying?"

"Oh no, sir. But all them French in Layou, sir."

"They come and they go. It's of no consequence." Carlton was adamant. This was one of his slave's stories that he was not going to accept. If he sent a runner to Roseau saying that he had heard that the French were going to attack and he was afraid of a few Frenchies camping on his boundaries, what sort of fool would he look?

Claudius, however, had other views. "Beg pardon, sir," he persisted, "if the French do come and if they take over the estate, what would happen to us slaves, sir?"

"Have I misjudged you, Claudius?" said Carlton, filling his glass with rum and taking the water goblet again. "I would have thought that your first concern would be what would happen to the Bondmaster and his family before considering the fate of the Negroes."

"Oh yes, of course, sir. You would escape with your wife and daughter and Massa Hayes, sir, in a vessel which I would endeavor to have standing by, sir."

"In that case, perhaps I would take my faithful Claudius with me."

"And Mingo and Tita, sir?"

"If you like. Mingo ain't so fast now, but I dare say we could train him up to earn prize money for us to survive," he humored the nigger.

"Sir, another question. If a slave like me were to ask you for his freedom, sir, to buy it, I mean, would you allow it, sir?"

Carlton's reaction was to choke, spluttering his rum over Claudius's face. "Freedom! What ails you today, Claudius? Who wants freedom? You do? I'll give you freedom with a lashing like you've never known before. Freedom, pah! If a white man offered me a thousand pound for you, I wouldn't think of it, so no nigger's going to buy his freedom for buttons and silver buckles he's stolen from my lady's chamber.

"Get out!"

Chapter 38

Claudius was used to his master's quick rages. He stood his ground. Carlton had closed his eyes in an effort to control himself and when he opened them he was surprised to see Claudius still there, pouring a measure of rum into his glass and proffering it to him. He scowled. Claudius placed the rum on the desk and stood back.

"Forgive me if I displeased you, sir. There does be slaves who buy their freedom, sir."

"But not you, my Claudius! You are worth real money, not paltry nail-parings and buckets of cock's blood. Don't think you can get one of your wretched obeah women to work some kind of potion that's going to make me suddenly turn around and manumit you." Carlton reached for the glass which Claudius had filled for him. He swallowed the contents and contemplated Claudius again, half closing his eyes as he did so. Claudius judged him to be more than a little drunk.

"I'll tell you, Claudius. About ten years ago—no, when I was thirteen—I had a slave of my very own. He grew up with me and we were like two peas in a pod except that he was black. He was more faithful than a dog, Claudius. He knew everything I wanted even before I did. He slept in my room, not on the floor but in my bed with me. Oh, yes," Carlton sighed, "he was a perfect slave."

Carlton got up from the desk and stepped unsteadily down from the dais. Then he did a strange thing. He put his arm around Claudius's shoulder and pulled the slave close to him, hugging him. "I vowed then, Claudius," he said as he released him, "that I would never part with a slave like him when I became Bondmaster. Well," he continued brusquely, "I'm the Bondmaster now, and you are that Prince!"

"Yes, sir," said Claudius, stepping back to the doorway. "If I was free, sir, I would not leave you, sir. I could still serve you, sir."

"Why this continued talk of freedom, Claudius? Is it your intention to rile me beyond tolerance?"

"No, sir. I've got a thousand pounds, sir. I'm asking you for my freedom, sir."

"What!" Carlton took a step backwards, colliding with the desk. He gripped the top, staring at his slave. "What foolishness is this? Don't you understand, Claudius? You are a slave. You cannot possess currency, you cannot buy your freedom. Now go, and leave me. I have work to do."

Claudius attempted to speak and then, thinking of a different tactic, bowed his head slightly in response and stepped out of the cabin. Carlton, looking up, realized he had departed and took up the rum bottle. He poured another measure and drank it eagerly. He felt as though he were in the middle of a situation he could not master as yet. First, the one slave he trusted came with a French invasion story he could not possibly believe and then the same slave claimed to have the money to buy his freedom.

"I've got it!" he said to himself, pounding the palm of his left hand with the fist of his right. "The nigger needs a little touch-up. I've been too easy on him. He has too many privileges. I've been treating him like a human being, and it has confused him."

He sat down on the top of the desk, thinking about where he had gone wrong with Claudius. Was he wrong to let the boy dress so smartly? No, his slave needed special raiment. Was he wrong to confide in him? No, a gentleman's personal slave was privy to innermost confidences. Was he too slack with him? Perhaps yes. He assumed that his slave was doing things when in fact he might not be. When he was supposed to be visiting the quarters, he might have been in Layou. Even the best cur needs a kick in the rear occasionally.

It was at this point in his thoughts that Claudius returned to the cabin, balancing on his shoulder a small wooden box such as a tradesman might use for his tools. He rapped on the door jamb and then entered, depositing the box on the desk top in front of Carlton.

"Here, sir," he said proudly. "This is to prove that I am not lying to you, sir."

"What's this?"

If Claudius had paid his usual attention to his master's moods, he would have noticed the danger sign of the rasping tone with which Carlton was speaking. But he ignored the menace in his master's drunken speech and pressed on.

"My treasury, sir."

Carlton's frown was eloquence itself. He did not speak, but watched the face of the Negro standing in front of him. He saw the broad brow capped by whorls of shiny black hair; he saw the ebony complexion and the smoothness of the boy's high cheeks; he saw the deep brown eyes watching him intently, and he saw the fat pouting lips stretched over glistening teeth. Slowly Carlton arose, steadying himself on the desk. He brought up his right hand across his chest and unleashed a forearm smash across the slave's cheek with all the strength his drunken fury gave him.

Claudius staggered back, the hope in his eyes rudely shattered. He rested against the cabin wall, horror spreading through his as he watched his master turn up his treasury box and empty its contents over the desk.

"So!" said Carlton, surprised at the amount of bits, gold pieces, and other currency which the box contained. "This is your treasury, is it? This is your freedom? No! No! No!" He hurled the box to the ground and turned to face Claudius. "This is treachery, not treasury!" He spat directly into the boy's face.

"See how you repay me. All the years I have kept you here, trusting you, treating you like a boy, not an animal. You come at me with a box full of money and demand your freedom."

"But the money's mine, sir!" Claudius dared to protest.

"And you are mine!"

Claudius lowered his head. "Yes, sir," he whispered, and Carlton could scarcely hear him.

"You lie to me about a French invasion, you are in possession of currency which you shouldn't have, and you ask for freedom without reason!" Carlton glanced out of the doorway of the cabin to see who was around. His eye fell on Mingo squatting under a flamboyant tree talking to young Caspar. He bellowed to him to come over.

"Claudius, I want you to know you are my slave for life." Carlton stood directly in front of the boy, noting how the self-confidence had oozed out of him as though, in rejecting his plea for freedom, Carlton had drained the boy of the very quality which endeared him to him. "I am keeping your treasury, and I want to hear no more talk of freedom, or French men of war, do you hear!"

"Yes, sir."

"Mingo! Come in. Take this nigger here and lock him in the hot house for a spell."

"Claudius, sah?" Mingo was incredulous.

"That's right! Claudius, and don't think it can't be you, as well. At Roxborough, we have only good niggers. That's what's going to make the Roxborough breed famous. So when a nigger is bad, he has to be punished, so he learns his lesson. I remember," Carlton added unexpectantly as he glanced around the cabin, "I had a tutor once. She was French, Claudius. She would rap me across my knuckles when I forgot what she was teaching me. I soon learned. A thrashing from

331

the flamboyant tree should help you to remember your place, now and for always."

"Yes, sir," said Claudius dully.

"Take him away, Mingo. But wait, there's no need to put him in the hot house. Take him straight to the tree. I'll warrant dinner isn't ready yet. There's time to etch your lesson in your backside before you have to serve us at table."

Beatings at Roxborough were a regular part of the day. There was not a slave who did not know the price of the lash across his back while he was working. The routine dusting by the drivers of the field gangs had accustomed everyone to the quick sting, then searing pain, of different kinds of whips, according to the driver's fancy. Major punishment, however, was reserved for Mingo to execute at the Bondmaster's command. Sometimes weeks would pass without anyone causing offense, while at other times the bell summoning all hands to the house to watch a whipping rang daily.

Cynics among the slave fraternity blamed the frequency of punishment on the prowess of Carlton's current bed wench, and each girl was schooled properly on how to drain the passion from the Bondmaster so that his energies could not be aroused to persecute them. The more astute may have observed that punishments were more frequent whenever Carlton felt his personal security threatened, from however remote a source. The fact that an invasion by the French was rumored contributed to his desire to inflict his will on Claudius. He had convinced himself that punishment was necessary, and now to force his decision through, he strolled over to the bell scaffold and began to pull the rope to ring it himself.

The sound of the big bell rolled over the savannah and cane fields. The tones reverberated down to the quarters and along the trail to the ferry at the river. The wind carried the ominous peals down to Layou Village, where the Negroes stopped what they were doing and twitched involuntarily. Outside her casino,

May Gregg heard the notes of the big bell and nodded her head. It was as sure a sign of Carlton Todd's uncertain conscience as was the sudden chill wind a sign of rainfall. May Gregg called her daughter over from where she was playing in the rutted street and held her close. "He must have heard the news, too," she murmured.

Sybil, who had been playing with Laura on the balcony, peered around the corner down into the yard. She saw her husband tugging the bell rope and wondered what catastrophe had stirred him to do that job himself. Glancing at the flamboyant tree, she was amazed to see that Mingo was tying a rope around Claudius, now naked and placid as he sat on the ground. Leaving Laura by herself, she ran around to her bedroom where Tita was resting on her bed.

"Oh, do come, Tita dear," she cooed. "Someone you know is to be whipped."

"Ah don't care about dat, ma'am," Tita replied lazily, not stirring from her mistress's bed. "It ain't me."

"You will care when you see! But stay there if you want."

"Who dat, den?" Tita sat up, now that her curiosity had been aroused.

"I shan't tell you!" Sybil hurried back to the corner where she could see, and then back to poke her head in her bedroom window again. "Oh, do come, you'll miss it! That gorgeous Mingo is to do the whipping. He has already stripped off his shirt and stands there in the sun flexing his muscles like some dusky Greek god. It is your Claudius he is going to thrash!"

"*Mon dieu!*" shrieked Tita, swinging off the bed and coming quickly to the balcony. She was dressed exactly like her mistress, not in a cast-off dress but one which the seamstress had made up for her. To the casual observer, Sybil and Tita could have been sisters, one tawnier than the other. Sybil, however, assured herself that there was a difference between them in the amount

333

of lace and jewelry with which she bedecked herself, while Tita was limited to a simple pendant.

The distinction between mistress and servant had been eroded by the bond of lust which still existed between them. Their intimacy had progressed to the sharing of fantasies about the various studs on the plantation, and Tita knew full well of her mistress's desire for Mingo, while she pretended that her own fantasy was for Claudius, never once revealing that with her it was more than a fantasy.

The two stood clasping each other on the balcony, Laura ignored as she ran up and down. "But what de nigger done do?" asked Tita. "Mas Carlton never done punish my Claudius befo'."

"Well, he is now, see him ringing the bell."

The slaves had begun to gather around the front square as was their habit on hearing the bell. The news that it was Claudius who was being punished spread among them, and many of the women in the quarters dropped their preparations for dinner to toil up the hill in the blazing sun to witness this strange occurrence.

"I think my husband must have had too much rum again," smirked Sybil, observing Carlton's flushed face.

"String him up, Mingo!" called Carlton, his chest heaving with the unexpected exertion of hauling the bell rope. "I want you all to hear," he shouted, glaring at the niggers around him. The low murmur of protest dropped as he spoke. "This slave here has lied to me. And he has money of his own in abundance with which he wanted to purchase his freedom. A slave is not entitled to property. You are all bondsmen, not freemen. That's why Claudius is being punished now."

Carlton stopped, out of breath. The murmur of resentment began again. Carlton strode off toward the steps, the crowd falling apart in front of him, each one afraid to restrict his progress in case he ordered them to be strung up too. Carlton reached the steps and climbed up slowly, turning to face the slaves when he reached the top. He did not look at his wife and Tita.

"Give him two dozen lashes!"

"Two dozen!" exclaimed Tita. "Dat must kill he." She clasped Sybil in her distress. "Oh, ma'am, can't you do somet'in' for him? Pray wid your husban' spare my Claudius."

"Your Claudius? I thought that he was just a dream man to you, Tita?"

"Oh yas, dat's de tru', ma'am. But I does have no use of a dead dream man, ma'am."

Sybil watched intently as Mingo hauled on the rope which was tied around Claudius's ankle and looped over the branch of the tree. As Mingo pulled, Claudius slowly rose feet first into the air. Mingo secured the rope when Claudius was hanging upside down above the ground, his hands dangling down but unable to touch the ground to support himself. A boy had brought Mingo the long leather whip he was to use, and he picked it up and made a trial flick, sending the whip cracking in the air with a sharp explosion which echoed in the sudden silence.

Sybil clasped Tita this time, thrilling at the sight of Mingo's muscular body wielding so much power. "Oh, he is magnificent!" she gurgled as the whip cut through the air and sliced into the soft flesh of Claudius's bottom, sending his body spinning.

"Oh ma'am," whined Tita. "Please stop he, if you love yo' Tita."

"I do love you," said Sybil caressing Tita's hair as the maid laid her head on her breast. "But don't you think Mingo has such style?"

Carlton, oblivious to everything around him, began to count the strokes. One, two, three. Something was pulling at his pants. Carlton looked down to see little Laura standing there. "Daddy, Daddy!" she was calling. He smiled and bent down to pick her up. Four.

"You want to see the bad nigger being beaten?"

"Look, Daddy! Look, Daddy!" said Laura pointing out to sea.

Carlton, amused by his daughter's inattentiveness, gave a quick glance in the direction she was pointing. The whip scorched the air again.

"Stop, Mingo!'

Carlton could not believe the sight. He rubbed his eyes and looked out to sea again. There were at least a dozen ships in full sail bearing down on the capital. They were so close inshore that if there were a cannon on the Roxborough hills, he could have sunk them. Even without a spy glass, he could make out five sail of the line, four frigates, and three smaller vessels. As he watched, the leading vessel hauled down the French tricolor she was flying and slowly ran up the English flag.

The invasion had come.

Chapter 39

Carlton gulped. What trickery it was to be exchanging flags, Carlton could not fathom. He looked around him helplessly. There must be two or three thousand men on so many ships. They would overwhelm General Prevost's regiment which was supposed to defend the capital. There was no way he could send a warning to the Governor now. The messenger would arrive after the enemy.

The slaves on the ground did not have the benefit of Carlton's view out to sea from where he was standing at the top of the steps. They were eyeing him uncertainly, wondering what ailed the master as he looked around himself in confusion. They saw him holding his daughter and looking toward his wife.

"Do you see that, Sybil?"

"Oh, my husband! What a lot of sail!"

"It's the French. They are sailing on to Roseau with the English flag flying. It must be a trick to fool Sir George Prevost into thinking they are English. The artillery won't be prepared. They'll take the town!"

"Do you think so, my husband? How tiresome." Sybil had released Tita, who was thanking unknown gods for this provident interruption. "Aren't you going to continue the whipping, Carlton? It was rather fun."

Sybil's request reminded him. He looked down at the grotesque sight of Claudius dangling upside down from the flamboyant tree, petals from its red flowers strewn on the ground. Mingo stood waiting patiently, the whip supple and easy in his hand.

"Cut him down!" ordered Carlton. "And bring him here."

Many hands reached up to lower Claudius to the ground and unbind him. Tita wanted to run over and lay her hand on his forehead, but knew that she might herself be flogged if she did so. Instead, she clutched at her mistress's hand as they both watched. The slaves attempted to carry Claudius up the steps to the Bond-master, but Claudius made them put him down.

"I am not so weak I cannot walk to my master," he told them, steadying himself on Mingo's shoulder while the blood settled down.

"I does be sorry I done lash yuh, Claudius," said Mingo in embarrassment.

"Lash me? If that's what you call a lashing, then the niggers here have the softest life I know. Mingo, you lost all your strength on them fillies. I scarcely felt the whip at all."

"Don't pain yuh den?"

"No," said Claudius, "not at all."

Mingo smiled. "We does still be friends, Claudius?" He put his arm around the smaller man's body as a gesture of affection.

"Always will be, you great makak," said Claudius as they mounted the steps. He was still naked and had not thought to put on his pants before standing in front of his master.

Carlton looked at Claudius. There was the usual alert willingness in his expression. What a remarkable nigger he was. "Turn around, Claudius."

"It's nothing, sir."

"I don't mean I want to see your damn black bottom, Claudius. Look behind you."

When he turned, Claudius realized what had saved him. The ships were awe-inspiring, sails billowing in the wind. He tried to count them all but some were so

338

close together it was impossible to distinguish one from the other. His eyes were blazing as he spun back excitedly to his master, the pain in his backside forgotten.

"The French, sir?"

"It is possible, boy. I want you to get Ma Phoebe to dress your bottom with some of her unguent. Make sure she does not bathe the welts with pepper! That's for the niggers that need it. I'm giving you a chance. I want you to ride to Roseau to see what's happening.

"Assess the situation and then ride straight back here. You'll confirm your story about the French if it's true. Do not stay in the town, though. Remain only long enough to see if the St. George's regiment is repelling the invasion. We must know here so we can make our preparations."

"Yes, sir!" Now Claudius was in a position to prove his worth. He realized that he was being entrusted with a mission that not even a freeman would be asked to do. "I will ride at once, sir. May I have Mingo with me, sir? In case I come under attack."

Carlton looked at him sharply. It could be a plan for the two of them to run away. On the other hand, there was sense in Mingo's going, for if the situation turned out as bad as the number of ships seemed to indicate, there would be a better opportunity for one of them to get back to Roxborough with the news than if Claudius went alone. He nodded. "You can take the fastest horses, but don't tire them, as you may have to ride straight back. I'll write you a ticket."

He spun around and went into the house, leaving Claudius and Mingo at the top of the steps. They gazed out to sea again. Claudius smiled at Mingo. "You see, brother, I knew they was coming. One of the Frenchies told me himself. Now is the time for the slaves to rise up and rebel, you know, Mingo. Ain' nothing Mas Carlton and the other buckras can do. They'll be busy defending themselves against the French." He allowed Mingo to help him down to the kitchen.

Mingo was horrified. "I don' wan' no part in dat. Not me dat does rebel against Mas Carlton. No way."

"That's right, Mingo. And the others?"

"Dey don't have no sense of rebellion."

Claudius nodded his head. It was true. He had already been trying to sound out the mood of the Roxborough slaves. There were many bands of runaways and maroons in the hills and they were getting more influential, with new slaves joining them every day. The Roxborough slaves, though, were not so interested in joining them, as the pattern of life at Roxborough was by no means unpleasant. The work was minimal now that Master Carlton had reduced the reliance on sugar and was concentrating on raising more Negro babies. No one understood why he wanted to do that, but it was all right with them all. There would be no uprising at Roxborough.

After Claudius had been treated by Ma Phoebe and Ella, he mounted the horse which Marmaduke had saddled for him. He was dressed in his best outfit and looked for all the world like a young gentleman of leisure. Mingo, in contrast, wore his usual calico pants and a shirt. Claudius hoped that he looked like a free Negro riding with a servant. He had secured his guarantee, the ticket for them both from the Bondmaster, inside his long coat in case he should be stopped by the militia. He tried to ignore the fire and tenderness in his bottom as he and Mingo galloped off down the hill to the ferry, waving jauntily to Mas Carlton watching from the balcony and much inspired by the cheers of the slaves lining the path.

"Hurrumph!" Hayes snorted as Carlton turned to face his father where he was seated in his chair. Sybil had retired to her chamber, clasping Tita, both of them shedding tears. "Never seen the like of that in my life!"

"At least twelve vessels, Father."

"I don't mean that pesky navy. I mean those two bucks what just rode out of here."

"How do you mean?" Carlton hated to hear criticism of his slaves.

"You send off your two best niggers to Roseau? If you see them again, it will be a fortnight next Tuesday, and without the horses. They'll sell them in Roseau and spend the money in the casinos, sure as dogs have tails. More like, they'll not even bother to come back, just hope that you think they've been killed when Roseau comes under fire. I declare, I never thought a son of mine could be so foolish.

"You think that's what will happen, Father?" Carlton sat down in the chair beside his father, automatically looking around for Claudius to bring him a drink. No one was there; Bo'jack was probably dozing in the kitchen. He decided to forget about a drink. "I think you're wrong, Father. We have to take a chance. We've got preparations to make if the French succeed."

"What kind of preparation is that, son?" Hayes sucked on his gums. "French were here before, never gave us a bit of trouble."

"My mother was alive then, wasn't she? She was French. This is 1805, Father. Times have changed. The English and the French are at war, Father. The French could sack the plantation, maybe free the niggers, too."

"Oh, aye, that's what you're doing anyway, only you give them horses to ride out on."

"We might have to flee, Father. Take the bullion with us. Go to Antigua."

"Flee from Roxborough? Never! I'll die here and be buried with the bullion under that flamboyant tree right there." Hayes pointed out to the yard. "No sense in fleeing only to let the niggers take over, is there? As long as the Bondmaster is here, there'll be no trouble with the slaves, son, even if the French do come."

"What about ourselves?"

"You scared of the French, son? Negotiate, that's all. That's what I did before, and I didn't even speak the lingo the way you do."

They exchanged the same conversation in different

syllables throughout the day. Sybil added her views when she joined them for dinner, but in private expressed her concern to Tita for the safety of her Mingo while Tita's anxiety was for Claudius. Tita knew that he was perfectly capable of taking care of himself, but she wondered if he would return. If not, she decided, she would leave Roxborough and find out where he was and join him.

Carlton had difficulty in falling asleep that night. There were so many possibilities racing through his mind. The sight of such an armed navy had convinced him of the plantation's vulnerability. He had sent Kingston to Layou for information, and the old bookkeeper had returned with the news that the casinos were packed with sympathizers ready to welcome the French. All vessels at the anchorage had shipped anchor and sailed away, so even escape by sea seemed to be cut off.

As he was at last drifting into sleep, cries outside the house disturbed him. He listened anxiously. The sounds of horses galloping into the yard were accompanied by the shouts of someone calling to Ella to open up the kitchen quickly. Was it Claudius returning so soon?

Carlton leaped out of bed and flung open the shutter. He could see nothing. He grabbed his lantern, padding in his nightshirt and bare feet into the drawing room. He turned the heavy wooden bolt on the front door and pushed it open, rushing to the balcony edge and peering out into the blackness below. Sounds were coming from the back of the house by the kitchen. When he reached the back steps, he saw that it was indeed Claudius who even now was helping Mingo off his horse and urging Ella to take him inside the kitchen.

Claudius struggled up the step to meet Carlton. His face was covered with dust and soot, his fine clothes were ripped, and he was near to collapse. Carlton hugged the boy to him, his nose wrinkling at the stench of his sweaty body.

"Come, come, Claudius, you are safe now." He led him into the drawing room and sat him in a chair, the first time that a slave had ever sat down in that room with Carlton's knowledge and consent. He went to the buffet and, finding some rum left from the evening session on the balcony with his father, he poured a large shot into his own mug and offered it to Claudius.

"Drink this, boy. It will give you strength."

Out of breath, his lips stretched across his teeth in agony, Claudius watched his master through glazed eyes. He took the rum and swallowed it quickly. He spluttered but kept it down.

"Dat's de buckra rum!" he panted. Carlton nodded his head encouragingly.

"Oh, massa!" said Claudius, after he had paused to catch his breath. "De town done burn, sah."

"Take your time, Claudius. Tell me in English."

"Yes, sir. I'm sorry, sir. Well, when we got to Roseau, the battle had been going strong, sir. We could see the vessels attacking the town before we reached it. And them Negroes, they were running away from the capital. Going into the bush. Well, when we reached there, the French were attacking from Woodbridge's Bay, sir, while the English were firing right across the town from Young's Fort. Then the town caught fire, sir."

Carlton nodded gravely. It was worse than he had expected.

"The whole of Roseau was burning. All the shingle roofs went up in flames. Seems like it was the wadding from the English cannonade what caused it, sir, and then all the people living in Roseau were fighting the French off, anyway, so no one could stop the fire, the niggers having run off already. You should have heard the noise. All them rum casks exploding in the stores and the people running everywhere."

"So Roseau has fallen to the French."

"Not exactly, sir. The General sir, that's Sir George Prevost, he did make a deal with the French."

"A deal? A surrender? So soon?" Carlton sank down in a chair in despair.

"No, sir. I spoke to him myself. I said that I came from the Bondmaster of Roxborough, and he sent you his compliments and says he is marching to Prince Rupert's to draw the French from the town to save it. 'Maintain the sovereignty' were his exact words, sir."

A hush fell on the drawing room. A suicidal moth crashed into the lantern glass. Claudius, still tense with exhaustion, waited impatiently.

Carlton was rubbing his hand through the blond curls at the back of his neck. Prince Rupert's was at the north of the island on the same coast as Roxborough. There was a fine anchorage there, and Fort Shirley was bristling with artillery. It was a sensible decision.

"How will he get there?" wondered Carlton aloud.

"He's marching up the Roseau valley, sir. We saw them all set off at sunset."

Carlton frowned. That was going to be a long march. The troops would have to pass inland to the east coast and then back along the north coast to reach Fort Shirley. It was an arduous journey but it would be safer than exposing the army to the French fire if they marched along the leeward coast. There was no trail, anyway. When Carlton had to go north, he took a boat. There was no chance of that this time.

"How do you feel, Claudius?"

"All right, sir," the boy grinned bravely. "It's Mingo that's hurt. A beam that was on fire fell on him, sir. Burnt his arm."

Carlton stood up. "I'll see him. I want you to go in my chamber and lie on my bed."

"Your bed, sir?"

"Yes, Claudius. No questions now, boy. It's softer than the pallet in the dressing room. Your arse must be burning you something terrible," he grinned, making amends. "You'll get two hours sleep, then we'll leave for Prince Rupert's."

"To fight, sir?" In spite of his exhaustion, Claudius's eyes blazed with excitement.

"Yes, nigger, to fight."

Chapter 40

While Claudius slept cautiously on his master's bed, the household was roused and soon bustled with activity. His father agreed with Carlton's decision to ride in pursuit of General Prevost and offer his services. The militia itself was composed of part-time soldiers obliged by law to train for the defense of the country. It was because of the location of Roxborough that Carlton had been excused his duty.

"You must go, son. Now is not the time to shirk your duty." Hayes sat up in bed, a nightcap stuck jauntily on his head, as he listened to Carlton.

"But what about you?"

"Me? I'm perfectly capable of taking care of the plantation while you are away. I did for twenty years, you know, and that's when we had sugar, not a breeding station."

"I must have a slave with me to prime the guns— two, really, but I'll make do with one. Mingo's the obvious choice, but he's burned his arm. Ella says it will heal in a few days' time, and she and Ma Phoebe are dressing it. Seems I'll have to take Claudius and leave Mingo here with you. He is strong enough once his arm gets better. You must put him to sleep in the cellar and have him help you move around and so forth."

"Dammit, Carlton Todd. You are worse than your

mother. I've told you I can take care of myself. It's you that's the one should look for assistance!" Hayes shook his finger in a warning at his son, who grinned at the old man's spirit.

"That's fine, Da. Remember to watch the Negroes, though. They don't have much work to do now, and they could get restless with all the activity. Kingston and Asaph and the drivers can keep them at the weeding or something."

"Get out!" said Hayes. "Make haste with your preparations or you'll never catch General Prevost until the battle's over."

Sybil's reaction to Carlton's proposed departure was one of feigned concern over his welfare. Her interest increased, however, when he told her of his decision to leave the house in Mingo's care. "If there is anything you want when I am gone, just ask Mingo to help you," said Carlton. "He is a good nigger and won't be disrespectful. Let my father deal with the field slaves, though."

"If you say so," answered Sybil, her mind racing at the new possibilities presenting themselves.

In the kitchen, the farewell was more concerned. Both Ma Phoebe and Ella rushed to give Carlton advice, and Ella particularly urged him to take great care. Mingo accepted his responsibilities as house protector gravely. "Whatever Massa Hayes or Mistress Sybil asks you to do, you must obey them," Carlton emphasized.

"Yassa, Mas Carlton, sah. I does understand."

"If he don't, Mas Carlton, Ma Phoebe de one dat does lay into him wid blows, yessa!"

Carlton laughed, thumping Ma Phoebe on her rump. "You'd be a match for any man, Ma Phoebe! Keep the niggers quiet and help Massa Hayes if he needs you."

"Yessa!" Ma Phoebe beamed proudly and threw a glance of haughty contempt at Bo'jack hovering at her side.

Carlton strode out of the kitchen. He had dressed himself and wore his best boots, shining brightly in the lantern glow, with a brace of pistols around his waist under his scarlet coat. Two horses had been saddled and waited at the front steps where Claudius, feeling a little refreshed after his rest but sustained more with the excitement of the trip, held them. Carlton kissed his wife, embraced his father, and then mounted his horse.

"Sir! Sir!" cried a shrill voice, tiny hands reaching up in the darkness to grip his leg. "Take me wid yuh. Please, sah, take me wid yuh!"

"Hush, child!" Ella ran forward, clutching her long dress above her ankles. She grabbed the child and pulled him away from the horse. "I does be sorry, Mas Carlton. He does be troublesome so."

"Huh!" Carlton looked down fondly at his son. "You're a good boy, Caspar."

The boy looked up adoringly at his father on the horse. "Yes, sir?" he replied hopefully.

"Your duty is here, Caspar. You must protect your mother, you hear, and help her well."

"If you does say so, sah! Always, sah."

Carlton's heart soared as he rode off into the night. It was curious how Ella and her son seemed to hold a far greater love for him than his wife and daughter did. It was fitting that they should be the ones to speed him on his way. He glanced back at the house. Already the lanterns were being extinguished. Sybil had left the balcony, and even her chamber was in darkness. A lantern still burned on the step illuminating the figure of Ella standing with Caspar clinging to her, peering out into the darkness.

Dawn broke as they headed east, the blackness of the sky punctuated with a set of bright stars which retreated as the pale light of daybreak spread over the island. The trail was overhung with thick bush, creepers, and branches dripping heavy dew on them as they passed. With the spreading light, they were able to make better progress, climbing steadily all the time. The horses were used to rough trails and picked their way carefully. Carlton warmed himself with rum from his flask, trying to forget the cold damp clothes which clung to him, soaked with dew and his own perspiration. He passed the flask to Claudius, who hesitated before accepting it.

"Go on, boy, take it." Carlton knew his slave's hesitation was not because he was reluctant to drink rum but because he was being offered his master's own bottle to drink from. They were going to battle together, they might die together, they were alone in the dense jungle together. Carlton could afford to breach the master/slave etiquette instilled in his niggers since birth. Besides, Claudius was an exceptional nigger, one who had somehow managed to acquire enough money to buy his freedom.

"If you still want your freedom, Claudius," he asked the boy when he returned the flask, "why did you return to Roxborough?"

"It was my duty, sir."

"You don't have to flatter me just because I let you drink from my flask, Claudius. You never will be free, boy. Not because I may refuse to manumit you. It's not chains which enslave you, Claudius. You are a Negro, descended from the blacks of Africa. Negroes can never be free in this world, even if they are not slaves."

"As you say, sir. I am yours. You have shown me I was wrong to ask you to sell me my freedom, sir. I will always serve you faithfully."

"Tell me something, Claudius." Carlton put his hand out to touch the boy's thigh as the trail broadened and they were able to ride side by side. "Where did a nigger like you get so much gold? Did you steal it from your president benefactor?"

"Sir!" Claudius was offended. "I may be a worthless nigger, and you were right to order Mingo to thrash me for my boldness. But I have never been a thief, sir."

"My! you protest too much."

"I cannot tell you where I got the money, sir. But it is mine."

"Yours, Claudius?"

"I'm sorry, sir," said Claudius quickly, noticing the telltale edge of rage which had crept into his master's voice. It must have been the rum, thought Claudius, to make him so stupid. His master was wrong to appear so friendly and trap him like that. "It is yours, sir. I am your property, and my property is yours."

Carlton rode on briskly, satisfied that he had imposed himself sufficiently and now the nigger knew his place.

There was no more welcome sight for Carlton than when his horse stumbled through a stretch of seemingly endless bush and he found himself face to face with a group of scarlet-coated soldiers holding guns at his chest.

Carlton was immediately attached by General Prevost to his forces, and the army made surprisingly good progress to Prince Rupert's under the General's ruthless enthusiasm. By sunset, they were within sight of the coast and burst through the bush surrounding the bay as the sun descended into the sea beyond the Cabrits. Prince Rupert's bay looked peaceful; the vast basin, which could accommodate the whole of the British navy safely riding at anchor all seasons of the year, was deserted. Fort Shirley, which lay between the two high mountains called the Cabrits north of the bay, exhibited the preparations caused by the General's advance warnings of the shifting of operations from Roseau to Portsmouth.

The General, who had expected to find the French fleet waiting for him, having sent a message to their Commander, General La Grange, that he was withdrawing to Prince Rupert's where he hoped to engage them, was puzzled by their absence. It was only later that Carlton learned that the French, furious at the accidental burning of Roseau, had stayed to try to stem the flames, possibly to preserve the value of their prize. Whatever the reasons, the delay gave the army time to make preparations. That night, Carlton slept with the officers in the fort while Claudius lay on his stomach on the stone floor of the store, trying to ease his aching backside.

The next day, the battle began anew with the French bombarding the fort and landing soldiers at various points around the bay to attack the fort from the land. Carlton had been assigned to a group under a regular officer whose job it was to man one of the approaches to the fort through the swamp and so repel any potential attackers. It was the first time that Carlton had been engaged in any battle. At the beginning, he found it enormous fun.

Quite secure behind a large boulder, a few yards from the group he was supposed to be with, but within shouting range, he wedged himself comfortably between the stones, overlooking the swamp and able to watch the exchange of cannonade between the fort and the vessels bombarding it. Claudius, lacking his master's self-confidence, cowered behind the boulder intent on performing his duties, priming his master's pistols and handing them to him as required. Carlton took out the flask and took a deep draft of his beloved Roxborough rum. He did not offer his slave any this time, although Claudius eyed the flask greedily.

The first assault on the path they guarded was repelled with ease. Taking the pistols handed to him by Claudius, Carlton stuck his head around the boulder, eyed a Frenchy as he dodged through the bush, took aim, and fired. He was careful not to remain exposed long enough to see whether he actually killed anyone, but the combined fire of the group was enough to send the attackers scrambling for shelter.

"Damn good sport this, Claudius."

"Yes, sir," gulped the slave, fumbling with the empty pistols.

"Of course, they know that we are here now," pointed out Carlton. "Next time may be fiercer. We can beat them, though, no doubt about it. Just keep those pistols primed, boy."

Claudius hardly had time to talk, so he nodded his

head emphatically as more buckshot flew overhead.

Carlton poked his head out and quickly withdrew it. "I say, there seem to be rather more of them this time."

He took the pistols Claudius handed him and peeped out more cautiously. He spied a figure wriggling up the side of the path, took aim, and watched in fascination as he blew a neat hole in the man's forehead.

"Sir! Sir! Behind you, sir!"

Hearing the cry from Claudius, Carlton turned immediately to see a Frenchman about to fire at him. Quickly Carlton lifted his pistol to eye level and pulled the trigger. Nothing happened. The man had ducked. Carlton spun around to where Claudius was fumbling to reload the spare pistol.

"A pistol, damn you!"

"I can't load it, sir."

"Quick!" Sensing that he was in the Frenchman's sights, Carlton threw himself on the ground, pulling Claudius down on top of him. In that instant, he heard the dull thud of the Frenchman's gun and then a twitch of surprise from Claudius, whose body was shielding him. Carlton lay without daring to breathe, awaiting the follow-up shot. When none came, he squirmed closer to the boulder, hugging Claudius close to him.

"Sir!" whispered Claudius huskily. "I'm wounded, sir."

"Shut your mouth, boy!" hissed Carlton, worried lest the Frenchman should decide to take a second shot. Firing had stopped from all the other posts guarding the path. Carlton realized in astonishment that he was covered with blood, spurting over him from a hole in his slave's chest.

"I'm dying, sir."

"Shhhh!"

"My gold, sir."

"I told you, Claudius, a slave don't have property. Will you never learn, boy? Keep quiet, for God's sake. I'll have Mingo thrash you thoroughly when we get back to Roxborough."

"I'm not going back, sir," croaked Claudius, a smile spreading across his young face. "Will you give Mingo his freedom, sir? Use that money, sir. Please, sir."

"What!" hissed Carlton again. "You still talking, boy?" Carlton shifted his body slowly to bring his face close to Claudius to make him understand that he must keep quiet. But it was too late. Claudius would never speak again. He was dead.

"Damn you!" said Carlton, cowering under the slave's body as shots began to pound the boulder. "Damn you, Claudius!"

BOOK THREE

Black Gold

Chapter 41

Perhaps it was natural for the mistress to seem so concerned about his arm, thought Mingo. But he knew that it was unusual for Mistress Sybil to descend to the kitchen. Yet no sooner had Mas Carlton and Claudius galloped off into the night to meet with the General's forces than Mistress Sybil came down the back stairs carrying a lantern. Mingo sat on a bench at the long wooden table used for the preparation of food. His arm was laid out on the top of the table while Ma Phoebe peered at it. The flesh of the upper side of his left forearm had been scorched, but the wound was not serious.

Sybil blanched to see it. "Oh, Mingo!" she cried, lifting her nightgown high to reveal her white ankles as she stepped into the kitchen. "You poor thing!"

"Yas, ma'am?" Mingo jumped to his feet quickly while Ma Phoebe shuffled forward protectively.

"De mistress like some coffee?" asked Ma Phoebe, wondering why Sybil had come down to her kitchen. She could have sent that girl Tita—or was the mistress waiting on her slave now? Ma Phoebe advanced to the end of the table, where she stood with her arms folded firmly across her massive bosom to emphasize who was in charge in the kitchen. Sybil ignored her and rushed up to Mingo, putting out a hand to touch his bare shoulder.

"Oh, sit down, boy," she cooed, pressing on his shoulder. "No need to stand up. I want to see what happened to you."

"Yas, ma'am," answered Mingo politely, glancing across at Ma Phoebe and wondering what she was thinking. Under the pressure of his mistress's hand on his shoulder, he sat back on the bench, laying out the arm for her to inspect.

"Was jest a piece of timber dat done fall on my arm, ma'am, when Roseau done burn. De shingle roof an' de trash roof all done ketch de fire from de wadding of de cannons, ma'am. Dis ain't nothing."

"Of course it ain't," chipped in Ma Phoebe, glaring from the end of the table. "I does have de remedy to fix him fine, Mistress. Tomorrow, he go'n be de new houseboy till dat Claudius come back, an' no trouble wid dat."

"That's all right, then," said Sybil, still with her hand on Mingo's shoulder, but preparing to leave. She smiled at something which had pleased her. "With Mas Carlton away, Mingo, we shall be relying on you. The master said that you must do anything we ask of you, you remember?"

"Yas, ma'am. I does be pleased to, ma'am." He tried to stand, but Sybil's hand on his shoulder urged him to remain in his place. Again he glanced at Ma Phoebe.

"That's good. You must remember that. I am a poor defenseless woman all alone here, and I will need your protection."

"Yas, ma'am."

"Massa Hayes does be here, Mistress." Ma Phoebe could not keep quiet in the face of such a slight to her real master.

Sybil turned on her quickly, a tight smile on her face. "I did not ask you to speak, Phoebe! If necessary you will have to be strung up and whipped, as fat as you are. There are plenty of bucks here could tear that black flesh off your fat carcass if Mingo's arm is sick. Do not feel that you are immune from punish-

357

ment. If my beloved husband does not notice your impertinence, I do."

Ma Phoebe's face began to fill with air like a balloon. She had never been spoken to so! And in her own kitchen, too! Her dark eyes blazed as she watched Sybil squeeze Mingo's shoulder and then draw away from him with obvious reluctance.

"You must call me at seven o'clock, Mingo. I shall leave my chamber open, so come right in. Bring me coffee, so that I can drink it in my bed." Sybil raised her head haughtily, hoisted up her nightdress, and picked her way out of the kitchen, collecting her lantern from the end of the table. At the door, she turned, inclined her head toward Mingo, and gave her tight smile again. "Do not be late, Mingo, nor you, Phoebe, in the preparation of the coffee, for you know what will happen."

Sybil groped her way out and up the steps, the torrent of angry patois unleashed in the kitchen telling her that she had managed to upset that dreadful cook's smug complacency. That fat Phoebe would soon see who was the mistress of Roxborough. And so would that adorable brute Mingo.

The rapping on the door surprised her. She had lain awake for so long planning the moment when Mingo would come that she had quite lost count of the time and fallen asleep. She opened her eyes. Tita had come through from the dressing room where she had been sleeping with Laura and removed the bar on the inside of the door to open it. Mingo entered.

Although it was already light outside, the shutters kept out the sun, and so the room was encased in soft shadows. Sybil edged herself up on her pillows to gaze more intimately on Mingo. He had dressed himself in a clean shirt and, she was amazed to see, a pair of breeches instead of his customary ragged pantaloons. But the breeches were tight, hugging his thighs like a white skin. The bulge of his crotch was quite the largest she had ever seen, and she was transported in her mind back to the days when she would supervise

358

his training sessions by the river. Then she had found his body grotesque, but now it inspired in her a fascination which made her yearn to reach out and touch it. Mingo balanced a silver tray in his large hand, and she noticed that his arm was now bandaged.

"How is your wound this morning?" she asked sweetly.

"It does be better, ma'am. Ma Phoebe and Ella done bind it good last night."

"Put the coffee down there." She pointed to a table near the bed, and Mingo cautiously placed the tray on it. "Tita," she ordered the hovering girl whose eyes were wide at her mistress's boldness in having the nigger in her chamber while she was still in her nightclothes.

"Tita! You may look about my daughter. There is no need to disturb us at all. Mingo will serve my coffee. You understand?"

"Yes, mistress!" Tita flounced out of the room, banging the door behind her to emphasize that she knew exactly what her mistress had in mind.

"There," said Sybil with a nervous giggle. "Now we are quite alone."

"Yas, ma'am."

"There is no one here with us at all, Mingo. Tita is in her room with Laura, and Phoebe is in her place in the kitchen. There is no one who can disturb us, Mingo."

"No, ma'am."

"For goodness' sake, you great black ox, don't just stand there."

"Ma'am?" Mingo shuffled his feet.

"Well, pour me a cup of coffee."

"Yas, ma'am." He reached down to the tiny table and picked up the pot and began to pour the coffee into the cup. Sybil noticed with amusement that his hand was shaking.

She took the cup from him when he proffered it, sipping daintily. It was just right. She raised her eyebrow at him and smiled in what she hoped was an alluring manner. "Why don't you sit down?"

He looked around. There was a chair by the wall. He walked over to it, knowing he must do whatever his mistress wished.

"Not over there, boy! Oh, what a silly nigger you are! No, come and sit here." She patted a spot beside her on the bed.

"It does be all right, ma'am."

"It is not all right! I order you to come and sit here on the bed."

Mingo's scratching of his thick curly hair indicated his puzzlement at his mistress's command, but he had to obey so he sat gently at the foot of the bed.

"Mingo," cooed Sybil, patting the space at her side once again, "you don't have to be scared of your mistress, you know. I am not going to have you whipped, unless you disobey me, of course. Yes, you do realize that, don't you, Mingo? If you disobey me, then I must have you punished. You wouldn't do that, would you, Mingo? You would do whatever I asked of you, wouldn't you?"

"Yas, yas, ma'am." Mingo understood orders. It was the gnawing suspicion which he felt in his heart that he should not be in Mas Carlton's wife's chamber at all which was troubling him.

"Well, come and sit here beside me. I want to look at your arm," she added as he hesitated.

Mingo moved further up the bed and offered the mistress his arm. She put her thin white hand over his powerful black wrist, which was almost as broad as her hand was long. She peered at the bandage on the arm, letting her eyes fall to where the bulge was bunched up in those beautiful tight breeches. She stroked his wrist.

"Does it hurt?" she whispered, her voice dropping a few tones.

He inclined his head forward to catch what she was saying. "No, ma'am, it does be fine." He could not remove his wrist without giving offense, as she was still stroking it, a tender motion which was making his flesh tingle. Her hand released his wrist and fell to his knee, resting there and then sliding up his thigh, brushing his inner leg.

"These are fine britches," she murmured in a husky voice. "The material is fine quality."

"Yas, ma'am." Mingo felt as though he was being strangled. Her hand continued to trace patterns on his thigh.

"They fit you so well."

Mingo gulped. If she did not stop, he knew that he was going to burst. The hand was moving faster now, in a circular motion, creeping up toward his crotch with each circle she made, the flat of her palm sending emotions soaring through him such as he had never experienced before. "Oh, ma'am," he whispered. "It does trouble me, trouble me."

"Trouble you, whatever for?" Her hand paused over the growing bulge in his breeches. The cloth was straining under the pressure, and her hand descended with determination to grasp him. "Oh, Mingo, Mingo!"

His eyes were half closed as he grappled with the feelings swamping him. He longed to seize her in his arms and pummel her body until she stopped. Instead, her hand was pawing at his *tuli* with a ruthlessness which would surely make it break. He felt her fingers pry inside his breeches and then her hand ripped the ties wide open and gripped the whole of him in her warm white fingers.

Sybil gasped as she saw the length of what she held. He was black and enormous, quite like a donkey. She trembled, wondering what it was going to be like with such a huge weapon inside her. She released him, moving over on the bed to make room for him beside her. He sat helplessly, not daring to move, his *tuli* dancing in front of him, his head held in shame and confusion.

"Come, Mingo," she said, tugging his shoulders. "Lie with me."

"Ma'am," he croaked, "de massa?"

"Mas Carlton told you to do what I commanded, did he not? Well, I am ordering you to lie down here on the bed and rest. Such a hard night you had, didn't you, Mingo?"

"Yas, ma'am."

He lay back on her pillows, closing his eyes and abandoning himself to whatever she wished to do. He kept his wounded arm hanging over the edge as he felt her hands exploring him again. She tugged at his breeches and began to peel them down his thighs. He arched his back to enable her to slide them under his buttocks, and he felt the gentle caress of her lips on his flesh. His *tuli* leaped in surprise.

Her long black hair tickled his thighs as she tugged the breeches right off his legs. He kept his eyes closed as he felt her straddle him. She gripped him desperately, guiding him, and then with a low moan began to ride him slowly at first, then gathering speed. Her hair brushed against his chest and face as she swept her head from side to side.

He remained as immobile as he could, allowing her to accommodate herself, but the pitch became too intense. A hand was caressing his groin, a finger tracing patterns between his legs. He did not know it, but another hand was fondling Sybil's bottom, a finger seeking out its intimacies. A mouth was nibbling his side with tiny bites, lips shivering the matted hair spreading out from his crotch. He reached up his hands to grasp the shoulders of the woman riding him and then, in a blind explosion, felt her collapse on top of him. The hand continued to caress his balls.

"Oh, Tita!" gasped Sybil.

Mingo opened his eyes. His mistress was stretched like a white wraith across his naked body, still clutching him inside her. Tita, also naked, lay on the bed with them, her hand plying his balls while her lips returned Sybil's deep and lingering kiss as both women lay with their heads resting on his chest. Mingo felt a stirring within him and put his arms with tenderness around the shoulders of both.

Laura, standing at the door of the dressing room, watched with fascination as her mother and Nanny Tita began to ride the black man like a horse.

Chapter 42

It was nearly two weeks before Carlton returned to Roxborough. A messenger had arrived, after the encounter between the garrison at Prince Rupert's and the French, to inform Hayes that his son was safe. That he should stay away so long did not worry Hayes, as he was aware of the damage to the island wrought by the French. There was much weeding and maintenance work to do on the plantation, and the slaves under the relentless eye of the overseers and drivers were content to perform their duties obediently.

Carlton's return was unannounced, and it was Mingo who noticed him riding up the hill. He was leaving his mistress's room by the gallery door and quickly stepped back into the room, surprising Sybil and Tita who had begun to embrace each other in the luxurious afterglow of Mingo's attentions.

"Ma'am!" His exclamation surprised them, both opening their eyes and staring at him.

"Fie on you, Mingo! You return for more?" laughed Sybil, clasping Tita to her and laughing.

"It does be Mas Carlton, ma'am."

"Indeed," said Sybil. "And what does be Mas Carlton?" It was late in the afternoon. The heat of the day was vanishing before the breeze which wafted occasionally through the shutters cooling the room. It was the lazy time of the day which Sybil loved to spend on her bed delighting in the diversions which her dear slave Tita could dream up to relieve the monotony of plantation life. The introduction of Mingo into these pastimes had been her constant dream now so wonderfully achieved.

"Oh, come back here, you gorgeous brute. I want you to bite me all over!"

Tita giggled with delight.

"Ma'am," said Mingo, waving his hand urgently in the direction of the gallery. "The massa does be comin', ma'am."

"What!" Sybil sat upright suddenly, clutching her naked bosom with her hands. "We are undone!"

"No, mistress!" Tita was more practical. "There is nothing amiss in you taking a sleep in the afternoon, ma'am. I shall be attending you." Tita got out of the bed and swept quickly across the room, her slim naked body distracting Mingo as he tried unhappily to contemplate his fate. She gathered up her dress from the chair where it had been thrown and was about to go into the dressing room when she remembered Mingo.

"Quick, Mingo, out through the back door and onto the gallery. Pass around the back of the house and then down the back steps. Remember, you have every right to be in the house, for you have been attending your mistress and Massa Hayes ever since Mas Carlton went away. Do not be afraid, Mingo." Tita looked at the giant, who was almost trembling at the thought of his master's return. "Nothing will befall you, donkey, if you keep your wits about you."

"Oh, Tita, how wise you are. Of course, Mingo," said Sybil, "there is nothing to fear. Look, you are dressed and perfectly decent. Be off with you this instant, and greet your master promptly." She paused to look around the cover of the bed for her own chemise, a thought striking her as she did so. She gazed at Mingo, a saintly smile on her thin lips. "And Mingo," she cooed, "if you fail us, I shall be obliged to tell Mas Carlton how you burst in here and raped me the night he left."

"And me!" chimed in Tita happily.

"What a slow and excruciating death would be your punishment, my black stallion!" Sybil laughed shrilly. "Now go!"

The inactivity of the house at this hour was no surprise to Carlton. The slaves, having finished their duties for the day, were scarcely in evidence as he rode the path toward the house. Smoke from the fires in the quarters drifted skyward, and those slaves who were around watched him noiselessly. He expected no joyful homecoming from creatures to whom his absence would mean only that there were fewer thrashings for their daily misdemeanors. Strangely, even Mingo's smile of welcome was curiously muted, and his eyes —which Carlton remembered as being direct and friendly—found difficulty in returning his own demanding gaze.

"How now, Mingo? Why this sullen look at my return?"

"Beg pardon, Mas Carlton, sah. I was be relaxin' an' sleep done take me, sah."

"Such a sweet life you've been living, I'll be bound." He jumped down from his horse and clapped the slave on his muscular back. "Fine clothes you wear now, Mingo."

"Miss Sybil done order de raiment for me, massa."

"Yes, yes," Carlton nodded. "Leave the horse for Marmaduke to stable. How is that arm of yours?"

Mingo pulled back the yellow sleeve of his silk shirt to show his master how well it had healed.

"H'm," said Carlton. "Silk, too? The mistress has taken a fancy to you, Mingo? Handing out fine clothes for ugly niggers to prance in? I hope you took good care of all the fillies while I was gone, eh?"

"Yas, sah," answered the slave, following his master up the front staircase.

"Are you serving in the house now, Mingo?"

"Yas sah," answered the slave, fear of what his master might find out making him stammer.

"Then you should know, boy, that upon his return

to Roxborough, the Bondmaster craves nothing more than an obedient tongue, which thank God you have, a welcoming smile, which seems curiously absent from your visage, and a glass of strong rum punch. Stop moping around my ankles like a chastised cur and jump to it, Mingo."

Mingo scuttled out as Ma Phoebe burst into the drawing room, her huge frame heaving with the effort of hauling herself up the back stairs. She held out her arms to embrace the Bondmaster, falling to her knees and grasping him around the waist, resting her sweating head on his stomach. She was sobbing, her cries muffled as she kept her head buried in Carlton's shirt. He drew her head away.

"For heaven's sake, Ma Phoebe! I am much touched by the fervor of your welcome, but I fear that you will convert a perfectly good shirt into a handkerchief!"

"Oh lord, yuh done come back, massa! I does be so glad! I never think I does live to see your safe return, Mas Carlton, sah."

Carlton broke away from Ma Phoebe and threw himself onto the sofa, stretching out his muddy boots over the worn fabric. Ma Phoebe struggled to her feet. "I'm weary, Ma Phoebe, we fought a fearful battle, but the French couldn't kill me. You need not concern yourself so. Tell me, Ma Phoebe, how are Ella and my son?"

"Dey does be fine, Mas Carlton. Ella does be preparin' de fire fuh de supper, sah. Caspar, he does kip axing where his massa does be, sah. Dat boy does be smart, sah."

Carlton grinned proudly. "Takes after his father," he smiled, pleased to be home at last. "Tell Ella I will see her tonight."

"Yassa."

"Carlton!" Hayes's shout brought Carlton to his feet. The old man embraced him, tears filling his eyes. "Yes, son," he said after contemplating him for a few seconds at arm's length, "you have seen a battle, I declare. You kill many Frenchies?"

"I cannot say, Father. I certainly shot at plenty. Until they overran us. That Prince Rupert's is a most frightful place. The swamp is very sickly. If you are fortunate to survive the enemy, the yellow fever gets you. The garrison was vastly understrength because of the black vomit, Father, and General Prevost's men were tired after the march from Roseau. But we acquitted ourselves well. The General negotiated a settlement."

"So I heard, son, so I heard." Hayes sank into the chair opposite his son while Phoebe stood forgotten, her mouth agape at the news.

"I returned to Roseau with the General. The town is in a ruinous state indeed. A third part is burned down, and the storehouses being consumed by the fire, both food and clothing were destroyed. The enemy demanded a large sum of money and took with him all vessels in the harbor except two, and those would not carry sail. They also seized many Negroes and plundered the residences that were not burned in the fire. So many Negroes fled into the hills, Father, it is doubtful if they will return. And if they return, how can they survive when their masters are so badly off?"

"Aye," Hayes nodded his head. "We are fortunate here, especially so now that you have returned." Mingo had entered quietly and set down the wooden tray with its pewter jug containing the punch and its two mugs on the low table between the two seated men. "We have fared all right here. This boy," he indicated Mingo, "has been broken in quickly. Your wife has been coaching him."

"Good." Carlton's reply was mournful.

"What ails you, son?" said Hayes sharply.

"Nothing, Da. We'll be needing Mingo, that's all."

"How so?"

"In the house, I mean. Claudius is dead."

"Whaaaaa!" Ma Phoebe's howl slipped out before

she could stop it. "Oh my gawd! Dat be de truth, massa?"

"Yes, Ma Phoebe. He died saving my life."

"Sorry to hear that, son. He was a gradely slave." Hayes sipped at the punch which Mingo had poured for him and began to talk plantation business. Ma Phoebe, her shoulders shaking with sobs, allowed herself to be guided out of the drawing room by Mingo. She had sensed that a tragedy would soon befall Roxborough, and now she could see her predictions coming true.

Hearing his father out, for he knew that the old man had done his task as caretaker of the plantation with zealousness even though his frailty prevented him from touring the estate, Carlton pondered. "It is a curious thing, Da," he said when his father had finished and he had expressed his satisfaction with the arrangements. "That nigger Claudius had somehow acquired almost a king's ransom in gold and currency. Well, a slave's ransom, at least."

"Stole it from you, I'll warrant."

"No, sir. Seems not, because I keep my own chest locked, with the only key right here on this gold chain around my neck. I believe that he was honest. How he acquired the money is not my concern now. Tell me, Da, when a man dies in your arms and he makes you pledge to do something for him, you are obliged to do it, of course."

"Why, yes."

"Now, what if a slave does the same thing?"

"A slave? In your arms?"

"That's what happened, Da. As Claudius died he asked me to use his money to free Mingo."

"What preposterousness next? You are too soft with your niggers, Carlton. What was the boy doing in your arms?"

"Dying, Da. He saved my life, you see. He shielded my body from the attack."

"Well, he was a slave. I would not let a slave's dying wish concern me, would you, Carlton?"

369

"No, Da. Thank you. Besides, it looks like we need that Mingo here."

"We certainly do, Carlton, my husband!"

"Sybil!" Carlton stood up, holding out his arms as Sybil ran prettily to him. She looked radiant, and it suddenly occurred to him how lucky he was to be married and have a wife to welcome him home. Her embrace was so warm and tender and happy that he had to hold her off and, with his arms on hers, he contemplated her. She had taken time with her hair and, as though in honor of his return, wore a full-hooped gown with all the accouterments. Standing demurely in the growing shadows behind her was Tita, looking as radiant as her mistress and clothed in similar luxury.

"My wife!" said Carlton. "You make me feel quite ashamed, standing before you in my traveling clothes."

"But you are my hero husband back from the battle! How can you be ashamed? It is I who should feel ashamed for such a tardy welcome. You must forgive me, I was resting when the slave brought the news of your return. Was all safe? Where is our dear Claudius?"

"Dead, Sybil. He died saving my life."

"Oh!" The gasp came not from his wife's lips, but from the lips of Tita.

"Let's not talk about the dead, Sybil. Let's talk about you. You look absolutely perfect."

"Aye," growled Hayes. "The woman has blossomed in your absence, Carlton, though I don't know why. You can even hear her singing in the mornings."

"Yes, it is true, Carlton. Not because of your absence, but to keep me cheerful for your return. We have such a lot to talk about, Carlton. With Claudius dead, what shall we do in the house? You'll have to keep on that boy Mingo, I suppose."

"Is that all right with you?" Carlton enquired anxiously. "We can get a young slave from the quarters to break in, too."

"Well, I shall miss Claudius, he was such a gentleman, but I dare say we can abide the rusticity of young Mingo." She glanced back at Tita now crying freely.

"Forgive me, my husband, I must take my maid back to my chamber. She seems quite overcome at the death of Claudius. Come, child." She put her arms around Tita's shoulder and led her away.

"Bah!" said Hayes, grasping his glass in anger. "Treating niggers like human beings ain't natural!"

Chapter 43

Layou was abuzz with rumor. With May Gregg, Carlton contemplated the fleet which even now was still visible from the window of her back room where it overlooked the sea. The first vessels, with sails flying full in the stiff September winds, had passed the bay just after dawn. Carlton had observed them as he made his early morning round to see that the slaves were doing their duties. It was the morning to take the rum wagon down to Layou, so Carlton decided to accompany the wagon in the hope of learning some news about this mighty armada in their waters.

"Busy days, Carlton," commented May Gregg, moving away from the window to return to her seat.

"That should delight you, May. More bits for your coffers." Carlton remained standing by the window, but faced May Gregg. Between the two, an easy familiarity had developed over the years. When he had newly become the Bondmaster, Carlton regarded May Gregg with a mixture of fear and repulsion. As his business involvement through the sale of rum for her casino enabled him to know her better, and as he himself got older the fear was replaced with respect, and the repulsion with affection.

A white girl, about twelve years old, entered the room without knocking. She smiled at Carlton and went over to a cabinet where she searched for something. Carlton appraised her. She had the sturdy build of her mother, with the delightful sheen of childhood still bright on her. Yet her body was firm and graceful, and she was quite aware of her femininity. She wore a long skirt which brushed the ground, and her straight fair hair was caught in a bunch over her head. Her cheeks had an attractive glow of careful exposure to the sun, and her lips, as she pouted at her mother's scolding, were round and sensuous.

"Oh, Mary," said her mother, "you know that you must knock before you enter the boudoir."

"Yes, Mummy."

"Why didn't you?"

"Because Mister Todd is here," she said. "I know Mister Todd is your friend, not a customer at all, so I did not think I would be interrupting."

"You're not, Mary. Not at all. Come over here." Carlton beckoned the girl to stand before him. He looked slowly up from her waist to her face, taking in her burgeoning bosom and the bright smile. "You are a credit to your mother, Mary!"

"She's a troublesome bitch at times," said May Gregg. "Go on, Mary, see about the customers. They'll drink grog in quantity this morning with the fleet to talk about."

The child's smile at Carlton as she tripped out of the room was not entirely innocent. It stirred him. He gulped and turned back to May Gregg who watched him cautiously. "Yes, a fine girl," he stammered. "Is she . . . eh . . . I mean, does she . . . eh . . . give you many problems? I mean with all the men around."

"Lord!" said May Gregg with a tiny shriek. "What's come over you, Carlton? You know this is a whorehouse! I've got six girls here, all kinds. The sailors want all kinds, too."

"But May," said Carlton, slightly shocked. "You surely don't—I mean, is she a virgin?" he blurted out.

"She ain't one of your niggers on the auction block, Carlton Todd, I'll tell you that. I'm not calling her back in here for you to finger her, if that's what you mean.

She's a pure-white girl, and her father was white, too. She's one of my assets, Carlton." As he looked abashed, May Gregg continued on another tack.

"I've started some tableaux now, just like they have in New Orleans. You must come here one night and watch. I'm going to be too old to run this casino soon, Carlton. The sailors don't come to see me any more, you know. It's the young girls they want. Mary's learning the business."

Carlton turned to gaze out of the window to the sea. The sun was beating down from his left, its rays highlighting the beautiful symmetry of the vessels streaming past. Every one of them flew the flag of England. "You're lucky, May. Wish I had a son to inherit Roxborough."

"Lord, Carlton! What are you, twenty-five, twenty-six? Plenty of fire in you for that."

"In me, sure, but what about my wife? She's changed, May. When we first got married, she wanted it worse than a slave wench. Since our daughter was born, I hardly enter her chamber. She spends all her time with that Tita wench I bought from you."

"Ah, yes," smiled May Gregg, recalling the delights of the vivacious Tita. "I know. Some women get like that. Woo her again, Carlton. And what about Tita? She give you a whelp yet?"

"No," said Carlton. "A disappointment, she is."

"Perhaps you haven't crossed her properly."

"Let me see. Maybe you're right. As she is in the house, it's been difficult. I can't have some ranky nigger slobbering all over the back steps. Claudius was mounting her, but his seed weren't good, I suppose. Yes." Carlton had been stirred by May Gregg's words. "I'll put Mingo to her. He's in the house now, and I know he's proven, so if she's any good, she'll soon take."

"That's right," said May. "All that romance might make your wife more willing."

"Romance? Is that what you call it when two niggers are rutting?" Carlton stepped away from the window.

"The last vessel's sailing past now," he said. "Suppose you're sorry none of them put in here?"

"Oh, Carlton, I don't think I could take on the whole of Nelson's fleet, do you? It's the French he's after, not May Gregg's doxies."

Carlton kissed the woman on both cheeks, and she patted his hand. "Remember what I said," she urged. "Mate that Tita wench and woo your wife. You'll soon have a son for Roxborough if you do."

"Aye," said Carlton, "maybe you're right." He backed out of the door, leaving May Gregg seated on her chair, her fat hands crossed in her lap, her thoughts on her own far-off days. Surely, she was thinking, rutting is romance, whoever is doing it.

As Carlton rode back to Roxborough at the head of a procession of rum wagons, Pipiritte, the new kitchen boy, came running down the path toward them.

"Mas Carlton," he called with relief as he sighted his master. He ran to the horse as Carlton halted and clasped his master's ankle for support. Carlton shook him off irritably, as he would an irksome fly.

"What ails you, boy?" he demanded angrily.

"Sah, Ma Phoebe, sah.'

"Ma Phoebe? Who sent you, boy?" Carlton amused himself by cuffing the boy on his chest with his boot, as the slave struggled to speak.

"Ella, sah, she done tell me ax yuh come quick."

"Indeed, Pipiritte?" Carlton continued to tap the boy on his chest with his boot. "And why should she say that, Pip, do you know?"

"No, sah," said Pipiritte, falling back at the last blow from Carlton's boot. "Yas sah, May Phoebe, sah. She done die, sah."

"Die? How do you know?" Carlton bent forward from the horse to listen to the boy more carefully.

Feeling confident now, the boy broke into his story. "She done say so, sah. She was be at de stove, preparin' de dinner, sah. Suddenly, she does gaze into de big pot, sah, where she does be stirrin' de broth. Den she does say 'Oh my gawd' like she does do, sah. But

375

she does stand still, sah, widout moving. Ella ax she what she could do for her. Ella does be dere wid Caspar an' Mingo, sah, an' she does be choppin' de chives fuh dinnah, sah, an' Caspar does be helpin' me to clean de dasheen."

"Oh, get on with it, boy!"

"Yas, sah, well, Ma Phoebe she jest starin' in de pot, sah, rockin' on her feet an' den she says 'Oh my gawd' again an' her eyes turn up an' she say 'I done die' an' she fall in a heap on de floor, sah. She does shake de kitchen, sah." Pipiritte finished and looked up at his master.

"It's a whipping for you, Pip, if you're lying. Get on the wagon there."

Carlton clapped his heels into his horse and galloped off up the hill without a glance behind him. If Ma Phoebe had indeed died, he wouldn't be surprised. He had no idea of her age, but she had been with his father for years and couldn't carry a weight like hers forever. Ella would have to be the cook, and the death would not greatly inconvenience the great house.

Carlton doubted if Pipirette's story was true, but as he passed the mill and neared the plantation trail to the house, he was puzzled to hear the wailing which was coming from the quarters. It was a kind of low moan which the breeze carried downstream, and he recognized the doleful tones of the Africans. Even though they had been seasoned on the plantation for years, they loved death and any excuse would bring them out chanting. It was unusual, though, for them to be so impassioned.

Hayes was waiting for him on the balcony. "Curious thing," he said as Carlton bounded up the steps. "Seems she knew she was going to die. You know, Carlton," the old man continued, shuffling to his seat as Carlton threw himself in his own chair to listen to his father's report, "Ma Phoebe was a strange woman. She had such a power over the slaves. They were all afraid of her, you know. I've heard some of them

376

say she was capable of magic, but that's just slave talk, of course."

"It was because you supported her, father. "That's why the niggers were scared. They knew if Ma Phoebe told you something about them, then you would punish them. Simple as that. Good house slave, she was. Fine cook, but we've got Ella, who'll take her place easily. Fewer mouths to feed now, too."

"Aye," said Hayes, mumbling. "Ma Phoebe was the one nigger I felt I could trust. She knew everything about this plantation."

"It's all right, Da. Ma Phoebe taught Ella all she knew."

"As you say, son. I'll miss her, though."

"Huh! Now I suppose dinner will be late. And we'll have to get our own drinks."

If Carlton had known about Ma Phoebe's reputation as an obeah woman and had paid it due respect, he would have taken charge of the disposal of his late cook's body. Instead, Carlton fumed upstairs about the disruption of his day's routine, while downstairs the slaves contemplated with awe the lifeless body of Ma Phoebe stretched out on the kitchen table. Ella, as though waiting for the moment, had risen from her chair the moment Ma Phoebe had collapsed on the ground, swept over to her, and clutched her head in her arms. She had bent down to suck her dying breath from her mouth with her lips fastened firmly over Ma Phoebe's. When she was sure she was dead, Ella had ordered Mingo and Bo'jack to lift the body onto the table and together with pushing from Caspar and Pipiritte, they had managed to get the cook's corpse onto the table.

Ella knew she had to work quickly. She dispatched Pip to inform Massa Hayes and Mas Carlton and then sent Caspar to tell Janus, the leader of the Ibos. She saw no reason to inform Sybil. Next, Ella reviewed the range of cutting knives which hung on the wall next to the store cupboard and selected the one with the thinnest and longest blade. Bo'jack was instructed to sharpen it. At first arrogant at the importance which Ma Phoebe's death would attach to him in the eyes of the other slaves, he now slunk away before the new light which had entered Ella's eyes. He was well aware of the powers of Ma Phoebe and was more than willing to believe that they had transferred themselves completely to Ella, especially when he recalled that Ella's mam was an obeah woman, too.

He kept his head down and muttered fervently to himself as he stroked the blade over the cutting stone.

Ella's next duty was to complete the lunch preparations, which she did calmly, slicing the chives by Ma Phoebe's ear before throwing them into the pot. The dasheen and tanias had been put on the fire to boil, and Mingo was told to keep his eye on them, because of the absence of Pipiritte. Mingo obeyed Ella quietly, wondering what she planned to do.

When Bo'jack had finished sharpening the knife, he handed it to Ella and withdrew quickly from the kitchen. Ella indicated to Mingo that he should leave, too. The door was locked after them and then, sitting on the back step, they heard Ella fasten the door at the other side of the house. They both pretended to have other affairs on their minds. After fifteen minutes, the door was unbolted. They hesitated before going in.

"Come, Mingo!" Ella called. "You must prepare the master's table. See, the tray is set up for you."

Cautiously, Mingo peered into the kitchen. Ma Phoebe lay still on the table and, true enough, the tray with the utensils and wares for dinner awaited him on the small serving table. Going to collect it, he stopped suddenly. Ma Phoebe's chest was covered with blood. A dark hole spread across the left side of her body, jagged flesh oozing around it. He averted his eyes and saw a calabash filled with a mass of blood and flesh on the floor under the table. Quickly, he grabbed the tray and escaped out of the kitchen before any harm could befall him. Ella, smiling, picked up the calabash and sipped the warm blood.

Ma Phoebe was buried that afternoon. Carlton rode over to the patch where the slaves were buried behind their quarters. He stuck his pistols into his belt before he went and made sure that Mingo carried the big whip with him. He was amazed to see that practically every slave on the plantation was present to watch Ma Phoebe being lowered into the ground. Religion was not encouraged at Roxborough and, with slaves from so many different tribes and many of them being third or fourth generation creole, there was no common ritual to be followed.

The slaves gathered around the hole which had been hastily dug and waited for Carlton. When he came, he stood over the hole and called out Ma Phoebe's name and her job, giving the year of her purchase and the year of her death. Then six Ibos gently lowered the wooden box (a special distinction because she was a house slave) into the hole. Carlton threw in a handful of dirt and beckoned to the Ibos to fill the hole quickly. He moved away through the gap in the slaves which opened up before him.

That night, the Ibo drums beat long on the plantation, and Ella, in a flowing white robe, tossed pieces of Ma Phoebe's heart to the naked Ibos gathered around her in the moonlit glade deep in the forest. Caspar, attending his mother, sucked at the raw flesh eagerly so that he, too, could acquire Ma Phoebe's obeah powers.

Chapter 44

All the children at Roxborough were reared communally in the nursery pen, a long building like a stable with a kitchen attached to it, set in a fenced-off area which allowed the children playing space. The nursery pen, or simply pen as it became known, was presided over by Congo Venus and her boyfriend, Chucco. Both were in their late forties, or so Carlton assumed, and between them they had at least fifteen children. Venus was also the midwife, and Carlton found her and her companion ideal for raising the whelps in the pen. They were assisted by six old biddies who helped train the young ones.

The pen was a happy place, constantly in an uproar, with children forever romping around the compound, shouting, singing, or playing. None of the children knew their parents and, with his constant switching around of partners and encouragement of breeding, few of the parents could recognize their own offspring. It was Carlton's policy to remove a child from its mother as soon as possible after its birth and give it to a wet nurse within the nursery. An advantage of his scheme, he soon realized, was a reduction in the loss of babies by unexpected death through disease or accident or even design. The reward of a bolt of cloth for the fillies and a gold piece for the stallions had encouraged his breeding program and every month there were new ones to add to his stock.

Of course, even Carlton could not police his breeding policy completely. There were some whelps who were unauthorized, but thanks to his gradual thinning down of his adult stock to leave only prime niggers, there were few complete failures. A slave who produced a deformed child was quickly sold to one of the itinerant traders while the child itself, if it was not interesting in its deformity, was quietly abandoned to the wild hogs in the bush.

Carlton loved to study his ledgers to see whom he could mount with whom, and to consider his successful crossings where a strong male whelp had been the outcome. He would not, perhaps have been quite so proud of his books if he knew to what extent the slaves deceived him. It was not difficult for the women, when they found they were pregnant by the buck of their own choice, to attribute it to the stallion with whom Carlton had ordered them to mate. They were often unsure, anyway, and the reward of cloth with which they could make a frock to show off in the quarters on Sundays became a coveted status symbol.

Although Carlton was delighted with the success of his program after eight years of breeding, it would take still another five to ten years before he could start to reap the rewards. He had around two hundred young niggers in the pen, an inconceivable fortune in black gold on the open market. This crop needed careful nurturing. A gang of slaves was employed full-time in raising provisions with which to feed them. The Wageny were engaged to the exclusion of all other work in fishing, while another gang reared domestic hogs and cattle.

The expense of rearing his whelps was minimal. The children all ran naked in the pen, there being no need for clothes. Roxborough was a completely self-supporting plantation as a result of his need to cater for the children at minimum expense. The adult slaves not only had plenty to occupy themselves in making it so, but also fared far better than those on the plantations where sugar or coffee was the crop and they were obliged to forage for food in their own time.

As he cut down on his export of sugar, Carlton was able to reduce imports. Being island-born himself, he found it easy to do without commodities which the white planters seemed to need to survive. He relished the local vegetables, wild pig meat, and river and sea fish. Only once a year he imported the flour and salt fish of the other plantations. Having long been deprived of such things in her own home, Sybil did not mind the concentration on local produce, especially as Ella turned out to be much better as a cook than Ma Phoebe.

Carlton was proud of his management of the plantation, and old Hayes grudgingly admitted that the estate was on a firm financial foundation. It seemed that whenever Carlton took a coffle of slaves to Roseau, he returned home with at least double what he had expected. The niggers being sold by auction, there was no question of the price he was receiving being less than fair. His slaves were getting a reputation, particularly as he introduced the young ones into the market. These were not the niggers he had bred himself, but those he had penned from the time he became Bondmaster. These slaves had a docility which the buyers liked, coupled with the strength of good feeding and exercise during their childhood. They had known no hardships, bathed daily, and smiled brightly.

Hayes could not understand the situation. He had made Carlton spread out his four thousand pounds in gold on the table at the end of his latest trip to Roseau. "It ain't as much as a sugar crop, Carlton, but I'll agree it was a damn sight easier to ship." Hayes contemplated the gold before him. "I don't know. All that gold just for a coffle of black niggers."

"It's the market, Father," explained Carlton, scooping the gold pieces back into the chest. "Everyone wants seasoned niggers now. There's no knowing when a vessel is coming from Africa. The planters are beginning to know a Roxborough slave; they know he is healthy and a hard worker."

Hayes sniffed. "He should be healthy. A dozen females to cosset him in that there pen. Don't know how he becomes a hard worker, though. You don't use the whip enough, son. Them English planters talk to their niggers with the whip, son."

"That's fine," said Carlton. "If the stock I'm selling ain't used to the whip, they'll respond quicker when they taste it. Don't worry, Father. The money is good and true. Not credit in a London merchant house, but gold right here." He held up the small wooden chest. "I'll sequester this tonight," he said. "Somewhere safe, and ain't nobody going to know but me."

Sybil viewed her husband's trips to Roseau with pleasure. There was always a danger when he was at home that he would demand his conjugal rights and make an unexpected entrance into her chamber. Infrequently Carlton, as though obliged to do so, did make efforts to fulfill the role of husband. So Sybil had to be very careful in her association with Mingo. As he was under instructions to mount Tita, there was every reason for him to be in her maid's room, but certainly not in her own. Carlton's absence enabled Sybil to throw caution to the winds and enjoy her slave.

"You used to insist on accompanying me to the capital," Carlton teased her when she joined him and Hayes on the evening of his latest return. "Now you say you prefer to stay at home."

"What about Laura? I could not leave her for so long."

"Nonsense," said Carlton. "Tita is here."

"So you would have me go to Roseau with all those fine people and no Tita to attend me," she pouted. "No, Carlton, dear, it is better for you, and better for Laura, if you go alone."

Carlton was inclined to agree, but he said nothing, merely handing to his wife the gifts of jewelry he bought her, and the different fabrics she ordered for even more dresses to be made up for herself and Tita.

Later that night, when the whole house was asleep, Carlton slipped out of his room with the chest of money and descended the back stairs to the kitchen. He had sent a message for Ella to wait for him there and, as he reached the bottom of the steps, the kitchen door opened, sending out a dim wedge of light into the night. He entered quickly and Ella closed the door and returned the wooden bolt to its position. He placed the box on top of the stove and embraced Ella fondly.

"My Ella!" he murmured. "How I longed to come back."

"Don't be *sot*, Carlton. All those soft brown-skinned girls in Roseau would never treat you so badly that you would want to leave them for your Ella."

"It's true!" Carlton held her at arm's length. Ella was still slender, her vivacious face beautiful and proud in the lantern glow. He pulled her to him and kissed her again. "One day you'll come with me, ride beside me like a queen, and stay in a grand hotel."

Ella smiled to humor him. "I hardly think that I would enjoy that, Carlton. A black queen with a white consort? Oh my—I'm sure the Governor would arrest you for treason."

"Why, Ella," Carlton sat down, "are you not pleased I'm back?" Her hands rested on his shoulders as she told him she was. He bent his head sideways and kissed her long fingers. "How's my son?"

"He demands to know why Mas Carlton did not take him, too," laughed Ella. "He said he wanted to sell niggers."

Carlton's eyebrow raised. "He did, did he? That's my son. Come," he pulled Ella from her position behind him and sat her down on his lap. "You smell good," he said, burying his head in her bosom.

"Well, I'm not one of your stinking field niggers. That's the expensive perfume from France you bought for me last time you went to Roseau. Anyway, you told me it was expensive." They laughed together.

"It was, it was," Carlton kissed her slim black neck. "Ella, you look lovelier each time I see you." He put his hand under her skirt to grip her ankle.

"Oh, Mas Carlton," she mimicked, "I know you does say dat 'cause yuh want yo' Ella."

"I can have you without sweet words, Ella."

"Yes, Carlton, I suppose you can."

There was silence as they stared at each other. Ella loved the white buckra with a passion she could not understand despite her knowledge of the mysteries of life. His golden curls were thinner than when she had first seen him, years before, and his tanned face was etched with maturity. His strong hands around her were masterful. For his part, Carlton saw the sable face and body which had captivated and held him so long ago. She was the mother of his only son and, incredibly, the only person at Roxborough, slave or white, whom he could trust.

Carlton caught up Ella from his lap and lifted her onto the scrubbed top of the pine table. She clung to him offering no resistance as he clambered onto the table and began a slow and gentlemanly lovemaking. She gasped as his lips hovered over her body, making her squirm with sensation. She arched her body as his cautious approach aroused her and clutched him to her in a fury that was uncontrollable. They rolled together on the table where Ma Phoebe had lain with her heart cut out. Ella sank her teeth into Carlton's ear as they reached a perfect climax.

Blood trickled down her mouth. Carlton's eyes were heavy as his head sang with mixed pain and pleasure. Ella quickly gulped and swallowed the piece of flesh she felt in her mouth and grinned apologetically as Carlton rolled off her to lie exhausted on the table. Shaking down her skirt, Ella lowered her feet to the floor and slowly stood up. She went to one of her cupboards fixed high on the stone wall, took out a jar of unguent, and coated Carlton's ear with the odd-smelling ointment where she had bitten off the lobe.

"Did you eat me?"

385

"Yes."

"Did I taste good?"

She did not answer at first, putting her head on one side to contemplate her man. "This unguent will still the bleeding and cure the cut," she said brusquely. "It's good. I made it myself. It's this I does use when the niggers does be bleeding from the lash, Carlton."

Carlton sat up. When he was younger, he would never have tolerated a slave calling him Carlton. Now he would be vexed if Ella called him anything else, except before others, of course. Once, having his face smeared with the same ointment as the niggers used after a whipping would have made him furious. Now he relished it. What changes had been wrought at Roxborough, he wondered, since the mantle of the Bondmaster had become his. And since Ella had become his, too.

"Come on," he said. "We've got work to do. Bring a spade."

"A spade?" Her eyes fell on the box on the stove.

"Of course, Ella. We've got to bury this money."

"Don't you want the lantern?"

"No," Carlton replied in a hushed voice, his fingers finding hers in the dark. "We can see by the moon. Let's go to the young mango tree at the corner of the house. It's about ten paces from the northeast corner. We'll bury the box in the middle of a line from the corner to the tree. You must remember that, Ella, in case anything ever happens to me. This money will be for our son."

"You'll free him?"

Carlton snorted. "He's not really a slave, is he? He should be in the pen running naked with the others if he is a slave. I don't know if I can free him, though, Ella. What would you do without him?"

They reached the corner of the house, and Carlton measured out five paces in the direction of the mango tree, which brought him equidistant from the tree and the house. He handed Ella the box and took the spade from her. The box was so heavy she had to put it on the ground.

He dug in silence for about fifteen minutes while Ella watched. "Claudius wanted to be free, Ella, did you know?" he asked after a while. "He saved an enormous sum. It's there in the box. I suppose he is free now."

"Yes, I suppose so," But, Ella wondered to herself as Carlton completed the hole, dragged the box over to wedge in it, and shoveled back the earth, what about the people you have sold to get that gold? Are they free?

She glanced out of the cave of darkness surrounding them toward the pen where a baby could be heard crying. Ella shivered. Would she or those children locked in the pen ever know freedom?

Chapter 45

The note from May Gregg had promised a *divertissement* such as Monsieur Todd had never witnessed in his life before. As his own visits to the capital were quick slave-selling trips, Carlton knew that he had never seen anything of a remarkable nature in entertainment at all. So he was looking forward to what May Gregg was laying on for her customers as he rode into the village. Mingo accompanied him, although Sybil had protested that she and Hayes would thus be left alone in the house to be protected by mere kitchen boys if anything happened. Reviewing in his mind the fears under which the white planters lived in the island—the fear of French invasion, of a slave uprising, or of a hurricane—Carlton decided that since none were likely to happen that evening, he could safely have Mingo with him.

It was an evening such as made the tropics so desirable a haven to strangers. The heat of the day had been cooled by a gentle breeze rustling down the valley, and the moon glowed vividly in a deep blue sky sprinkled with stars. Three ships were anchored in the river mouth, their lanterns swaying regularly, their creaks and cracks echoing across the river to the wharf. Pausing at the top of the street that wound through the village, Carlton was amazed at the activity. The street was probably not more than nine hundred feet long as it hugged the curve of the coast, almost pushed over the edge and into the sea by the weight of the dense jungle around it. In that short distance, every house seemed ablaze with the light of lanterns. Music and singing came from some, women sat at the doorways of others, and the shouts and clatter of the casinos overflowed into the road from others. It was a stimulating sight after the austere evenings at Roxborough.

"I'm ready for whatever May Gregg has to offer, Mingo." Carlton turned in his saddle to address the slave riding a few paces behind him.

"I does hear dat she does have one heap of nigger girls in a show wid a white man, massa."

Carlton was surprised. "You know more about it than I."

"Oh no, sah. When de boys does bring de rum dey carry back de news, sah."

"Hmm!" said Carlton. They had reached the casino, and Carlton dismounted eagerly. He threw his reins at Mingo and stepped inside to join the throng of white sailors.

Mingo tied the horses leisurely and looked around him. In his bright livery and tight breeches, he was aware he aroused the interest of the whores sauntering nearby. But they were not for the likes of him. Instead, he eyed a pair of black girls leaning against the railing on the other side of the street. He strolled over to them, and they giggled as he spoke.

"Night, missies," he said, bowing before them in the manner of white people. "I have not had de pleasure of seein' you in dis village befo'." With more coaxing and banter, he learned that they were both from a plantation some miles along the coast. They had accompanied their mistress and, like Mingo himself, were awaiting their owner's pleasure before returning home.

"It does be far to ride at night," said Mingo, leaning on the railing beside them. He could manage both, he was thinking, if there was time.

"Oh, we does have a carriage," said one of the girls

haughtily. "An' a groom an' a footboy," added the other.

"An' where dat be?" demanded Mingo, who did not believe them.

"At de end of de village. As soon as she have finish her show, de mistress does come runnin' out de back door an' we runs to de carriage an' we does ride like de night wind. We does reach de plantation in an hour an' de massa don't know nothin'."

"Pray," laughed Mingo at the earnestness of the two girls, "an what should de massa suspect?"

"Why, what de mistress does do, of course."

"My, Carlton!" cooed May Gregg, enfolding him in her arms while he pecked her on both cheeks. "I'm so glad you've come at last. You won't regret it, I assure you."

He could scarcely hear what May was saying above the shouts of the customers and the banging of tankards on barrel tops. The stench in the casino reminded him of his odorous niggers at sugar time. He peered through the crowd toward the bar.

"Where's Mary tonight?" he shouted at May Gregg.

"Mary?"

"Your daughter," he bellowed again.

May squinted at him and then smiled. "Bless my soul, Carlton, you'll see her tonight. Oh, yes." She broke into a wheezy chuckle. "You'll be seeing her all right. Now fill up your glass and come and sit by me. The show will take place over there."

She pointed at a dais constructed from planks laid across upturned rum barrels which, he knew, had been fashioned by his own coopers at Roxborough. One of the burly Negroes who kept order among May Gregg's clients lifted a pygmy onto the stage. He held a squeeze box in his hand and without waiting for the noise to die down in the bar, began to play a tune. His rhythm was lively and as they recognized the tune, the men at the packed bar began to concentrate on the action in the corner. The staff dimmed the lanterns until the casino was in darkness except for the stage.

"Egad! That's enough of the music!" shouted one.

"Yes, let's see the doxies!" chorused another.

A bamboo screen had been constructed beside the makeshift stage, and as though in answer to the crowd's request, May Gregg's daughter came on stage. She was dressed to look the picture of innocence and sat demurely on the edge of a bed and passed a comb through her hair. Carlton glanced at May Gregg, his eyebrow raised, but May just smiled enigmatically.

A white woman wearing a mask and enveloped in petticoats was the next entrant, and she sat on the bed beside the girl. She began stroking the girl's hair and then, in response to the roars from the crowd, began caressing her body. Little Mary, Carlton was amazed to see, appeared to be enjoying it hugely and was soon returning the white lady's kisses, even to the extent of lifting the woman's petticoats high to her waist revealing her nakedness underneath. She was applying her lips to the most intimate parts of the lady's body, and the lady was reacting with ecstasy when onto the stage strode a Negro, naked, his ebony skin glistening with oil. The crowd gasped, and even Carlton was impressed.

"You see," May Gregg prodded him in the ribs, "I said you'd never seen anything like this."

"Where did you get him?" demanded Carlton.

"Trader. It measures fourteen inches."

"What's he going to do?" asked Carlton, watching the Negro standing by the bed.

"You'll see."

As though reaching out to pull a bell cord, the white lady grabbed the Negro's penis and pulled it. Behind the screen a bell rang. The crowd laughed. As if only then becoming aware of the Negro's presence, both the lady and the young girl pulled the Negro onto the bed with them. The crowd were getting excited at the thought that a white woman would allow herself to be entered by a Negro of such donkey-like proportions.

While May Gregg's daughter held the Negro, the woman positioned herself to accept him.

Carlton was disgusted. "Who's that whore you have there! Letting herself be mounted by a Negro. She should be burnt to death. No wonder she wears a mask."

"Just one of my girls, Carlton. Some white women quite like a Negro's loving."

"It ain't natural, and you know it. That's an animal."

"But isn't he rather gorgeous?"

To the amazement of the crowd, the white woman had managed to accommodate the Negro, and the show proceeded for a few minutes as the two main performers reached a pitch of ecstasy that, on the woman's part at least, was not faked. Just then, a white man, obviously recognized by the sailors, came onto the stage. He, too, was naked.

Presumably meant to represent the woman's husband, he expressed indignation at what he saw on the bed, then leaped on top of the Negro and proceeded to force himself into the Negro's buttocks. Pinioned under the two men coupled on top of her, the woman moaned and thrust, while the crowd roared their delight.

Carlton was profoundly disturbed. The sight of a Negro bracketed by the white couple unnerved him, and he lost interest in the action. Somehow the woman detached herself at a point in the action and ran off behind the screen to applause while her place on stage was taken by a bevy of May Gregg's regular bar whores, all of whom were naked. A most complicated tableau ensued involving both the white man and the Negro.

As Carlton watched and sipped his grog, Mingo saw from the back door, which was ajar, the white woman with the mask bend down and kiss little Mary Gregg. "That was wonderful, *chérie*," she whispered. "One night you must come to our plantation, and we will spend the whole night in *l'amour!*"

"That's all right," said the child. "You'll arrange the fee with my mother,"

"Mais oui, chérie! Oh, but that nigger has set me on fire!" She kissed little Mary passionately on the lips, which the child accepted passively. *"Oh, mon dieu!* I must fly before anyone recognizes me. My husband will find me out if I am late."

Mingo held open the door and watched curiously as the masked lady met her two little slave girls and rushed into the night in search of her waiting carriage.

The show was ending. Mingo took up his stance by the door as the customers began to drift out of the casino. Carlton stumbled out through the swing door and onto the hard mud of the street, and Mingo ran forward to support him.

"Don't need your help, boy. Where's the horse? Got to get back."

Carlton followed Mingo up the trail to the hall, a foolish smirk on his face as the breeze began to work on his befuddled brain. He didn't resist Mingo's strong hands lifting him off his horse and guiding him up the stairs to his chamber. Mingo helped him off with his boots while Carlton rambled on about the *divertissement* he had seen, with niggers mounting white women. The angry tone of his voice made Mingo wonder if his master was somehow referring to him. As quickly as he could, Mingo escaped from his master's room and went back along the balcony where he was supposed to sleep with Tita. She was waiting for him.

"The mistress wants you," she said icily.

He grinned. "Wha' de matter, Tita? You does be sorry you not gittin' it?"

Tita's hand slashed through the air and slapped him on his cheek. "It's not a great codfish like you I would ever want, boy. The massa says you supposed to be loving me. I praise the Lord you ain't! Me and the mistress was fine until you came in the place!"

"Well, it does be me she does want now, Tita, you does say. I does be goin' to her. You can go 'n' find yourself a field hand!" he laughed.

Mingo pushed open the connecting door into Sybil's bedroom, stepping carefully over the floor to reach

393

the bed as Tita muttered an oath under her breath and closed the door.

Maybe I will go 'n' find myself a buck, she thought. There was one particular buck she could have which would give her such sweet revenge on her mistress for discarding her in favor of that great monkey, Mingo. She opened her own door onto the balcony very quietly and eased herself past her mistress's window, treading carefully so none of the wooden boards would creak. Reaching Mas Carlton's door, she tried it and stepped boldly in. The lantern was still lit and Carlton lay on top of the bed, fully clothed.

"Oh, Mas Carlton," crooned Tita, soothing his forehead with her hand. "Is that the way Mingo does treat you? Let me help you remove your clothes before you sleep."

Carlton, vaguely aware in his drunken stupor of an attempt to remove his breeches, endeavored to help. Only when he recognized the touch of a woman's hands on his thighs did he respond.

Quickly, he grabbed the filly's waist and pulled her on top of him. Now he would have his own *divertissement!* Tita, spurred on by vengefulness, coaxed Carlton to such a delicate pitch that he eventually fell back on the bed completely exhausted. Sometime later Tita crept back to her mistress's room, strangely absolved, and uncannily aware that she had the Bondmaster's child in her womb.

Chapter 46

Sybil gazed intently at her reflection in the mirror while Tita brushed her hair. It was a hot morning and the sun which always hit her room early in the day pounded down and burned up whatever air there was in her chamber. She fanned herself in desperation as she watched. Although she was forced to accept that the sheen of her youthful beauty had changed to a more mature attractiveness, no one would take her for the mother of a six-year-old daughter and certainly not the bed-partner of a slave. She shuddered.

"What ails you, Sybil?" Tita asked immediately, ever sensitive to the moods of her mistress.

"Tita, I'm pregnant."

"Why," Tita burst out, "so am I!"

"You!" Sybil swung round to look at the slave standing beside her. "By Mingo, too? After two years of his favors, that brute has to make us both pregnant!" She laughed ironically. "I should have known this would happen!"

"You're not vexed, Sybil?"

Sybil pulled Tita close to her and nestled her head in the slave's bosom. "You do not understand, my love. There is nothing wrong in you having a child by Mingo. Carlton has ordered you to lie with him, anyway, so when you have Mingo's child you'll get a bolt of cloth for a new dress. "Sybil's shoulder shook as sobs overtook her. Tita hugged her closer.

"What's the matter, Sybil?"

"It's my child, Tita. Mingo is its father, too. What happens when I give birth to a little black baby? A slave's child?"

Tita began to grasp the situation. In the islands it was not a scandal for a white woman to have a child by a black man as it was in the American plantations. But when the white woman had a husband and he was the Bondmaster, it was a perplexing situation indeed.

Sybil was sobbing on her chest. "Can you help me, Tita? I'll give you anything to help me."

"I could ask one of the quarter's women for a potion."

"What will that do?"

"It can help you lose the whelp before it's born."

"No!" Sybil was tearful again. "I don't want to do that to Mingo's child."

"Does the master know you does be pregnant?"

"Heavens, no!" The mention of Carlton made Sybil look at herself in the mirror again and start to dab her eyes and re-apply powder where the tears had smeared her face. Carlton was probably in the pen, counting his stock. It would soon be time for breakfast, when she must make an appearance.

Tita smiled, putting out her hands to touch her mistress, stroking her arm. "I think I know what to do. It's a few weeks since you slept with Carlton. Lie with him tonight and then in a few weeks you can tell him you are pregnant. Then everything will be all right."

"You think so?" Sybil watched her features in the glass again. She frowned. "Yes, that will explain my condition but what will happen when I give birth?"

Tita shrugged. "Give the child away before he knows. Say it died."

"But Tita, the Bondmaster knows everything, you know that. How can I give birth to the child at Roxborough and say it died? Even if I could buy silence from all the slaves, Carlton will still want to see the child's body if I say it died. He's that kind of man."

Tita had lost interest. She crossed over to the bed and started to pull at the sheets. She would certainly kill her own child if she had to, and throw the body into the bush before anyone knew. Why not?

"Oh, Tita!" Sybil's exclamation of joy bounced around the wooden walls, startling the birds on the balcony rail outside. "I know! We'll go to Antigua, where I can have the baby and let my mother care for it. Carlton will never know. Then I can say it died."

Tita looked at her mistress with doleful eyes. But what will you say, she was thinking to herself, when you discover that my child is your husband's?

"Tita, I know why you are sad. Do you think I will go to Antigua without you? Give me a kiss, my darling. You shall come with me. We shall have Mingo's babies together, with doctors to attend us and white nurses." She pressed herself eagerly on Tita's lips, hugging her closely.

Tita, trying to put her own troubles out of her mind until such time as she could see a way out of the situation, began to respond. It would, she thought, be nice to visit another island, anyway.

Ella had no doubt that her mistress was pregnant. What she had not learned from Ma Phoebe, Ella had garnered herself through experience. Nothing that happened at Roxborough escaped her, whether it was in the quarters, the pen, or the house. When she felt there was an event which could affect her own life, she would inform Carlton. About the quarters, Carlton knew very little. He saw that his niggers were clothed and fed and assumed that because of this they would have no inclination to disobey him. He did not know that Ella's ministrations to their simple beliefs kept them in check.

Ella, too, studied the young ones in the pen with as much interest as Carlton and advised him on the niggers which could be sold and those which he should keep for breeding. She helped him pair up the adults, spending endless evenings discussing with him the adaptability of one slave to another.

After Ma Phoebe died, Ella had expanded her influence over both the slaves and the whites far beyond anything Ma Phoebe had achieved. She was intelligent and was able to be a companion and partner to Carlton, whom she also loved. She shared his desire to breed perfect slaves, and the decreeing that one Negro should mate with another added to her power. As the quarters slaves realized the influences which Ella could exert on their behalf, they made requests to her for mates and, if she saw it as a good thing, she would suggest the union to Carlton as her own idea. In this way, the creation of the Roxborough breed which was to become so famous throughout the Caribbean owed as much to her machinations as to Carlton's charts, ledgers, and pedigrees.

In the house, Ella had achieved the removal of the old Bo'jack to the pen. Mingo who he no longer trained for fighting, had assumed the role of butler. Carlton had not secured a replacement for Claudius, but rode about the estate by himself or accompanied by Caspar. The boy was nine and showed such a lively and pleasant disposition that Carlton was quite taken with him. He was permitted to wait at table and run messages and, in the evening, to serve the punch to Mas Carlton and Massa Hayes on the gallery.

"That's a smart lad, there, Carlton," observed Hayes one evening when Caspar had returned to the kitchen. "A pity he ain't your heir."

"My son," smiled Carlton. "Yes, I like the lad. Always asking me questions on the plantation, he is. Wants to know how many hogsheads of sugar from the acre, what price a slave brings, and so on. He seems to have inherited his grandfather's brain!"

"Aye." Hayes did not laugh, but sucked on his gums. "Don't forget that his grandfather on his mother's side was a naked black savage devouring raw flesh in the jungles of Africa. As long as there is nigger blood, it's going to come out. Somehow. Mark my words, son.

That Caspar of yours is as black and as evil as any Negro, even though his skin is light and his hair straight like your'n. There's animal in him, you see."

"All right, whatever you say, Father. Ella has told me that her own father was an African chief, just like a Prince, who was descended from a royal line bred from the purest stock over the centuries."

"You always talking about breeding, son. You should go to a university and get a doctorate in that nigger-breeding!"

Carlton chuckled. "I'll be glad when I have a son of my own, though." He paused. "Sybil says she's pregnant again at last."

"I'm glad, boy. Ain't no life for a woman like her to be stuck out on this plantation without some interest. A son will burn up her energy."

"A daughter didn't."

"I can't understand that. She does not spend much time with Laura at all, does she? And that Laura is a nice little girl. I see your Caspar playing with her in the yards in the afternoons."

"So Ella tells me." Carlton poured more drinks for them.

"You must make sure that you have a doctor here in time for the confinement, Carlton. Ma Phoebe ain't around no more, nor that Congo Venus. We can't do it ourselves, you know."

"I was going to ask you about that, Father." Carlton leaned forward in his chair. "Sybil has a mind to go to Antigua for the birth. Her mother is there, and she says that if I won't let her mother come here, then she would like to have the baby in Antigua, where she says there are some good English doctors."

"It's true. Antigua is very English in ways. Should be some excellent doctors there, not like this forgotten island."

"What do you think, then? I certainly don't want her mother here."

"Hmm!" said Hayes, thinking, idly watching the fireflies darting through the night around the house.

"It could be a good idea. You can arrange it through our agents in London. They have a representative in Antigua who can advance her money and deduct it from the London account. There should not be any difficulty."

"You approve, then?"

"And why shouldn't I? Probably do your wife a power of good to see her mother after all this time. When does she want to go?"

"She says as soon as possible, so she has time to settle in before the birth. She'll return after the baby is a few months old so he won't have a bad journey."

Hayes nodded his approval. Life was good at Roxborough. At times he had wondered if he had given up work too early, but his son had managed such a successful transition in affairs that it was a pleasure just to enjoy the fruits of three decades of work. None of the old faces were around any more; even the niggers had passed on. But the replacements were satisfactory. Ella cared for him more than Ma Phoebe ever did, fussing over him and entertaining him with her tales of happenings in the quarters. His grandson, Caspar, was a bright little scamp, while Laura, although a little crosspatch at times, would grow into a beautiful young lady. With a proper grandson about to be added, the Bondmaster line would be complete.

Ella viewed the preparations for the departure of Sybil and Tita with misgiving. She had known almost at the same time as Sybil had of her pregnancy, and she had been more than a little puzzled. She kept her suspicions to herself. Mingo, when she taxed him about the situation, would only shrug his shoulders and make a playful grab for her.

Ella had to content herself with the thought that whatever happened in Antigua, she would find out from the slaves. However, Sybil was adamant that she would not take any Roxborough slaves with her, saying she would hire any they needed in Antigua. It was curious for a white lady to travel with only a female slave to accompany her, and Carlton agreed only when he had made satisfactory arrangements for his wife's passage with an old Captain whom May Gregg recommended as a man of honor.

Carlton and Caspar rode down to the wharf with Laura and a gang of slaves to carry the luggage when the time came for his wife's departure. The leave-taking of the Bondmaster and his wife, watched by most of the inhabitants of Layou, was touching. Sybil was in tears and nearly suffocated Laura with her embraces. She lingered long in the arms of her husband, and to all who watched they seemed an idyllically happy couple. While Sybil's pregnancy was not yet noticeable, and neither was Tita's, the rumor had already spread through Layou and the plantation that Mistress Sybil was going to have a child in an English hospital in Antigua.

As the ship weighed anchor, Sybil watched from the deck. Carlton turned and mounted his horse. Sybil waved and he returned the farewell. She stepped back into her cabin as the boat began to roll.

"Oh, Tita!" she cried, clutching her maid. "We are free at last!"

"Yes, ma'am," answered Tita dutifully.

Chapter 47

The Negro sitting in the shade of the tavern awning, his legs resting on the barrel which served as a table, passed his long fingers over his chin thoughtfully. Keeping two fingers resting on his cheek, he waved an elegant hand to dismiss the boy who had been whispering in his ear.

The Negro sat alone while around him the other tables were occupied by seamen and their women. As though superior to the noise and surroundings of the tavern, he gazed across the wharf to where the vessel his messenger had spoken about was tied. He had been informed that two women were on board and, even as he looked, they were descending the plank to *terra firma*. They were accompanied by an anxious white man with spectacles, greasy hair, and no wig. who looked most uncomfortably warm in the heavy English clothes he wore. The Negro recognized him as a clerk from one of the sugar merchants in St. John's.

The confidence with which the white woman conducted herself showed she was a creole, not English-born. The presence of the merchant's clerk indicated wealth, he thought, although the absence of personal slaves meant either poverty or discretion. The lady's companion, who was a darker version of the white, appeared to have considerable status, for the white lady conversed with her and clutched at her as she would an intimate.

The Negro continued to stroke his cheek, intrigued by this couple. It had been weeks since a pair of ladies either one of whom would deserve his attention, had descended on Antigua. He rose from the table, smoothing down his well-cut coat and drawing himself up to his full impressive height. Tossing a coin at the white serving wench who bustled forward, he strode across the wharf to take a better look at the visitors.

They were about to enter the merchant's carriage, the clerk holding open the door while the white lady prepared to ascend.

"Bonjour, m'selle!"

Sybil paused, her leg raised onto the step revealing her ankle. She glanced to her side to see who was addressing her. The sight of a black gentleman sweeping off his hat and bowing low was so unexpected, she was at a loss for words. She hopped quickly into the carriage and then peered out at the fellow. His gorgeous clothes marked him as a person of distinction. She beckoned to Tita to jump in beside her and then urged the clerk to close the door so at least there was some barrier to separate her from this remarkable personage. It suddenly occurred to Sybil that she might have caused offense to her unknown admirer for she saw the black man's eyebrows rise as she shut the door. So she tilted her head politely at him, reaching for Tita's hand as she did so.

"Good morning," she said, a slight query in her voice. Observing then the curious behavior of the English clerk who was now standing behind the Negro and making frantic gestures of warning, Sybil decided to be much bolder. She withdrew her hand from Tita's grasp and extended it from the coach window. The Negro bent forward and kissed her fingers briefly.

"Prince d'Anjou at your service, *m'selle*. May I welcome you to Antigua?"

"You may," said Sybil, withdrawing her hand and regretting the presence of the English clerk which pre-

vented her from carrying out her plans for a pseudony-
mous existence which she had made.

"Grosvenor," she addressed the clerk on the dock.
He stood a good eight inches shorter than the splendid
Negro fellow and was far less impressively dressed in
his English browns. "Most kind of you to meet us,
Grosvenor. Do we depart now?"

"But madam, I am supposed to accompany you to
St. John's," protested the clerk unhappily, wiping his
brow.

"Then you shall," smiled Sybil tightly. "But do you
mind riding with the coachman? It is rather cramped
inside."

The Negro smiled and cocked his head in admiration
while Sybil, leaning forward as Grosvenor scrambled on
top of the covered coach, bade him draw closer. "We
are strangers here, *m'sieur*, and it seems we are to be
chaperoned."

"There is no one better in Antigua than I to be of
such service to you, *m'selle*."

"I am sure," said Sybil, a wave of excitement almost
engulfing her as she returned the Negro's challenging
stare. "We are to live in St. John's, my companion
and I. Will you call on us?"

"This very afternoon, *m'selle*."

"I shall look forward to it." Sybil extended her hand
again. This time, the black man's fingers held her own
tightly, and his lips stayed longer on her hand than
was necessary. He kept his eyes on hers as the coach
started up at Grosvenor's insistence and broke their
embrace.

"Oh, Tita!" exclaimed Sybil as she sank back into
her seat. "Isn't he gorgeous! Isn't he the most exciting
blackie you've ever seen!"

Tita sniffed. He was certainly handsome and well-
dressed and courteous. "How can a nigger have such
airs and graces, Sybil?"

"Hush, Tita, dear. You must not call me Sybil
again. I am to be Belle while we are here. Belle Lugay,

I think. I do not want anyone to know I am Mistress Todd, nor to know that I was once Vandy."

"That clerk, Grosvenor knows."

"So he does. Then I will convince him of the virtues of silence. A man like that earns so little he will have debts up to the top of his flannel collar. I will give him a substantial tip which will buy his silence and his loyalty. But what about that blackamoor, Tita?"

"As I said, Sybil, I mean, Belle, I think the nigger is too grand for a nigger."

"But Tita, that's what I've tried to tell you. In Antigua, the Negroes are not like they are in Dominica. They are far more advanced in education and manners. They are quite like people. Many of them are free, Tita, and have established themselves. That's why you can be my companion while we are here, and not my slave. I shall expect you to call me Belle all the time, and never mistress. We are going to have such a time!"

Sybil lapsed into silence, a smile stealing across her face as she thought of the suave Negro who had kissed her hand. He was one, and there would be others like him. Antigua, for Sybil, was going to be the reward for years of neglect and frustration she had suffered first at Vandy Hall and then at Roxborough. Even her darling Mingo could not match up to the genteel ways of Prince d'Anjou.

The visit to St. John's of Belle Lugay and her companion, the fair-skinned Negress called Tita, seized the imagination of the populace. Unknown to Sybil, the impact of her arrival was helped by the rumor, begun by Prince, which quickly spread through the Negro quarters, that she was a mistress of the Prince of Wales. She made no attempt to enlighten anyone about her background, and her eccentric life style served only to add to her reputation.

The house she leased in St. John's resounded with music and laughter every evening. While the white residents, who had also heard the rumor, grew more curious about the mysterious Belle day by day, they were unable to penetrate the circle of black admirers with which she quickly surrounded herself. When the whites sent her invitations, she refused. When they tried to pry information about her from Grosvenor, who was the only white man who seemed to have access to her, they were rebuffed with such vehemence that they were more convinced than ever that Belle Lugay did, indeed have royal connections. Certainly her behavior showed no regard for convention.

Her constant companion, the English community was aghast to note, was the notorious Prince, who squired her everywhere as if she were his queen. As the months passed, Belle and Prince were seen less and less driving around the streets of St. John and the gossipers noted that Prince was now ensconced within the house itself. In Antigua, it was no more than a passing scandal when a white woman had a black lover, but Belle Lugay's deliberate snubbing of people of her own race and wanton disregard of the rules of convention were regarded as intolerable. If she were simply a paid whore, the white residents could have understood and dismissed her from their mind. But there was the lingering rumor of her "connections" which Prince continued to encourage.

One thing that Prince did know, even though he himself was ignorant of Belle's true identity, was that she was pregnant. She was growing rounder day by day, and so was Tita.

"I shall have to give a prize to the winner," announced Prince one evening. He lay on the sofa, his head on Belle's lap, caressing the bulge in her stomach.

Since the day she arrived, Sybil had craved Prince's constant attention. The occasional requests which he made for money to help him with his various "business enterprises," as he called them, did not deter her at all. Although he was a Negro, Sybil could see no connection between the blacks she ruled at Roxborough and this carefully manicured tawny god whose proficiency at loving combined the ardor of a Frenchman with the stamina of an athlete. That she was using Prince as much as he was using her stabilized the relationship at a level they both understood.

"And is the prize you?" asked Sybil coolly.

"Can either of you think of anything better?" laughed Prince.

Sybil smiled down at him as she twisted his hair in her fingers. Why could not her husband have such gaiety? Prince was about the same age as her husband, and he had a zest for life which Carlton, with his obsession for breeding pure niggers, could never have. If she had had a husband as attentive as Prince she could never have got herself pregnant by Mingo. She sighed.

"What ails you, precious?"

They had both avoided questioning each other about the past. Sybil sensed that there were things she did not want to know about Prince, and he, for his part, did not want to dispel the security which he felt with Belle. She was the first woman who did not try to own him and make demands.

"Nothing ails me, Prince. I'm so happy, that's all."

"Then I am happy, too."

"I'll have to go back one day, Prince, after the baby is born."

"I know, Belle, I know."

"It does not worry you? Are you not curious?"

"Why should I be? Fate has brought us together. We are together, and we understand each other. What more is there to know? I can help you, and you can help me."

"Yes," said Sybil, wondering just how much the Prince's help was going to cost. He had already arranged for a midwife, whom he described as the most discreet in the West Indies, but there would be other matters for which she would need his help. She would have to find a family to take care of her child as soon as it was born. She had never had the slightest intention of contacting her mother as she had told Carlton and Tita she would. The only solution was to count on the connivance of Prince. She was sure that Prince would know what to do when he saw the color of her baby, and would not think less of her. She would reward him handsomely.

"You are so kind, Prince. It is going to be such a comfort to have you here when the baby is born. There are many thing I shall want you to do for me. You must not be shocked."

"Shocked? Can I be? If the child's father is not at your side, you can have no one better than Prince."

The weeks leading up to the confinement were quiet ones. The musicians who used to serenade during the riotous evenings which Belle kept for Prince and his cronies no longer came. The slaves who had been hired to attend Sybil when she first arrived were sent back to their owners, leaving only Tita and a small kitchen staff. Sybil wanted no one present for the birth apart from the midwife, for not a word must ever reach Carlton. Remembering also the crudities of Laura's birth, Sybil demanded that the midwife, who was a free mulatto from Jamaica, should move into the house to live at least two weeks before the birth was expected.

It was Tita who won the race. Her confinement was so easy that Prince and Sybil, who were waiting in the drawing room watching the view from the fine casement windows overlooking the town's square, were astonished when the midwife entered with a lusty child whom she proclaimed as Tita's son.

"But he's white!" exclaimed Sybil.

The midwife beamed. "Sometimes it does happen so. A white child from a black mother. She's fair herself, an' if de fader was white it ain' surprisin'."

Sybil steadied herself on Prince's arm. "White?" She thrust aside the midwife and stormed into Tita's bedroom, where her slave companion smiled meekly at her. "Why have you got a white child?" Sybil shrieked.

"Oh, forgive me, mistress," cried Tita, horrified by the contortions of anger in Sybil's face. "It wasn't my fault, mistress."

"You told me that Mingo was the father!"

"Mas Carlton, ma'am. Mas Carlton made me do it."

"Carlton!"

Sybil lunged at Tita as much to keep her quiet as in anger. Prince tried to hold her back, but she wrenched herself free, falling on the bed and pounding Tita with clenched fists. As Prince fell on top of her to drag her off, she gave a startled moan, rolling over onto the floor and clutching her groin.

Prince leaped up, startled. "Hush now," shushed the midwife busily. "She does be startin' now. 'Bout time. I'm tired of all dis. Help me carry her to de chamber. First, one, den de other. Let's see how de Prince's child does be."

"What?" said Prince in amazement.

"Not you, yuh great fancy nigger. I does mean de Prince ob dat Wales dey does be talkin' about all de time."

Prince grinned, not at the midwife's gossip but at the recollection of the name the white woman and her slave or companion or whatever she really was had called out: Carlton. There was a Carlton he remembered dearly from the time he had been torn from his home and sold to Captain Loring. If this white woman was anything to do with the same Carlton, he would see that her secret was kept. He had the secret of his slave birth to hide, himself.

Sybil's child was long in coming. The midwife was amazed at his size, clucking professionally throughout the delivery. It was only when the baby had cried and she held it in her arms that it occurred to her that the child was as black as the other one was white. With the child in her arms, she rushed to consult Prince.

"Lord, I don't know what dese two women does be doin' an' it ain't no concern of me. One black, one white." She held out both babies to Prince as though he was the one responsible.

Prince's delicate fingers stroked the side of his cheek thoughtfully. "M'selle Lugay?"

"She does be out cold. I done give her a draft to ease de pain. Dis one sure a gigantic brute."

"And the Tita wench?"

"She does be sleepin'."

Prince looked at the midwife and shrugged his shoulders elegantly. The woman looked from one child to the other, the pretty white one with blond hair and the heavy black one, eyes screwed up and soft black curls on his head. She looked back at the white one and held him out again for Prince. Taking the white baby in his arms, he carried him gently into the white woman's room, laying him beside the woman whom he knew as Belle.

"Dere, dere," he urged as the child started to cry. "Go to your mama, little one."

Tita, waking as the midwife entered her room, saw the black baby in the midwife's arms and smiled. She held out her arms and the baby gurgled as he snuggled up to her breast.

"He's so handsome and big," she smiled. "Just like his father. And see, he has my hair," Tita said proudly.

Chapter 48

Hayes enjoyed being fussed over by Ella. The wench appealed to him, and in the absence of Sybil, she had become like a daughter-in-law, permanently ensconced in Carlton's chambers while his son, Caspar, had the freedom of the house. In the tranquillity of Sybil's absence, Hayes regretted that Ella was not white. Had she been, Carlton would have made a contented marriage, with an heir for Roxborough. But Caspar, for all his winning ways, was a mulatto and a slave. Ella was so efficient that he and Carlton had precious little to do. The niggers coupled, produced whelps, changed mates, and coupled again. There was peace.

From his vantage point on the balcony, Hayes watched the procession which wound slowly up the mill toward the house. Sybil was returning after an absence of eight months. Hayes was eager to see the son which they had been informed by letter, she had given birth to. Carlton, who had gone to meet the party at the jetty, detached himself from the procession and galloped up to the house.

"Da! Such a beautiful boy! Golden curls and the Todd eyes. Such a son!"

"Aye. I expect no less."

Ella, watching from the side of the house, frowned. Of course, she was delighted that her Bondmaster was happy, but there was something about the episode which she still could not understand. She caught Caspar as he ran to her. He had golden hair and the Todd eyes, too, but there was also the unmistakable glow of his royal Negro heritage in his copper complexion. She ran her fingers through his hair, reassuring herself that one day it would be Caspar who would inherit Roxborough, not this Antigua-born child.

"Go 'n' tie Mas Carlton's horse, Caspar."

"Son, we've got a new baby here today," Carlton said delightedly as he dismounted and patted Caspar's head. "He's your half-brother, I suppose, but he's the heir to Roxborough."

"Yas, Mas Carlton."

The carriage drew up to the steps, and Carlton helped his wife out. Ella's heart sank. Sybil had totally changed. She radiated happiness and an alluring femininity which had been missing before. Proudly, Sybil reached back into the carriage and took her child in her arms. She walked slowly up the steps to the balcony, conscious of the attention she was attracting from the slaves who had gathered in the forecourt. It was her moment of triumph. She walked over to Hayes, holding the baby out for him.

"Aye," said Hayes. "A bonny baby. A grandson at last."

From her place beside the house, Ella watched Tita descend from the carriage with her own child. The baby was bigger than Sybil's and was crying loudly. Tita flashed a glance at Mingo, who stood holding the carriage door open. "Look your son!" she hissed at him accusingly. Mingo regarded the child with an air of disbelief and closed the carriage door. He followed Tita around the side of the house to the kitchen.

"Such a big baby," said Ella, welcoming Tita back casually.

"A noisy brute, he is."

"No mistaking that you be the father, Mingo," commented Ella. "Look, the child wants to be a fighter."

Mingo growled a response, flinging himself onto a

chair, legs stuck out in front of him as he had seen Mas Carlton do. Tita stood by the table holding the babe.

"What you does relax in de chair for now? De buckra does wan' a drink now dat de mistress does be home," chided Ella.

"Da's all right," yawned Mingo. "Yuh boy does be do dat. Mas Hayes done say dat Caspar mix de punch like Claudius, so I does be out of dat. Ah does be tired."

"Tired!" exclaimed Ella, "Is now de mistress does be back dat yuh sure go'n be tired!"

"Dat more dan you then. De massa sure does be pleased to see his missy an' she look so sweet an' fair dat he go'n forget about his Ella."

Tita, smelling scandal, let her eyes widen. "Things done change 'round here while de mistress 'way?"

"How does it be in Antigua?" demanded Ella. "De Vandys, dey does hab a big plantation?"

"De Vandys?" Tita was puzzled. "I don't remember de Vandys."

"Yes," said Mingo. "Dat's de mistress family. I does be raise on deir plantation."

"Oh, yas," said Tita thinking quickly. "I done forgot their names."

Although Tita swung the conversation around to the highlights of St. John's and the beautiful house where they stayed, Ella was still puzzled. She looked again at the child she was holding. That it was Mingo's baby, there was no mistake. She wondered if it would be put in the pen with the others. She doubted if Mas Carlton would like two screaming babies in the house. The bell tinkled twice, which meant that she was wanted upstairs. Mingo was smiling smugly, so Ella thrust the child at him as she rushed out of the kitchen.

To see Carlton, his child cradled in his arms, striding up and down the gallery shouting out his orders to Ella, no one would have guessed that only three hours before she had been nestling snugly in his bed.

Now Sybil was back, Ella knew she must revert to her position as kitchen slave.

Tita's child will go to a wet nurse in the pen," decreed Carlton. "Tita will nurse this son of mine."

"Oh, no!" interrupted Sybil.

"Why not? You want another nurse? I thought Tita was ideal. She was considerate enough to have her baby at the right time."

"Yes, yes," said Sybil, perched on the edge of a chair, eyeing the baby as Carlton paced up and down. "But do you have to put Tita's son in the pen? I mean, he could quite easily stay here. Ella has her child here."

Carlton looked at Hayes, who returned his glance blankly, and then at Ella. "Well."

"Please, Mas Carlton. De house be a little small for two babies." Ella ignored the glare directed at her by Sybil. Hayes, as though hearing talons being sharpened, sipped slowly at his drink.

"Exactly!" Carlton paused, bouncing his son. "I'm going to call this boy Hayes, after you, Da." He proffered the child to his father, who put his glass on the long arm of the chair and took the baby in his own arms as required.

"What about Tita's baby?" It was Ella who asked.

"Oh, yes," said Carlton. "Any ideas?" Ella shook her head, still conscious of Sybil's malevolent stare. "Let's see. He's Mingo's son, so we'll call him Mingoson."

"You like your son? Sybil asked Mingo as they lay in her bed that night. Carlton had got drunk celebrating his son's arrival and passed out early. After Mingo and Caspar had put him to bed, Mingo had crept along to her chamber as she had instructed him. Sybil had been eager to renew her relationship with Mingo but was disappointed to discover that, after the refinements of Prince, Mingo was rather boorish.

"My son?" said Mingo slowly, lying completely naked on top of the bed while Sybil's fingers toyed with the tight whorls of hair on his stomach. "I don't believe he does be different from de others."

"I suppose not," said Sybil, the little hope that she had that Mingo would show some concern for her vanishing. "Am I different from the others?"

"Huh?" This time Mingo did sound a bit interested. He turned his head to look at her on the pillow beside him. "How you mean?"

"You said the baby is the same as the other whelps you've sired. Well, am I different from the other wenches you've mounted?"

"Of course!"

Sybil was happier, but oh, how she yearned for the sophistication of Prince's conversation. "How is that?" she probed, just to find some sign of affection.

"You be white, of course. All dem fillies be black."

Mingo slept in the cellar with the other house slaves, and it was easy for Ella to keep track of his movements. When he left his room at night, Ella had only to wait a few minutes and then steal quietly up to the balcony and listen outside the window of Sybil's room. If she heard the sounds of the bed creaking, she knew that Mingo was there. Now that her mistress was back from Antigua, it seemed that nothing had changed. No, thought Ella as she lay in bed with her son Caspar sound asleep beside her, some things have changed. She could no longer sleep in the house now that Carlton's wife was back and Sybil had brought back a white heir.

Ella could not rid her mind of the feeling that something was wrong somewhere. She blamed Mingo. The new heir might rob her own son of what she considered to be his birthright. Lying in her bed trying to sleep, Ella hugged Caspar closer to her. The boy was growing fast. He slept naked and she could feel his warm hard flesh pressing against her. She turned her back on him while she pondered again the problem which, even though Sybil and Tita had been back three months, she had still not been able to solve. Damn Mingo, she thought. The brute had become impossible and arrogant. He was lazy, too, leaving the work to Caspar to do.

Perhaps she was the one to blame, she thought. Maybe she had tolerated for too long what she knew went on in her mistress's chamber. Perhaps she should have told Carlton of Mingo's visits.

Caspar's arm fell across Ella's body, causing her to smile in the darkness. The boy stirred, curving his body around her as she lay with her back to him. She moved away but the boy clung to her, seeking comfort as he dreamed. Ella felt the strength of his young body pulsing against her own naked flesh. She arched her back against his groin and his hand crept down to lie on her own stomach as he thrust himself into the warmth of her bottom. In the daze of encroaching sleep, she began to twitch her body almost automatically, taking up the languid rhythm of her son as he pushed into her.

They lay still together, sleep claiming them when suddenly Ella heard the muffled creak of a door being opened. She listened again and caught the soft footfall of Mingo on the flagstone floor outside her own room. She waited until she heard the bolt being gently drawn on the door to the yard and then heard the door being shut as carefully as it had been opened. If Mingo had gone to Sybil's chamber, it would be a few minutes before she could check.

Ella eased herself away from Caspar and wrapped a sheet casually around her body, wiping the stickiness between her legs with the edge. She padded barefooted out of the cellar and up the stairs to the balcony. Outside Sybil's door she heard a woman's voice whining as though pleading, and the deep grunts of Mingo. It seemed that he was demanding something before he would let Sybil have what she wanted. Ella smiled to herself. She knew what to do now.

Returning to the cellar, she shook Caspar awake. He clung to his mother, kissing her affectionately in his sleepiness. She forced him to stand up. "Come on, Caspar, wake up! Your master is in trouble."

"What, what?" the little fellow responded, his heart beating faster against Ella's hands as she held him upright. He opened his eyes and concentrated on her. "I done have such a lovely dream, mam."

"I know," said Ella softly. "Keep your voice low. Now listen to me carefully."

"Yas, mam."

"I want you to go upstairs and wake Mas Carlton. But you must go up the grand staircase so that you do not disturb anyone else."

"Mas Carlton done tell me don't use de grand stairs unless he does tell me."

"He will be plenty pleased with yuh tonight, Caspar, if yuh do as I say."

"Yas, mam."

Carlton groaned as he felt his shoulder being shook. A voice was whispering in his ear. He forced open his eyes to see Caspar standing naked beside his bed, a lantern in his hand. " 'Swounds, boy! What are you disturbing me for?"

"Please, sah! Don't make no noise, sah, or de thief take off, sah."

Carlton understood. He eased himself out of bed and reached for his pistol under his pillow. Caspar watched with growing fright. "How many, boy?"

"One, sah. Come."

The dark of that night was unrelenting. Long afterwards, Carlton recalled that noiseless walk along the balcony as the blackness engulfed them trying to smother the weak glimmer of Caspar's lantern. He would always remember the disbelief at first and then the fear as Caspar stopped outside Sybil's door. He had expected him to walk on, at least to the kitchen stairs, but the boy was waiting patiently, holding up a warning finger when Carlton tried to speak.

When he put his ear to the door in the manner indicated by Caspar, Carlton heard the horrifying sound for himself. The rhythmic creak of boards rapidly increasing in intensity and the low soft moans and yelps. For a second, Carlton checked himself. He stared at

Caspar as though seeking assurance that what he could hear was not true. The boy nodded his head, turning up the lantern.

Bursting into the room, Carlton saw Laura first. She was watching the scene with such painstaking concentration that she did not recognize her father. She gave a shriek of terror and collapsed on the floor writhing. Carlton snatched the lantern from Caspar and held it remorselessly over the bed, forcing himself to take in the sight which was to etch itself on his memory until the day he died. In the sudden light, the sweat on the shoulders and black buttocks of Mingo, his prize slave, glistened as the nigger lay on top of the naked whiteness of his wife.

Chapter 49

The silence which descended on Roxborough Hall was ominous. Hayes, sitting on the gallery as he was accustomed to do, could feel the silent terror in the air. The slaves, who knew far more about life on the plantation than their masters ever did, avoided passing close to the house lest some unexpected wrath should descend on them. Even the children in the pen seemed muted as they played under the stern gaze of Bo'jack and Chucco. The very air itself was heavy with the threat of an impending thunderstorm.

Hayes was listening thoughtfully as Ella related the events of the previous night. She sat in Carlton's chair beside him, her voice low, recounting what she had seen from the shadows. "Mas Carlton," she whispered, "took a look at that nigger on top of his wife, then he done stride out of the room without a word."

"He didn't say anything at all? Not even to Sybil?"

"No. He just took off. I was expecting his fury, that's why I stayed hidden, because when a buckra is vexed all us niggers feel it, but he just go with his gun still in his hand and lock himself back in his room I hear him set the bolt."

"What happened then, Ella?" Although it was after breakfast time, no one had eaten that morning. Hayes permitted himself a small sangaree, for medicinal purposes he assured Ella, and sipped carefully at it.

"I took Caspar back to the cellar. The child started to cry, that's Hayes, not Laura, and Tita supposed to nurse him. I hear Laura shrieking, but I'm afraid to go in that chamber and quiet her myself. I stay in the kitchen, although I'm in time to see Mingo come out and the mistress kiss him."

It was too much for Hayes. He smothered his face with his hands, his glass of sangaree completely forgotten on the arm of his chair. He shielded his eyes with his hands while Ella continued.

"It's true, sir. Sybil kissed the nigger on his cheek and I hear her tell him to go into the hills and join the maroons, them runaways. Mingo stood there like he did not know it's night or day. Then he tells the mistress that he is not running nowhere 'cause it was she that call on him, and he ain't done nothing. He say how he go'n tell Mas Carlton how it be."

Hayes dropped his hands and stared out at the hills lining Roxborough beyond the river. He had often found comfort in the majestic beauty in that ragged range of hills which marked the boundary of his secure kingdom. Now it seemed as though the very hills were closing in on him, and where once they protected Roxborough from the outside world, they now seemed to imprison the plantation. The sky above the hills was almost sinking with the weight of livid clouds which scudded down the valley to the coast. It would not be long before the storm engulfed them.

Hayes turned his head to gaze at the black girl sitting in the chair beside him. How things had changed since the days when he was young. No slave would dare to sit in his presence then, and now one was doing so and recounting how another had been mounting his son's wife, apparently with the connivance of all concerned. On reflection, he was not surprised. This breeding farm had been his son's idea, and now he was seeing the harvest. If they had kept to sugar, Hayes was sure that this would never have happened. Great drops of rain began to thud against the shingles of the roof. Hayes shrugged his shoulders, knowing that if they had kept to sugar, the plantation would be mortgaged and he himself would probably be dead with worry.

"Where's Mingo now?" he asked Ella, wondering if he should go and hunt the nigger down himself. "He run?"

"No, Mas Hayes. He down in the kitchen, saying all kinds of things about how the mistress made him do it."

Hayes was astonished. "Does he not know he was wrong?"

"Perhaps, sir. But he's a spoil' nigger so he never go'n say so."

Hayes nodded sorrowfully. Carlton really had himself to blame, cultivating the slave to be a prize-fighter then pampering him with any wench he wanted. He was damn useless at any kind of work, and Hayes had long realized that it was Ella and her bright-eyed kid who kept the household running.

He stared back at the rain as it accelerated, pounding against the roof of the house and streaming down in front of the balcony, blocking off the view of the distant hills as though it was a curtain. It was impossible to see the river mouth or the shacks of the village, and the spray as the rain hit the edge of the balcony was forming puddles on the decking.

Ella stood up. "Won't you come in? The rain go'n wet you out here."

Hayes was about to snap at the woman for her impudence. He paused and licked his dry old lips. He shook his head, then reached for his glass of sangaree and drained it. Carefully, he stood up and allowed Ella to help him, although he knew he was perfectly capable of moving inside without her aid. It was a comfort sometimes to have another's support. Perhaps his son needed his support right now.

"Is Carlton still in his room?"

"Yes," said Ella, easing him into his chair in the drawing room. "He's all right."

"How do you know?"

"I can hear him breathing. Sometimes he sleeping, sometimes he waking. He's just brooding. And this is the time for that, with the rain." The sound of the rain beating against the house was making Ella shout.

"We must wait, then," he said. "Carlton will decide what he is going to do." He paused at the sound of the wind rushing down the valley, gathering speed as it raced toward the coast. Suddenly, the wind buffeted the house, howling around it and blending with the rain to create a cacophony which made Ella smile.

"The niggers are frightened today," she said. "When they are afraid, they behave."

Hayes had been wondering how it was that Ella had ingratiated herself to such an influential position within the Roxborough hierarchy without his noticing. Now he was startled by her confidence. "What about you, Ella? Are you not afraid?"

"Not now, sir. The storm is here now. It's the waiting that does be troublesome." She looked toward Carlton's door.

Hayes had been with niggers long enough to appreciate that some of them had qualities which made them superior to other niggers, yet he could not believe that some slaves could have qualities which placed them above their white masters. But something about the assurance in Ella's voice, as though she knew what was going to be the outcome of all these dreadful happenings, sent a chill through him. And it had nothing to do with the rushing of the wind and rain against the house. Beside this slave with her extraordinary confidence Hayes felt curiously inferior. It was as though what was happening between Carlton and his wife, even the storm itself, was somehow at the control of the slave.

It was nonsense, of course. "Be off with you!" he said, rousing himself and sitting up in his chair. "Get my coffee at once! We haven't had breakfast yet."

"Yes," said Ella, gliding silently out of the room. Seemingly within seconds, Caspar stood beside him with a large wooden tray loaded with pungent coffee and cream and a bowl filled with thick grains of sugar.

Hayes spent that day confined to the drawing room

while the storm raged outside the house. He was accustomed to spending hours in the house, dredging his mind and reliving past experiences. For him, time passed quickly. Carlton, too, stayed in his room but in a trance-like state as he reviewed the unbelievable sight and consoled his wounded pride. The hours, like the storm, passed unnoticed.

Sybil, in her own chamber, clung to Tita and sobbed and then, when no more tears would come, railed against the nigger who had forced her to submit. By the evening, when the storm had abated, she had formulated her tale of persistent rape under duress and was prepared to convince her husband of her own innocence and wounded dignity.

It was three days before Sybil, or anyone apart from Caspar and Ella, saw Carlton. He permitted Ella to bring him some juice in the evening as the storm blew itself out, and then the next day he took a little callalou. Ella reported to Hayes that Carlton was just lying on his bed, saying nothing, with a curious smile on his face. The third day, with everyone in the house and on the plantation nervously awaiting developments, Carlton threw open his door and clomped out onto the balcony dressed for riding.

"Mingo!" he bellowed. "Mingo!"

The sound of his voice slicing through the still morning caused all the slaves within sight of the house to scuttle into the bush to hide. Mingo himself, whose moods had fluctuated from wounded arrogance to fear as the days passed without anything happening to him, felt his throat tighten and his heart leap inside him. Ella turned from the stove to face him as he sat stupidly in the kitchen.

"De massa does be callin' yuh, Mingo."

"Ah hear."

Caspar burst into the kitchen through the front door. "Mas Carlton does be dress' fuh ridin'. He standin' on do balcon' shoutin' for yuh, Mingo. Best you go fast, for he vexed."

Mingo stood up, pursing his lips. "Chupes. Wha for

he wan' me? I always too damn slave for de buckra. Dis be Mingo he does be callin'—de Dominique champyon what sired a score of whelps for de Roxbruh herd. And he does be shoutin' for me like I does be a field hand. I be de bes' niggah on de plantation. De buckra done tell me so himself."

"Den go," said Ella. "Yo' massa does be callin yuh."

"Ella," he said, his eyes pleading. "I does not be afraid. Is de mistress dat made me do dat thing."

"Go!"

Chapter 50

Carlton Todd, the Bondmaster of Roxborough, stood at the top of the grand steps of his house, his legs apart, his hands behind his back. He wore his riding boots and held his riding crop loosely in his right hand. He stood straight, staring out at the hills beyond the river, an expression of ruthlessness on his face. Mingo, who padded nervously around the gallery from the back steps, paused at the corner. He had never realized that Mas Carlton was so tall. He shuffled reluctantly along the balcony and cowered at his master's side, waiting.

"Boy!" Carlton spoke without looking round. "Saddle my horse."

"Yas, sah, Mas Carlton, sah." Mingo scuttled away.

At the sound of his son's voice, Hayes peered out of his window onto the balcony. Carlton was contemplating the spread of Roxborough below him, draped in its lush greenness. The rains of the past three days had ceased and the thick foliage of the bush glistened as the sun picked out the drops of rain hanging from each leaf. The air was fresh and clean.

Carlton was glancing down the trail through the young royal palms he had himself planted nine years before on the birth of Caspar. He turned his head to follow the path through the trees to the slave quarters and then glanced over the buildings clustered around the house, the office, the workshops, the pen with the young ones, and the stable with the stallions and the stable with the horses.

Following his glance, Hayes observed Mingo walking toward the stable. There was no other slave in sight. "Son," said Hayes cautiously, still leaning out of his window, "you done brooding?"

When he turned to face him, Hayes was amazed to see that his son was clean-shaven, his hair freshly combed, and he even wore a clean shirt with a new stock at his throat. His eyes were bright, and he smiled boldly. "Why, good morning, sir!" he said. "I hope I did not disturb you. Is it not a fine day, now the storm has blown itself out?"

"Aye, son. How are you feeling?" Hayes anxiously scanned Carlton's face.

"Fit as a fighting buck, father. Such a lovely day, thought I'd take the wife for a picnic. Just sent the slave there for a horse. Think I'll go 'n' shoot a pig for a *cochon boucan*."

Hayes shook his head. He had expected his son to emerge from his room full of either anger or remorse, but to propose taking Sybil on a buccaneer picnic with roast pig was beyond his comprehension. If it weren't for the wild brightness in his eyes, Hayes would have thought his son was serious. "You tell Sybil?"

"You tell her, Da. Tell her to make her preparations for a picnic. I'll come for her this afternoon. I'm going to hunt my pig now while the Negroes build the fire in the charcoal pit. When all is ready, I'll come for her. She should leave the girl Tita here, and Laura, too, of course. We have some things to talk about, Da."

Carlton's rueful smile made Hayes want to lean out of the window and embrace his son. He was taking it like a real man, he thought, as Carlton ran easily down the steps and strolled over to the stable. The tiny figure of Caspar ran after him from under the house where he had been waiting.

"Mas Carlton, sah," Caspar called, catching up with Carlton. "May I come with you, sir?"

Carlton paused and looked down at the boy, smiling

at him. "No, son." He ruffled his long yellow hair, gripping the boy at the back of his neck and kneeling down to face him, eye to eye. "I'm going hunting, son. Tell your mam to meet me by the coal pit. You stay home and look after your grandfather."

"Yes, Father." Caspar hesitated, then ran quickly back to the house where Ella was watching from the kitchen, a mortar and pestle gripped between her knees as she squatted on the step and pounded berries and herbs into a paste.

Mingo brought Carlton's horse for him, and his master mounted quickly without speaking. Uncertain what he should do, Mingo pawed the ground waiting for an order. Carlton watched him, recalling the day he had found him locked in that coffin jail on the Vandy estate. How the nigger had grown since then. His muscles still bulged on his arms and across his shoulders, as the result of all the early training he had given him, but now his trunk had thickened and, Carlton suspected, he would have difficulty sustaining himself for a few rounds without being short of wind.

"Take off that fancy shirt and roll up them britches!" Carlton barked. "You need training, nigger, to trim up that body of yours."

Startled by the unexpectedness of the command, Mingo quickly pulled off his shirt and looked around for somewhere to hang it, as he had been taught.

"Drop it there, on the ground!" ordered Carlton. "Now roll up them britches fast. You can run behind the horse, nigger. Get that surplus fat off you."

Hayes saw this strange performance from the balcony as Carlton galloped off up the path to the savannah behind the house, followed by Mingo scrambling to keep up with the horse. The shirt which the slave left behind lay screwed up in a heap in the center of the path. Hayes frowned. His son hated the niggers to maltreat their clothes. He would send Caspar to retrieve it and keep it until Mingo returned.

Carlton galloped across the savannah as fast as the condition of the trail would allow, with Mingo trotting after him. To his left, the sea sparkled in the morning sun, and the busy sounds of the bay-front village drifted up in the clear air. He plunged straight into the woods surrounding the open savannah cutting off the light and the noise. He began to work his way along the trail, slowing the horse while Mingo caught up with him.

There was a charcoal pit to the east where the slaves prepared charcoal for the house kitchen, and Carlton branched off the main trail to follow a footpath through the undergrowth. With the horse reduced to a walking pace by the overhanging trees, it was not long before Mingo caught up. He was panting and fell in quietly behind the horse. As they walked, Carlton whistled softly to himself as though unaware of the slave behind him who was keeping a sharp lookout through the ferns and grass in the hope of seeing a pig for his master to shoot. Perhaps if he saw one, his master would feel more kindly towards him.

"Yassa! Dere so, sah! Ah hear one, sah!"

Carlton twisted around in the saddle and regarded Mingo with amazement. "What ails you, boy?"

"A hog, sah. Ah done see a hog through de trees, over there, sah!"

"A hog, you say?"

"For de *boucan*, sah."

"Oh, yes, how foolish of me, boy. We can't have a *boucan* without a pig, can we?" He rode on without stopping. Mingo scratched his head before following dutifully.

When they reached the charcoal pit, the coals were already glowing in the mound of earth. There was nobody there, a group of slaves having followed Carlton's instructions relayed to them earlier by Ella and built up the fire. Carlton halted his horse and dismounted. Mingo took the bridle and secured the horse to a tree, wondering what was going to happen next.

Once before, Mingo had accompanied his master on one of these pirate-style picnics. There had been a big crowd of white people, and they had spent the whole day drinking and laughing and eating slices of the pig which had been shot that same morning and roasted in the fire. It had been a gay and happy time, quite different from the eerie loneliness of this charcoal glade, far from the house with only the noise of a near-by stream and the rustle of the undergrowth for company. Mingo would be pleased to go home. And what about the pig, anyway?

Carlton sat down with his back against a tree. He had placed a blanket on the damp earth, and he relaxed with his long legs stretched out in front of him. Although Carlton's eyes were closed, Mingo did not think he was asleep. He had the air of a man waiting for something. Mingo was puzzled. He squatted down on his haunches to wait. It was cool in the shade with the leaves of the heavy branches overhead preventing the sun penetrating through to warm him. He shivered. Suddenly a twig snapped. It was a clumsy, irregular sound, not a natural one. Mingo's hackles prickled with fear. His master had heard it, too, for his eyes were open now, and he was watching Mingo steadily.

The foliage at the corner of the glade sprang apart. Ella stepped into the clearing. She carried a basket on her head, and she gently lowered it to the ground in front of Carlton. "I came as fast as I could," she panted. "You chase the boy here?"

"No, he ran behind the horse. A little bit of training!" He chuckled with a bitter note. "You bring everything?"

"Oh, yes, the seasoning paste, salt and crushed peppers. And," she said, reaching into the basket and pulling out a flask which she handed to Carlton, "a bottle of your old rum."

Carlton uncorked the flask and took a swig while Mingo, still on his haunches, scratched his head again. He was feeling cold now and would not object to a shot of rum himself. And why, he was thinking, had Ella come so soon with the seasoning, when they did not have the pig yet? This was a strange hunt, to be sure. He watched Ella hand Carlton a container which the master sniffed.

"Smells good," he said. "Boy, take this cup and rub the paste onto you. It's good for the cold." Seeing the bowl thrust at him, Mingo had no alternative but to jump up and accept it. His experiences with the mad Major Vandy had taught him that buckras had some crazy ideas at times and you just had to do what they told you. He looked at the sauce, then back at Carlton.

"Go on, boy, rub in in."

Gingerly, Mingo dipped his finger in the cup and patter himself on the chest with the paste. It was cool. He would have preferred a drink to keep him warm.

"Go on, boy, all over. Ella, help him."

Ella took some of the paste on her hand and rubbed it across Mingo's shoulders and down his back to his waist.

"Keks," said Carlton, his voice tighter. Mingo looked in surprise at his master. Carlton had pulled out his pistol from his saddle bag and was examining it. "Step out of your britches, boy."

It was nothing for Mingo to be ordered to strip down. In his fighting days, his master proudly showed off his body to his cronies and visitors to the estate. He was the prize nigger on the whole plantation, and Mingo was proud to have the buckras fingering him, exclaiming at the length and girth of his prick. He let his breeches fall, unrolling them below his knees where they had got caught up, without a second thought. It was only when he stood naked before his master with Ella rubbing the sauce over his buttocks and down the back of his thighs that Mingo began to wonder what it was all about. It was not the same as the snake oil rub Ma Phoebe used to give him. Ella poured the remainder of the sauce over his prick, slapping it viciously as it danced to life.

"Is this the potion?" Carlton asked, holding up another container he extracted from Ella's basket.

"Yes."

He handed it to her. "Now, Mingo," he said, casually pointing the pistol, which he had finished priming, at the slave. "A toast. Give him the potion, Ella."

Mingo was still uncertain about what was happening to him. He took the cup from Ella's hands, beseeching her with his eyes to enlighten him. She held her head aloof. When Ella had first appeared at the pit, Mingo had been surprised, until he realized that the house cook had a right to be there to prepare the pig. But now, too late, he remembered that she was also an obeah woman.

"Miss Ella, Miss Ella," he whimpered. "What's dis for?"

"Drink it!" Carlton ordered. "It's a toast, Mingo. See, I have my rum here, too." He waved the flask at Mingo, holding it by the neck and preparing to drink from it. "Drink your grog, boy, and I'll drink mine."

"Sah, sah! I don't want drink, sah! I done do nothin', sah. It was be de mistress, sah. Miss Ella! Tell de massa how it was be. De mistress, she dat make me do dose things, sah!"

"A toast, Mingo." Carlton leveled his pistol at the slave's heart. "Let us drink to my wife, shall we? You're not refusing to do that, are you, my fine buck? Drink!"

Mingo looked around him in despair. The sun had found a way to stream through the leaves which formed the roof of the glade, throwing shadows which flickered across his face. Ella had withdrawn to crouch over the glowing coals where she seemed to be mumbling to herself. Carlton faced him, a rum flask in one hand and a pistol pointing straight at him in the other. The bush around them was dense. If he broke away and ran, his master could shoot him in the back. If he drank the potion, he did not know what would happen. He bit his lip.

"What, slave! You insult my wife by refusing a toast? A toast, I say, to my wife, Mistress Sybil Todd, mistress of Roxborough! Drink, or I'll have to shoot you, Mingo."

Seeing a gleam of hope in his master's words which indicated that he would be shot only if he didn't drink the potion, Mingo gulped down the unwholesome liquid. It tasted harsh, but slid down his throat quickly, even though he tried to restrain it. He felt it seeping through his body down into his stomach and then into his limbs.

He dropped the cup as the strength drained out of his arms. His legs collapsed beneath him and he slid slowly to the ground. He saw Carlton walking slowly over toward him, tucking the pistol into his belt. Mingo tried to apologize for collapsing, to explain that suddenly he felt so weak, but his mouth wouldn't open. With his hands and legs utterly limp, he lay at the feet of the Bondmaster, his eyes staring upwards as his master's shadow fell across him.

He heard Mas Carlton hawk, and then a glob of spittle hit him in his eye. Another rasping throat and then a stream of phlegm descended on him, landing on his forehead and trickling slowly down his cheek. Another shadow flickered across his face, and Mingo cast his eyes to his side to see Ella standing there, the short knife which she used for gutting fish, in her hand. She handed the knife to Carlton, who accepted it wordlessly and crouched down beside him.

Chapter 51

Carlton's face was close to Mingo's. He looked into the slave's eyes as they stared helplessly upwards.

"But what's happened to you, Mingo?" he crooned mockingly. "No strength left? You can't move your head? Is this the way my prize slave behaves on a picnic?" Carlton looked at Ella. "This stuff really works," he said with amazement in his voice. "You can tell by his eyes that he hears me, and yet he cannot move or speak at all."

Ella gave a vague grin; she would only have been surprised if she had failed. She walked back to her wicker basket and took out a bundle of green and red peppers which Caspar had picked for her that morning, and a jar containing crushed salt.

Carlton was idly surveying his Negro's body. It was black and massive without a scar. With rigorous training and discipline, Mingo could still be a champion fighter. Using the blade of his knife, Carlton lifted up the dead weight of Mingo's penis, bouncing it, anger building up within him. This nigger was the animal who had destroyed Roxborough. Carlton let the heavy penis fall back to Mingo's thigh.

"Damn your heart, Mingo! Why did you do it?" Only the stirring of the forest in the breeze answered.

"Wretched, loathsome animal!" Carlton shrieked, jabbing the knife into Mingo's stomach, drawing the

433

blade over the flesh. The small incision began to bleed. Ella watched with interest.

"Damned odorous nigger!" The knife jabbed into Mingo's skin again, making another wound. "Heinous black toad!" This time the knife cut into Mingo's chest, slicing through the flesh from his left nipple to the right.

The excruciating pain made Mingo's eyes cloud over with tears. Carlton lunged at Mingo repeatedly, making nicks all over his body. Ella came forward and began to jam the cuts with split peppers, sprinkling the salt crystals over the incisions with the same lack of emotion she exhibited when seasoning a pig for roasting in the Roxborough kitchen.

Carlton picked up Mingo's penis again, biting his lip in his rage as he gripped it in his fist. "That poisonous snake!" he gasped, tugging at it. When a slave mounts a white woman that's an animal and a human together. That's bestiality! The punishment for bestiality is death!"

He pulled Mingo's penis like a piece of rubber until it extended about eighteen inches. Holding the top of it in his left hand, and the knife in his right, he slashed at the base, hacking at it until it separated from the slave's body. With his finger, he parted Mingo's lips and jammed the severed penis between them.

"Roll him on his side," suggested Ella, heaving the still conscious slave toward her, blood smearing her long apron. Carlton helped, then gave some half-hearted stabs at Mingo's rear before falling back and reaching for the rum flask which Ella had placed near him. She was working on the slave's back to season it properly, finally jamming a large red pepper into his moist anus and pronouncing the job finished.

Together, Carlton and Ella rolled Mingo's body over the ground to the charcoal hole. The coals within were glowing brightly, and the pit, which had been lengthened under Ella's instructions the day before, was long enough to accommodate Mingo. They tipped him in, and then Ella took up the spade to cover the body with the hot earth.

Mingo's eyes were no longer seeing, but the tremor in his bleeding chest revealed that there was still life in his mutilated and highly seasoned carcass. His lips were drawn across his face, giving the appearance of a grotesque grin with his penis hanging out like an elephant's trunk. Carlton cleared his throat and spat out a spittle of his hatred straight at the penis where it stuck, dripping down like a glob of semen.

Sybil was delighted when Carlton, who had by then sluiced the blood off his hands and donned a fresh outfit of clothes, appeared so charming and conciliatory as he escorted her out of the house for the picnic he had promised.

"We'll have a chance to talk," said Carlton casually as they rode up the path to the savannah.

"Where's Mingo?" asked Sybil, trying to appear just as casual.

"He's gone to Roseau on an errand, my dear. He'll be back tonight."

Restricting their conversation to trivialities, the couple would have seemed to any observer a perfectly matched pair as they rode into the bush at the edge of the savannah to find the picnic site. Carlton led Sybil to a small glade not very distant from where, he said, the pig was being boucanned.

"Uummm! I would love to see it," said Sybil, sniffing the scent of charring meat.

"So you shall, my dear, so you shall. The slaves are preparing it now, but we don't want them watching us, or we them, so we are better away from the jungle kitchen for now." He spread a rug on the ground and helped his wife to be seated. "Would you take a punch?" he offered, unpacking the basket he had brought with them.

"Did you shoot a big pig?" she enquired politely.

"An enormous brute."

"Oh, good. I do so enjoy wild boar."

435

"Ella has seasoned it perfectly—a little salt, a little pepper, a little lime. You'll find it delicious. It's amazing, really," he said, settling down beside his wife, "that such an obnoxious and troublesome animal should be capable of yielding such a piquant flesh."

The conversation which followed took Sybil's mind back to the wonderful days she had spent in Antigua. She used to converse a lot with Prince, something she rarely did with her husband. And yet Carlton was really quite sophisticated and charming when he forgot about his odious slave-breeding habit and found other matters to discuss. Looking at husband with his silver-gold hair and tanned face with its forceful expression and challenging green eyes, she knew that others must envy her for having such a man for her husband. Maybe he was not such a dull buffoon, after all.

"I must go and see about the dinner," he said, jumping up quickly as her fingers strayed to his thigh. He replenished her glass, smiled in a weirdly condescending manner, and stepped into the bush, spreading the foliage in front of him as he walked.

Sybil had only a few minutes to reflect on the tranquillity of the scene. The tiny glade he had chosen was such a private place. She realized that it had been especially cleared by the slaves, and logs had been placed around for seats. A tiny table about twelve inches high had been constructed on the ground itself on which to place the picnic dishes. A few yards away from where she sat was a tiny stream, water gurgling over stones as it hurried down to join the river far below. The earthenware jar of punch had been placed in the stream to keep cool. It was an idyllic setting.

When Carlton returned, Sybil was surprised to see he was accompanied by the slut Ella. She had a bowl of sauce in her hand, while behind her followed a slave, naked except from a loincloth carelessly draped around his waist. He carried an enormous silver platter laden with chunks of steaming meat. Sybil had not seen the slave before and eyed him with interest. He was about her height, with muscles rippling over his body under a midnight blue skin. As he crouched down to place the platter on the low table, his sex protruded from the loincloth and scraped against the ground. Sybil licked her lips nervously.

"I see you are going to enjoy the dish!" said Carlton kneeling down beside her. "That's all right," he said to Ella. "You may go now, I will serve the mistress."

"Yas, massa." Ella withdrew, beckoning the slave to follow her.

"Who is that?" asked Sybil, trying to follow the slave with her eyes as he threaded his way through the bush.

"One of the Roxborough herd," said Carlton. "I have some fine animals here, you know. You haven't seen him before, my dear? He's one of the Ibos from the quarters."

"An Ibo? How interesting."

"Why?" Carlton handed her a plate full of meat, garnished with watercress. "Sauce?" Sybil nodded, and he poured some onto her plate for her.

"I've heard that the Ibos are cannibals." Sybil picked up a piece of meat with her fork and put it in her mouth and began to chew.

"I don't know about that," said Carlton softly. "They are good scavengers, clear up all the rubbish and keep the plantation clean. Not so good for breeding, though. Anything wrong?"

Sybil had stopped chewing and swallowed the meat. "No, nothing, just the flavor of the pig meat."

"That's the wildness of it, dear. And it was such a big animal." He sipped his punch while Sybil put another piece of meat in her mouth. "I saw you liked the Ibo. Thinking he might be a replacement for Mingo?"

"Mingo?" Sybil choked, gulping down the meat. "What do you mean?" She observed that Carlton was watching her, his usually frank eyes squinting at her in a fashion new to her. He had not eaten anything, not even put meat onto his plate. Instead, he was gripping his glass of punch until his knuckles were white. She noticed his pistol in his belt and suddenly, as though a cloud had blocked out the sun, the atmosphere of trust which he had lulled her with darkened forebodingly.

"I want to talk to you about that," she said, putting down her plate on the little table. "I don't know what silly nonsense that slave told you. He came to me that night saying you had sent him. I let him in—why shouldn't I? Perhaps when he saw me *déshabillée*, he was overcome. I don't know. He just grabbed me and forced me onto the bed. I ask you, Carlton, what could I do? His hand was on my mouth so I couldn't scream. I was so glad when you burst into the room, Carlton, before anything really terrible happened."

"Really terrible?"

"I mean before he was able to do what he had come to do."

"Oh, I see."

"I expected you to shoot him dead there and then, Carlton. I must confess I don't understand you. A slave rapes your wife, and you tell me you've sent him to Roseau on an errand. You might have told me."

"Whatever for?"

"I wouldn't have advised it at all."

"Of course you wouldn't! Now you are wondering what has happened to your accursed black lover. Yet the moment he is out of sight, you cast your eyes on a cannibal Ibo! Your heart leaps with excitement. You are nothing more than a rutting whore, worse than any of my breeding fillies."

"How dare you say that to me! A gentleman wouldn't."

"Since when did any gentleman pay attention to you, you slave's strumpet?"

"I tell you, in Antigua plenty of gentlemen sought my favors. Black ones, too!"

"Oh, yes, I'm sure they did. And slaves, as well, no doubt."

"You misjudge me, Carlton. I resisted them. I remained true to you, as I always have."

438

"The way you resisted Mingo, I suppose."

"Mingo raped me!"

"Night after night since we were married?"

"That's not true!"

"So you say, but I have found out all about your ways, believe me. You like Mingo, admit it. You like him enough to eat him, don't you!"

"Mingo? Mingo is a lovely boy whom you've abused since you've had him, forcing him to breed with just anyone."

"Instead of keeping him for you? Come on, Sybil, admit it. I have nothing against you for it. If you consider yourself low enough to let my slaves enter you, that's your affair. And maybe it wasn't Mingo alone."

"I would not disrespect Mingo like that. He is a pure and simple boy whom you corrupted."

Carlton sighed. "So you do admit it?"

"Very well! Yes, of course, I admit it. Why not? You have always treated me like a slave, so I have chosen to live like one. Mingo is my slave lover!"

"You worship him, do you? Carlton pressed. "You devour him with the intensity of your passion?"

"How funny to put it like that. Yes, if you like."

"Come," said Carlton quietly.

"Where to?" Sybil drew back for protection to the shaded spot of the glade.

"Oh, nothing will happen to you," Carlton said with a laugh. "I want to show you the animal you have just dined on. You said you wanted to see the beast." He held out his hand to help her up, but she declined, scrambling to her feet by herself, suspecting some trickery. "Come," continued Carlton, "your Ibo is tending the fire. You can have a second look at him."

Sybil lifted her head haughtily. "I'll come," she said, "but I am not one of your breeding mares you can bed with whomever you like."

"Now, that's an idea," said Carlton sarcastically. Bright-skinned mulatto whelps would fetch a good price in Trinidad. Perhaps you and your Ibo would make an interesting combination. You could always say he raped you."

Sybil followed Carlton uneasily through the bush to the glade where smoke rose up from the charcoal pit. Ella was standing beside the pit, looking into it, a knife in her hand. The Ibo was there as well, crouching on his haunches at the edge of the clearing. There were six other Negroes with him, all of them naked, ash from the fire daubed on their faces and across their chests. Carlton stepped aside and let Sybil pass. She went over to the pit idly, more to satisfy her husband's demand than to see the pig.

She stopped in horror, staring at the hole. The creature inside was burnt black and unrecognizable, slices of charred flesh hacked from its thighs. It was a man.

"There's your precious Mingo!" Carlton crept up behind her and whispered in her ear. "Burned like a beast. Devour him now if you will!" He pushed her at the same time as she swooned, tumbling forward at the edge of the pit.

Carlton turned away in disgust. "Come, Ella," he said. "The Ibos. Let the Ibos have him and," he added, pointing at the Ibo who had attracted Sybil's interest, "let him have her."

Chapter 52

Hayes had watched Carlton and Sybil ride off for their picnic and now he rubbed his eyes as he saw Carlton returning with Ella. He reached for the silver bell on the table beside him, but Caspar was by his side before he had a chance to ring it. He too was puzzled.

"Mas Carlton does be comin' back, sah," Caspar confirmed, "with my mam. I don't see Miss Sybil, though."

"Go hold their horses, boy, and shout for the groom. Tell Mas Carlton that I desire a word with him."

Carlton bounded up the steps more by habit than enthusiasm. He walked over to his father and sank down into the chair next to him, reaching for the rum bottle and pouring himself a half-gill. He knocked it back in one long gulp and then faced his father, who was waiting to speak.

"I see you ride back with Ella on Sybil's horse. Where's Sybil?"

Carlton looked at his father, trying to find his reply. The silence between them was interrupted by the rising sounds of excitement from the cellar. Loud explanations in patois reverberated around the house as the slaves gathered in the kitchen to speculate on what had happened. Carlton smiled at the sound of Ella's strident voice reprimanding the niggers for troubling her and driving them out of the kitchen. He seemed to draw strength from her example.

"Sybil had an accident, Da."

"Dead?"

Carlton nodded, a triumphant grin spreading over his face as he added: "The Ibos were always a pesky set of niggers. They ain't even left a body to bury. Ate every piece of her. Afterwards."

"Mingo?"

"Same thing, not a bone, not a trace."

Hayes nodded his head slowly. Of course, he thought, Carlton would have to report the matter to the authorities. They would round up a couple of the Ibos and hang them. No problem in that.

"I'm going away, Da."

It was Hayes's turn to reach for the rum bottle. Again there was a silence between the two men, as Carlton waited for his father to finish his drink.

"Perhaps it's best," agreed Hayes at length. "For a few weeks."

"I want to go to England, Father. I want to learn."

"Learn, boy! What can they teach you in England about running a plantation?" Hayes sounded offended.

"Nothing you ain't told me already, Da. It's not just that. This nigger-breeding. I'm just experimenting, and sometimes things go wrong. I was thinking what animals they breed to a pedigree, Da. There's race-horses, fine animals. Perhaps I could learn something from all those stables in England?" Carlton poured himself a drink, warming to his theme.

"Things are quiet here now. We don't have trouble with the slaves, and sugar is not our concern. The slaves we've been breeding ain't going to be ready for the market for some years yet, so there is time for me to go."

Carlton was encouraged by the enthusiasm which seemed to be entering his father's eyes. "You could run Roxborough again, Father, couldn't you? Ella knows everything I am trying to do here. She knows every slave on the plantation, and they all respect her because they believe that she is an obeah woman. We can send to Roseau for a white overseer to supervise the field work so you won't have to ride at all."

Hayes willingly accepted Carlton's proposal and was eager that his son should get away. Immediate preparations were made, and Roxborough was plunged into activity which reduced the impact of the disappearance of Sybil and Mingo. Apart from the Ibos and Ella, no one really knew what had happened in the bush that day, and it was weeks before some of the braver slaves ventured up to the charcoal pit. The two skulls they found there, lying together, ensured that no slave would visit the glade again. By that time, Mingo and Sybil had passed into memory.

Carlton insisted on putting Sybil's son, Hayes, into Tita's care, even though Ella repeatedly advised against it. "He needs a wet nurse," Carlton reasoned, "and who better than Tita? She can live in the house and help you take care of Massa Hayes and Laura. But you," he assured the proud Ella, "will be in charge of all the slaves, whether here or in the fields, after Massa Hayes, of course. You are my eyes and ears, Ella. You are my partner."

He was holding Ella in his arms in the privacy of his chamber. It was an extraordinary thing for him to be doing, he reflected, handing over the future of Roxborough to a slave. But, in fact it had always been so. At least in Ella, Carlton was confident that he had someone who shared his ambition for the plantation. His father and a white overseer would handle the administration of the estate, and with Ella to control the Negroes, there would be a chance for him to spend at least a year in England.

Caspar, it was decided, should accompany him. Although they had heard rumors that a slave could be freed once he landed in England, Carlton was emphatic that he needed a servant to attend him. The boy was ten and an ideal age to perform his duties properly. The fact that he was also Carlton's son would prevent the interference of any nosy abolitionists. Hayes was sorry as he had grown attached to Caspar, but he recognized the advantages and did have Laura and his real grandson to keep him company. Ella and he would have to train some new house slaves to make punch the Roxborough way.

Within three days of his decision to leave, Carlton was riding out of Roxborough and down the trail to the river wharf where a passage had been secured for him on a schooner bound for Antigua. From there he could pick up an English ship for the voyage to Bristol. His farewell to his father was perfunctory, for both of them tried to hide the emotion they really felt. As he was about to leave, Ella called to him from where she stood at the corner of the house.

"Carlton," she whispered so all the slaves who were gathered around the front yard would not hear. "When you return, there will be a brother for Caspar. My belly full for you."

"Come on, Father!" cried Caspar anxiously. "I see de vessel does be ready to leave."

"Yes, Ella," said Carlton, withdrawing from her to mount his horse. "If you make another one like this Caspar, then Massa Hayes go'n be so proud." He looked up at his father for the last time, waved, and rode down the hill.

Captain Loring was pacing the deck impatiently as the skiff came along side. Another minute and yer'd be swimming ter Antigua, sir!" he said as Carlton hauled himself up the side and jumped on board. "We leave immediately." The Captain barked his orders and curses at the crew, and slowly the ship set sail out of the river mouth.

Carlton kept his eyes on the coast. Roxborough Hall stood out among the cane fields and palm trees like a beacon marking the river entrance. As usual, the crest of the ridge of hills bordering the valley through which the river flowed was capped with clouds. The sun shone from above the sea, spotlighting the home he had known for twenty-seven years. Although he was leaving Roxborough and did not know when he would return, Carlton sensed that his destiny was truly linked with that fertile plantation beside the Layou River. Wherever he roamed, he knew that he would die there and that his progeny would make Roxborough renowned throughout the islands.

Caspar was standing beside him, and he rested his hand affectionately on the boy's shoulder. "See your mam? There! Standing on the balcony, waving!"

"She too far now, Father."

"Oh-ho! That's a fine mulatto slave yor've got yerself there, Mister Todd!" It was Loring who spoke, joining them at the ship's rail as Carlton quickly withdrew his hand from Caspar's shoulder. Over the years, Carlton had seen Loring occasionally, either when the Captain called to purchase slaves or visited his daughter by May Gregg in the village.

"Slave, Captain Loring?" said Carlton coolly. "This lad is my son. He is one boy your gold and ideas cannot buy. And," he added, suddenly recalling the Captain's callused hands on Prince years before, "he ain't for fingering, either!"

"Hey! Hey!" laughed Loring suggestively. "Yer got yerself a choice companion fer those long nights on the voyage to England, anyhow."

"Tell me," said Carlton, not understanding the remark. "Do you remember when you first came to Roxborough? My father sold you my playboy, a slave fourteen years old, fine youth. Know what happened to him? Who bought that nigger?"

"Name of?" Loring scratched his beard, sending a shower of tiny scabs drifting into the breeze.

"Prince."

"Prince!" Loring cleared his throat and spat eloquently away from the wind. Almost absent-mindedly, he put his hand on Caspar's shoulder, letting it run slowly down the boy's back. "Prince d'Anjou he calls himself now, the toast of the ladies of St. John's." He clutched Caspar's bottom in his hand, squeezing it, pressing his finger between the boy's legs.

"He's in Antigua?" asked Carlton excitedly.

445

"Aye. Probably be on the wharf waitin' fer this ship ter see what pickings I've brought. No fancy ladies fer him this voyage, though."

"I must see him!" said Carlton. "I've only had two buck slaves ever worth a bit. A lively buck called Claudius, and he's dead now, and that playboy Prince, whom I haven't seen since you took him away. So much has happened since then. I miss him, you know. I must see him, Loring, I must!"

"I understand," said Loring with a leer, still fondling Caspar's bottom. "I understand."